What gives this story legs is Paul's character. Like a Dick Francis protagonist, he's a plucky amateur whose persistence only grows as more cards are stacked against him.
—*People*

"The author makes you feel the intensity of the trading floor, the combination of number-crunching and gut instinct that leads people to take big risks, the thrill of playing a hunch and getting it right."
—*Los Angeles Times Book Review*

NEW YORK   TOKYO   LONDON   FRANKFURT

FREE
>>> to <<<
TRADE

A NOVEL OF SUSPENSE

Michael Ridpath

HarperPaperbacks
A Division of HarperCollinsPublishers

HarperPaperbacks *A Division of* HarperCollins*Publishers*
10 East 53rd Street, New York, N.Y. 10022

Copyright © 1995 by Michael Ridpath
All rights reserved. No part of this book may be used or reproduced in any manner whatsoever without written permission of the publisher, except in the case of brief quotations embodied in critical articles and reviews. For information address HarperCollins*Publishers,*
10 East 53rd Street, New York, N.Y. 10022.

A hardcover edition of this book was published in 1995 by HarperCollins*Publishers.*

Cover photographs by Christian Michaels and Richard Laird/FPG International and Bill Binzen/The Stock Market

First HarperPaperbacks printing: January 1996

Printed in the United States of America

HarperPaperbacks and colophon are trademarks of HarperCollins*Publishers*

❖ 10 9 8 7 6 5 4 3 2 1

To Candy

FREE

>>> to <<<

TRADE

I HAD LOST HALF a million dollars in slightly less than half an hour and the coffee machine didn't work. This was turning into a bad day. Half a million dollars is a lot of money. And I needed a cup of coffee badly.

The day had started off well enough. A quiet Tuesday in July, at the investment management firm of De Jong & Co. Hamilton McKenzie, my boss, was out. I yawned as I reread the *Financial Times*'s tedious descriptions of yesterday's nonevents. The dealing desks around me were more than half empty; people were away either on business or on vacation. Phones and papers lay scattered across abandoned desktops. Chaos at rest. The office felt like a library, not a trading room.

I looked out of the window. The tall gray buildings of the City of London pointed silently upward out of the listless heat of the streets below. I noticed a kestrel gliding around the upper reaches of the Mercantile Union Insurance building a hundred yards to the west. The great financial center slumbered on. It was difficult to believe anything was happening out there.

A solitary light flashed on the telephone board in front of me. I picked up the phone. "Yes?"

"Paul? It's Cash. It's coming. We're doing it."

I recognized the broad New York accent of Cash Callaghan, the "top producer" at Bloomfield Weiss, a large American investment bank. The urgency in his voice pulled me up in my chair.

"What's coming? What are you doing?"

"We're bringing the new Sweden in ten minutes. Do you want the terms?"

"Yes, please."

"Okay. It's five hundred million dollars, with a coupon of nine and a quarter percent. Maturity is ten years. It is offered at ninety-nine. The yield is nine forty-one. Got that?"

"Got it."

The Swedes were borrowing $500 million through the means of a eurobond issue. They were using Bloomfield Weiss as underwriter. It was Bloomfield Weiss's job to sell the bonds to investors; the term *euro* meant that it would be sold to investors all over the world. It was my job to decide whether to buy it.

"Nine forty-one is a good yield," Cash went on. "Ten-year Italy yields nine thirty-eight, and no one thinks Italy is as good as Sweden. Canada is a better comparison, and that's yielding nine twenty-five. It's a no-brainer. This one's going to the moon, know what I'm saying? Shall I put you down for ten million?"

Cash's enthusiasm to make a sale was extreme at the best of times. When he had $500 million of bonds to sell, it knew no bounds. He had a point though. I tapped some buttons on my calculator. If the yield on the new bonds did fall to the level of Canada at 9.25 percent, that would mean the price would move up from ninety-nine to one hundred. A nice profit for any investor quick enough to buy bonds at the initial offer price. Of course, if the issue was a failure, Bloomfield Weiss would have to lower the price until the yield was high enough to attract buyers.

"Hold on. I've got to think about this one."

"Okay. But be quick. And you should know we have already placed three hundred million in Tokyo." The phone went dead as Cash rushed on to his next call.

I had very little time to gather information and make a decision. I punched out the number of David Barratt, a salesman at Harrison Brothers. I repeated what I had heard from Cash and asked David what he thought of the deal.

"I don't like it. It sounds good value, but remember how badly the World Bank issue that was launched two weeks ago did? No one's buying eurobonds at the moment. I don't think any of my clients in the UK will touch it." David's clear unhurried tones carried the weight of experience and a sound analytical mind. He had built up a loyal following of customers by being right most of the time.

"That's very useful. Thanks," I said and hung up.

Another light flashed. It was Claire Duhamel, a persuasive French woman who sold bonds for Banque de Lausanne et Genève, known as BLG.

"Hello Paul, how is it with you? Are you ready to buy some bonds from me today?" Her low throaty accent was carefully designed to demand the attention of even the hardest-hearted customer.

That morning I had no time for Claire's line of flirtatious chat. Although she did her best to hide it, she had excellent judgment, and I needed her opinion quickly. "What do you think of the new Sweden?"

"Boff! A dog. A howling dog. I hate the market at this moment. So do my customers. So do my traders. In fact, if you want any, I am sure they will be offering bonds very cheaply."

She meant that her traders disliked the issue so much that they would try to sell bonds as soon as the issue was launched, in the hope that they might buy them back cheaper later.

"Bloomfield Weiss claims that most of the deal has been placed in Tokyo already."

Claire's reply was tinged with anger. "I'll believe that when I see it. Careful Paul. A lot of people have lost a lot of money believing Cash Callaghan."

For the next few minutes the board in front of me flashed constantly as salesmen called in to discuss the deal. None of them liked it.

I needed to think. I asked Karen, our assistant, to put off all the incoming calls. I liked the deal. It was true that the market was very quiet. It was also true that the World Bank issue of two weeks ago had fared poorly. However, there had been no new issues since then, and I had the feeling that investors did have cash waiting for the right bond issue. And this could be the right one. The yield was certainly attractive.

Most intriguing was the Japanese angle. If Cash were right and they really had already sold $300 million of a $500 million issue in Japan, then the deal would go very well. But should I trust Cash? Wasn't he just taking me for a sucker; a twenty-eight-year-old with only six months' experience in the bond market? What would Hamilton do if he were here?

I looked around me. I supposed I should really discuss it with Jeff Richards. He was Hamilton's deputy and responsible for the strategic view the firm took on currencies and interest rates. But he liked to do things based on thorough economic analysis. Trading a new issue was not his cup of tea at all. I looked over to his desk. He was tapping figures from a booklet of statistics into his computer. Best to leave him out of it.

Apart from Karen, the only other person who was in the office was Debbie Chater. Until recently she had been involved in the administration of the funds managed by the firm. She had moved on to a trading desk only in the last two months and had even less experience than I had. But she was sharp, and I often discussed ideas with her. She sat at the desk next to me and had been watching what was going on with interest.

I looked at her vaguely, searching for a decision.

"I don't know what the problem is, but suicide isn't the answer," she said. "You look like you are about to jump out of a window." Her broad face split into a grin.

I smiled back. "Just thinking," I said. I briefly explained what Cash had said about the new Sweden and the lack of enthusiasm from his competitors for the deal.

Debbie listened closely. After a moment's thought she said, "Well, if Cash likes it, I wouldn't touch it with the proverbial ten-foot pole." She tossed me a copy of the *Mail*. "If you really want to gamble our clients' money away, why don't you do it on something safe like the four-thirty at Kempton Park?"

I threw the paper in the wastepaper basket. "Seriously, I think there might be something in this."

"Seriously, if Cash is involved, drop it," she said.

"If Hamilton were here, I am sure he would get involved," I said.

"Well, ask him. He should be back at his hotel by now."

She was right. He had spent the day in Tokyo talking to some of the institutions whose money our firm managed. He should have finished his meetings by now.

I turned to Karen, "Get hold of Hamilton. He's at the Imperial I think. Hurry up."

I still had a couple of minutes. It only took Karen one of them to track Hamilton down at his hotel.

"Hello, Hamilton. I'm sorry to disturb your evening," I said.

"Not at all. I was just catching up with some reading. I don't know why I bother. This so-called research is all drivel. What's going on?"

I outlined the deal and repeated the negative comments of David, Claire, and the others. I then told him what Cash had said about the Japanese.

After a few seconds' pause, I heard Hamilton's soft, calm voice with its mild Scottish intonation. Like a good malt whiskey it soothed my nerves. "Very interesting. We might have something to do here, Paul, laddie. I spoke to a couple of the life insurance companies this morning. They both said that they were worried about the stock market in America and have been selling shares heavily. They have several hundred million dollars to put into the bond market, but have been waiting for a big new issue so that they can buy the size they want. You know how the Japanese are, if two of them think like this, then there are probably another half dozen with the same idea."

"So maybe Cash was telling the truth?"

"Extraordinary as it may seem, that might be the case."

"So shall I buy ten million?"

"No."

"No?" I didn't understand. From what Hamilton had said it looked as though this deal was going to work.

"Buy a hundred."

"A hundred million dollars? Are you sure? It seems an awful lot of money to invest in a deal that nobody likes. In fact it seems an awful lot of money to invest in any deal. I'm sure we don't have that much cash available."

"Well, then sell some other bonds. Look, Paul. Just once in a while we get the chance to make some real money. This is it. Buy a hundred."

"Right. Will you be at the hotel for the rest of the evening?"

"Yes, but I've got some work to do, so don't disturb me unless you really have to." With that, Hamilton hung up.

Buying $100 million was a big risk. A huge risk. If we got it wrong, our losses would ruin our performance for the whole year. It would be very difficult to explain this to the institutions that entrusted us with their money. On the other hand, if the Japanese really had bought $300 million, and we bought $100 million, that would only leave $100 million for the rest of the world. Hamilton had a reputation for occasionally taking large, calculated risks, and getting them right.

A light flashed. It was Cash.

"We are launching it now. What do you think,

buddy? Do you want ten? I feel lucky on this one. Let's make some dough here!"

I felt my throat tighten as I said slowly and deliberately, "I'll take a hundred."

Even Cash was silenced by that one. I could just hear a whispered "Wow!" He put me on hold for five seconds.

"We can't do a hundred at ninety-nine. We can sell you fifty at ninety-nine, but we will have to do the second fifty at ninety-nine twenty."

I was damned if I was going to let them get away with that.

"Look. You know and I know that the rest of the market hates this deal. I just happen to like it, but only at a price of ninety-nine. It's a hundred at ninety-nine or none at all."

"Paul, you don't understand the way these things work. If you want to buy that many bonds, you've got to pay up for them."

Cash's wheedling voice was irritating me.

"A hundred at ninety-nine or you have a dog on your hands."

A pause. Then, "Okay, you're done. We sell you one hundred million dollars of the new Sweden at a price of ninety-nine."

My hand shook as I put down the phone. This was by far the biggest position I had run in my life. Betting a hundred million dollars against the opinion of the rest of the market made me more than a little nervous. My mind conjured up the awful possibilities. What if we had got it all wrong? What if we were to lose hundreds of thousands of dollars in the next few minutes? How would we explain it to Mr. De Jong? How would we explain it to the institutions who trusted us with their money?

This wouldn't do. I had to banish all the what-ifs from my mind. I had to transform my brain from an emotional jumble of wild conjectures, to a totally reliable calculating machine. I had to relax. I noticed that my knuckles were white as they clutched the handset of my telephone. I forced my fingers to loosen their grip.

The lines were all flashing. I picked one up. It was Claire.

"What did I tell you. A howling dog. Did you buy any?"

"We did buy some, actually, yes."

"Oh no." She sounded sympathetic. "You really must be careful of that Cash. But, if you want any more you know where to come. We are offering them at ninety-eight ninety."

"No thanks. Bye."

So BLG was already offering bonds below the initial offering price of ninety-nine. But Claire had mentioned that they would try to sell short bonds they didn't have in the hope of buying them back later. No wonder their offer was low.

I picked up another line.

"Hi Paul, David. Have you bought any of these new Swedens?"

"A few."

"Well, this thing is falling out of bed. We are bidding ninety-eight seventy-five and offering bonds at ninety-eight eighty. None of my customers like it."

Oh, God. This was all going horribly wrong. The price was falling fast. At a bid price of 98.75, I was down $250,000. Should I take my loss? I remembered an old maxim: "Cut your losses and let your profits roll." Then I remembered another: "If you have a view, stick with it." Great help. Think, Paul, think.

Another line flashed. Claire again. "This doesn't look good, I'm afraid. We are now bidding ninety-eight fifty. There are sellers of bonds everywhere. This bond is only going to go down. Do you want to do anything?"

A bid of 98.50! My losses were now half a million dollars. A voice inside me screamed, "Sell!" Fortunately, I managed to answer in a quiet, hoarse voice, "No, nothing right now, thank you."

I called Bloomfield Weiss. Cash answered.

"What's going wrong with this deal? I thought you had placed most of it?" I asked, just winning the struggle to keep my voice below a shout.

"Relax, Paul. We sold the three hundred million into Japan. We sold you a hundred million. We sold an American fifty million. And we just bought about fifty million from the other dealers. That makes five hundred million. There are no other bonds around."

I could have screamed at him. I could have shouted foul abuse at the telephone. But I didn't. I just murmured good-bye.

I felt cheated, betrayed. Worst of all I felt stupid. Anyone can read a market wrong. Only a fool would trust a hundred million dollars to Cash Callaghan. He hadn't even admitted his lie when the collapse of the bonds had shown it up for what it was. I tried to call Hamilton in Tokyo, but couldn't reach him. I left Karen to keep trying while I tried to work out the best way to limit the damage of this mess.

During all this I had been totally absorbed in the world at the other end of the telephone. For the first time I looked up to see Debbie watching me. She had been following everything. The smile that always seemed a second away from her lips was nowhere to be seen. Her face was concerned.

"What was that you said about jumping out of a window?" I said, struggling to keep my voice steady.

She forced a brief smile and then the worried look reappeared.

"Any ideas?" I asked.

Debbie frowned for a moment. It was wrong of me to ask her. There was no magic solution to this problem, and I couldn't shift the burden of responsibility for such an enormous screw-up onto her. But as she paused, I found myself daring to hope that she would point out a simple solution that I had overlooked.

"You could sell," she said.

I could sell. And lose half a million dollars. And

maybe my job. Or I could do nothing and risk losing more.

I developed a sudden craving for a cup of coffee to help me think, or to at least occupy my hands with something. I stood up and walked over to the corner of the trading room where a machine dispensed "real" filtered coffee. It tasted worse than instant but was strong on caffeine. I pressed a button and pulled a lever. Nothing. I banged the machine with the side of my hand. Still nothing. I kicked the base of the machine hard and, deriving some satisfaction from the small dent that appeared, stalked back to my desk.

Think! If Cash had lied, which seemed most likely, then there would be a lot of unsold bonds for sale, and the price would not move up for a while. But at a price of 98.50 the bonds now yielded 9.49 percent, which was more than any other eurobond of similar quality. In time they would trade back up in price. If Cash had lied, I shouldn't sell, but should hang on. With patience I should be able to recoup my losses and maybe even make a profit.

What if Cash had not lied? What if all the other dealers were wrong? What if Bloomfield Weiss really had sold $300 million of the issue into Japan? Then, once the other dealers had realized their mistake, they would be forced to cover their shorts, in other words buy back the bonds they had sold short earlier. The price would scream upward. There would be a fortune to be made for anyone brave enough to buy more bonds now.

The more I thought about it, the more possible it seemed that Cash was telling the truth. I didn't trust him, but I did trust Hamilton. If Hamilton believed the Japanese would buy an attractive new issue, there was a strong probability that they had. How could I tell who was right?

I had an idea. It was an enormous risk, but the payoff would be big if it worked. I had no time to check it with Hamilton. If it was going to work I would have to act now.

I rang Cash. My heart rapped half a dozen times in the second it took him to answer the phone.

"I'd like to buy another fifty million if the price is right." I was amazed at how steady my voice sounded.

Cash laughed, "Way to go, Paul! Let's make some money here! Hang on."

That didn't tell me anything. More sales meant more commission for the salesman. Cash, at least, would be making money. The real test would be when Cash came back with a price. If there were still millions of the bonds to sell, then he would be right back with a cheap offer. In that case I would have a fight on my hands to wriggle out of my purchase. If they really had sold the whole issue then there would be lots of excuses and a higher offer.

I hung on for what was probably only a minute, but seemed like ten. Finally Cash came back on the other end of the phone.

"I'm sorry about this. I'm afraid we can only manage ten million, and then only at a price of ninety-nine."

I could tell from Cash's voice he was expecting protests from me for offering fewer bonds than I wanted at a price half a point above his competitors' offer. He didn't get any. I wasn't angry. Here was an opportunity and I was going to make the most of it.

"Okay, I'll take ten at ninety-nine."

I had to move fast. Next call was to Claire.

"Are you are still anxious to sell the new Sweden?" I asked.

"Oh, but yes, of course," she purred. "I can get you some at ninety-eight fifty."

"Fine. I'll buy twenty."

After two more phone calls I had managed to buy another $15 million at 98.60. That took my total holding to $145 million. I sat back and waited. I still felt tense, but this was the tension of the hunter, not the hunted.

It didn't take long. Within two minutes the lights began to flash with dealers bidding for bonds. Their bids rose from 98.60 to 98.75 to 98.90. Then David Barratt called.

"I'd like to buy twenty million of those Swedens at ninety-nine ten," he said.

"That's a very high price for a bond with such limited prospects," I teased him, unable to keep the euphoria out of my voice.

"It's a funny thing," he said. "The price fell as I thought it would. Then someone somewhere bought some bonds. Since then the dealers have been scrambling to cover their shorts, but haven't been able to find bonds anywhere. So they have driven the price up. The really funny thing is that a couple of my English clients who have been sitting on their hands for a month have just taken it into their heads to buy. They think the bond has value, and the rapid run up in price makes them afraid they might miss a move up in the whole market."

I sold David $20 million and unloaded a further $75 million over the rest of the day. Claire had been especially imploring. BLG had lost a lot on that one. I decided to keep $50 million on the basis that it could move up even more over the next week or two and sold some other bonds to raise cash for the purchase. I totted up my profits. I had realized nearly $400,000 profit over the day and had unrealized profits of $300,000 on the remaining $50 million.

I slumped back in my chair. I felt drained. It was as if I had been physically beaten up. The tension, the adrenaline, the sweat of the last few hours had left me limp. But I had got it right. In a big way. No matter what Hamilton might say, he couldn't deny that. For the first time in my life, I knew what it felt like to take on the market and win. And it felt good. I had shown myself that I could be a good trader, as good as the best. I hoped I had shown Hamilton too.

"Come on Smug Features," Debbie interrupted. "If you have any more afternoons of successful spivving, let me know. I am sure the secondhand car business would give anything for one as talented as yourself. In the meantime, why don't you buy me a drink."

"How come I always get to buy the drinks? Don't they pay you a salary here?" I said, putting on my jacket.

I had a thought. "Just a moment, I have got to make one more phone call."

I dialed the Imperial Hotel. When I asked for Hamilton McKenzie the operator told me he had left a message specifically asking not to be disturbed. I marveled at the man's coolness. So much at stake, and he had deliberately taken steps to avoid hearing about the outcome. He had enough confidence in me to let me handle it by myself. As usual, he had been right.

With my smug look intact, I switched off the machines and followed Debbie to the elevators, leaving Jeff still engrossed in his statistics.

THE TRAIN LURCHED to a halt at the Monument station. Silently, about a quarter of the passengers stood up and picked their way through the car to the doors. I was one of them. We dropped onto the platform and climbed the short flight of steps through the ticket barrier and out into the July sunshine. There our company of office workers split and was met by a much larger battalion marching out of step across London Bridge. I joined a contingent striding up Gracechurch Street toward my offices on Bishopsgate. A few lost individuals struggled against the advancing army in an attempt to fight their way down the street. They were jostled and pushed for their temerity. Since "Big Bang" the commuting crowd had started earlier and earlier, as salesmen, traders, and settlements staff struggled to ensure that they were not the last to their desks to talk to Tokyo, or Australia, or Bahrain.

Although the army seemed unified by one purpose—getting to work and making money—each individual carried his own concerns, worries, and responsibilities with him. Some days I would thrust myself through the crowd, eager to get to my desk and work on the problem that I had mulled over in my disturbed sleep the previous night. Other days I would drag my feet, jostled from behind, as I delayed the inevitable confrontation with yesterday's bad position. Often, I would just drift along with the others, my mind still asleep, shutting out the expected events of the day until I was sitting down with a cup of coffee in my hand.

Today, though, I rode above them all. I had made $400,000 in the last twenty-four hours; who knew how much I would make in the next? I had an irrational conviction that any trade I did would turn money into more money. I knew this would not last. But I should enjoy it while I could. Eventually luck would abandon me. Fifty-fifty trades would all go against me. Certainties would be blown away by the unforeseen. My computer would develop undetectable bugs. My job was like a drug with highs and lows. Was it addictive? Probably.

It was certainly more exciting than the large American bank I had joined after Cambridge. I had spent six years in the credit department, analyzing companies that borrowed from the bank. I had to decide whether the companies would be in a position to give the money back. The job was intellectually interesting, but the bank had done its best to make it boring. It felt like a gray factory, staffed with gray workers who had weekly quotas of a certain number of pages of analysis to produce.

It had suited me though. The bank had been very understanding about the hours I kept. They obviously thought it was good public relations. The general manager of the London office was an American, an ex-college football player and a devoted sports fan. It was fine with him if I arrived at work late or left early. Holiday days were not counted scrupulously; I could have as much unpaid leave as I wished. The whole office was proud of its Olympic eight-hundred-meter bronze medalist.

They hadn't understood when I had given up running. None of them had. The general manager had taken it personally. There was nothing wrong with me. I was still young. In four years' time the gold medal was mine for the taking. How could I let him down like that?

The gray work got grayer. I was expected to work a full day. With nothing else to distract me, the drudgery became unbearable. I needed something new, a challenge, something to win.

So when I saw an advertisement in the *Financial Times* for a junior trader I put together a CV and sent it in. The ad said that a small fund management firm, De Jong & Co., was looking for someone with good credit experience whom they could train to become a portfolio manager. After two more weeks of tedium, I had received a reply. They wanted to see me! I liked the people I had met at my interviews. I thought them both bright and friendly, people from whom I could learn a lot.

I was particularly impressed with the man I was to work for, Hamilton McKenzie. He was a neat, slim Scot of medium height, in his late thirties. His prematurely gray hair always looked as if it had just been cut, and he wore a beard that was carefully trimmed close to his chin. His blue eyes were cold and aloof until he focused them on you. Then they seemed to bore right into your mind, exposing everything, evaluating what was revealed. Indeed Hamilton appeared to be thinking all the time, judging, calculating. At first I found this intimidating and could not feel comfortable in his presence. But he was an excellent teacher. He saw things clearly, and he explained things clearly. He often made me feel like an idiot for not reaching his conclusions, but he always took the time to lay out how he himself had arrived at them. His criticism, although harsh, was always constructive, and he was determined to teach me all he knew about portfolio management.

And he knew a lot. He had the reputation of being an inspired taker of risk. Much of modern portfolio theory emphasizes the hopelessness of trying to beat markets that are efficient. Many modern portfolio managers concentrate on matching or narrowly outperforming the market. Hamilton thought this was ridiculous. His view was that the institutions who gave their money to De Jong to manage paid their fees for ideas. He believed his duty to them was to make as much money for them as he could, any way he could. This meant he took risks, big risks. But he did not take them indiscriminately. Rather, he would wait until an attractive opportunity arose, analyze all the risks, avoid or hedge as many as he could, and then, when he was sure the odds were in his favor, make his move. De Jong & Co.'s clients were happy with the results, and gave him more money.

The firm had been founded by George De Jong twenty years earlier. It had originally managed the funds of a number of prominent charitable trusts. In the eight years since Hamilton had joined, the firm had attracted clients from overseas, especially Japan, bringing the total funds under management up to £2 billion. For the last five years Mr. De Jong, who was now in his late sixties, had come into work only three mornings a week. He still retained total control of the firm and made a very good living out of it. The funds were invested in bonds in a range of currencies, and the management of these was left entirely in Hamilton's hands. Six people worked for him, including me.

Jeff Richards was the most senior of us, with two decades of investment experience. His job was to determine which way exchange rates and interest rates would move and position his portfolios accordingly. A mild-mannered man with a very academic approach to the markets, he was generally quite successful. Rob Greenhalgh helped him in this and was also responsible for managing the nondollar bond positions. He was about my own age and had been with the firm two years. We also had a "chartist," Gordon Hurley. He used the technical analysis of historical prices to forecast future prices. This seemed to me little better than reading tea leaves, but Gordon got it right more often than he got it wrong.

My role was to look after the dollar portion of the portfolio, which represented more than half our funds.

This was Hamilton's area of interest, and one in which he still played an active part. Eventually, the idea was that I should share this role with Debbie, who was even newer on the desk than I. At the moment she spent most of her time on administration and legal documentation and on some of the more harmless trading. We all shared one assistant, a quiet but highly efficient young woman of twenty named Karen.

I had been part of this team for six months, and I loved it.

I continued up Bishopsgate until I reached the tall, black-glassed headquarters of the Colonial Bank. As the Colonial Bank's fortunes had dwindled, so had its use of its headquarters, to the point at which it now rented out the top half of the building. De Jong had the twentieth floor, two from the top. I took the elevator up and entered the plush reception area, all polished mahogany, worthy leather-bound books, and eighteenth-century prints of old trade routes and sleek tea clippers in full sail. The room gave the impression of solidity, of distinction, of wealth earned a century before by the financiers of imperial trade, of conservative investment decisions quietly taken. The reality was that the firm was only twenty years old, and its customers' money was daily wagered against the market by Hamilton and his team behind the oak doors.

I went through those oak doors and entered the trading room of De Jong & Co. This was much smaller than the trading rooms of the investment banks or brokers that bought and sold securities from customers round the clock. As a relatively small investment institution, De Jong did not have many people. Although it was more active than other investment managers, the firm did not trade round the clock. We only bought or sold bonds when we had a particular view on the market.

Nevertheless, even in its quieter moments, the room exuded an atmosphere of suppressed tension, which I found exhilarating. Here the fate of £2 billion was deliberated.

Information flowed in from all over the world, either through the telephones, through the screens, or on paper. It was analyzed, debated, picked apart and then put together. A decision was made: to buy one security, to sell another, or simply to do nothing. Each decision resulted in the movement of millions of pounds. If we got it right, our clients would be tens or hundreds of thousands of pounds to the good. If we got it wrong . . . The responsibility was taken seriously by all of us.

The room had two external walls that were entirely made up of thick glass windows. They faced southeast and southwest. From twenty floors up you could see right over the City of London to the low hills beyond Upminster in the east, the needle of the Crystal Palace mast in the south, and the tower blocks of Middlesex to the west. The internal walls were bare except for the obligatory clocks telling the times in Tokyo, Frankfurt, London, and New York and a large white board covered in blue scribbles recording a trade we had executed months ago.

There were eight desks in the room. Each was equipped with the paraphernalia that is necessary to move money around the world: Reuters and Telerate screens that provide up-to-the-minute information on prices, news, and markets; personal computers for analyzing portfolios and historical price data; a complicated phone system with a board displaying a dozen or so lines that flash rather than ring; and large wastepaper baskets for throwing away most of the two-foot-high pile of research received every day with the mail.

One of the desks was larger than the others, slightly less cluttered, and was positioned a little away from the rest. Empty at the moment, it was the point from which Hamilton controlled the room and devised his next strategy for beating the markets. Close enough to keep informed, far enough away to keep in control.

It was five past eight, and I was the last in this morning, as I thought I had every right to be. The room was fuller, and more active than it had been the day before. Rob was back from his holiday and Gordon from his seminar. They were both on the phone, and Rob's voice was raised to a level that suggested he was already exercised about something. Jeff was glued to his computer, in exactly the same position I had left him the night before.

"Morning," I said as I passed. I got a grunt in return.

I walked over to my desk and turned on the array of switches above and below it. As the machines whirred into life, Debbie greeted me, "Morning, Smuggerlugs. Thanks for the drink last night."

"Give me a break," I said. "Everyone gets lucky sometime."

I opened my briefcase and threw the previous evening's reading onto the desk.

"Don't tell me you actually enjoy that stuff," said Debbie, pointing to a yellow pamphlet carrying the Bloomfield Weiss logo. She walked round to my desk and picked it up. "'The Volatility of Volatility: How Information Decays over Time,' by George Feuchtwanger, Ph.D. That sounds a bundle of laughs." She opened it up to a page covered with long equations each interspersed with tortuous sentences. "Okay, so what does that one mean?" she asked, pointing to a particularly long string of Greek letters and Arabic numerals.

"It means, 'Good morning, Paul, please can I get you a cup of coffee,'" I said.

"And this one means, 'Go and get your own coffee, you lazy bastard,'" she said, pointing to almost as intricate an equation just below it. But she tossed the research paper onto the desk and turned toward the coffee machine.

I liked Debbie. We had worked together for only two months, but in that time we had developed a good understanding. She thought I was too dedicated to my work; I thought she was not dedicated enough to hers. But she was fun. She put the minor ups and downs of the bond market into perspective. You never got a chance to take yourself too seriously with her around.

She was in her mid-twenties, small, with light brown hair, which she wore tied up in a ponytail. She was probably a little overweight, although this gave her a softness that was attractive. A broad smile was never far from her lips, and her bright brown eyes never kept still, dancing from one object to the next.

She was a lawyer by training. After a couple of years of articles for a middling firm of solicitors, she had had enough of the law and joined De Jong & Co. There she had not entirely escaped, because she spent her first couple of years in our "back office" devoting much of her time to working on the legal structures of our funds and on compliance with the stream of new regulations, which were intended to make sure we didn't steal any of our clients' money. Eventually, she had persuaded Hamilton to take her on as a junior trader. Despite giving the appearance of doing almost no work at all, she had been quick to learn.

She got on well with everyone in the firm. Even Jeff Richards warmed to her banter. Only Hamilton seemed to have equivocal feelings toward her. For him, there could be no excuse for a lack of commitment.

I looked at the research paper lying open on my desk. Debbie had happened to pick the exact point in the article where I had finally lost track of Dr. Feuchtwanger's argument. I had wrestled with it for an hour and a half the previous night before giving up. Although the article had no direct relevance to what we were doing, I was eager to learn as much about the bond markets as I could. There is a limit to how much you can pick up about bond trading from reading, but I wanted to reach that limit. However complicated or arcane the article, I would plow through it in my attempt to catch up with the combined knowledge of all those traders and fund managers out there.

Debbie soon returned, bearing two plastic cups of

gritty black liquid. She handed me one and sat at her desk, the television review section of the *Financial Times* spread out in front of her. During the day, she would get through the *FT,* the *Times,* and the *Mail.*

One of our lines flashed. It was Cash.

"Boy, you guys at De Jong are getting real lucky," he started. "Yesterday I bring you the sweetest of trades. Today I get you out of a hole."

"And what hole is that?" I asked, slightly worried. I didn't realize we were in a hole. I ran through our various holdings in my mind, trying to think of what Cash could mean.

"I've got a bid for your Gypsums," Cash said, a note of triumph in his voice. "I will bid eighty for all your bonds."

"Hold on," I said. At first I wasn't sure what he meant. Then, rifling through the papers on my desk, I dug out one of our client portfolios. There among a group of odd-lot holdings was "Gypsum Company of America 9% 1995." The purchase date was three years before, and the purchase price was 96.

Covering the mouthpiece with my hand, I leaned back and shouted, "Hey Jeff!"

Jeff looked up from his computer, slightly annoyed at being disturbed in his analysis. "Yes?" he replied.

"Do you know anything about half a million dollars of Gypsum of America? It looks like we bought them three years ago."

Jeff frowned for a moment. "Yes, I think I know what you mean. Not one of Hamilton's best positions. I think he bought them close to par. Then the company got into trouble, and they were last seen trading in the sixties."

"I've got a bid here at eighty," I said.

"Then take it."

I thought for a moment. If Cash was suddenly bidding eighty for a bond that had been trading at a price of sixty, there must be something he knew that I didn't.

"Is there anything I should know about Gypsum?" I asked him.

"No, nothing I'm aware of. Hey, Hamilton was belly-aching at me all last year to come up with a good bid on this position. Well, I've finally got one. He'll be pleased when he hears."

This was the old tactic that salesmen used on junior portfolio managers when their bosses were away. Tell the junior what the boss would do in a similar situation, and make him think there is more risk in not doing a particular trade than in doing it. I had fallen for this once or twice in my first couple of months. Hamilton had given me a lecture about how I should always trust my own judgment, and never believe what others might say his views were.

"Hmm," I said. "I am going to need some time to think about this. I'll call you back."

"Well, get back to me by this evening. The bid may not be there tomorrow," Cash said.

"Okay. I'll talk to you this afternoon," I said and hung up.

I needed to find out more about the Gypsum Company of America. I left my desk, and went through a door at the back of the trading room to the library.

Library was probably too grand a name for the small, windowless room. There were hardly any books. The walls were stacked high with files, and there was a computer in the middle of the room, which was linked to a range of different information databases. Allison, the part-time librarian, was out, but I knew my way round most of the sources of information. Within twenty minutes I had extracted the prospectus for the Gypsum bond we held and reports from stockbrokers on the company. I also printed out the accounts for the last five years and press reports over the last year from the computer.

I carried the armfuls of paper back to my desk.

Debbie looked up from her *Times*. "It's not that cold in here. No need to start a bonfire."

"I just want to see if there is anything going on with this company," I said.

"Typical Paul," Debbie said. "Anyone else would just have read the latest *Value Line,* and then sold the bonds."

I smiled. Debbie was probably right. But then, as she well knew, I wouldn't be satisfied until I had analyzed the accounts going back five years and read all the press and analytical comment on the company I could find.

I spent the next three hours going over the material, stopping only for a quarter of an hour to get a sandwich from the small shop across the street.

As I read, I began to build up a picture of a company that had started off mediocre and over the last two years had become a basket case. It wasn't all the company's fault. Its main product, wallboard, had been in less demand as housing construction had declined sharply. However, the company had not been helped by the actions of its chairman and 30 percent owner, Nat Morrison. He had borrowed heavily to build factories that were now operating at half capacity. He had also fired a succession of chief operating officers over "policy" differences. As the company's earnings had turned to losses, the prices of Gypsum's shares and bonds had fallen sharply. The market thought there was a strong likelihood the company would not survive.

The company had received a number of overtures from large conglomerates, looking to buy its modern factories cheaply in preparation for the upturn in the economy that must eventually occur. But Nat Morrison would not give up his chairmanship. And no buyer in his right mind would want the company with Nat Morrison in charge. But, because his support was crucial for any takeover to succeed, none could occur, and the company's position continued to deteriorate.

Then, going through the press reports, I came across a headline dated about a month ago: "Wallboard King Dies in Helicopter Crash." Wallboard King was perhaps a flattering term for Nat Morrison, but it did mean him. He had died in his helicopter while visiting one of his factories. I read the reports of the following few days closely. Not surprisingly, the share price had risen 10 percent on the news. He had apparently left his money in a trust. His son, a successful Chicago lawyer with absolutely no interest in wallboard, was the trustee together with a local bank president.

I stood up from my cluttered desk and wandered over to the window. I stared at the silver line of the Thames cutting its way through the tall black and gray buildings of the City, past the more sedate St. Paul's Cathedral and Houses of Parliament and on toward the squat lump of Battersea Power Station. Why was Cash bidding so high for the bonds? Who was the ultimate buyer? And why?

With old man Morrison gone, a takeover would be a possibility, especially because a lawyer and a banker would be more likely to see the financial sense in the sale of the family firm. I supposed that if Gypsum was taken over by a sounder company then the bonds would move up in price. But a takeover was far from certain, and the company could easily go bankrupt in the meantime. If a speculator wanted to gamble on a takeover, it would make more sense to buy the stock, which could easily double. In comparison, however strong the acquiring company was, the bonds would always be redeemed at 100, which was just a 25 percent profit on the price of 80, which Cash was bidding.

So who would want Gypsum bonds? Perhaps the company was buying back its own bonds cheaply? No, Gypsum didn't have the cash.

I watched a barge push its way under Blackfriars Bridge.

Of course! There was only one logical buyer! Someone was about to take over Gypsum. But before they made their intentions known to the market, they would gather as many Gypsum bonds at a discount as they could. There were $100 million in Gypsum bonds outstanding. If they could buy them at an average price of 80, then that 25 percent profit when the bonds were redeemed would be worth $20 million, a significant sum. The more I thought about it the more I was sure that this was the most logical explanation. To work!

I strode back to my desk. I called David Barratt. "Harrison Brothers," I heard him say.

"David, have you heard of an issue for the Gypsum Company of America?" I began.

David had an excellent memory and knew the details of most of the bonds still in existence.

"I certainly have," he said. "The nine percents of 1995. Last I saw, they were trading at sixty-five, but that was six months ago."

"I wonder if you could get hold of five million for me?" I asked.

"It's going to be difficult," David said. "The issue hardly ever trades. I'll see what I can do."

I put the phone down. Debbie, as usual, had heard it all. "I thought you were supposed to be selling these bonds, not buying them. Hamilton will have a fit when he finds out."

I explained what I had discovered about Gypsum and the conclusions I had drawn. "If I'm right, and the bonds are being bought by someone who is about to take over the company, then they are going to trade right up to par. If I can buy any at eighty, that's twenty points profit."

Debbie listened carefully. "Sounds like a great idea to me. I still think Hamilton will have a fit."

I winced. She might be right. Technically, I was not authorized to increase De Jong's exposure to any company that did not have the top credit ratings of AAA or AA without Hamilton's permission. But I knew what I was doing made sense.

The phone flashed. It was Cash. "Have you made up your mind on the Gypsums yet?"

"Not yet. Give me another half an hour."

"Okay. But my bid isn't going to be around forever.

Half an hour is all you have got." Cash hung up. He was just a little tenser than usual. There had been none of the usual banter.

It was twenty-five minutes before David came back. "There's something going on. There is an eighty bid in the street for these things, God knows why. Do you know what's happening, Paul?"

"I don't know, but I can guess," I said.

"Well?"

"Sorry David, I can't say. Did you find any bonds?"

"Only two million. We can offer them at eighty-two."

Harrison Brothers was probably taking at least a point out of the price, but now wasn't the time to quibble. "I'll take them," I said.

"You buy two million Gypsum of America nines of ninety-five at eighty-two," David said. "Thanks for the trade."

"Thank you," I said. "If you come across any more, let me know."

"I will," said David. "But I think it unlikely. We had to scour Switzerland for these two. Someone has cleared up all the available bonds. Everyone we spoke to had sold in the last day or two."

Still, at least I had amassed $2 million. That should make a tidy profit. I remembered my promise to call Cash back.

"Well?" he asked.

"I'm sorry, Cash. Thanks for the bid, but I think I would rather keep them."

"Hey, Paul buddy. Think this through. Hamilton's going to be awful sore with you when he hears you didn't hit my bid."

And when he finds out I bought two million more, I thought.

"Sorry Cash, but we can't help you."

There was silence for a moment. Then Cash's voice came back on the phone, disappointed, but friendly. "That's your decision. Just remember the trouble I went to to help you out of a bad position. Speak to you later."

As I put the phone down, I marveled at Cash's ability to make you feel guilty, even when he was trying to rip you off.

"Did you get any?" Debbie asked.

"Only two million," I said.

"That's not bad. You should make some decent money out of that." She sat back in her chair. "It's a shame we can't buy any of the bonds ourselves," she said. "It looks like easy money."

"Of course you can," I said. "All you need to do is take a couple of million out of your building society account."

"We could try to buy a smaller amount. An odd lot," she said.

"Would that be ethical?"

"I don't know."

"Well, you ought to know, you are the compliance officer after all," I said. Every fund management company appointed a compliance officer to ensure that insider trading and conflicts of interest were avoided. With her legal background, Debbie had become ours.

"I suppose I am." She paused. "Thinking about it, it would almost certainly be a conflict of interest."

"Shame. It's not a bad idea," I said.

"Of course, we could buy the stock," Debbie said. "That should move up sharpish if the company is taken over."

"Why not?" I said. "Seems like a great idea to me." I had £10,000 in the building society. It seemed to me that Gypsum shares would be a good place to put half of it. "But how the hell do you buy American shares?"

Debbie and I mulled over this problem for a minute or two. Then Debbie laughed, "This is ridiculous! We've got ten lines all plugged in to the biggest stockbrokers in the world. One of them should know!"

"Of course!" I said. "I'll ring Cash. He's bound to know all about that sort of thing."

I got through to Cash. "Changed your mind about the Gypsums?" he asked.

"No, I haven't," I said. "But I wonder if you could do me a favor?"

"Sure," said Cash, perhaps a little less enthusiastically than usual.

"How can I buy some stock on the New York Stock Exchange?"

"Oh that's easy. I can get an account opened for you here. All you have to do is call Miriam Wall in our private client department. Just give me five minutes and I'll warn her you are coming through."

Ten minutes later Debbie and I were proud owners of a thousand shares each of Gypsum of America stock bought at a price of $7 per share.

TAP. TAP. TAP.

I was in full stride now. My feet were making the lightest of sounds as they touched the pathways of Kensington Gardens. I focused on the Round Pond in the distance, pleased to see that it seemed to remain stationary. When I ran, the world glided by. No movement up or down. My body just moved horizontally forward, driven by the regular strides of my legs. Any jogging, any rolling, meant a loss of energy. And a loss of energy meant a loss of speed.

I enjoyed the discipline of running. Not just the willpower required to force yourself to keep going when your body told you to stop. But the discipline of ensuring that every muscle in your body was moving as it should, when it should.

The commentators had raved about my running style. But I was not a natural. I had learned it through years of single-minded concentration. And through Frank.

I had first come across Frank when I was running at Cambridge. He coached middle-distance running at a club in north London. Occasionally, he would come up to Cambridge to coach some of us. More often, I would travel down on Sundays to learn from him.

I certainly had some natural talent. I had enjoyed cross-country running even as an eleven-year-old. I would voluntarily run for miles over the moors at home in Yorkshire, something my friends found very difficult to understand. As I had passed puberty, I had filled out. My leg muscles had grown in size and strength, and I had picked up the speed you need to be a good middle-distance runner. At Cambridge, I had thrown myself into athletics and had achieved a blue in my first year.

But it was Frank who had really taught me how to run. Not just in the body, but also in the mind. I had the necessary determination; he knew how to channel it. We worked long and hard at my technique. During speed training, he exhorted me to put 100 percent into each leg, when my body told me to go 90 percent. And he taught me how to race, how to ration not just my physical energy, but my mental energy as well.

And it worked. It was hard and slow, but every year I ran just that little bit faster. A year after I left Cambridge, I ran for Britain for the first time. The next season I just missed selection for the Olympics. Over the next six years, my speed and consistency improved just enough to win me a place.

That year Frank and I put everything we could into getting me to the peak of my mental and physical fitness. The bank was very understanding, my job became at best part-time.

The heats went well. I managed to run them hard enough to qualify for the final while still leaving a lot in reserve.

On the day of the final, I felt as ready as I ever could be. I was fit. I was determined. There were four other runners who had done times faster than me, but I was going to beat them all. My plan was simple. I would start the race fast and lead from the front. There were two or three faster finishers than me. I had to make sure they were beaten by the last hundred meters.

I followed my plan, but for the first six hundred meters, most of the field kept up with me. Whenever I drew away, the others would catch up. Then, with two hundred meters to go, I lengthened my stride slightly and began slowly to pull away from the others. For a hundred and fifty meters I was running five yards ahead of the best runners in the world. The crowd in the huge Olympic stadium cheered me on—I was convinced they were cheering just me alone. It was the best fifteen seconds of my life.

Then, fifty meters from the line, two green shirts barged past me as a Kenyan and an Irishman battled for the line. I told my legs to move faster, stride longer, but they didn't obey. Suddenly, the crowd were cheering for the two backs a yard or two ahead of me, not for me. It was as though I were slowly moving backward.

I made it over the line in third place and won a bronze medal.

For several months afterward, I basked in the attention I received. From the media, from people at work, people I met in business, even from people in the street. But despite the euphoria I could not hide a simple fact from myself. I had lost. I had put everything into that race, a year of my life had been devoted to that one-and-a-half-minute period. And I had lost.

My time was easily my personal best. As I resumed training and racing the next season, my times came nowhere close. It began to depress me. I became more and more sure I would not be able to better that one effort. And it would take all my energy just to get close.

I wanted time for other things. For friends. I wanted a job that would stretch me. I wanted a new challenge.

So I quit.

When I told Frank, I expected him to be furious with me. But he took it very well. In fact, he was very supportive.

"I've seen too many young men sacrifice their lives to athletics," he said. "Go out into the world and do something."

Secretly, I think he knew, as I did, that I had got as far as I was going to go. He didn't want me to lose years of my life aiming for the gold medal that would never come.

So I gave up. And I had gone out into the world to win at something new. Trading.

I sped toward the pond, passing a couple of middle-aged, wheezing joggers moving at walking pace. A red setter bounded up toward me, ignoring the shouted plea of its owner to heel. He bounced up and down beside me for a few yards before darting off after a terrier yapping at a squirrel in a tree. He leaped over an embracing couple under a tree, who took no notice.

I still needed to run. I ran three or four times a week, usually the three or four miles round the perimeter of Hyde Park as fast as I could. I needed my fix of adrenaline, the masochistic pleasure of feeling totally exhausted.

I thought of yesterday's Sweden trade. A smile came to my lips as I recalled the sweet feeling of knowing I was right and the market was wrong. Or rather Hamilton and I were right. I had done well for a rookie trader. It had been the first time I had been under pressure, real pressure, and I had come through it well. I had been scared at one point, but I had held my nerve. The fear had been a necessary part of the exhilaration. Just as a runner had to go through the pain to experience the adrenaline rush, so a trader had to feel fear.

I looked forward to what Hamilton would have to say to me when he returned. It had been my first real opportunity to prove myself to him, and I had taken it. I hoped he would appreciate it.

I dodged a gaggle of chattering Arabic women out for an evening stroll in their black yashmaks and gold face masks and veered left toward the exit of the park. I lengthened my stride as I ran the last couple of hundred yards to my flat, nagging doubts snapping at my heels.

I pulled the keys to my building out of the pocket of my shorts, my chest heaving, sweat soaking my exhausted muscles. I opened the door, stepped over the debris of unopened junk mail, and pulled myself up the stairs to the second floor.

I let myself into my flat, quickly stretched my muscles, and collapsed on the sofa. I stared around me, too tired to move. It was a small, convenient place. One bedroom, a living room with an alcove kitchen just off it, and a hallway. I kept it tidy; I had to because it was such a small space. The furniture was simple, practical, and cheap. On the mantel was a small selection of my most treasured running trophies and a black-and-white photograph of my father and mother leaning against a drystone wall. They smiled down at me with the lost happiness of twenty years ago.

It wasn't much, but I liked it. A convenient bolt hole.

Groaning, I pulled myself up off the sofa and hobbled on stiffening muscles into the bathroom for a soak.

As soon as I got to work the next day, I grabbed *The Wall Street Journal* from Karen's desk where it was left every morning. I was surprised to see the newspaper shaking slightly as I looked down the column of stocks for the ticker GYPS.

There it was. $11 1/4. The stock had risen by more than 50 percent overnight! I turned round to see Debbie coming into the trading room clutching a cup of coffee. She saw the page I was reading.

"Well?" she said.

"Eleven and a quarter," I said with a grin.

"I don't believe it!" she said, grabbing the paper from me. She let out a whoop, and threw the paper up in the air. Everyone turned round to look.

"I'm rich!" she screamed.

"Not very rich," I said. "It's only a few thousand dollars."

"Oh be quiet, you old misery," she said. "I'm going right out to get some champagne. We've got some orange juice in the fridge. Buck's Fizz all round." I was dubious about this but Gordon and Rob made smacking noises with their lips. Even Jeff rubbed his hands in anticipation. He had his own reason to be happy. Overnight, the dollar had finally done what his economic model said it should.

She was back in quarter of an hour clutching an ice bucket in which nestled a bottle of champagne. I had no idea where she had gotten it from at that time of the morning. Glasses and orange juice were fetched from the fridge, and within a couple of minutes we were all toasting the Gypsum Company of America.

"We should have this every morning," said Rob, staring appreciatively at the bubbles rising in his glass.

"Our lord and master would have a fit," said Gordon.

"No chance," said Debbie. "I can't imagine him actually having a fit about anything. It would be more a cold stare and a quick lecture, 'De Jong and Company prides itself on its professionalism, and you, Robert, are not acting in a professional manner,'" she said in a prim Scottish accent, which somehow managed to capture the essence of a typical Hamilton putdown.

Rob laughed. "Well, you had better get rid of that," he said, pointing to the empty magnum on Debbie's desk.

"Oh, he won't be in till lunchtime," Debbie said.

"Oh won't I now," said a quiet, measured voice from the door of the trading room. Instantly, the room was silent. Jeff turned to his sheets of computer printouts and Rob, Gordon, and Karen all melted back to their desks. It was as though the Upper Fifth had been caught misbehaving by the headmaster.

This was ridiculous. We weren't schoolchildren, and Hamilton was not a headmaster.

After a long silence, I raised my glass to Hamilton. "Welcome back. Cheers."

Hamilton just looked at me.

Emboldened by my greeting, Debbie approached Hamilton with the bottle and a glass. "Won't you have one?" she asked.

Hamilton's gaze turned to her. He ignored her offer. "What are you celebrating?" he asked.

"I have just made a killing!" said Debbie, her enthusiasm undimmed.

"That's good to hear," said Hamilton. "What was the trade?"

Debbie laughed. "Oh no, it's not De Jong that made the killing, it's me. I bought some shares yesterday, and they are up fifty percent today."

Hamilton stared at Debbie for a few seconds. Then he said in a quiet, reasonable voice, showing no trace of anger, "Just let me put down my things and let's go into a conference room."

Debbie shrugged, put down her glass, and followed him to his desk and then out of the trading room.

"Whew," said Rob, "I wouldn't like to be in there."

Ten minutes later Debbie came out. She stared at a fixed point on her desk and walked straight toward it, looking neither left nor right. Her cheeks were slightly reddened. Her mouth was clenched firmly together. There was no sign of tears, but she looked afraid that if she relaxed one muscle in her face, they would break out. She sat down, stared at her screen, and began to tap bond yields furiously into her calculator.

Hamilton entered the room and walked through the silence over to his own desk. He took some papers off the pile that was his in-box and began to read. The tension was only broken by Rob, who answered a call from a broker with an elaborate display of cheerfulness.

After half an hour or so, Hamilton came over to my desk and sat in a chair beside it. Debbie studiously ignored him, punching numbers into her calculator. Although I had worked with Hamilton for six months, I always felt nervous talking to him. It was difficult to have a casual conversation; he seemed to listen to everything I said so carefully that I was always scared of saying something foolish or banal.

He just sat there leafing through the position sheets that outlined all the trades we had done while he had been away.

"You were back a little earlier than we expected," I said, to break the silence.

Hamilton smiled slightly. "Yes, I got an earlier flight."

"How was the trip?"

"Good. Very good. De Jong is beginning to build a bit of a name for itself in Japan. There is one insurance company, Fuji Life, that I have high hopes for. They sound as though they might give us some money to manage, and if they do, it will be big."

"Great." It was good news. A fund management firm like De Jong is only as good as the size of funds that it manages. A big new investor could really put us on the map.

"How have you been doing here?" Hamilton asked, running his finger down the position sheets.

"Well, we had some fun with a new issue, as you know."

"Ah, yes. How is the Sweden doing?" he asked.

"Moving up slowly but surely," I said, trying to keep the pride out of my voice.

"Well don't be too quick to sell it, it has got a long way further to go."

"Okay."

"And watch out for any other new issues. After the success of the Sweden, people will be looking to buy anything as long as it is at a halfway decent price. Now what are these two million Gypsum of America's I see we have bought? I have been trying to sell our position for over a year."

I paused for a moment, disappointed and a little angry. No "well done." Not even a smile. I realized I had been looking forward to Hamilton's return and the approval I felt I deserved. More fool me. In Hamilton's world, taking risks and getting it right was taken for granted.

Trying to keep the indignation out of my voice, I described Cash's excited bid for our bonds and my decision not to sell. I then told Hamilton why I had decided to buy some more.

"Hmm," said Hamilton. "And where are they trading now?"

"They are still bid at the price I bought them, eighty-two," I said. "But the stock is up to eleven and a quarter. The bonds should follow soon."

"Yes, Debbie told me you had bought some stock as well for your own account." Hamilton looked hard at me. "Be very careful, Paul. You won't be lucky all the time. And when you do get unlucky, make sure it doesn't wipe you out."

I could feel my face getting hot. I had made good money on the Swedish issue and it looked very much like I was going to make some more on the Gypsums. I deserved some encouragement, for God's sake! Of all people, Hamilton was the last person to criticize anyone for taking risks.

"Thank you," I said. "I'll remember that."

"Good," said Hamilton. "Now, have you got anything interesting coming up this week?"

"Actually, yes," I answered. "Cash is coming in this afternoon with his sidekick to try to sell us a new deal."

"Not another one," said Hamilton. "I would have thought one would have been quite enough for one week."

"No, this is different. It's a junk-bond issue. It's for the Tahiti, a new hotel in Las Vegas. It's a risky deal, because almost the whole cost of the construction of the casino has been financed with debt. But it yields fourteen percent."

"Now that is a lot. I hope we can live with the risk. This is where you earn your crust."

I sincerely hoped so. Junk bonds, or high-yield bonds as they are sometimes more politely called, can be very profitable. They can also be very dangerous. The name *high yield* comes from the high-interest coupon that these bonds pay. The name *junk* comes from the high risk that they represent. They are usually issued by companies burdened with high levels of debt. If everything goes well, then everyone is happy; the investors in the junk bonds get their high coupon, and the owners of the company make a fortune out of an often small initial investment. If everything does not go well, then the company is unable to earn enough cash to meet its interest bills, and it goes bankrupt, leaving its junk-bond holders and its owners with paper fit only for the wastebasket. The secret to investing successfully is picking those companies that will survive. This was where my experience as a credit analyst came in. Hamilton wanted to begin buying junk bonds, and he had specifically hired someone with credit skills to help him do it. I was looking forward to my first opportunity to display those skills, although I knew nothing about casinos and was more than a little suspicious of Bloomfield Weiss's new deal.

"Well, let me know how it goes," Hamilton said. With that, he stood up and went back to his own desk.

Debbie muttered something that sounded very much like "Bastard!"

"What was that?" I asked.

She looked up just for a second, her face still clenched with the effort of keeping control.

"Nothing," she said and bent over her calculator. The anger radiated from her desk.

I looked at my watch. It was a quarter to twelve.

"Look, it's almost lunchtime. Why don't we go out and get a sandwich?" I said.

"It's too early," said Debbie.

"Come on," I said firmly.

Debbie sighed and threw her pen down onto her desk. "Okay, let's go."

We ignored the usual Italian sandwich shop across the road and instead walked to Birley's in Moorgate. Clutching our absurdly expensive turkey and avocado sandwiches, we walked on to Finsbury Circus.

It was a gorgeous day. The sun was out and a gentle breeze ruffled the dresses of the secretaries who were making their way to the lawn in the middle of the circus for a lunchtime's sunbathing. We found an empty patch of grass with a view over to the bowling green. Young men in bright blue-striped shirts and red suspenders were playing. The gentle murmur of relaxed conversation hovered over the lounging office workers scattered over the lawn, pale limbs and faces turned toward the July sun.

We chewed our sandwiches in silence, watching the people go by.

"Well?" I said.

"Well, what?" said Debbie.

"Do you want to tell me about it?"

Debbie didn't answer. She leaned back on her elbows and raised her face to the sky, her eyes closed. Finally, she opened them and squinted sideways at me.

"I think I should give all this up," she said. "Hamilton's right, I'm not suited to it."

"Bullshit," I said. "You are picking it up very quickly. You're a natural."

"A natural dilettante, according to Hamilton. I have the wrong attitude. Traders with my attitude are dangerous. They're careless. They lose money. Unless I improve my attitude, I have no future. And you know what, I don't care. I am damned if I am going to become an anally retentive Scottish robot, just so I can earn De Jong's clients an extra half a percent. It's all right for you. He loves you. All that dedication and hard work. The sun shines out of your arse. But that's just not me. I'm sorry."

She looked away from me as she blinked away a tear.

"Look around you," I said, inclining my head toward the crowd of prone bodies. "Do you think all these people are failures? The City isn't full of people like Hamilton or even me. There are hundreds of people who enjoy a good laugh and who spend their lunchtimes lying in the sun and who are very successful, thank you very much."

Debbie looked at me doubtfully.

"Look," I said, "you are quick on the uptake, you always get the work done, you are ninety-nine percent accurate, what more do you want?" I put my hand on hers. "I'll tell you what you have got that the rest of us haven't," I said. "People love to work with you. They like to deal with you. They tell you things. They let you get away with things they probably shouldn't. They do you favors. Don't underestimate how important that is in this business."

"So I shouldn't just get married, have two point two children and eat ice cream in front of *Neighbours* every afternoon? I would be good at that. Especially the eating ice cream bit."

"You can if you want, but it would be a shame," I said.

"Well, it may not be my decision," she said. "Unless I 'sharpen up' in the next month, I will be out."

"Hamilton said that?"

"Hamilton said that. And I am damned if I am going to change my personality just for him."

She put her head on her knees, and examined a daisy two feet in front of her.

"What did he say to you about buying the Gypsum stock?" she asked.

"He wasn't too happy," I said. "He didn't exactly tell me I was wrong to do it. He just said I should be careful. Come to think of it, I don't know whether he was talking about the stock I bought for my own account, or the bonds I bought for the firm. Either way, it's a bit much for him to criticize anyone for taking risks."

"You like him, don't you?" Debbie asked.

"Well, yes, I suppose I do," I said.

"Why?"

"It's difficult to say. He's not exactly a warm and loving person, is he? But he's fair. He's honest. He's professional. And he is probably the best fund manager in the City."

I watched a couple slowly get up from a wooden

bench opposite us, their places soon taken by two young bankers, there to check out the talent. There was plenty to look at, dotted about on the closely cut grass.

"I doubt there is anyone else like him in the City," I went on. "It really is a privilege to work with him. When I see him in action, I am amazed. He always sees angles others don't. And he has this way of drawing you into his thought process, making you an accomplice in whatever brilliant trade he is working on. Do you understand what I mean?"

Debbie nodded. "Yes, I suppose I do." She looked at me closely. "Why do you come in to work every day?" she asked.

"To earn a crust," I replied.

"That's not all, is it?"

I reflected a moment. "No, I want to learn how to trade. I want to learn how to trade better than anyone else out there."

"Why?"

"What do you mean *why?* Isn't it obvious?"

"No, not really."

"I suppose it isn't." I sat back and rested on my elbows, squinting into the strong sunlight. "I need to push myself all the time, as hard as I can. And then a bit harder. I have always been like that, ever since I was a boy. When I ran, I wanted to be the best. Not second or third, but the best. I suppose the habit just doesn't go away."

"I envy people like you. Where do you get all that drive from?"

"Oh I don't know," I said. But I did know. There was a reason for those bitter hours of self-inflicted pain I had suffered as an adolescent, that single-mindedness which Debbie said she envied and which had cut me off from the carefree enjoyment of life that I saw in other "normal" people. But I wasn't going to tell Debbie or anyone else at De Jong what that reason was.

Debbie was looking at me intently. Then her face

creased into a broad smile. "You're weird. No you're not, you're nuts. You should see a psychiatrist immediately before you end up as a Hamilton Mark II. You are the one with an attitude problem."

She stood up and wiped the grass off her dress. "Anyway, I have got to go back to the office to polish my nails, and you have got to charge into battle for your lord and master. Let's go."

We walked back to the office in much better spirits. It was difficult for Debbie to be depressed for long.

I stopped at the coffee machine to replenish my caffeine level. As the gritty brown liquid flowed into my plastic cup, Rob came up beside me. "Did you see Reuters?"

"No," I said, my curiosity aroused.

"Have a look." He grinned at me. Bad news, I thought.

I returned to my desk and looked. There was a message on the screen that Congress was considering a change in the U.S. double-taxation treaty with the Netherlands Antilles, a favorite tax haven and domicile for entities that issued bonds. IBM, General Electric, and AT&T had all issued bonds through their Netherlands Antilles subsidiaries, as had a lot of less well known borrowers.

I sighed. We would have to analyze these tax changes. Someone would have to go through the prospectus of every Netherlands Antilles issuer in our portfolio. It was a pig of a job.

"Debbie? A very interesting situation has just arisen . . ."

Debbie interrupted. With her legal background, and the time she had spent in De Jong's administration department, she was uniquely qualified, and she knew it. "I know what you want me to do. You want me to read every Netherlands Antilles prospectus ever printed."

"Well, er . . ."

"Don't deny it. The things I do for this firm. Morons

like you blow bucketsful of money on silly trades, and I get left to do the really glamorous stuff."

But she seemed in good humor as she set off to collect the prospectuses.

Rob had followed me to my desk and perched himself on it, cup of coffee in hand. He grinned at Debbie's retreating figure and began idly leafing through some of the research that had accumulated on my desk. Boring stuff. He had his own pile to go through should he be so inclined.

"Can I help you?" I asked.

"No. Oh no. Just looking," Rob said.

After a minute or so, he said, "Up to anything?"

"Not really. This and that. And you?"

"Nothing much. Are you doing anything interesting today?" he asked.

"Just the usual." I wasn't going to help him.

Silence. More leafing through pages. Rob coughed slightly. "Did I hear you say Cash Callaghan was coming in with his sidekick today?" he asked.

So that was it. "Yes," I answered.

"By 'his sidekick,' do you mean Cathy Lasenby?"

"I think that was her name. Why do you ask?"

I smiled. I could guess very well why Rob asked. He had an intense passion for women. It was not the sort of passion that lies inside most young single men. It was not at all physical. Rob was always in love. The more unattainable the object of his love the better. In fact, whenever he got too near to consummating his desire, his ardor would cool, and he would find someone new. He had only just recovered from Claire Duhamel. Having finally persuaded her to have dinner with him, he had been driven wild with jealousy by her constant references to a boyfriend in Paris. She had told him that Gaston was the only man for her. He had been inconsolable for two weeks.

He carried his energy and enthusiasm into areas other than his love life. He was a very emotional trader. He had a "feel" for a market. He would claim his views were based on logic, but that was just rationalization on his part. He either loved the market or he hated it. He was by no means always right, and when he got it wrong the world was a very dark place. However, like Gordon, our chartist, he got it right more often than he got it wrong, which was the important thing.

Looking at him, you would never have guessed that he was tormented by such strong emotions. He looked very ordinary; light brown to fair hair, a chubby face, a little under medium height. But the frankness with which he displayed his passions had a certain charm. Women found him "sweet" and seemed to be drawn to him, at least at first. I must admit that over the last few months I had found myself developing quite an affection for him. He was fun when he was making money, and I had learned to avoid him when he wasn't. I am afraid to say I often found his romantic tussles amusing, there was always a new crisis to hear about.

Rob ignored my expression. "I've always been fascinated by junk bonds. It sounds as though it will be an interesting meeting. Do you mind if I join?"

I laughed. "No, of course not. It's at three o'clock. Plenty of time to get to the flower shop across the road."

Rob scowled at that but couldn't prevent his scowl spreading into a grin as he walked away. I was looking forward to the meeting. Partly I was eager to get my teeth into some credit analysis again. Partly I was curious to see the woman who had aroused so much interest in Rob.

They arrived at three on the dot. It was difficult to imagine two more different people. Cash led the way, bustling his short, slightly overweight frame through the door of the conference room and bellowing hellos in his hoarse, loud Brooklyn voice. Cash Callaghan, originally Charles Callaghan, had established a reputation in New

York that he had built on since he had moved to London. He was the top producer in Bloomfield Weiss, meaning he sold more bonds than any of the other hundred or so salesmen at the firm. His lifestyle matched this success. The name *Cash* reflected the large amounts of cash he earned, and the large amounts he so obviously spent. If ever anyone was larger than life, it was he. His personality seemed to fill any room he was in. His good humor and his throaty chuckle drew people toward him. He made you feel that you were a special friend of his and that it was an honor to be a friend of someone so popular who had so many other friends who were not quite as important to him as you. You wanted to please him, show him you appreciated his friendship. You did business with him.

Everyone felt this pull, me included. I did my best to fight it. I didn't trust him. Partly it was because his small, blue piggy eyes seemed totally detached from his wide grin and bright white teeth. When he and everyone around him were smiling and laughing, those hard little eyes would be darting around, weighing up those around him, looking for opportunities to make the sale. Partly it was because I had suspected him of trying to pull one over on me once or twice. No doubt he succeeded with other clients, and no doubt they were still drawn back to doing business with him.

Behind this rush of energy came Cathy. She was tall and walked into the room with an awkward, angular grace. Her dark hair was tied tightly back behind her neck. She wore a crisp white blouse under an expensive-looking blue suit, with a delicate set of small pearl earrings. She had a figure designed to wear elegant clothes, slim with sharp edges. But I couldn't help noticing her eyes; large and brown, they carefully avoided contact with anyone in the room. I could see what Rob meant. She had a mixture of untouchable beauty and vulnerability, which must have been giving him all sorts of problems.

As we sat down, Cash began, "Paul, I'd like you to meet my new colleague Cathy Lasenby. Cathy, this is Paul Murray, one of our more successful clients." He gave a broad grin in my direction. "Rob I believe you have met before."

Cathy gave us both a thin smile, barely twitching the corners of her mouth. I nodded to her, and Rob smiled inanely and mumbled something incomprehensible in her direction.

"It's not many of our customers who are able to spot opportunities as good as the recent Swedish deal and have the balls to make as much out of it as Paul here did," Cash continued.

"Even the foolhardy get it right sometimes," I said. "There was that other customer, the American who bought fifty million. He must have made good money. I wonder who that was."

"Oh, that was a small savings and loan bank from Phoenix, Arizona," Cathy answered. Her clear English diction contrasted sharply with Cash's gruff New York patter. Her voice was deep, and slightly haughty, betraying an expensive education. I have a weakness for voices like that; hers struck me as remarkably sexy. "He often takes that sort of risk. Actually, he is quite good at it."

For a moment Cash frowned in evident disapproval. Customers are not supposed to know what other customers are doing. In theory it is supposed to protect client confidentiality. In practice I suspected that it was to prevent them ganging up on the investment bank in the middle. Cathy had shown her inexperience by breaking this rule.

She noticed Cash's disapproval and reddened. "But I am sure you can keep that to yourself," she added, glancing toward, but not quite at, me.

"Oh, of course," I said.

Cash's grin returned to his lips. He cleared his throat. "As you know, we have come here today to talk about the new high-yield bond issue we are going to launch for the Tahiti Hotel. Cathy will outline the details of the deal to you. Before she starts, I just want you to know that we at Bloomfield Weiss think that this is a great deal. It's going to be oversubscribed several times. This'll be a blowout. There's a lot of money to be made here for the smart guys who can decide fast."

I wondered if there were ever any deals Cash sold that were *not* blowouts. "Please go on," I said.

Cathy began. "You may be wondering what can be riskier than investing in a casino. You've heard about 'The Man who broke the Bank at Monte Carlo.' Why should you finance an operation that can be bankrupted by any lucky punter coming off the street?

"Well, when you are on the side of the house at the gaming tables, then your winnings no longer depend on luck, they depend on reliable percentages. Over the long run the proportion of total bets placed that is won by the casino is remarkably constant. Different games have different percentages. Slot machines are a high-volume, low-margin business. The biggest profits are made from the high-rollers, the top thousand or so gamblers in the world who bet, and lose, large amounts of money.

"So the secret to running a very profitable casino is to make sure that when the high-rollers come to town, they spend as much time in your casino as possible. It is with this in mind that the Tahiti was conceived and built. It will be the most exciting and luxurious hotel and gaming complex in Las Vegas. The hotel has a south sea theme with palm trees, lagoons and a specially regulated indoor climate that adds to the effect."

She handed Rob and me a folder with glossy photographs of models of the new casino. The building did look impressive. Its two most distinctive features were a tall white tower and a large glass atrium filled with trees and water. Rob, I noticed, scarcely looked at the folder, but kept his eyes firmly on Cathy.

"A good location is important to ensure that the casino attracts as many of the casual passers-by as possible," she went on, handing us maps of Las Vegas. "The Tahiti is located on the Strip, between the Sands and Caesars Palace. These are two of the most popular casinos in Las Vegas, and we expect that many visitors to these locations will want to step into the Tahiti to see what it is like.

"The casino has two and a half thousand hotel rooms, including twelve luxury imperial suites that will be made available free to the target list of the biggest high-rollers in the world. There is also parking space for four thousand cars and a one-thousand-seat showroom, where famous entertainers will perform every night. The aim of all this is not to make money, but rather to attract people to the tables.

"The whole complex will cost three hundred million dollars. It is just being completed now and is due to open at the beginning of September. I would like you to look at the financial forecasts I have here." Cathy passed Rob and me two documents. "As you can see, the casino's cash flow is expected to be twice as high as its interest costs in the first year. As you look further into the future you will see that this ratio rises as the casino becomes more profitable.

"The new bonds will have a coupon of fourteen percent and a maturity of ten years. They will be secured with a first mortgage on the casino, so that if it does not make enough money to pay back debt, then you will become owners of a very attractive property.

"Any questions?" The haughtiness in Cathy's voice rose a notch as she threw this out like a challenge.

There was silence for a minute while I quickly looked over the numbers in front of me. The deal did look as though it might be interesting, but there was a lot more I would have to find out.

"I have to admit that I don't know very much about the casino business," I said. "And there is a lot more research that I will have to do. But I do have a couple of initial questions. Firstly, what happens to these wonderful forecasts if there is a recession?"

"It's well known that the industry does not suffer in a recession," said Cathy. "In fact, occupancy rates increased in the recession of the early 1980s. The reason is that people actually like to gamble more when times are hard." She looked at me, daring me to contradict her.

I looked steadily back at her and didn't say anything for a moment or two. I don't like being patronized, however good-looking the patronizer may be. I wasn't going to let her put me off. "I can see that may be true," I said. "But hasn't much of the development in Las Vegas in recent years been aimed at making it a destination for the family holiday?"

"Yes. In fact in addition to attracting wealthy gamblers, the Tahiti is expected to be one of the top destinations for families in the next decade."

"Little junior has got to learn his poker game somewhere," said Cash with a laugh.

"I see," I said. "But isn't the family vacation one of the first things to be cut back in difficult times?"

"Perhaps."

"In that case won't there be fewer people coming to Las Vegas in a recession, and won't profits fall sharply?"

There was a short silence as Cathy shuffled the numbers in front of her nervously. "As you yourself mentioned, you are new to this business. Analysts are unanimous that the effect of a recession on the gaming industry would be negligible. It is well known that during the Depression of the 1930s gambling actually increased."

She was floundering, but she clearly wasn't going to concede my point, so I let it drop. "I have a second question. Whenever you are lending money to someone, no matter what business they are in, it is important to know something about them. Who owns the Tahiti?"

Cathy was quick to answer, on surer ground again. "A man named Irwin Piper. He is a well-known investor on Wall Street. He is generally recognized as a winner, his purchase of Merton Electronics ten years ago was one of the great successes of the 1980s; he quadrupled his money in three years. He has also been involved in a number of leisure projects in the past, and he has made money out of them. He is a good man to back, believe me."

"I see." I asked another question, "Doesn't Las Vegas have a reputation for attracting organized crime? How do I know this man is clean?"

"Just because he owns a casino, it doesn't mean he is a crook," said Cathy sniffily. "It's true that there were cases of organized crime in Las Vegas in the 1950s and 1960s, but nowadays the Nevada Gaming Commission runs very strict checks on people before granting them licenses to own or manage a casino. If an applicant has ever been involved or has even been suspected of involvement in any criminal activities at all, then the commission won't grant a license. I can assure you Irwin Piper is clean."

"Nevertheless, I feel uncomfortable lending someone money if I have never met them," I said.

"Look, if the Nevada Gaming Commission's thorough investigations aren't good enough for you, then you will never be satisfied," Cathy snapped.

This was getting seriously annoying. After all, I was the customer. And I wasn't going to buy these bonds until I could get completely comfortable with the owner, his casino, and the industry.

Cash sensed this. He had not become Bloomfield Weiss's top producer by bludgeoning alone. New junk-bond issues carry the highest sales commission, and he was prepared to go a long way to try to land a sale, even if there was only a half-chance of success.

"Look, Paul. If we can get satisfactory answers to your questions will you buy these bonds?"

"Well, I would need to think about it some more. But there is a good chance I would, yes," I said.

"Okay. Let me suggest two things. First, Irwin Piper

is passing through London in a couple of weeks' time. I've met him. He's a great guy. I may be able to fix for you to meet him. Have an informal drink. How does that sound?"

"That would be very helpful. Thank you."

"Okay, I'll call you tomorrow to tell you where and when. The other thing I wanted to mention was our annual high-yield bond conference. It will be in Phoenix at the beginning of September. There will be an opportunity to visit the Tahiti in Las Vegas at the end of the conference. You will also get a chance to see the management of a number of other companies that issue high-yield bonds. Would you like to come? It should be fun. Cathy and I will be going."

"Well, thank you very much," I said. "I will have to check with Hamilton first, but that does sound interesting. I suppose I will get a chance to see the savings and loan Cathy mentioned earlier."

Cash's blue, piggy eyes looked at me questioningly for a moment. Then he coughed uncomfortably and looked at his hands clasped in front of him.

"I'm sorry, client confidentiality. I understand," I said, although I didn't quite understand.

With that the meeting broke up.

As soon as the elevator doors had closed on Cash and Cathy, Rob turned to me. "Phew! Don't you think she's gorgeous? Can you believe those legs?"

I couldn't argue about the legs. I could argue about the woman.

"She's all yours Rob. Talk about arrogant. She makes Cash look as sweet as a kitten."

"You just didn't like her showing you up like that," said Rob. "She obviously knows her stuff. Beautiful and intelligent too. I'm sure she was looking at me all through that meeting. I think I'll give her a call and see what she's doing tonight."

"You must be out of your tree. She'll eat you alive," I said. But I knew it was no use. When it came to women,

Rob was definitely out of his tree, and he would probably enjoy being eaten alive.

As we walked back into the office, Hamilton called me over. "How did it go?" he asked.

"Pretty well," I said. "I'll need to do a fair bit more work on it, but I may well get comfortable with the credit in the end." I told him some of the details of our discussion. "It certainly will be worthwhile seeing the owner. Cash also invited me to their high-yield conference in Phoenix. He said there would be a number of companies that issue junk bonds present. What do you think?" Hamilton could be tight on expenses, and I feared the answer would be no.

But I was wrong. "You should go. I'd like to begin buying a few junk bonds soon, and it will be a lot easier if you have seen the managements speak. You might learn something from other investors, too. It's always worth gathering information."

"Fine," I said. The idea of going to Arizona appealed, although I wasn't sure whether I would be up to prolonged exposure to Cash's geniality and Cathy's lectures.

"While you are over there, you may as well stop off in New York. It's always worth finding out what's going on there."

"I will. Thank you very much."

I had been to New York before, but I had never visited any of the investment banks there. Their trading rooms were legendary, the center of the world financial markets.

I went back to my desk, and opened the Tahiti documentation. I could use some help with this.

"Debbie?"

"Yes?"

"Are you feeling helpful?"

"No."

"Would you do me an enormous favor?"

"No."

"See what you think of this." I tossed her the prospectus

for the Tahiti. "I'll do the numbers, but see what you think of the covenants."

"Oh great, thanks," she said, waving at the pile of prospectuses already surrounding her. "I'll squeeze it into the half hour between when I go to bed and when I get up."

For all her complaining, I knew she would do a thorough job. And although she would never admit it, she approached the Tahiti documents with obvious enthusiasm.

"Oh, by the way," she said, "Did you see the Gypsum of America stock price is up to thirteen dollars this morning. Not bad, eh?"

"Not at all bad," I smiled.

At least that little investment seemed to be going right.

I WAS APPROACHING HOME. The road became wilder as it made its way up the dale where I was born. Gently sloping banks grew into towering hillsides, a tartan of close-cropped grass, bracken, and heather. It had rained earlier in the day, but the clouds had disbanded leaving a pale blue sky. The bright green of the grass and the bracken glistened in the sunlight; even the usually dour drystone walls shone like streaks of silver along the hillside. This drive up the dale never failed to invigorate me, no matter how long I had been cooped up in the car.

Eventually I came to a T junction with a sign pointing straight up the hillside announcing, "Barthwaite 3." I turned up an impossibly steep road. In five minutes I topped the crest of a hill and looked down into the small valley in which the village of Barthwaite nestled. I drove down past the hard gray stone cottages, brightened up here and there by geraniums or lobelia sprouting from window boxes. I slowed down as I passed a narrow lane that led down to a large farm. The words *Appletree Farm* were clearly painted on the white gate. It looked just as well kept as it had when I had lived there as a child. A new shed, some modern machinery, but otherwise the same.

I drove on through the village, crossing the small river and up the hill on the other side. I stopped in front of the last cottage, where village turned to moorland. I

walked through the small front garden, brimming with
hollyhocks, lavender, roses, gladioluses, and a host of
colorful flowers whose names I did not know, and
rapped the iron knocker of the front door, which was
guarded by half a dozen tall foxgloves.

The small, bustling form of my mother was in the
doorway in a moment.

"Come in, come in," she said. "Sit yourself down. Did
you have a good journey? Can I get you a cup of tea?
You must be tired."

I was ushered into the living room. "Why don't you
sit in Dad's chair," she said as she always did. "It's nice
and comfortable." I sank into the old leather armchair
and within a moment I was plied with scones and straw-
berry jam, both homemade. I commented on the garden,
and we spent a few minutes chatting about my mother's
plans for it. Next came the village gossip, where I caught
up on the latest scandalous activities of Mrs. Kirby,
Barthwaite's answer to Pamella Bordes. Then there was
a long story about the problems my sister, Linda, was
having getting the right fabric for her settee and the
usual mild nagging that I hadn't dropped in to see her.

My mother didn't keep still for a moment during this
conversation. She illustrated every point with elaborate
hand movements and every minute or so got up to refill
my cup, straighten up something in the room, or rush
out to the kitchen to get some more scones. Her face
was slightly flushed as she talked rapidly on. She was a
very energetic woman, throwing herself into everything
that went on in the village. Everyone liked her. Despite
her tendency to be a busybody, most of what she did or
said was motivated by kindness or a genuine desire to
help. And people still felt sorry for her. Seventeen years
is not a long time in a Dales village.

The afternoon passed pleasantly. Then, after she had
come back from the kitchen with some more tea, she
said, "I do wish your father would write. He has been in
Australia a while now. You would have thought he

could write. I'm sure he has found a lovely sheep farm. I saw one on the telly last week which I am sure would do for us."

"I am sure he will write soon. Let's go out and see the garden," I said, trying to change the subject. But it was no use.

"It really is inconsiderate of him, you know. All I need is a quick letter. I know it's expensive to phone from that distance. Have you heard from him?"

"No, Mum, I'm afraid I haven't," I said.

Nor was I likely to. My father hadn't gone to Australia. Or Argentina, or Canada as my mother had suggested over the years. He had died.

It had happened when I was eleven, and although I hadn't actually seen it, what I had seen would always remain with me. Something had caught in the combine harvester on our farm, and he had tried to free it. But he had left the engine on. I was kicking a ball against the wall on the other side of the barn. I had heard a shout over the noise of the engine, which cut off abruptly. I ran round the barn to find what was left of my father.

Eventually, I had come to terms with the shock. My mother never did. She had been devoted to my father and could not accept his death. She had created another world for herself, one in which he was still alive, and one in which she could be comfortable.

My father was the tenant of one of the largest farms on an estate and was respected by everyone in the village. This had made the lives of my mother, my older sister, and me easier. Lord Mablethorpe, the owner of the estate, had spent a lot of time on my father's farm, discussing with him ever more efficient ways to get the maximum yield from it. They had become firm friends. When my father died, Lord Mablethorpe had given us a tied cottage to live in, promising it to my mother for as long as she lived. My father had taken out a generous life insurance policy, which gave us enough to live on, and the neighbors were all kind and helpful.

My father was a good man. I knew that because everyone always said so. I remembered him as a big, fierce man with a strong sense of right and wrong. I had always done my best to please him and I had usually succeeded. On the occasions when I failed to meet his expectations, there was all hell to pay. At the end of one term I had come home from school with a report criticizing me for playing the fool in class. He had given me a lecture on the importance of learning at school. I was top of the class the next term.

His death, and the effect it had on my mother, seemed so unfair, unjust. I was stricken by my inability to do anything about it. It made me angry.

It was then that I had started running. I ran for miles over the hills, pushing myself to the limit that my small lungs could bear. I would battle my way through the cold wind and gloom of a Yorkshire winter, seeking some solace in the lonely struggle against the moors.

I also worked hard at school, determined to live up to what I imagined my father would have expected of me. I had struggled into Cambridge. Despite spending so much time on athletics, I had managed a respectable degree. By the time I started my Olympic campaign, determination and the desire to win had become a habit. It would be wrong to say that I had driven myself to an Olympic medal just for him. But I secretly hoped he had seen me crossing the line for my bronze.

My mother had never come to terms with my ambitions. While my father was "away," she had wanted my sister to marry a local farmer and myself to go to agricultural college so that I could look after the farm. My sister had obliged her, but I had not. After the accident, I could not face farming. But, to make her world habitable, my mother had decided that I was studying at an agricultural college in London. At first I had tried to contradict her, but she hadn't listened, so I gave up. She had been proud of my achievements on the track, but worried in case they were interfering with my studies.

"It's a lovely afternoon," I said to try to change the subject. "Let's go for a walk."

We left the cottage and struck up the hillside. My mother was a regular walker, and we soon made it to the saddle between our valley and the next. We looked down onto Helmby Hall, an austere mansion built at the beginning of the twentieth century by an earlier Lord Mablethorpe with the profits from his textile milling interests.

My mother paused for breath. "Oh, I didn't tell you did I? Lord Mablethorpe died last month. A stroke. Your father will be sad when he finds out."

"Oh, I'm sorry to hear that," I said.

"So am I," she said. "He was always very good to me. And to lots of people in the village."

"Does that mean his moronic son has taken over Helmby Hall?"

"Paul, really. He's not daft. He's a charming young gentleman. He's clever too. He works in a merchant bank in London, I believe. I hear he is still going to spend most of his time down there. He'll just come up here at weekends, like."

"Well, the less he has to do with Barthwaite the better," I said. "Has Mrs. Kirby met him yet? I wonder what she thinks of him," I asked my mother innocently.

My mother laughed. "I wouldn't put even that past her," she said.

We got back to the cottage at about seven, tired but contented with each other's company.

Then, just as I was getting in the car for the drive home, she said, "Now then, make sure you study hard, dear. Your father told me before he left that he was sure you would make a good farmer, and I am sure you can prove him right."

I drove home as I often drove home after visits with my mother, sad and angry at the unfairness of life and death.

>>>

I was sitting at my desk early on Monday morning when Rob arrived, a huge grin on his face. I knew that grin of old. He was in love again, and things were going well.

"Okay, what happened?"

He was bursting to tell me. "Well, I called Cathy yesterday and persuaded her to go out with me. She made all sorts of excuses, but I wasn't going to let her get away with any of them. She finally gave in and we went to a film she said she had wanted to see for years. It was some French rubbish by Truffaut. I thought it was extremely boring and lost all track of what was going on, but she was glued to the screen. Afterward we had dinner. We talked for hours. She really seems to understand me in a way no other girl ever has."

Or at least not since Claire last month and Sophie three months ago, I thought a little cruelly. Rob could get quite carried away when he poured his heart out to women. The funny thing was, often they would get carried away too. But I wouldn't have put Cathy down as a pushover for Rob's technique.

"So what happened?" I asked.

"Nothing," Rob smiled. "She's a nice girl. She doesn't go in for that sort of thing on a first date. But I'm seeing her on Saturday. I'm going to take her sailing."

"Good luck," I said. This was shaping up to be like Rob's other affairs. He was at the pedestal-building stage, I thought. You had to hand it to him, though. He seemed capable of cracking even the toughest nut.

The light flashed on my phone board. It was Cash.

"I got a couple of things," he began. "First, are you coming to our conference?"

"Yes, I'd love to come. Thank you very much," I said.

"Good," Cash said. "And I promise I will set up a meeting with Irwin Piper when he is over. Now, I have another suggestion. Would you like to come to Henley as a guest of Bloomfield Weiss? The firm has a tent every year, and I hear it's a blast. Cathy and I will be there. Bring someone from the office if you like."

My heart sank. I had no interest in rowing. And I had no interest in this kind of corporate entertainment. It would involve lots of drinking with a crowd of people I didn't know and didn't want to know. The only good thing was no one would be paying any attention to the rowing. I wanted to say no, but it was always difficult to say no to Cash.

"Thank you very much, I'll have to check whether I am doing anything that weekend. I'll let you know."

"Okay. Give me a call."

I hung up. Effusive American meets polite Englishman, and neither is comfortable with the result, I thought, feeling slightly guilty.

"What's up?" asked Rob.

"I've been invited to Henley by Bloomfield Weiss, and I feel bad about saying no."

Rob perked up. "Bloomfield Weiss, eh? Will Cathy be there?"

"Yes," I said.

"Well, I think you should go. And I think you should take me with you."

I protested, but it was useless. The persuasive powers of Rob and Cash combined were too much for me. I rang Cash back to say I was delighted to come, and I would bring Rob. Cash sounded pleased.

I was sitting at my desk watching the market struggle through the summer doldrums, ably assisted by Debbie. I was bored and irritated. Debbie seemed quite happy with the situation. I watched her work her way through the *Financial Times* crossword. I was struggling to keep myself busy. I scanned our portfolio, hoping for some ideas.

There were one or two bonds with *NV* after their name. That reminded me.

"Debbie."

"Not now, can't you see I'm busy," she said.

"Did you check the Netherlands Antilles issues? Do we have to worry about those changes to the tax treaty?"

Debbie put down her paper. "Amazingly enough, I did." She pointed to a pile of prospectuses. "I've checked over all our portfolios, and we are all right. None of our bonds are affected. The only Netherlands Antilles bonds we hold are trading below a hundred, so we will make money if the issuer calls them at par."

"That's a relief. Well done. Thanks very much for doing all that," I said.

"Hang on a moment. We may be okay on the tax legislation, but I have stumbled across one bond that smells fishy, very fishy indeed."

"Go on."

"It's this one."

She put a bond prospectus down onto the desk in front of me. I picked it up and looked at it. Written on the cover in bold was "Tremont Capital NV secured 8 percent notes maturing 15 June 2001," and underneath in slightly smaller type was, "guaranteed by Honshu Bank Ltd." Beneath that was, "Lead Manager Bloomfield Weiss."

"Well, what's wrong with this?" I asked.

"It's difficult to say exactly," Debbie began. Then she sat up bolt upright in her chair. "Christ! Did you see that?"

"What?" I said.

"On Reuters." She read from the screen in front of her, "'Gypsum Company of America announces agreed offer from DGB . . .' Who the hell are DGB?"

"It's a German cement company, I think," I said. "We were right. There was something going on."

The lines began to flash. I picked one up. It was David Barratt.

"Did you see DGB has bid for Gypsum?"

"Yes," I said. "Reuters suggests it's a friendly. Any reason why the bid shouldn't go through?"

"I don't think so," said David. "DGB doesn't have

any U.S. operations, so there won't be any antitrust problems."

"What's DGB's credit like?" I asked. If DGB was a strong credit, then the risk on our Gypsum bonds would be much less. The bond price would soar.

"Double A minus," said David. He was like a computer when it came to the details of even the most obscure companies. "Hold on, my trader is shouting something." I could hear a fair amount of noise in the background. "He says DGB is paying for the acquisition with cash and a share placing. That shouldn't harm the credit."

"Where are the bonds trading?" I asked.

"Hang on." He was back a moment later. "He's bidding ninety-five. Do you want to sell your two million?"

I thought for a moment; ninety-five was too low. "No thanks. They should be higher than that. Let me know if they move up."

I put the phone down and shouted across to Debbie. "What are you hearing?"

"Everyone is looking for these Gypsums. Bloomfield Weiss is bidding ninety-seven. I have got Claire on the line here. She is bidding ninety-seven and a half. Shall I sell?"

I tapped the buttons of my calculator. By my reckoning we should be able to get 98 1/4. "No, hold on."

"Let's just take the profit," said Debbie.

"No, these things are worth three quarters of a point more."

"You are so greedy," she said.

We spoke to three more salesmen, but none were bidding more than 97 1/2. I was close to giving up when Karen shouted, "Debbie, Leipziger Bank on four!"

"Who the hell is Leipziger Bank?" said Debbie. "Tell them to go away, we're busy."

Leipziger Bank? Now why would an obscure German bank want to talk to us, I wondered. "I'll talk to them, Karen," I shouted.

"Good morning. This is Gunter here. How is it with you? It is a fine day here."

"Good morning," I said. Come on, Gunter, get to the point.

After a little more polite conversation Gunter asked me if I had heard of an issue for the Gypsum Company of America.

"As a matter of fact, I happen to own two and a half million dollars of that issue."

"Ah good. My trader is bidding ninety-five. This is a very good bid, I believe."

An appalling bid—at least two points below the market! "Listen very closely, Gunter," I said. "My colleague is on the other line and is just about to sell these bonds to an old friend of ours at ninety-nine. If you bid ninety-nine and a half right now, then I will sell them to you. Otherwise you will never see these bonds again."

"Can I have an hour to work on that?" asked Gunter, shaken.

"You can have fifteen seconds to work on it."

Silence. I looked at my watch. After thirteen seconds, Gunter was back on the line. "Okay, okay we will buy two and a half million Gypsum of America nine percent of 1995 at ninety-nine and a half."

"Done," I said.

"Thank you," said Gunter. "I look forward to doing a lot more business with you in the future."

Fat chance, I thought, as I put down the phone.

"How on earth did you get him to pay ninety-nine and a half?" asked Debbie.

"The only reason I could think that an outfit like Leipziger Bank should be buying these bonds is if it is DGB's local bank. If DGB is desperate to buy the Gypsum bonds, then it can afford to pay up for them. Can you believe that guy bid only ninety-five when he was prepared to pay ninety-nine and a half? Remind me not to deal with them again."

"So how much are we up?" asked Debbie.

"We bought those two million at eighty-two and sold them for a seventeen-and-a-half point profit," I said. "That's three hundred and fifty thousand dollars we've made! Not bad. And we got rid of our original half million position. I wonder where our shares will be when New York comes in?"

Debbie looked thoughtful.

"What's up?" I said.

"Someone must have known about the takeover," she said.

"Of course they did," I said. "They always do. That's the way the world works."

"Maybe we shouldn't have bought those shares," she said.

"Why shouldn't we? We had no knowledge there was going to be a takeover. We just guessed. We haven't broken any rules."

"Somebody knew. Why else would the stock shoot up?"

"Look," I said. "You are the compliance officer. You know the rules. Have we broken any of them?"

Debbie thought a little. "Technically, I suppose not," she said.

"Good. Now pass me some tickets so I can log this trade."

The next day, Wednesday, was an infuriating one. I was supposed to produce a report for one of our clients, and I was having severe trouble reconciling the performance figures produced upstairs with what I knew we had achieved. I spent two hours in the afternoon staring at the same columns of numbers before I spotted the mistake, which had been staring back at me the whole time. Cursing myself for my stupidity, I went upstairs to administration to point out the error. There was still many hours' work involved to straighten it out, and what with constant interruptions from salesmen, I would be lucky to get out before midnight. Debbie offered to help me, and I accepted with relief. Even so it was not until eight o'clock that we had finished.

I put the report on Karen's desk, ready to be sent out first thing the next morning. Debbie and I looked at each other. "Drink?" she said.

"Somehow I thought you would suggest that," I said. "Where shall we go?"

"Have you ever been on that boat on the Thames? You know, the one by the Temple tube station?"

"That's fine with me," I said. "Just let me get my briefcase."

"Oh sod your briefcase!" said Debbie. "All you are going to do is take it home and bring it back to work unopened, aren't you?"

"Um, well . . ."

"Come on!"

I looked round the trading room. Rob and Hamilton were still there, Hamilton going through piles of papers, Rob fiddling with his computer. It was no surprise at all to see Hamilton at this time of night, but Rob was a rarer sighting after six o'clock. It was dusk, and the red evening sunlight shot into the trading room driving a broad band of orange between city and sky, both looming shapes of gray and black.

"It's going to rain . . ." I said.

"Oh, do come on."

We got to the boat just before it started to rain. We sat at a table in the main cabin, looking out at the gray Thames rushing up toward Westminster on the flood tide. Powerful eddies whirled around the poles driven into the riverbed just next to the boat. It was strange to see such a wild, untamed force in the middle of a late-twentieth-century city. Humans might be able to build river walls and elaborate barriers to contain or channel the flow, but there was nothing we could do to stop it.

Just then it started to rain, lashing down onto the

water, so that river, city, and sky became blurred in the gathering darkness. The wind had got up and the boat began to rock back and forth gently, creaking as it did so.

"Brrr." Debbie shivered. "You would hardly think it was summer. Mind you, it's quite cozy in here."

I looked round. The varnished wooden interior of the boat was softly lit. There were a few small groups of people at the tables running up both sides of the cabin, and a larger group of drinkers at one end. The swaying and creaking of the boat, the murmur of relaxed conversation, and the damp but warm atmosphere did make it snug.

We ordered a bottle of Sancerre. The waiter returned with it right away and poured us both a glass. I raised mine to Debbie. "Cheers," I said. "Thank you for your help this evening. I would still be there now if you hadn't done your bit."

"Not at all," Debbie said, taking a sip of her wine. "You see, I'm not quite the lazy slob I'm cracked up to be."

"Well, I'm sure Hamilton noticed."

"Oh, screw him. I only did it because you looked so miserable all day. The language you used about that accrued interest reconciliation made me blush."

"Well, thank you anyway," I said. I thought it highly unlikely that any language I could use would make Debbie blush, although looking at her now, her round cheeks were beginning to glow in the fuggy, alcohol-ridden atmosphere.

"You do seem to have been working abnormally hard recently," I said. "Are you sure you are all right?" Debbie had kept her head down all day.

"Well, it's you who gave me all those prospectuses to read, thank you very much." She frowned. "There are a couple of things that bother me, though. Bother me quite a lot."

My curiosity was aroused. "Such as?"

She thought for a moment, then shook her head. "Oh forget it. I've spent enough time worrying about those bloody prospectuses today, it can wait till tomorrow. We'll have a chance to talk about it soon enough."

I could tell she was worried about something, and for Debbie to be worried, it must be something interesting. But she clearly didn't want to talk about it now, so I changed the subject. "You know some of the traders at Bloomfield Weiss, don't you?"

"Yes, why?"

"Do you know which one trades the Gypsums?"

"Yes, Joe Finlay. He trades all Bloomfield Weiss's U.S. corporate book. He is very good. He is supposed to be the best corporate trader on the Street, makes money month in and month out. Traders at the other houses try to keep him sweet."

"Why is that?"

"He is a total bastard." Debbie said this with such certainty, that I assumed she had come to this conclusion from personal experience. Something about the tone in which she said it put me off asking her to explain more.

"Is he honest?"

Debbie laughed. "A trader from Bloomfield Weiss? I would think that highly unlikely, wouldn't you? Why do you ask?"

"I was just wondering why Bloomfield Weiss showed so much interest in the bonds just before the takeover announcement."

"You mean you think Joe might have known about it? I wouldn't be at all surprised."

I refilled both our glasses. "What are you going to spend your Gypsum profits on?" she asked, mischievously.

"You mean from the shares we bought? I don't know. I suppose I will just save them."

"What for? A rainy day?" said Debbie, nodding toward the driving rain outside.

I smiled, feeling foolish. "Well, what am I supposed to spend it on. My flat is perfectly adequate. De Jong gave me a car. I don't seem to get time to take any holiday."

"What you need is a very expensive girlfriend," said Debbie. "Someone you can lavish with your ill-gotten gains."

"None of those about at the moment, I'm afraid."

"What, an eligible young financier like you? I don't believe it," said Debbie in mock astonishment. "Mind you, you are a bit rough around the edges, and that nose could do with improvement. And it is a while since you last had a haircut, isn't it? No, I can quite see your problem."

"Thank you for the encouragement. I don't know, I just don't seem to get the time."

"Too busy working?"

"Too busy working, too busy running."

"Typical. So what are you? The virgin toiler?"

"It's not quite that bad," I said, smiling.

"Oh yes? Tell me more," said Debbie, leaning forward, all curiosity.

"It's none of your business," I said half-heartedly.

"Of course it isn't," said Debbie. "Tell me."

She was leaning across the table, her bright eyes dancing over my face, begging me to talk. Despite some reluctance, I couldn't disappoint her.

"Well, there was a girl at university called Jane," I said. "She was very nice. Very patient."

"Patient?"

"Yes. I was almost always in training. I used to run at least forty miles a week, and that didn't include weights and sprint training. And then I was trying to get a good degree. There wasn't a lot of time for much else."

"And she put up with that?"

"For a while. She was really very good about it. She would always watch me compete, and sometimes she would even watch me train."

"She must have been quite taken with you," said Debbie.

"I suppose she was. In the end she had enough. It was either my running or her. You can guess which I chose."

"Poor her."

"Oh, I don't know. She was better off without me. Two months later she met Martin, one year later and they were married. She probably has two kids now and is very happy."

"And no one else since then?"

"One or two. But none of them really lasted." I sighed. Every relationship I had started had soon become a struggle between the woman and my running, and I had never been willing to compromise on my running. Sometimes I regretted it, but it was just part of the price I had to pay to get to the Olympics. In the end I was always prepared to pay it."

"Well, what's to stop you now?" Debbie asked.

"Stop me what?"

"You know, getting a girlfriend."

"Well, you can't just go out and get one, just like that," I protested. "I mean it's not that easy. There's no time, what with work and everything."

Debbie laughed. "Surely you could fit in some time between nine and nine thirty on Tuesdays and Thursdays. That should be enough, shouldn't it?"

I shrugged and grinned. "Yes, you are right. I am just out of practice. I will rectify the problem immediately. By this time next week I will have three women ready for your inspection."

We polished off the bottle, split the bill, and got up to brave the wind and the rain outside. We walked along the covered gangway, bucking on the choppy water, and stood under the awning on the pavement.

We were standing staring in dismay at the cold wet night, when a man pushed past us. He stopped for a second in front of Debbie, thrust his hand up to her blouse and squeezed. "Miss me love?" he said and gave a short, dry laugh. He turned to me for just a second, looked at me with strangely limp blue eyes, twitched the corners of his mouth in a fake smile and ducked into the rain.

I stood still for a moment in surprise, my reflexes

dulled by the wine. Then, as I lunged out into the rain to catch him, Debbie caught my sleeve. "Don't, Paul! Stop!"

"But you saw what he did," I said, hesitating, with Debbie pulling on my arm.

"Please Paul. Don't bother. Please."

I looked into the gloom, but the man had already disappeared. Debbie's face was pleading and, for once, dead serious. And she was afraid.

I shrugged my shoulders and got back into the shelter of the awning, soaked from just a few seconds in the rain.

"Who the hell is he?"

"Don't ask."

"But he can't just do that to you."

"Look, Paul. Please. Just drop it. Please."

"Okay, okay. Let's get you in a taxi."

Not surprisingly, given the rain, no taxis appeared, and after five minutes we agreed to depart to our respective tube stations. Debbie, hunched under her umbrella, dashed off to get the Northern line from the Embankment and I sprinted through the rain to the Temple.

As the underground train lurched westward on its never-ending journey round the Circle Line, I wondered about the man I had seen grope Debbie. Who could he have been? A former lover? A former work colleague? A total stranger? A drunk? I had no idea. Nor had I any idea why Debbie refused to tell me anything about him. She had looked scared, rather than shocked or offended. Very odd.

I had caught a good glimpse of him in the moment he had turned to me. He was thin and wiry, about thirty-five, and wearing an unremarkable city suit. I could still see his eyes. Pale blue, dead, the pupils almost invisible pinpricks. I shuddered.

The train stopped at Victoria. A crowd of people barged off, and one or two got on. As the train jolted into motion again, my mind wandered. I tried to read the newspaper of the old man sitting opposite me, but I couldn't quite make it out. The conversation I had with Debbie about my girlfriends, or rather lack of them, drifted back into my mind. I had just not tried over the last few years as far as women were concerned. It wasn't that I disliked female company, far from it, it was just that so many relationships had started with high hopes and ended in disappointment that it did not seem worth the effort. Well, I should probably change that. Debbie was right; however single-minded I was about succeeding at work there had to be time for some other things.

The thought of Debbie made me smile. Her good humor was irrepressible. I realized that I looked forward to facing her wide grin and gentle teasing as I came into work every day. I had grown very fond of her over the last few months.

Hold on. Had Debbie anyone in mind when she was encouraging me to find myself a girlfriend? It would be typical of me to miss a come-on like that. No, I was just imagining it, surely. Not Debbie. Not me. Still, in some strange way, the idea appealed.

I WAS BUSY the next morning. The phones didn't stop ringing. The market was active. Institutional fund managers were switching out of Deutsche marks into dollars ahead of what they believed to be an interest rate cut by the Bundesbank. The Street had been taken by surprise. The buildup of supply of eurobonds that had preceded the recent Sweden issue had almost all been bought, and a number of brokers had been caught short. Salesmen were calling us to try to tempt us to sell our positions to them. But we were hanging on. Let them sweat.

Debbie was late, so I had to answer all the phones myself. It was hard work.

At nine I called over to Karen, "Heard anything from Debbie?" We hadn't had that heavy a night's drinking last night, she should have been able to make her way in.

"Nothing yet," she said.

At nine thirty, Hamilton wandered by my desk. "Any sign of Debbie?"

"Not yet."

"You would think she would at least have the good grace to call in sick," he said.

I didn't argue. If nothing else, it was a bit stupid just not to show up. Any excuse was better than no excuse. Debbie had days off sick quite frequently, but she usually called in with a story.

The morning progressed. I had managed to hold on to

all our positions, despite the best efforts of Cash, Claire, David, and the other salesmen to tempt them away from me.

My concentration was broken by Karen's voice. A note of concern, almost fear, in it attracted my attention and that of the others in the room.

"Hamilton! It's the police. They want to talk to someone about Debbie."

Hamilton picked up the phone. We all watched him. Within a few seconds, his eyebrows had pulled together slightly. He talked quietly for five minutes or so. Then he slowly replaced the handset. He stood up and walked over to stand by my desk, by Debbie's desk. He motioned for everyone to gather round.

"I have some bad news. Debbie is dead. She was drowned last night."

The shock of these words hit me hard in the face, leaving my ears singing and my eyes out of focus. I slumped back in my chair. When Hamilton was talking to the police, wild fears of what might have happened to Debbie had run through my mind, but they hadn't prepared me for this blow. I felt the emptiness of the desk behind me, usually the center of gossip and laughter, now silent. I only half heard Hamilton continue.

"Her body was found at six o'clock this morning in the Thames by Millwall Docks. The police will be round this afternoon to talk to us. They asked me to check who was the last to see her last night."

"I was," I said, or rather I meant to say. What came out of my mouth was just a croak. "I was," I repeated, more clearly this time.

Hamilton turned to me, his face grim. "Okay, Paul, they'll probably want a statement from you."

Everyone looked at me, inquiringly. "I last saw her about half past nine last night," I said. "We had just had a drink. She was walking along the Embankment. I didn't see anything else." Despite the turmoil inside me, I managed to keep my voice under control.

"Do they know how it happened?" asked Rob.

"Not yet," replied Hamilton. "They are not ruling anything out, according to the policeman."

How it happened? She fell in, surely. But how do you just fall into the Thames? That would have to be very difficult, however windy the night. That meant she either jumped, or she was pushed. The dead eyes and thin face of the man who had groped Debbie just before she left the boat loomed up in front of me. I bet he had something to do with it.

The phones were flashing angrily. Hamilton said, "We had better answer those."

None of us talked to the others. It was difficult to think of anything to say. We each suffered our shock privately. Karen sobbed quietly into a handkerchief. Rob and Gordon stood around, looking for something to occupy themselves with.

I just stared across at Debbie's desk.

Until last night, I hadn't realized how close we had become over the last couple of months. I could still see her round cheeks glowing in the soft light of the boat, eyes bubbling with laughter. That was only hours ago, fourteen hours to be precise. How could someone who had so much life in her suddenly not be? Just cease to exist. It didn't make sense. I could feel my eyes smarting. I put my head in my hands and just sat there.

I don't know how long it was before I felt a hand on my shoulder. I looked up. It was Hamilton.

"I'm sorry," he said. "You were a good team."

I looked up at him and nodded.

"Do you want to go home?" Hamilton asked.

I shook my head.

"Can I suggest something?" said Hamilton.

My voice cracked as I said "What?"

"Pick up the phone and talk to people."

He was right. I needed to enmesh myself in the safety of the daily routine. Prices, gossip, yields, spreads.

I couldn't bring myself to tell people about Debbie.

But it was not long before word got around the market. The rest of the morning was more difficult as I spent most of it agreeing with everyone what a wonderful, fun-loving person Debbie was and how awful it was that she was dead.

At lunchtime the police came. They spent half an hour with Hamilton. He then called me into the conference room where two men sat waiting for me. The larger of the two introduced himself as Detective Inspector Powell. He was a stocky man in his mid-thirties with a cheap double-breasted suit hanging open and a loud tie. He moved quickly as he stood up, his stockiness was muscle, not flab. He looked like a man of action, uncomfortable in the rarefied atmosphere of De Jong's conference room. His colleague, Detective Constable Jones, merged into the background, pencil at the ready to take notes.

"Mr. McKenzie says that you were the last person here to see Miss Chater alive?" Powell began. He had a flat London accent and a tone that made a simple question sound more like an accusation. He oozed impatience.

"That's true. We went out for a drink last night." I told them all about the previous night. The constable took copious notes. The questioning became closer when I got to the man who had accosted Debbie and disappeared into the night. I answered well under pressure, giving a pretty accurate description, and said I would spend some time with a police artist if necessary. Then Powell's questions changed tack.

"Mr. McKenzie said that you were the closest to Miss Chater?"

"Yes, I suppose that is correct."

"Would you say that Miss Chater was depressed lately," he asked.

"No, not really."

"No problems with boyfriends?"

"None that she told me about."

"Any problems at work?"

I hesitated. "No, not really."

"None at all?" Powell looked me straight in the eye. He had caught my hesitation.

"Well, she was a little upset recently." I told him about Debbie's disagreements with Hamilton and her conversation with me in Finsbury Circus. "But she wasn't nearly upset enough to commit suicide," I said.

"It's always difficult to tell that, sir," said Powell. "It's surprising how often apparently stable people take their own life because of something that friends or relatives think of as trivial."

"No, you don't understand," I said. "She was never depressed. In fact, she was always having a laugh. She enjoyed life."

Powell looked as though he only half heard this. He nodded to his colleague who closed his notebook and then said, "Thank you for your time, Mr. Murray. You will of course be available should we have any more questions?"

I nodded, and with that the two policemen left.

I struggled through the day somehow. At about six, I turned off the machines and went home.

As I was waiting at the elevator, I was joined by Hamilton. There was an awkward silence. Small talk with Hamilton was tough at the best of times. In the present circumstances, I did not have the energy to think of anything bright or interesting to say.

Eventually the elevator came, and we both got in. As the elevator descended, Hamilton spoke. "What are you doing now, Paul?"

"Nothing. Going home," I said.

"Do you want to stop in for a drink at my place on the way back?" Hamilton asked.

I didn't answer at first. I was amazed by the invitation. It was completely unlike Hamilton to invite anyone to do anything socially. A half hour of difficult conversation with Hamilton was the last thing I felt like right then, but I couldn't refuse.

"That's very kind of you," I said.

Hamilton lived in one of the gray-streaked concrete towers of the Barbican, which guard the northern approaches to the City. It was only a fifteen-minute walk from the office, which we spent almost in silence as we dodged through traffic and commuters. The Barbican is a maze of concrete walkways and towers that wind round the old walls and churches of the City at about twenty feet above street level. It is so disorienting that yellow lines have been painted on the walkway to guide you to various places you may or may not want to go. A soulless place to live.

We eventually came to Hamilton's tower and took an elevator to the top floor. His flat was small and convenient. Expensive, but unremarkable furniture provided most of the functions that someone needs to live, but little more. The only pictures were a set of nineteenth-century prints of the abbeys of Scotland. Walls have to have pictures, but it would be difficult to find any grayer than these. I looked curiously through an open door where I could just see a desk.

"That's my study," said Hamilton. "Let me show you."

We went into the next room. There was indeed a desk facing the window. The walls were lined from floor to ceiling with shelves and filing cabinets. Thousands of books and papers were held in that small room. It was a bit like a professor's office at a university, except that it was perfectly tidy. Everything was in its place. The desk was completely bare except for a computer.

I scanned the shelves briefly. The titles of nearly all the books I saw had something to do with finance or economics. Many of them were written in the nineteenth century. There was one set of shelves that aroused my interest. It held titles such as Gleick's *Chaos Theory*,

Rudé's *The Crowd in History,* and even Darwin's *The Origin of Species.* There were works on psychology, physics, religion, and linguistics.

Hamilton drew up beside me. "You should read some of these. It would help you understand our job better."

I looked at him, puzzled.

"Markets are about movement of prices, about groups of people interacting, about competition, about information, about fear, greed, belief," he went on. "All these things are studied in detail by a range of academic disciplines, each of which can give you an insight into why the market behaves the way it does."

"Oh, I see," I said. Now I understood. In Hamilton's world the great scholars of matter and the mind had made a significant contribution to financial theory. They did have some use after all.

I pulled out *The Prince* by Niccolò Machiavelli. "And this?" I said, showing it to Hamilton.

He smiled. "Oh, Machiavelli understood power. That book is all about power and how to use it. And so are the financial markets. Money is power, information is power, and analytical ability is power."

"But doesn't he write about how to become a ruthless dictator?"

"Oh no, that's much too simplistic. Certainly, he believes the end justifies the means. But although a successful prince will do whatever is required to achieve his goal, he will always maintain the semblance of virtue. That is vital."

I looked puzzled.

Hamilton laughed. "In the markets that means be smart, be imaginative, but at all costs keep your reputation. Remember that."

"I will," I said, putting the book back on its shelf.

"I like this room," Hamilton said, relaxed. "I spend most of my time here. Look at that view."

It was indeed a remarkable view, looking out over the offices of the City from St. Paul's to the East End.

De Jong's offices were clearly distinguishable. A source of inspiration for Hamilton whenever he was bogged down in his studies of the markets.

We went back into the living room. "Scotch?" he asked.

"Yes please."

He splashed generous portions into two glasses and added a small amount of water to each. He handed me one, and we both sat down.

After a moment's appreciation of his drink, Hamilton asked, "Do you think she committed suicide?" He studied my face closely.

I sighed. "No," I said. "No matter what the police said, Debbie would never do anything like that."

"She was concerned about her job, though, wasn't she?" said Hamilton. "I don't know whether she told you, but we did have a slightly difficult discussion about her future not long before she died."

"Yes, I know," I said. "She did tell me about that conversation and it did upset her for a bit. But she soon forgot it. She was not the kind of person who would allow a little thing like work to get in the way of her enjoying life. I am quite sure that is not the reason she died."

Hamilton relaxed. "No, suicide doesn't seem like her at all," he said. "It must have been an accident."

There was silence for a moment.

"I'm not so sure," I said.

"What do you mean?"

"I saw someone just before she died."

"Saw someone? Who?"

"I don't know who it was. It's probably someone who works in the City. Thin. Mid-thirties. Very fit. Mean looking."

"What was he doing? Did you see him do anything to her?"

"It was just as we were leaving. He just walked up to her, groped her breast, and walked off into the night. A couple of minutes later, she set off as well."

"What an extraordinary thing to do! Didn't you do anything?"

"Debbie stopped me," I said. "And she looked frightened. I don't blame her. There was something very strange about that man."

"Have you told the police?"

"Yes."

"What did they think?"

"Well, they took lots of notes. They didn't actually say they thought anything. But it looks to me like he must have pushed Debbie into the river. Don't you think?"

Hamilton sat for a moment, gently touching his chin, in his habitual thinking pose. "It certainly looks like it, doesn't it. But who is he? And why would he do it?" We sat in silence for a minute, each wrapped in our own thoughts. Hamilton was no doubt trying to figure the problem out, I was missing Debbie. It had been a long day.

I gulped my whiskey. "Let me get you another," said Hamilton.

With another glass safely in my hand, I changed the subject. "How long have you lived here?" I asked.

"Oh, about five years," Hamilton answered. "Since my divorce. It's very convenient for the office."

"I didn't know you were divorced," I said, tentatively. I wasn't sure how personal Hamilton would allow the conversation to become. But I was curious. No one at the office knew anything of Hamilton's life outside it, but it was something about which we all speculated.

"Didn't you? I suppose you wouldn't. I don't talk about it much. But I have a son, Alasdair." He pointed to a photograph of a smiling seven- or eight-year-old boy kicking a soccer ball. I hadn't noticed it before. The boy looked a lot like Hamilton, but without the gloom.

"Do you see him much?" I asked.

"Oh yes, every other weekend," he said. "I have a cottage in Perthshire near where his mother lives. It's very useful. And it's much better for him to be up there rather than in this dreadful city. It's lovely up there. You can get up onto the hills and forget all this," he gestured out of the window.

I told him about Barthwaite and my own childhood there, roving over the moors. Hamilton listened. It was strange to be talking to Hamilton about something like that, but he seemed interested, and as I talked on I began to relax. It was good to talk about a place hundreds of miles and ten years away rather than about today, here.

"I sometimes wish I had stayed in Edinburgh," Hamilton said. "I could have had a nice easy job up there, managing a few hundred million for one of those insurance companies."

"Why didn't you?" I asked.

"Well, I tried it for a bit, but it didn't suit me," he said. "Those Scottish funds are good, but they have no sense of adventure. I needed to be down here. At the sharp end." He looked into his whiskey glass. "Of course, Moira didn't like it. She didn't understand the hours I worked. She thought I could do my job properly between nine and five and spend the rest of my time at home. But this job requires a lot more than that, and she just didn't believe me. So we split up."

"I'm sorry," I said. And I was sorry for him. He was a lonely man, and cut off from his wife and son, he must be lonelier still. Of course it was his own decision; he had put his work squarely before his marriage. Nonetheless, I sympathized. I could see myself in the same situation in ten years' time. I shuddered. I remembered my conversation with Debbie. I was beginning to think she was right.

Hamilton looked up from his whiskey. "So how are you finding De Jong, now you have been here six months? Enjoying it?"

"Yes, I am. Very much. I am very pleased I joined the firm."

"How do you find trading?"

"I love it. I just wish I was better at it. Sometimes I think that I am getting the hang of it, and then it all goes wrong. I wonder if it isn't just all about luck."

Hamilton laughed. "You shouldn't ever think that, laddie. Of course, it's all about luck, or at least each individual trade is. But if you discipline yourself to trade only when the odds are in your favor, in the long run you will certainly come out ahead. It's basic statistics."

Hamilton saw my expression and laughed again. "No, you are right, it's not quite that easy. The trick is to work out when the odds are in your favor, and that can take years of experience. But don't worry. You are on the right track. Just persevere, keep thinking about what you are doing and why, learn from your mistakes, and you will turn out very well. We will make a good team."

I hoped so. I felt a surge of excitement. Hamilton wouldn't say something like that unless he meant it. I was determined to keep trying, and to do all he said.

"I remember seeing you run," Hamilton said.

"Oh, I didn't know you watched athletics."

"Well, everyone watches the Olympics, even me. And I do like athletics. Something about the sport appeals. I watched you a number of times, but what I really remember is the final, when you pushed yourself into the lead. The television had a closeup on your face. Total determination, and pain. I thought you were going to win, and then that Kenyan and Spaniard drifted past you."

"Irishman," I mumbled.

"What?"

"Irishman. It was an Irishman, not a Spaniard," I said. "A very fast Irishman."

Hamilton laughed. "Well, I'm very glad you are working for me now. I think together we can really make something of De Jong."

"I would like that very much," I said. Very much indeed.

>>>

Debbie's funeral was in a quiet churchyard in a small village in Kent. I was there representing the office. It was a gorgeous day, the sun beating down on the mourners. I was hot in my suit, and I could feel the sweat trickling down my back. A group of rooks cawed halfheartedly in a small coppice by the gate to the churchyard. The noise complemented the silence rather than disrupting it. The perfect accompaniment to a small country funeral.

The vicar did his best to relieve the sadness of the occasion by saying that Debbie would have wanted her mourners to smile and that we should give thanks for the time she spent with us. Or something like that. I didn't quite follow his logic, and anyway it didn't work. There is something heart-rendingly sad about the death of any young person; nothing you can say can change that. That it was Debbie who had been taken so early from a life she had enjoyed so much, did not make it any better.

Her parents were there. There was something of Debbie in the face of each of them. Two small round figures, drawn together in their grief.

As we all made our way slowly back toward the road, I found myself walking next to a tall, thin red-haired woman. She was wearing heels and got one of them caught in the paving stones of the path. I bent down to help her free her shoe.

"Thank you," she said. "I hate these bloody shoes." Then, looking around, "Do you know all these people?"

"Very few," I said. "And you?"

"One or two. I shared a flat with Debbie, so I got to know a number of her boyfriends."

"A number?" I said, surprised. "How many are here?"

She looked around. "Just one or two that I knew. You weren't one of them, were you?" she said, her eyes teasing me.

"No," I said sharply, a little shocked. "I worked with her."

"No offense meant. She usually had good taste," said the woman. "Are you going past the station?"

"Yes I am. Can I give you a lift?"

"That would be very kind. My name is Felicity, by the way."

"Mine's Paul." We walked on out of the churchyard and into the road. "This is it," I said as we came to my little Peugeot.

We got in the car and headed for the nearest station, which was three miles away.

"I must say, I never realized Debbie had many boyfriends," I said. "She seemed to me to be the stable relationship kind."

"She wasn't entirely a loose woman. But she did enjoy herself. There were different men in and out of our house all the time. Most of them were okay, but some were quite unsavory. I think one or two may have been from work."

"Not the unsavory ones, I hope?"

Felicity laughed. "No, I don't think so. Although there was one who gave her a hard time very recently. I think he may have had something to do with work."

I wondered who on earth that would be. Unable to restrain my curiosity, I asked her.

"I can't remember his name," she said. "I last saw him a couple of years ago. He was a right pain."

I let it drop. "How did you meet Debbie?" I asked.

"Oh we both did articles at the same law firm, Denny Clark. I still work there, but Debbie went on to do greater things, as you know. Since we were both looking to rent accommodation in London, it seemed natural to share if we could." She bit her lip. "I shall miss her."

"You are not the only one," I said as we approached the station. I pulled up in front of the entrance.

"Thanks very much," she said as she got out of the car. "I hope we'll meet again on a slightly happier occasion." With that she disappeared into the station. As I drove back to London I tried to come to terms with the picture Felicity had given of Debbie sleeping around with a succession of men. It didn't seem in her character. But, on the other hand, why shouldn't she?

Debbie's desk looked just the same. It was scattered with the debris of half-done tasks. There were notes on little yellow stickers reminding her of things to do and people to call back. The AIBD directory of bonds lay with its pages open, face down, waiting for her to pick it up again at the page she left it. I would have preferred it to have been tidy, the desk of a life ended rather than a life interrupted.

She had a large black desk diary, which had the Harrison Brothers logo on it. Last year's Christmas present. I leafed through the pages. Nothing very interesting. The appointments were quite densely packed over the next week, and then thinned out as July became August. September on was just blank white paper.

There was one entry that caught my eye. It was a meeting with Mr. De Jong. It was for the day after she died, at 10:30 A.M. It was strange that Debbie should have an appointment fixed up with him. We hardly saw him. Although he would have meetings with Hamilton occasionally, the only time I had been in his office was the day I joined. He was a nice enough fellow, but hardly what you would call approachable.

I began to put everything in order. I started by putting all Debbie's personal belongings into an old copier paper box. There wasn't much; certainly nothing that would have value to anyone else. An old compact, some tights, three yogurts, a horde of plastic spoons, a letter opener with the name of a deal she had worked on during her legal days engraved on it, some packets of tissues and a well-thumbed Jilly Cooper novel. I considered throwing it all away, but couldn't bring myself to. With the exception of the yogurts, I packed it all into a box. I would take it round to Debbie's flat to put with her other belongings.

I then began the task of sorting out all her papers and

files. Most of them I threw away, but I put some to one side to take to the library for filing.

I came to a pile of prospectuses. They mostly related to bonds that were issued by Netherlands Antilles companies. On top of the pile was the Tremont Capital prospectus that Debbie had thrown on my desk. She had said it was fishy. I picked it up and flicked through. There didn't seem much odd about it to me. There were one or two lightly penciled notes in the margin. None of them seemed to have any startling meaning.

I put the prospectus down on one side and worked my way down the pile. I soon came to the Information Memorandum for the Tahiti. I leafed through it slowly. Debbie had used a yellow highlighting marker on it. There were only two or three passages marked. These were much more interesting. She had highlighted Irwin Piper's name and also references to the Nevada State Gaming Commission. One statement in particular was picked out in fluorescent yellow:

> Potential investors' attention is drawn to the policy of the Nevada State Gaming Commission to refuse a license to any person convicted of a criminal offense. The good character of the applicant is an important consideration in the granting of any license.

Cathy Lasenby had referred to this policy in our meeting as evidence that Piper was straight. Maybe her confidence was misplaced. Maybe Debbie had discovered something that suggested this was far from the case.

Maybe that was why she was dead.

I stood up and looked out of the window westward over London. I was sure Debbie wouldn't kill herself. An accident was possible, I supposed, but I didn't believe it. Someone had pushed her, and it was almost certainly the man who had frightened her so badly as we left the boat. And if she had been killed, it must have been for a reason. There was no obvious reason why anyone should want to kill Debbie.

I sat down again and continued the job of sorting through papers. After an hour and a half I had just finished when Karen came over with a letter.

"What shall I do with Debbie's mail?" she said.

I wondered how long dead people continued to receive mail. "Give it to me, I suppose," I said.

Karen handed over a white envelope with Bloomfield Weiss's logo stamped on it. It was marked "Private and Confidential: To Be Opened by Addressee Only." Not much chance of that, I thought, gloomily. I opened it.

> Dear Ms. Chater,
> Thank you for your recent correspondence regarding trading in the shares of the Gypsum Company of America. We have started our own investigation into possible irregularities by employees of Bloomfield Weiss regarding this same stock. I suggest that we should meet to share information on this matter. I will call you early next week to arrange a time.
>
> Yours Sincerely,
> Ronald Bowen
> Senior Compliance Officer

I was intrigued. Gypsum's shares certainly had moved up sharply before the takeover by DGB was announced. This letter suggested Debbie was right to be suspicious. I wondered who should deal with it at De Jong. I supposed I should really give the letter to Hamilton, because we no longer had an official compliance officer. But I was curious. I was dealing with all the rest of Debbie's work, why shouldn't I deal with this as well?

I picked up the phone, dialed Bloomfield Weiss, and asked to speak to Mr. Bowen.

"Bowen here." His voice was gruff and officious. Large firms such as Bloomfield Weiss took compliance seriously. A scandal could cost them not only a fine of several million, but also the loss of their reputation. After the Blue Arrow affair when a compliance officer at County Natwest had been ignored and overruled, big institutions ensured that their compliance officers had teeth. They were the sort of people who did everything by the book and who could not be pushed around.

"Good morning, Mr. Bowen, this is Paul Murray from De Jong and Company," I said. "I'm calling regarding your recent letter to Debbie Chater, our compliance officer."

"Oh yes."

"I am afraid to say Debbie died very recently." Several days and many explanations after the event, it was getting easier to say this bit.

"I'm very sorry," said Bowen, sounding as though he didn't care in the least.

"I wonder if I can help you regarding the Gypsum Company of America? Debbie and I worked on that together. I read your letter to her this morning."

"Perhaps you can. Let me just get my file." There was a rustle of papers down the phone line. "Yes, one of my colleagues in New York alerted us to the unusual movements in the Gypsum share price. Our investigation has turned up a few useful facts, but nothing we can take action on yet. We were very interested to receive Miss Chater's letter outlining her own suspicions. You will appreciate that the whole investigation is still very confidential at this stage?"

"Yes, of course," I said.

"Good. We are investigating two employees of Bloomfield Weiss and one client of the firm. There is also someone else . . ." His voice trailed off as I heard him turning the page.

"Mr. Murray, didn't you say your name was?" said Bowen, his voice a note lower, a note graver.

"Yes," I said. I swallowed.

"Ah, I'm sorry, I am afraid we don't have anything more on file. Good-bye, Mr. Murray."

"But shouldn't we meet as you suggested?" I asked.

"I don't think that will be necessary," Bowen said firmly. "Good-bye." He hung up.

I slumped back in my chair to think. I didn't like the sound of this investigation.

Vague thoughts of trials and prison floated round my head. Then I pulled myself together. I hadn't done anything wrong. Debbie had said so, and she did know the law. I had no inside information. It was only natural that people would check me out, given my purchase, but I had nothing to worry about. Nothing at all.

Still best to make sure. I rang Bloomfield Weiss again. Cathy answered the phone.

"Is Cash there?" I asked.

"No, he has just popped out to fetch a cup of coffee," Cathy's clear voice replied. "He'll be back in a minute."

"Perhaps you can help," I said.

"If you think I can," said Cathy, a hint of sarcasm in her voice.

She was probably offended I had asked for Cash instead of her, I thought. Perhaps she thought I doubted her capabilities. I was about to apologize when I stopped myself. Screw it. Some people are just too touchy.

"I was curious about all those Gypsum bonds you were buying last week," I said. "Were they for your own books?"

"No, they were for a client."

"He must have done very nicely," I said.

"He certainly did," said Cathy. "In fact . . ."

I heard Cash's growl interrupt her. "Hold on," she said and clicked her phone onto hold. A moment later she was back. "I'm sorry, I've got to jump. I'll tell Cash you were after him," and hung up.

Rob walked past my desk and saw me staring gloomily into the receiver. "What's up? Seen a ghost?"

His smile only lasted a second. "Sorry. Stupid thing to say."

"Life goes on," I said. "But I will miss her."

"So will I," said Rob.

"She had a lot of boyfriends, didn't she?"

"Some, I suppose." Rob caught my glance. His cheeks reddened. "Some," he said again, and turned away.

I shrugged my shoulders and got back to work. I looked at the small box of Debbie's possessions at my feet. I should take them over to her flat, I thought. I pulled out the phone book and rang Denny Clark. I asked to speak to Felicity. There was only one woman of that name who worked at Denny Clark, and she was in.

"Hello, it's Paul Murray," I said. "We met at Debbie's funeral."

"Oh yes," she said, "you are the guy she used to work with."

"That's right. I've got some things of hers. Not much and none of it's very important. Can I bring them round?"

"Sure, when would you like to come?" she said.

"This evening okay?"

"Fine. Come round at seven. The address is twenty-five Cavendish Road. Clapham South is the nearest tube stop. See you then."

CHAPTER

> > > > > **6**

CAVENDISH ROAD TURNED out to be part of the South Circular, one of the most clogged of London's tired old arteries. Cars and trucks crept forward and then, as a light changed, hurtled along the street for fifty yards or so before slowing to a crawl again. The July evening air was full of dust and carbon monoxide fumes and throbbed with the sound of revving engines.

Number twenty-five was a small terraced house similar to all the others on the street. There were two bells by the door. I pressed the one with *Chater* and *Wilson* written in smudged blue ink. The door buzzed to let me in.

Debbie and Felicity had the upstairs flat. It was cheaply but attractively furnished, untidy but not a mess. Felicity came to the door in tight blue jeans and a sloppy black T-shirt, her red hair falling in a tangle onto her shoulders. She showed me through to the living room. There was one sofa and a series of large cushions on the floor. Felicity motioned for me to sit on the sofa, while she curled up on a cushion.

"Sorry this place is a bit of a tip," she said.

I handed her the box I had brought. "Thank you," she said. "Debbie's parents will be down this weekend to collect her things. Can I get you a glass of wine?"

She disappeared to the kitchen and came back with a bottle of Muscadet and two glasses.

"So, you have lived here with Debbie since you both came to London?" I asked.

"Oh no," answered Felicity. "When we first moved down here we rented a flat in Earl's Court. Well, it really wasn't much more than one bedroom. But a couple of years ago, we bought this place jointly. It's a bit noisy, but you get used to it."

"You and Debbie must have been very close," I said.

"I suppose we were," said Felicity. "She was a very easy person to live with and we had some good laughs together. But in a way she was a very private person. So am I, come to think of it. I think that's why we got on together. We liked living with each other, but respected each other's privacy."

"I hope you don't mind me asking this," I said, "but I think I met someone the other day who might have been a boyfriend of Debbie's. He was thin, mid-thirties, blue eyes, dark hair?"

Felicity thought for a moment. "Yes, there was one who fits that description. She had an affair with him last year some time. It didn't last long. I really didn't like him at all. I remember the way he used to look at me." She shuddered.

That must have been the man on the boat. "What was his name?" I asked.

Felicity screwed up her face in an effort to remember. "No. Sorry. I know she met him through work somehow or other. He was a nasty piece of work. Charming at first. But very soon he was ordering Debbie about. At breakfast it was embarrassing to watch. And Debbie did everything he asked! It was very odd. You know Debbie, she was hardly your average meek house slave. This man did exude a sort of violent power. Debbie found it fascinating. It scared me.

"Then one evening I came home at about ten o'clock to find Debbie in a terrible state. She had a big bruise on her forehead and her eye was puffed up. She was sobbing quietly, as though she had been crying for a while.

"I asked her what had happened. She said that—oh, I wish I could remember his name. Anyway whoever the bastard was had beaten her up. She had found out he was married and had confronted him with it. He had hit her and walked out.

"Over the next few days this man would telephone or come round in person. Debbie never talked to him or let him in. She nearly gave in once or twice, but in the end she had too much common sense. We were both scared. I certainly didn't want to have anything to do with him and we were both frightened in case he was waiting outside our building to follow us when we went out. I think he did once follow Debbie, but she screamed and he slunk off. After a week or so he gave up calling and we didn't see any more of him."

Until the other night on the boat, I thought. It seemed to me more likely than ever that this was the man who had pushed Debbie into the river. I wondered how I could find out who he was. "You can't remember anything more about him. Where he lived, what he did, who he worked for?"

"I'm sorry. That was one of the main areas in which we respected each other's privacy. I would occasionally bump into Debbie's boyfriends, but she rarely talked about them. And I did my best to avoid him."

"It wasn't the same man you mentioned at the funeral? The one who was bothering her lately."

"No, no. It wasn't him. He wasn't quite so scary. Although he was a bit weird perhaps. Oh, I've remembered his name by the way. It was Rob."

Rob! Incredible! I had never noticed anything between him and Debbie. They seemed to treat each other perfectly naturally. Still, if you thought about it, it wasn't so surprising. In a way, it was inevitable that Rob would make a play for Debbie at some time.

Felicity had noticed my initial surprise. "Of course, you must know him. You obviously didn't know about it."

I shook my head.

"Well, they went out together just after Debbie joined De Jong and Company. It only lasted a couple of months or so, and then Debbie called it off. She said it was getting a bit heavy. Rob took it badly for a bit, but after a while Debbie said they could treat each other normally at work."

Felicity took another sip of wine. "Then, about a week before Debbie"—Felicity paused—"fell into the river, this bloke rang up. It was late, just after midnight, I think. He said they should get back together again. He said they should get married. Debbie just told him not to be so silly, but he kept on ringing night after night. It began to get to Debbie. She told him to get lost, but it didn't seem to have any effect."

"But why did he suddenly decide he wanted to marry her?" I asked. "It sounds a bit odd."

"Yes. As I said, a bit weird. Debbie said this guy was like that. Isn't he?"

I nodded. I had to admit Rob was like that. "I still don't quite understand why Rob waited until now."

"He was jealous. At least that is what Debbie said."

"Jealous? Of whom?"

"I don't know. Debbie said she was getting interested in someone else at work, and Rob didn't like it. He was getting possessive and it annoyed her."

For a second I cast around thinking who Debbie could have been talking about. But there could only be one person. Me.

I felt very foolish. The closening of our relationship must have been obvious to Debbie and even to Rob. But it was only just beginning to sink in to my thick skull when she died.

The depression that had been stalking me wherever I went since then enveloped me again. With Debbie had died an opportunity to break out of the straitjacket of my life, the self-discipline, loneliness, hard work, and dedication to a goal. She had offered irresponsibility, fun, easy companionship. And just as all that had been in my grasp, it had been pulled away. Pulled away by the thin man with the dead eyes.

I drained my glass and got up to leave.

"Thank you for bringing her things round," said Felicity, nodding toward the box, "I will be sure to pass them on to her parents."

The box reminded me of Debbie's cluttered desk. And the prospectuses lying on it. I paused at the door. "You haven't heard of someone called Irwin Piper, have you?"

"Yes, I think I have." Felicity thought a moment. "I am pretty sure Denny Clark was involved in defending him a few years ago. Why do you ask?"

"Oh, just something Debbie was working on before she died. I would like to tidy it up. Can you remember anything about the case?"

"No. I had nothing to do with it. But I think Debbie might have done. If it's important I could find out who was involved with it. Debbie must have been working with one of the partners."

"That would be very helpful," I said. "I would love to talk to someone about it. It would make things a lot clearer." I opened the door. "Thank you very much for the wine."

"Not at all. It's nice to have some company. You can spend too much time in this flat, alone."

I said good-bye and let myself out.

I arrived home with my mind spinning. Part of it was the wine. Most of it was with the whirl of information I had received in the last few days. The last days of Debbie's life had been far from uneventful. Her row with Hamilton, her concerns about Piper and the Tahiti, and Rob of all people pestering her to marry him.

All this mingled with the jumble of feelings I felt toward her myself. It was only since her death that I was really getting to know her. I wished it was possible to talk to her about all I had found out. There was a lot we could talk about. If only that bastard hadn't killed her. I was more and more sure that her death was not an accident.

I pulled on my running clothes and set off round the park. The wine in my stomach made it tough going, but I didn't care. I ran fast until it hurt, and then I ran a bit more. I made it back to my flat exhausted, had a bath, and went to bed.

There were things I wanted to do at work the next morning, but it was difficult. With Debbie gone I had enough phone calls for two to answer. The markets were choppy. The Japanese were sellers because the dollar was weakening against the yen, but there had been some buying programs overnight from the States. This was the sort of market that presented plenty of opportunities for those who were quick enough on their feet. I found it hard to concentrate and missed all of them.

I looked over to Rob's desk. He was staring at his screen and biting his lip. He had a position that was going against him. His line flashed and his hand shot out to pick up the receiver. He listened for a few seconds, scowled, and flung the receiver to his desk. Rob was not happy this morning.

I tried to remember any telltale sign of something between Rob and Debbie, but I couldn't think of anything. No sideways glances, no attempts to avoid one another, no embarrassed silences. They were always friendly toward each other. I hadn't heard any gossip about them either, but then Debbie herself would have been the principal source of gossip. I wondered if anyone else had known.

I stood up and walked over to the coffee machine. "Would you like a cup?" I asked Karen as I passed her desk.

"Oh, yes, please. Cream, no sugar."

I returned a minute later with two cups and gave one to Karen. I perched on her desk. She looked surprised. I was not really one to stop and chat.

"I heard something very strange yesterday," I said quietly.

"Oh yes?" said Karen, her interest aroused.

"It was about Debbie. And Rob."

Karen raised her eyebrows. "Oh, is that all? Didn't you know? Mind you that was a long time before you joined here. Must be two years."

"I would never have guessed it."

"Well, it didn't last long. They tried to keep it a secret but everybody knew. But it's old news now. Poor Rob, he must have taken what happened to her very badly."

"Yeah. Poor guy," I said and walked back to my desk. You did have to feel sorry for him. He was seriously confused.

I was still struggling to focus my mind on the market when Felicity called. "I found out who was dealing with the Piper case," she said. "It was Robert Denny, our senior partner."

"Oh," I said. "Would he have time to see me, do you think?"

"Don't worry," said Felicity. "He's a very nice man, not a bit self-important. And he was fond of Debbie. He was quite upset that she left. I mentioned that you might want to talk to him, and he said all you had to do was arrange an appointment with his secretary."

I thanked her and did just that. Mr. Denny's secretary was friendly and efficient. Thursday at three o'clock.

Then I called Cash. There was a lot I wanted to talk to him about. Like what did he know about the investigation into Gypsum of America share purchases? Who had he been acting for when he had bid for our Gypsum bonds? Could he tell me some more about Irwin Piper's background?

"Bloomfield Weiss, purveyors of fine bonds to the gentry," he answered.

"Hello, it's Paul. I wonder if I could ask you a few questions?"

"Sure, fire away."

"No, not on the phone. I think it would be better if we met up for lunch or a drink or something."

Cash caught the serious tone of my voice. After a pause he said, "I'm a bit tied up this week. Can it wait until Henley on Saturday?"

"No, I'd like to see you much sooner. Like today or tomorrow," I insisted.

Cash sighed. "Okay, okay. You are seeing Irwin Piper at his hotel this evening, aren't you? How about after that. I'll join you there, and we can go on for a quiet drink afterward. How's that?"

"Fine," I said. "See you then."

Irwin Piper was staying at the Stafford, a small but elegant hotel just off St. James's. We were supposed to meet at seven. I arrived a few minutes early. I made my way to the bar. The room was softly lit with wood-paneled walls and green leather upholstered chairs. It achieved the effect of warmth, comfort, and exclusivity. It was almost empty except for an elderly American couple sipping martinis in a corner. I felt like asking for a pint of Young's, but that didn't really seem appropriate in a place like this so I asked the bartender for a malt whiskey. He showed me a menu with an impressive list of spirits, the cheapest being a Glenlivet and the most expensive being an 1809 armagnac. Not having the £89 necessary for the armagnac, I settled for a glass of Knockando, and sipped the light gold liquid carefully while I waited for Piper.

I didn't focus on the tall, expensively dressed man who entered the bar until he approached me and said, "Mr. Murray?" He was not the kind of man who you would have thought would own a casino. He was dressed from head to toe in English clothes, all hand-made, no doubt, and probably bought within a quarter of a mile of the hotel. But no Englishman would wear them the way he did. The sports jacket, the brogues, the green tie with pheasants on it, were all worn with a gloss that belied their "casual" status. Piper was an inch or two taller than me, with iron gray hair, carefully combed back, and a film star's jaw. A waft of expensive after-shave followed him in.

"Yes, I'm Paul Murray." I descended from the barstool and held out my hand.

"Good evening, Paul. Irwin Piper. Pleased to meet you." We shook hands. "Why don't we sit down over there." He led me to the corner of the room opposite the American couple. He beckoned a waiter and ordered a whiskey and soda.

"Have you been in London long?" I asked.

"Just a week or so," Piper answered. "I am planning to come back next month. I will be going grouse shooting in Scotland."

My own experiences of beating grouse moors in Yorkshire for £5 a day and a bottle of beer came to mind, but I thought it best not to mention them. My immediate problem was how to question Piper to find some clues to any weaknesses in his past. If he had been intimidating, that would not have bothered me. I was quite happy to match aggression with aggression. The difficulty was that he had a mixture of charm and authority that made awkward questions seem very awkward.

"Thank you very much for taking the time to see me," I began. "I wonder if we could start with your own background in casinos."

Piper's brows came together in a sign of mild disapproval. "I wouldn't say I have a background in casinos. Sure, the hotels I build have casinos in them, but they are primarily centers for entertainment, not gaming." His voice was cultured, almost English in intonation. It sounded like the accents of wealthy men in prewar

American films. To one of his countrymen, I guessed it sounded affected.

"But you do make your money from the gambling, don't you?"

"Yes, that's true." Piper held out his fingers in front of him and examined his manicure. They were clean hands, he was saying. "But I don't get involved with the gambling much myself. I'm an organizer. I hire the best."

He was getting in his stride, beginning to talk faster now. He counted off on his fingers, "I have the best showman in the casino industry working for me, Art Buxxy. I have a guy with a Ph.D. in mathematics from Princeton who makes sure that the odds are always, how shall we say, correctly balanced. I hired the manager of one of the top hotels in Geneva, and I have a software genius who has built up the most advanced customer information database in the industry."

"So what's your role in all this?" I asked.

"I put them all together. Arrange the financing. Make sure the numbers add up," Piper smiled. "Art takes most of the operational decisions. He's the front man."

"So you have no interest in the Tahiti itself?" I asked.

"Oh no, you misunderstand me," he said. "I wanted to build the greatest hotel in the world. The Tahiti is the greatest hotel in the world. It may not suit my tastes exactly," he glanced approvingly around the Stafford's bar, "but people will flock there, believe me."

"Have you invested in casinos, I mean hotels, in the past?" I asked.

"One or two."

"Could you be more specific?"

"I'm afraid not. They were private investments." Piper saw my concern. "Everything was declared to the gaming commission if that is what you are worried about," he said, sounding offended. He looked at me questioningly.

"Oh no, I am sure there's no problem there," I said,

and as soon as I had said it, cursed myself. Piper had challenged me to question his probity, and I had backed down from that challenge.

Piper leaned back in his chair and smiled.

"You do make a number of more passive investments, don't you?" I asked. "Aren't you what they call an arb?" I was referring to the risk arbitrageurs of Wall Street who at the first sniff of a takeover would pile into a target company's stock in the hope of making a killing.

Not surprisingly, Piper didn't like that word either. "I have a large portfolio, which I manage aggressively," he said. "When I see strategic value which the market has not seen, then I will take a sizable position in the stock, yes."

"Has that strategy worked?"

"I have made one or two mistakes, but mostly it has worked admirably," said Piper.

"Have you had any recent successes?" I asked.

Piper smiled apologetically. "I'm afraid I don't discuss individual investments. It's not a good idea, it gives people too much of an insight into how I operate. A poker player never shows his hand after he has folded."

I wasn't getting anywhere. Piper could play the honest, wealthy American gentleman all night. Who knows, maybe he really was an honest, wealthy American gentleman. There was just one last thing I wanted to try.

"Well, thank you for your time, Mr. Piper. You have been very helpful," I lied. "One final question before I go. Have you ever had anything to do with Deborah Chater?"

Piper looked genuinely puzzled. "No, I don't think so."

"Or Denny Clark?" I looked hard at Piper, who noticed my stare and bridled. He didn't like being interrogated. "No, or Denny Clark, whoever they might be. Now, I think we have finished here."

We both stood up, and I made my way to the door of the bar.

Before I could get there, Cash's squat form bustled through. The aura of calm serenity was shattered as his hoarse voice cried, "Paul! There you are! Irwin! How are ya? You guys all done?"

I didn't say anything. I just stood there. Someone had come into the bar behind Cash.

I recognized him.

This time I had a chance to take a good look at him. He was six feet tall, lean with a narrow face. Deep lines ran down from the bridge of his nose to the corners of his mouth. Despite his spare frame, his shoulders were square, and his suit seemed to hang uselessly round his athletic body. He looked fit. And strong. And his eyes, a washed-out light blue, looked at nothing. No discernible expression. No curiosity. The whites were yellow near the pupils and were crossed by one or two thinly penciled veins.

I had seen those eyes before.

"Irwin, you know Joe," Cash continued. "Joe Finlay, Paul Murray. You two guys don't know each other, do you? Joe trades our U.S. corporate book."

I didn't say anything, but shook Joe's reluctantly offered hand. Joe didn't say anything either. He looked at me, but with no hint of recognition. No hint of anything.

"How did you two get along?" asked Cash. "Happier, Paul?"

I shook myself to respond. "Yes, thank you. It was very useful. Thank you very much for your time, Mr. Piper."

Piper's earlier irritation had not survived the onslaught of Cash's good humor. "Not at all. I hope you will understand that the Tahiti represents a truly outstanding investment opportunity."

"No kidding," said Cash. "And Paul here doesn't miss too many of those. Come on, let's go. The night is young."

We left Piper in the lobby of the hotel. When we were

out on the street Cash ran into the middle of the road to hail a cab. Joe paused to light a cigarette. He saw me looking at him and reluctantly offered me one. I shook my head. We both stood in silence, uncomfortable for my part, for the minute it took Cash to catch us a taxi.

"The Biarritz," Cash shouted to the driver.

"What's that?" I asked Cash as we climbed into the cab.

"It's a champagne bar," he said. "You'll like it. There will be a bunch of traders from Bloomfield Weiss there. It will be a good chance for you to meet them."

"Never meet the traders" was one of Hamilton's dicta. Let the salesmen deal with them. The less they knew you, the less they could take advantage of you. But I was glad for the opportunity of finding something out about Joe.

As we came to some traffic lights, the taxi driver turned round, looked at Joe, and said, "Can't you read?"

There were NO SMOKING signs all over the cab. Joe took a deep drag on his cigarette and blew out smoke, never moving his gaze from the driver. The driver was a big fat man. He was angry.

"What's wrong with you, mister? I said can't you read?"

Nothing.

"Joe, how about putting out the cigarette, huh?" said Cash quietly.

No reaction.

The lights turned to green and the driver turned forward to drive off. "If you don't put that cigarette out, you can get out of my cab."

Joe very slowly took the cigarette out of his mouth. I could feel Cash relax slightly. Joe held the cigarette in front of him, smiled a thin mirthless smile, and leaned forward to stub the cigarette out on the back of the beefy cabby's neck.

"Fuck!" the driver screamed as he swerved over to the side of the road.

Joe swiftly opened the cab door and dropped to the sidewalk. Almost in one motion he stopped another cab and jumped in. Cash and I followed in a hurry, our previous driver swearing at the top of his lungs and rocking up and down as he gripped his neck.

"What's he excited about?" asked our new cabby.

"Maniac," said Joe, smiling gently to himself.

The journey to the Biarritz continued in silence. When we entered the bar it was full and smoky. The floor was black and white squares, the fittings chrome, the furnishings art deco. Cash propelled us through to a table surrounded by half a dozen eurobond traders. You could tell they were eurobond traders. They came in different sizes, big and small, old and young. But they were all jumpy. Eyes darting around, laughter snatched for a few seconds and then dropped. Many were going prematurely gray. Young men's faces with old men's wrinkles.

There were already three empty bottles of Bollinger on the table. The unwinding process had begun. Cash introduced me to everyone. I attracted one or two suspicious glances. Traders are just as wary of their "customers" as their customers are of them. But everyone was having a good time and they weren't going to let me spoil it. Cash's back-slapping welcome was returned. Joe was greeted with a nod.

Luckily, I was not let loose in the middle of this pack alone. Cash sat me at one end of the table, and sat himself firmly next to me. I was grateful for the protection. As the traders screamed across the table at each other I leaned over to Cash.

"Do you often drink with these guys?"

"Once in a while," he said. "It's just as important to keep the traders sweet as the customers."

I sipped my champagne. "What was that in the cab?" I asked.

"That was typical Joe," said Cash, taking a large gulp from his glass. "He is weird. Seriously weird. It's best to keep out of his way when he gets like that."

"So I can imagine," I said. "He's not like that at work, is he?"

"I don't think he has ever actually injured anyone at work yet," said Cash. "Apart from himself, that is."

"What do you mean?"

"Well, I remember once he was long twenty million ten-year euros. He was underwater, but the treasury market was ticking up. He had spent an hour or so staring at the Telerate screen, waiting for the market to reach his ownership level so he could get out flat. Then his screen froze. There was some problem with the terminal connection. I was watching him. He didn't shout or scream or anything. There was no reaction at all on his face. He stood up and slammed his fist into the screen. He cut his wrist quite badly. He just picked up the phone, sold his position at a loss, and walked out. Blood was pouring from his hand but he didn't seem to care.

"The story is he used to be in the army. The SAS, so they say," Cash continued. "Then one day he shot an unarmed sixteen-year-old boy in Northern Ireland. There wasn't enough evidence to show conclusively that he knew the boy was unarmed. But he left the army soon afterward."

"How did he end up working for Bloomfield Weiss?"

"Oh, he was hired by an ex–U.S. Marine, who thought he recognized a kindred spirit. He's been with us four or five years now."

"Is he any good?" I asked.

"Oh yeah, he's good. Very good. The best on the Street. No one likes him but they have to put up with him. He has a very sharp brain and a good nose for value. But I try and keep him away from customers."

"Apart from me?" I said.

"Yes, sorry about that." Cash swallowed some of his beer. He leaned forward. "So, you said you wanted to talk to me urgently. What do you want to talk about?"

I told Cash about my discussion with Bowen, the Bloomfield Weiss compliance officer.

Cash listened carefully. When I had finished, he whistled through his teeth. "You'd better be careful. That Bowen is an officious bastard. He won't let things drop easily."

"What do you know about all this, Cash?" I asked.

"Well, nothing," he said, as innocently as a schoolboy caught with a packet of cigarettes in his jacket pocket.

"Oh, come on, you must know something," I persisted. "Who were you buying all those bonds for? It wasn't DGB was it? It must have been someone else."

"Now, Paul. You know I can't tell you that."

"Bullshit. Of course you can tell me. This is serious. Do you know who bought those Gypsum shares before the takeover was announced?"

"Gee, Paul, I'd really like to help you," said Cash, still the sweet innocent. "But you know how it is. I don't know anything about the share price going up. I don't even know who we were buying the bonds for. Another salesman was talking to the other side of the trade."

I gave up. Cash was a professional liar. He lied day in, day out, and he was paid a lot of money for it. He was not going to give in, I could see that. I had no idea whether he was just hiding the identity of the buyer of the Gypsum bonds or whether he was doing more than that.

We sat in silence, watching the group around us. People were more relaxed now. The discussion had moved away from bonds and on to women and office gossip.

Joe unsteadily got to his feet, and came over to sit by Cash and me. Although I wanted to talk to him, his presence next to me made me nervous. He was unpredictable and dangerous.

"So, are you enjoying yourself?" he asked, his dead eyes locked on my face. He was clearly drunk. His delivery wasn't slurred, but overly slow and deliberate.

"Oh, it's nice to see my adversaries in the flesh," I said lamely.

Joe never removed his eyes from my face as he took a long slow swig from his champagne glass. Oh Christ, I thought, he has recognized me.

Cash did his best to break the tension. "Paul used to be an Olympic runner, you know," he said. "You remember Paul Murray? The eight hundred meters? He won a bronze medal a few years ago."

"Oh yes?" said Joe, still staring at me. "I thought I recognized the face. I am a keen runner myself. Do you still keep fit?"

"Not really," I said. "I still run a bit, but for relaxation rather than fitness."

"We should race sometime," said Joe flatly.

I wasn't sure how to respond to this. Joe's eyes hadn't moved from my face since he sat down. It was making me very uncomfortable. I suppose he must have blinked, but I hadn't noticed it if he had.

I looked around the room, trying to throw his gaze, but it didn't work.

"So you work for De Jong?" he said.

"Yes."

"Hamilton McKenzie is a bastard, isn't he?"

I laughed, trying to keep the tone conversational. "He may seem that way, but actually he is a very good boss. And he's an excellent portfolio manager."

"No he's not. He's a spiv. And a bastard."

There didn't seem much I could say to that.

"That tart Debbie used to work for you, didn't she?"

I didn't say anything. Joe continued. "I hear she fell in the river the other day. Tragic that." All this was delivered in a slow matter-of-fact way that gave his last comment an unpleasant irony, which I pretended to ignore.

"Yes, it was," I said. "A terrible tragedy."

"Did you fuck her?"

"No, of course not." I fought hard, and succeeded in controlling my anger. I held his stare and returned it.

"Didn't you? That's funny, everyone else did," said Joe, a thin smile curled on his lips. "She was a popular girl, that Debbie. She was always begging for it. I fucked her myself a few times. Slut." He smiled a bit more.

There was silence round the table. All eyes were on me. I knew he was goading me, spoiling for a fight. And I was angry.

Slowly, I stood up. He just looked up at me, that thin smile still on his lips.

Then Cash jostled into me. "Hey, come on Paul, you told me you wanted to get an early night. Let's share a cab."

I knew he was right. I let him push me out of the bar.

"Man, let me tell you, the last thing you want to do with that guy is get into a fight," Cash said as we climbed into a passing taxi. "Look at it this way. He wanted to pick a fight with you, and he didn't succeed."

"Scum," I said. "That man is scum." I sat in the cab fuming, acting over in my mind the things I would have done to him in the Biarritz if Cash hadn't stopped me.

After a couple of minutes, I asked Cash, "Is it true what he said about him and Debbie?"

"Well, I don't know. I think he was seeing her for a few weeks a year or two ago. But I think she told him where to get off. Maybe that's why he is still sore at her." Cash touched my arm. "Look, forget what he said. She was a good kid."

"Yeah," I said as the cab drew up outside my flat. "Yeah."

I WAS STILL furious the next day. I had seen that bastard at the scene of Debbie's death. He was obviously the violent boyfriend Felicity had referred to. The one who had ordered Debbie around and who had beaten her when she had confronted him about his marriage.

The more I thought about it, the more annoyed I was that I had walked out the night before without hitting him. I resolved to go round to his house that night and find out what had really happened. I knew it was stupid, but I was determined to do it.

I called Cash for Joe's address. He didn't want to give it to me, but I insisted. I waited until seven o'clock, by which time I judged Joe would be home, and set off for the Wandsworth address.

He lived in a cul-de-sac. The small road was lined with large red Edwardian houses, the dwellings of middle-ranking bankers at the turn of the century.

It had been a hot day, and the air was still stifling. It was very quiet in the little road. The houses were not in good repair, windows were smudged and dusty and some were cracked, paint peeled from doors and sills. Most had been converted into flats for single people or unmarried couples commuting into the City. I was startled by something small and lithe darting between some trash cans. A cat? An urban fox?

I began to feel uneasy. I had no idea what Joe's

reaction to me would be when I met him. All I knew about him was that he was unpredictable, and sometimes violent. All day the words I would use to confront him had been running through my mind; suddenly they had lost their conviction. I stopped in the middle of the silent street. Then I saw Debbie leaning back at her desk, the *Mail* spread out in front of her, her eyes shining and her broad grin teasing me. The anger welled up in me again.

I strode up the road. Joe's house was at the end. Tall, thin, and red, it stood alone, decorated with two minia-ture Victorian-Gothic turrets. I walked up the short drive and was immediately hidden from the street by a cluster of large rhododendron bushes, their shiny dark green leaves providing some shade.

I could hear the muffled sounds of a baby crying, probably from the back of the house. I rang the doorbell. No reply. The baby had heard, though, and put new force into its screams. Hoarse and angry, they cut through the stifling silence of the close.

Had Joe left his child to scream alone in the house? Possible, but what about his wife? I picked my way through the beds in front of the house to look in the windows. I saw a large kitchen with the debris of a half-prepared meal all over the counter. On the floor were scattered pieces of chopped onion and a kitchen knife. Some ground beef mixture bubbled over the edge of a frying pan on the stove, dripping meat and grease onto the gas flame.

I moved on to the next window. There she was, huddled up on a sofa in the living room, a woman sobbing silently. Her knees were pulled up to her chin, and I couldn't see her face, but her shoulders were shaking unevenly.

I knocked on the window. No response from the body on the sofa. I knocked again, hard, rattling the glass. A thin, tear-stained face looked up between damp wisps of light brown hair. Her eyes struggled to focus on me, and then she let her head flop back onto the cushions.

I saw some French doors at the back of the room,

opening out onto a small garden. I walked around the side of the house and climbed over a locked side gate into the garden.

I stood at the threshold of the French doors, the evening sun streaming over my shoulder into the prettily decorated sitting room. I could just see the woman's sandaled feet from where I stood. The baby had shut up for a moment, no doubt listening for more signs of adult life. I could hear the woman sobbing, deeply, quietly. I coughed. "Hello?"

No reply. She must have heard, but she was ignoring me.

I moved around to the front of the sofa. "Are you all right?" I said, touching her gently on the shoulder.

She pulled herself up awkwardly, so she was sitting upright on the sofa, her arms still wrapped round her knees. She took some deep breaths and the sobbing stopped. "Who the hell are you?"

She had a thin face that was pretty but pale and washed out. It was a face that had felt tears many times before. Now they streaked her cheeks, running in thin rivulets from her red, puffed-up eyes down to her quivering lips. As she rocked backward and forward, I could see that one hand was grasping her upper arm, and the other her ribs. She was in pain.

"My name is Paul Murray. Are you hurt?"

She looked at me doubtfully, clearly weighing up whether to tell me to go to hell. She sobbed again and clasped her side.

I crossed the room to the sofa. "Are you hurt?" I repeated softly. Silence. "What's your name?"

"Sally," she said. She sniffed and wiped her nose, trying to sit up straight. "Now go away! I'm all right. Leave me alone!"

Just then I heard the light tumble of steps down the staircase.

Joe! He must have heard the doorbell and decided to ignore it. A look of terror crossed Sally Finlay's face. I stood up straight, ready.

He was surprised to see me but only for the barest of moments. His eyes flicked quickly from my face to Sally's and then rested again on mine. A cold, unmoving, lifeless stare.

Joe smiled his thin smile. "I see we have a guest. Can I get you a beer? Let me put these in the fridge." He showed me the six-pack in his hand and disappeared into the kitchen.

Sally and I waited, motionless.

He was back in an instant with a knife. It was the one that had fallen to the floor in the kitchen. It was small, but I could see it was sharp. Two cubes of onion clung to the lower edge of the blade.

"Why don't you go up to bed, darling? You look tired," he said.

Sally stood up shaking, threw me a glance mixing fear with pity, and slunk out of the room into the hall. I heard her feet tapping quickly up the stairs.

Joe had a knife, and he probably intended to use it. I couldn't kid myself that I could protect his wife and this wasn't the time to ask difficult questions.

Stay calm and get out.

Joe blocked my path to the French doors. My eyes flickered over his shoulder. Three strides would take me to the hallway. I took two of them, but Joe had seen my eyes move. I stopped my headlong dive for the door just in time to avoid impaling myself on his knife.

Joe slowly waved the knife in front of me, forcing me to back up into the corner. The sun flooded into the room, bathing Joe's face in a yellow light. His eyes narrowed, and the pupils shrunk to tiny black pinpricks. The knife flashed white in the sun.

The clamor of the blackbirds' furious evening chorus rang in my ears from the garden. I could feel the fabric of my heavy white cotton shirt, sticky under my suit jacket. A bookcase jutted into the back of my legs. And my eyes kept following the knife.

Dive for his knife hand. It's only a small knife, it

wouldn't hurt much if it grazed me, would it? Unbalance him and then run. Fast.

His wiry frame was perfectly weighted on the balls of both feet. The knife was held loosely in his right hand. Relaxed, but ready to move in an instant. Joe knew how to fight with a knife.

I looked at Joe's eyes. He's daring me. He wants me to jump him.

So, I let my hands flop down by my sides. "Just let me go," I said in as reasonable a voice as I could muster. "I won't tell anyone about Sally."

"You annoy me, Murray," hissed Joe. "Why did you come here anyway?"

"To talk to you about Debbie's death," I said.

"And what should I know about that?"

"I was with her when you walked past her on the boat. The night she died."

Joe chuckled. "I thought I recognized you. So you think I killed her, don't you? Well, if you want to know whether I killed her, ask me." He was smiling now. Enjoying himself.

I said nothing.

"What's the matter? Are you afraid that if I killed the slut, I might kill you? Perhaps you are right. Go on. Ask me. Ask me!" he shouted.

I was scared. Really scared. But I thought I had better humor him. I swallowed. "Did you kill her?"

"Sorry, I didn't hear you. What did you say?" Joe said.

I stood up straight. "Did you kill Debbie?"

He smiled. There was a long pause. He savored it. "Perhaps," he said, and chuckled to himself. "But let's talk about you. I don't like you very much, Murray. I don't like you nosing round here talking to my wife. I think I will have to give you something to remind you to keep out of my way."

He moved closer to me. I stayed absolutely still. He slowly raised the small knife toward my neck. The bottom of the blade had the gray-white shine of truly sharpened steel. I could smell the chopped onion inches from my nose.

I didn't move.

Panic. Stay calm. No, panic! Don't just stand there while he cuts your throat. Move!

I snatched at the knife. As I moved my hand up, he caught it with his free left hand, twisted and pulled me over his shoulder. I found myself pinned to the floor.

He grabbed the little finger of my left hand. "Spread out your fingers," he ordered. I tried to clench my fist, but he pulled back on my little finger. "Spread out your fingers or I will break it!"

I unclenched my hand. "You don't really need that little finger, do you?" Joe chuckled. "You don't use it for anything. You wouldn't miss it. I want to give you a little reminder to stay clear of me."

I tried to move my hand, but it was pinned tight to the floor, right in front of my face. I saw the blade move down until it gently brushed the skin below the knuckle. I felt a small sharp stab of pain as my skin was lightly punctured. A line of little droplets of blood welled up across the back of my finger.

Then he leaned down on the knife, and very slowly moved it backward and forward, carving into the skin. The pain shot up my hand. I clenched my teeth and pushed my chin into the carpet, determined not to cry out, my eyes still fixed on the blade. I tried to wriggle, but Joe had me pinned to the floor. My legs were free, and I kicked them uselessly.

There was nothing I could do but watch Joe cut my finger off.

Suddenly he removed the knife and laughed. "Go on, get out of here," he said, standing up.

The relief rushed through me. I did exactly as he said, picking myself up off the floor, and running for the door, gripping my bloody finger with my right hand. I left Sally's sobbing behind me, as I sped out of the house, ran down to the end of the street and into the main road.

As I came to a row of shops I stopped running. God, that man is a psychopath, I thought as I gathered my breath. And a strong one too. I could feel the blood from my finger trickling down my forearm. The wound was deep and it hurt. I noticed a drugstore across the road. In a couple of minutes my finger was clean and bandaged.

I sat down on a low wall to collect myself. My finger throbbed with pain, but at least I was still attached to it. My heart was beating wildly, and not just from the running. It took ten minutes for my hands to stop shaking, and my heartbeat to slow to its normal rate.

I was very tempted just to go home and forget about Joe. But I could still hear Sally Finlay's deep sobs of pain and see her face wracked with tears of misery. What I had seen of Joe made me feel physically sick. He was inhuman. I couldn't let him just hit his wife whenever his sick mind felt like it. God knows what he did to the child. Like it or not, I was the one who could do something to stop it, and if I didn't it would be my conscience which would suffer. So I resolved to tell the police about him. I hoped that he would never find out who had told them, but I knew I was kidding myself. At any rate, I resolved to make sure never to find myself alone with Joe again.

I asked an old lady for directions to the local police station. The nearest one was only a quarter of a mile away.

I told the desk sergeant about how I had found Sally beaten up. I didn't tell him about the struggle I had had with Joe. He seemed efficient and concerned, which was a relief. I had half expected a brush-off. The sergeant did say it would be difficult to prove anything, unless the wife was willing to testify. He said that the station had set up a Domestic Violence Unit recently, and he would pass on what I had reported to them. He assured me that they would get a police constable round to the Finlays' house that evening.

I then asked if I could phone Inspector Powell, because I had some information relating to a murder investigation. This took the desk sergeant back a bit, but once he had decided I wasn't just another nut case, he found me a small room with a phone and, after a few minutes, located Powell.

"Hello, it's Paul Murray. I am calling you about the death of Debbie Chater."

"Yes, Mr. Murray. I remember you. What have you got for me?" Powell's voice was impatient.

"You remember the man I told you about, who groped Debbie the night she died?"

"Yes?"

"Well, I met him a couple of days ago. His name is Joe Finlay. He's a trader at an investment bank called Bloomfield Weiss. He had an affair with Debbie about a year ago." I gave Powell Joe's address in Wandsworth.

"Thank you very much, Mr. Murray. We will follow up this lead. However, it seems clear that we are looking at an accident, or perhaps suicide. I will be in touch with you in the course of the next few days." The note of irritation in Powell's voice was clear. He had probably dismissed my description of Joe as unimportant and made up his own mind about how Debbie had died. He would have some more work to do now.

"I will be happy to help any time," I said, and put the receiver down.

As I left the police station and headed home, I wondered what Joe's reaction to being questioned by the police would be. He wouldn't be very pleased with me, I was sure. Still, I hoped they would nail the bastard.

I WAS RIGHT on time for my appointment with Robert Denny. Denny Clark's offices were in Essex Street, a tiny lane winding down toward the river from the Strand. They were in an old red brick Georgian building, with only a small brass nameplate to identify them. The receptionist, a well-groomed blonde with a plummy accent, took my coat and asked me to take a seat. I found a comfortable leather armchair and sank into it.

I looked around me. Books rose from floor to ceiling, old leather-bound books. In front of me on the mahogany table, next to a vase of orange lilies, were copies of *Country Life, The Field, Investors Chronicle,* the *Economist,* and the *Times.* It was clear what kind of client Denny Clark catered to. I was not surprised that Irwin Piper would seek the firm out. I was slightly surprised that they would feel comfortable with him, but then a fee is a fee.

After five minutes I was ushered into Mr. Denny's office by the efficient secretary I had spoken to on the phone earlier. It was on the second floor, large and airy, with a view out onto the quiet street below. There were more bookcases with stacks of leather-bound books, although these looked as though they were actually used from time to time. On one wall, above a long conference table, hung a portrait of an imposing-looking Victorian gentleman, brandishing a quill. A former Denny, I assumed.

The current Denny was sitting behind his huge desk, finishing off a note. After a couple of seconds, he looked up, saw me, smiled, and got up from behind his desk to welcome me. He was a neat, gray-haired, slightly small man. Although he was clearly in his sixties, there was none of the wise old senior partner put out to pasture about him. His movements were agile, his eyes quick, his manner assured. A competent lawyer at the height of his career.

He held out his hand to me. "Paul Murray, it's an honor to meet you."

Slightly confused at this, I said rather lamely, "I'm glad to meet you too."

Denny laughed, his eyes twinkling. "I like watching athletics on TV. I always admired your running. It was a sad day when you retired. I had you down for a gold in two years' time. Have you given up athletics entirely?"

"Oh, I still run regularly, but just to keep fit. I don't compete anymore, though."

"Shame. Would you like some tea? Coffee perhaps?" he asked.

"Tea, please," I answered.

Denny raised an eyebrow to his secretary, who left the room swiftly to reappear with a tray, tea, cups, and cookies. We sat in two armchairs next to a low table. I leaned back and relaxed. Denny was one of those men, confident in their abilities, who use their intelligence and charm to make you feel at ease, rather than intimidate you. I liked him.

Denny took an appreciative sip of tea. "Felicity tells me that you were a friend of Debbie Chater's," he said, eyeing me over his cup.

"Yes, I was," I said. "Or at least I worked with her. We only worked together for two months, but we got on pretty well."

"That was at De Jong and Company, presumably."

"Yes, that's right."

"I'm sure Debbie was a real asset to you," Denny said

earnestly. "I was very sorry to see her go. She was a brilliant lawyer." He must have seen a slight look of surprise on my face. "Oh, yes," he continued. "She lacked a little in application, I suppose. But she was always able to grasp the core of a problem remarkably quickly for someone of her experience. And she never missed anything. It's a shame she gave up the law." He coughed, leaving unsaid the thought that crossed my mind. Not that it mattered now. "What can I do for you?"

"I wanted to ask you about something Debbie was working on before she died," I began. "Something that was a little odd. It may be nothing important. But then again it may be."

"Could it be connected with her death?"

"Oh no, I'm sure it's not," I said quickly.

"But you think it might be?" Denny was sitting back in his chair listening, picking up not only what I said but how I said it. There was something about his posture that encouraged me to talk.

"Well, I may just be being fanciful, but yes, I think there might be. I really don't know yet. That's why I'm here."

"I see," said Denny. "Go on."

"It's to do with an American named Irwin Piper. Felicity said that you handled a case in which he was involved. Debbie worked with you on it."

"Piper was a client of this firm's. I believe Debbie and I did act for him on one occasion," Denny said.

"I was looking at a new bond issue for a casino in America," I continued. "The owner of the casino is Irwin Piper. I asked Debbie to go through the information memorandum. After she died I looked at the document myself. She had marked one or two passages. In particular a paragraph explaining that a gaming license would not be granted to someone who had a criminal record."

I looked at Denny, who was listening just as intently as before.

"Does Piper have a criminal record?" I asked.

"Not that I am aware of," said Denny.

"Can you tell me anything about the Piper case that you and Debbie worked on?" I asked.

Denny was silent for a moment, thinking. "It's difficult. Piper was my client. I wouldn't want to harm his reputation or disclose any of his private affairs."

"But you will help me," I said firmly. "This isn't the time for legal niceties."

"It is always the time to respect the law, young man," said Denny. But he smiled. "I will do my best to help you. Most of what happened is a matter of public record. I will leave out as little as possible.

"Irwin Piper had bought a large country house in Surrey with a partner—an English property developer. It was called Bladenham Hall. They refurbished the house and created the Bladenham Hall Clinic. It was ostensibly an exclusive clinic for executive stress. It never had more than a dozen or so 'inmates.' It was like a health farm, providing rest and relaxation for overstressed businessmen. Needless to say, it was very expensive. Naturally, given the nature of the facility, it was sealed off from the outside world.

"Well, after a year or so, the police raided the establishment and arrested the manager and a number of female staff. They subsequently charged my client and his partner with running a brothel. At the trial, this allegation was never proved. The prosecution's case was shown to be a mixture of inconsistencies and inadmissible evidence."

"Due to your efforts," I interrupted.

Denny smiled. "Well, we don't usually do criminal law here, so I referred the case on to a firm I know who does. But I thought it best to keep a watching brief, and I did point out some rather obscure inconsistencies that the prosecution had overlooked. Although, I must admit several of them were uncovered by Debbie."

"So Piper was set free?" I asked.

"He was acquitted, yes," Denny replied. "He sold the

house. I believe it is now a hotel. And a very good one too."

"And were the police right? Was it a brothel?"

Denny hesitated. "The evidence submitted by the police would suggest it was, but that evidence was not admissible."

"So it was a brothel," I said. "Did Piper know what was going on?"

"He spent very little time in this country. Had it been proved by the police that Bladenham Hall was a brothel, I would have then shown that my client knew nothing about it."

This was exasperating. Denny's evasiveness goaded me into being more direct. "Is Piper a crook?"

"From what I learned during that trial, I wouldn't accept him as a client again," said Denny. His strongest reply so far.

I thought for a moment. "If this was brought to the attention of the Nevada Gaming Commission, would it cause Piper to lose his license?" And the Tahiti, I thought.

Denny touched his fingertips together and tapped his chin. "It's difficult to say. I know very little of Nevada law specifically. Piper was never found guilty, so he would not automatically be disqualified. It would depend on how much discretion the commission has to judge good character, and how they choose to use it. But it obviously wouldn't help an application."

I rose from my chair. "Thank you, Mr. Denny. You've been very helpful."

"Not at all. Any time." We shook hands and I walked toward the door.

Before I got there, Denny called after me. "Oh, Paul."

I turned round.

"I don't know what you meant when you said that this might have something to do with Debbie's death," he continued. "I caught a glimpse of how Piper operates. For all his gentlemanly affectations, he is dangerous. I liked Debbie. I am very sorry she died. If you need any more help, give me a ring."

"Thank you," I said.

"Be careful."

Denny's words followed me as I left the room.

It rained that evening, but I went for a run anyway. In the warm August evening the rain kept me cool as it seeped through my running vest and shorts. I came back to my flat wet, tired but refreshed.

As the effect of the endorphins wore off, my finger began to throb. I carefully peeled off the bandage and looked at the wound. It was deep, but because the knife was so sharp, the incision had been a narrow one and already the skin looked like it was joining back together. I leaped into the bath before I had a chance to get cold, dropped my finger underwater for a good soak, and let my muscles relax.

The phone rang. I cursed softly to myself and just lay there. It didn't stop. Reluctantly I hauled myself out of the bath and dripped over to my bedroom. "Hello."

"I told you not to interfere." The drops of hot water suddenly chilled on my skin. It was the flat tones of Joe Finlay.

I grabbed for words. He had a point there. He had told me not to interfere. Why on earth had I? My mind went blank. Finally I said, "How did you get my number?"

"How did you get mine?"

Good question. It would be easy for him to have got my number off Cash, like I had his. In which case, he probably had my address. My skin felt colder. I picked up the duvet from my bed and wrapped it round myself.

"I told you not to interfere," Joe repeated. "I have had two lots of policemen round here in the last twenty-four hours. First there was a police tart asking about me and Sally. Sally didn't tell her anything. And she's not going to. She knows what would happen to her." Menacing words delivered in a dull monotone. "Then there was a plod detective asking me questions about that slut's death. Well, he didn't get anywhere either. But it got me annoyed. Very annoyed. You were lucky not to lose your finger. You will lose more than that, unless you back off. Do you understand me?"

I was scared. Why had I got mixed up with him? Because I thought he had killed Debbie, I reminded myself. Well, if the police were already talking to him about it, then perhaps I could leave it all to them. "I understand you," I said.

Joe's voice lowered an octave, which somehow added a touch of extra menace. "Look, Murray, I don't want to hear anything more about the slut. And if you go anywhere near my wife again, or talk to anyone about her, you are dead."

I was frightened, but I didn't want him to know it. I was determined not to be intimidated. "If you just treat her properly, then no one will bother you," I said. "Threatening me won't help now." With that I hung up. I dried myself off, and rang Powell at the home number that he had given me. I was curious to find out what Joe had told him about Debbie.

"Powell." His voice was gruff, irritated at being disturbed.

"It's Paul Murray here."

"Yes, Mr. Murray?"

"I just had a phone call from Joe Finlay. He says you have been in touch with him."

"Yes, that's right. We interviewed him today."

"How did it go?"

"A dead end. Finlay says he shared a taxi with the two people he had been drinking with immediately after they all left the boat. They both corroborate his story. None of them say they saw Debbie after they left her with you."

I protested. "That can't be right. Have you found the taxi driver?"

Powell's sigh echoed down the phone. "No, Mr. Murray, we have not. That would be next to impossible without major publicity. But unless you think all three of them did it together, I think we can rule Finlay out."

"But, you can't! You should have seen him. I'm sure he must have killed her. Have you checked into his relationship with her?"

"We have spoken to Felicity Wilson. It's clear Finlay is a nasty piece of work, but there is no evidence at all that he murdered Debbie Chater. In fact there is no evidence she was murdered at all. And if she was, you were the last person seen with her before she died."

"You don't think I killed her?"

"No, Mr. Murray, I don't think you killed her either," said Powell, his voice long-suffering. "Personally, I think it was suicide, but there is precious little evidence of that either. The inquest is tomorrow and I wouldn't be surprised if an open verdict was returned. They don't like classifying cases as suicide unless they are sure, it causes unnecessary grief for the relatives. Now, thank you for all your help in this enquiry, Mr. Murray. Good night."

"Good night," I said, and put the phone down. So somehow Joe had got himself ruled out. I didn't believe it. I didn't believe it one bit.

I poured myself a large whiskey, drank it, and tried to get to sleep. The nursery rhyme "Three Blind Mice" swirled through my mind as I finally dozed off. I dreamed of a thin farmer's wife running around brandishing a carving knife.

Cash picked me up on Saturday morning. He was dressed in his Henley gear: blazer; white trousers; and a garish purple, gold, and silver striped tie. He drove a gray 1960s Aston Martin. I am no expert on classic sports cars, but it looked to me to be the same model as appeared in the James Bond films. I couldn't hide my admiration for the vehicle. I almost expected to see the controls for the machine guns and the ejector seat.

Cash saw my reaction and grinned. "Like it?" he asked. "I'm a sucker for old cars. I've got an old Mercedes and two Jaguars back in the States. I just love to drive around in the Merc on the weekends in the summer with the roof down."

"Gray old London must be a bit of a change," I said.

"Oh yes. But I like it here. Mind you, it takes a bit of time to get used to Europeans, especially the Brits."

"What do you mean?"

"When you first meet them, they all seem unfriendly. You feel like you are breaking some social taboo just by saying hello. Once you get to know them, they are good guys. No offense meant."

"None taken. I think I know what you mean. People here are wary of dealing with people they don't know." I could imagine the most aloof of Cash's clients being horrified of him when they first met him, and then falling gradually under his spell.

"You're telling me. At first they feed you some bull about how cautious and conservative they are. They make it sound like buying a T-bill was the most adventurous thing they have ever done in their lives. But after a little coaxing they just gobble up those bonds. I've been over here a year now, and I have already done some sweet trades."

We were at a traffic light. He paused to concentrate on accelerating away from it as fast as possible, leaving the Porsche in the next lane standing. As he wove between the traffic he continued, "Some of these guys in London don't know what selling bonds is about. They think if they stuff some Swiss gnome with a million dollars of some issue they are selling bonds. They don't know nothing. Selling bonds is about moving big blocks of money around the world. It's about making one part of the world finance another. Know what I'm saying?"

I nodded, cowering in my seat as we sped up the

wrong side of the road to get by a particularly congested stretch.

Cash seemed unconcerned by the horns blowing around him. "I'll tell you something about moving money round. I once had a guy in Boston who wanted to put five hundred million dollars into the eurobond market. So we launched three new issues, and gave him half of each issue. Three months later we own five hundred million of mortgage-backed bonds we can't get rid of. Triple sales credits on those. So, I make this guy in Boston realize he didn't want eurobonds after all, he wanted mortgages. He sells his eurobonds, and buys our mortgage-backed bonds.

"The firm has solved one problem. Trouble is we now have five hundred million eurobonds nobody wants. So I wait a week. The trader gets desperate, he can't sell his eurobonds. Then they put the sales credits up to triple again. So then I decide to ring another friend of mine at a Californian insurance company, who has a billion dollars in cash that he wants to invest and doesn't know what to buy. It so happens I have the ideal investment for him." Cash laughed as he recounted this.

"You want to know why they call me Cash? You ever heard the saying 'Cash is King'? Well, I'm the king of cash. I control it. These portfolio managers think that they control the cash in their funds. But they don't, I do. It's guys like me that move cash around the system, and I'm the best of them. And every time it moves, some of this cash rubs off on me. Any idea how much the commission is on a five hundred million dollar trade on triple sales credit? Think about it."

I thought about it. Different houses have different formulas, but my calculations made it just under a million dollars. I began to see how Cash could afford his expensive toys.

"But I can see you are different from the others, kid," he continued. "You're not afraid to take risks. You are prepared to bet big money when the opportunity is there. I think you and me are going to do some good business together."

Here was a man who really was at the center of the bond markets. This was the world that I had left my staid old bank to see. Certainly I could become a big player in the market. Cash and I together would make fools of the rest of the crowd.

Then I snapped out of it. Cash probably talked to all his customers like this. Not that he was making it up. Cash's reputation preceded him. But I couldn't help wondering whether when Cash was driving his Boston customer around in his Mercedes convertible he wouldn't talk about his clients in London in such a disdainful way.

"Do you still talk to any of your American customers?"

"Only the one on a regular basis. I have what you might call a 'special relationship' with him. But if I ever wanted to renew the relationship with any of the others, all I would have to do would be pick up the phone. People don't forget me."

We drove up the ramp onto the M4. There was a lot of traffic, but it was flowing steadily. Cash moved the Aston Martin into the outside lane, and worked his way through the cars in front, flashing his headlights to intimidate them out of the way.

"How did you get into the business?" I asked.

"I met a man in a bar. He was Irish. We came from the same part of the Bronx, only I hadn't seen him before. We got on great. We got drunk together. The only difference between us was that I was twenty and in jeans and he was fifty and in an expensive suit. He had had a bad day. I was sympathetic. He asked me what job I did. I told him I worked in a hardware store. He asked me whether I would like to work in his store for a while. So I did. I started in the mail room and worked my way up from there. It was a ball all the way."

"What was it like in the Bronx then? Wasn't it dangerous?" I asked.

"Sure it was dangerous, but only for people from a different neighborhood. In your own neighborhood you were safe. Everyone would protect you. Of course, it's all different now, now that there is crack all over the streets. Before there was violence, but there was always a reason for it. Now there can be violence for no reason. It makes me sick." I looked at Cash and saw his jaw clenched and the color beginning to rise in his cheeks. He was angry.

"Some of the greatest people in the world live in my neighborhood," Cash continued. "But we are all ignored by the rest of the country. I never forgot what that guy in the bar did for me. Did I tell you I bought my own bar?"

"No," I said.

"Yeah. It was a great little place right by my neighborhood. I had to close it down a few years ago. With crack things were getting just too wild. But I put thirty kids on Wall Street. Some of them are doing real well."

Cash looked at me and smiled. There was no doubt that he was proud of what he had achieved and also of what he had helped others achieve. And I thought he had a right to be proud.

Henley was just as bad as I feared. It was a typical July day in England. A blustery wind and rain showers, which were more on than off. All pretense of watching the rowing was forgotten. About a hundred people, employees of Bloomfield Weiss and their clients, were crammed into the tent, gobbling down cold salmon and champagne. The air was damp and oppressive; it was difficult to breathe in the clammy atmosphere. There was a constant din of rain drumming on the roof of the tent, caterers clanking plates and fifty people talking at once, interspersed with the hysterical cackle of champagne-induced laughter. A great day out.

Over the heads of the crowd I saw the tall figure of Cathy talking to a group of Japanese. She caught my eye, extricated herself, and slowly made her way through the crowd over to me. Oh God, here we go.

"I hope you are enjoying yourself," she said.

I mumbled something about how it was good of Bloomfield Weiss to arrange such a nice occasion.

She looked at me and laughed. "Yes, ghastly isn't it? I don't know why we do it. Still, I suppose there are always some people who will take any excuse to get drunk on a Saturday afternoon. But I have to be here. What drags you out?"

I hadn't seen her laugh before. It was a relaxed, genuine sound, not a bit like the drunken braying around us. I thought I had better not go into the details of Rob's pleading, so instead I said, "Cash is very persuasive, you know."

"I certainly do," she said, smiling. "I'm the one who works with him all day."

"That must be a joy," I said.

Cathy grimaced and then smiled at me over the lip of her champagne glass. "No comment," she said.

"So who is this American client Cash has a 'special relationship' with? Is it the savings and loan in Arizona that bought the fifty million Swedens?"

Cathy's smile disappeared. I had overstepped a boundary. "Now I really can't comment," she said brusquely, the imperious saleswoman again. "I can't discuss one client in front of another." She had taken to heart the reprimand Cash had given her earlier. My curiosity would have to go unsatisfied.

Chastened, I was searching for a less controversial topic of conversation, when Rob appeared at my elbow.

"Hello, Paul," he said. Then he looked hard at Cathy. "Hello."

"Hello," she replied coldly.

"How have you been?"

"Fine."

"Why haven't you answered my phone calls?"

"Oh, I didn't know you had called," she said.

"I called four times last night, and six times the night before. Your flatmate took the messages. She must have told you. Didn't you get the note with my flowers?"

"I'm afraid she's very forgetful," Cathy said, looking around her with an air of desperation.

"Well, what are you doing tonight? Perhaps we could get a bite to eat."

Cathy caught the eye of someone at the other end of the tent, and then turned to Rob and me. "I'm terribly sorry. There's a client of mine over there who I simply must see. Bye."

With that she was off.

"You know, I think she might be trying to avoid me." Rob looked puzzled as he said this.

I couldn't help smiling at this. "Do you really think so?"

"But you don't understand. I don't understand. She's a marvelous woman. We've been out together three times. She's not like any other girl I've ever met. There is something special between us. I'm sure of it."

"You haven't proposed to her, have you?" That was the usual reason why Rob's girlfriends ran away from him, but I thought a proposal on the third date might be too fast going, even for Rob.

"No, we haven't got that far yet," he replied. I could tell, though, that for his part Rob didn't have much further to go. "But I did tell her exactly how important she was to me."

"Rob, I've told you before, you've got to pace yourself," I said, exasperated. "That's the third girl you have frightened off like that."

"Fourth," said Rob.

Ordinarily I would have had the strength to console Rob. But I had a lousy week, the weather was awful, and I just wanted to go.

I knew Cash wouldn't be leaving for several hours yet, and I couldn't face his bonhomie on the way back. So I sneaked out of the tent, caught a bus to the station, and then a train home. As I stared out of the window across the rain-drenched Thames floodplain, my thoughts drifted toward Cathy. For a moment there I had thought she was almost human, and I had liked what I had seen. Perhaps Rob wasn't so daft after all.

AUGUST IS ALWAYS a dead month in the eurobond markets. There are plenty of reasons for this. The Continentals are all on vacation, as are the bureaucrats who work in the government agencies that issue eurobonds. The summer heat in Bahrain and Jeddah dulls even the most hardened Arab's gambling instincts and many of them travel to London, Paris, and Monte Carlo, often to play with chips instead of bonds.

Of course, many of the traders and salesmen in London are unmarried, or at least have no children. There is nothing they would like to do less in August than join the screaming families at the beach. But the month is a good time for a rest. There is an unspoken pact not to rock the boat, not to create the volatility that would require us all to spend the month thinking hard about work. The market recharges itself, and everyone makes plans for what he or she will do in the first week of September.

Normally, this seasonal pattern irritates me. But this time my mind was on other things, and so I was glad for the cover that August brought.

Specifically, I was thinking about Debbie. And Joe.

It had seemed to me obvious that Joe had lain in wait for Debbie that night and thrown her into the river. He was there, and he clearly had the capacity to kill. But why did he do it? Even someone like Joe didn't just wander round London murdering his old girlfriends on a whim. He must have had a reason. What could that be?

And then there was the business of the shared taxi taken by Joe and his two friends just after I had seen him leaving the boat. It was possible that his friends were covering for him, but the police believed that they were telling the truth. If the police were right, how did Debbie die?

I didn't believe she just fell into the river by mistake. And I couldn't believe that she killed herself. I refused to believe it. So who else might have wanted Debbie dead?

As I mulled over this problem, my thoughts turned to Piper. Debbie's knowledge of the Bladenham Hall case was of real concern to him. He did not sound like the most upright of citizens. If he were to lose his license from the gaming commission, then his plans for the Tahiti would have to be shelved. At best, he could try to sell it; it would be difficult to recoup most of his costs. Another dangerous enemy.

Then there was also the investigation into the Gypsum Company share price. Was that in some way connected to Debbie's death?

I needed to find out more.

I searched the pile of prospectuses on my desk for the information memorandum for the Tahiti. Before I came to it I uncovered the prospectus for Tremont Capital. I stopped my search and picked it up. It was thin and innocuous. No logos, certainly no pictures. I began to read it. Carefully.

Tremont Capital NV was a shell investment company set up in the Netherlands Antilles as a means for wealthy individuals to shelter their tax. The company invested in securities, about which there were no details. The company had issued a $40 million private placement of bonds through Bloomfield Weiss. De Jong & Co. had bought $20 million of these. What had made an investment in the bonds of such a flimsy offshore vehicle attractive was the guarantee from Honshu Bank, Ltd.

Honshu was one of the largest banks in Japan, and had the top rating of AAA assigned to it by the credit agencies. Investors didn't have to worry about the details of the structure, or what Tremont Capital invested in, as long as they had that guarantee.

But Debbie had worried about details.

I read the whole prospectus through carefully. Lots of tedious legal language, but nothing out of the ordinary that I could see. The sole shareholder of the shell company was listed as Tremont Holdings NV. That didn't tell me anything, and I guessed that under the Netherlands Antilles secrecy laws that would be the most I would ever find out about the ownership structure.

Still nothing strange.

Then I noticed a telephone number penciled in the margin under the section titled "Description of the Guarantor." I recognized the area code as Tokyo. It must be the number for the Honshu Bank. I looked at my watch. It was late in Tokyo, but I might still catch someone. I tried the number not knowing what it was I was supposed to be asking.

After a few false starts, I was finally put through to someone who understood English.

"Hakata speaking."

"Good afternoon, Mr. Hakata. It's Paul Murray from De Jong and Company in London speaking. I wonder if you can help me. I am inquiring about a private placement you have guaranteed for Tremont Capital."

"I am very sorry," said Mr. Hakata.

Damn, I thought. Just when I needed someone helpful. "I would very much appreciate some information, Mr. Hakata. You see we are a major investor in this private placement."

"I should like to help, Mr. Murray, but we have no record of giving such a guarantee."

"No, you don't understand. I have the prospectus in front of me. And someone from your bank spoke to a colleague of mine, Miss Chater, about it last week."

"It was I who spoke to Miss Chater. And I spoke to a Mr. Shoffman about it a few months ago. We are quite sure we have given no guarantee to this Tremont Capital. Indeed we have no record of such a deal existing. If you have some information on this company, we would like to follow up. We don't like people misusing the name of our bank."

"Thank you very much, Mr. Hakata. I will send you some information if I can. Good-bye."

This didn't make any sense. How could Honshu Bank be unaware of a guarantee they had given? Hakata had clearly checked his files quite carefully. Still, Honshu Bank was a very big bank. Perhaps the guarantee had somehow got lost. Unlikely, but just about possible, I supposed.

If Honshu Bank hadn't heard of the issue, then Bloomfield Weiss certainly should have. I decided to call them. I didn't call Cash. If Debbie was right and there really was something wrong with this issue, I didn't want to alert Cash to it at this stage. So I called the Bloomfield Weiss library, which would have complete information on every bond issue they had ever managed.

A young woman's voice answered the phone, "Library."

"Good morning. It's Paul Murray from De Jong here. Can you please send me all the details you have on a private placement you led for Tremont Capital NV. It was about a year ago."

"I'm afraid we have no details on that issue," the librarian replied immediately. No pause to check files or cards.

"But you must have. Can't you check?"

"I have checked. Your colleague Miss Chater called a few weeks ago. We have no details on the issue. And the reason is that the issue does not exist."

"You must have made a mistake. You can't be so sure. Please check again."

"Mr. Murray, I have checked very thoroughly," the

librarian's voice rose. She was obviously not a woman who liked her professional pride to be questioned. "Miss Chater was just as insistent as yourself. The issue just does not exist. Either our records are wrong, or yours are. And we have spent hundreds of thousands of pounds on modern relational database retrieval systems. No mention of Tremont Capital anywhere. When you have found the correct name of the bond you own, please call. We will be delighted to help." With that the librarian hung up, sounding anything but delighted to help.

I leaned back in my chair, stunned. How could the lead manager and guarantor have no knowledge of this bond? Did it really exist? I thought for a moment. Because it was a private placement, it didn't have to be listed on any stock exchange. But there were always lawyers involved in these sort of transactions. I grabbed the prospectus and leafed through, looking for the name of the law firm who had put the transaction together. I quickly found it. Van Kreef, Heerlen, in Curaçao. Odd. I would have expected a London or New York firm. A few more minutes' examination of the prospectus showed me what I was looking for. "This agreement shall be interpreted under the laws of the Netherlands Antilles." None of the customary mention of English or New York law.

Why hadn't this been picked up before? I supposed that if everyone was busy, the documentation might not have been read as thoroughly as it should have been. After all, the Honshu Bank guarantee had probably made it seem unnecessary to check the fine print.

But there was no Honshu Bank guarantee. De Jong & Co. had loaned $20 million to a shell company we knew nothing about. We didn't know who owned it. We didn't know what had been done with our money. We certainly didn't know whether we would ever get it back. The legal documentation was probably full of holes.

I made a quick phone call upstairs to check to see

whether we had received our first interest coupon payment. We had. At least we hadn't lost any money yet. Whoever had set up the company would probably pay at least some interest to avoid arousing suspicion. It looked very much as though we were victims of an elaborate fraud.

I couldn't ask Cash about it directly. If he were implicated in some way it might tip him off, and I couldn't risk that. But I somehow needed to find out more about Bloomfield Weiss's involvement. I had an idea. I picked up the phone and punched out a number.

"Allo. Banque de Lausanne et Genève."

"Claire, it's Paul. Are you free for lunch today?"

"Oh, what a nice surprise. Of course, I should love to have lunch with you."

"Great. I'll see you at Luc's at quarter past twelve."

Claire had worked at Bloomfield Weiss until six months ago. She ought to be able to tell me something about Tremont Capital and Cash's involvement with it. Besides which, it was nice to have an excuse to take her to lunch.

I got to Luc's Brasserie early and was shown to a table by the window. The restaurant was on the third floor of a building in the midst of Leadenhall Market. The sun streamed in through the open window, bringing with it the noise of the shoppers below. The restaurant was only half full; it tended to fill up around one o'clock with underwriters from nearby Lloyds.

I had only been waiting a couple of minutes when Claire arrived. The loud clack of her high heels on the black-and-white floor, the tight short skirt hugging her thighs, and the trace of expensive but subtle perfume following her captured the attention of every man in the room. As she came to my table, she held out her hand in greeting, smiled, and sat down opposite me. I could not help feeling a touch of pride at the envious glances in my direction. Claire was not classically beautiful, but she was desperately sexy.

We ordered and shared complaints about how quiet the market was. After a few minutes, I came to the point. "Claire, I did actually have something specific to talk to you about. But it's very delicate, and I would be very grateful if you wouldn't mention it to anyone."

Claire laughed. "Oh Paul! How exciting! A secret! Don't worry, I won't tell a soul."

"It's about Cash."

All trace of laughter disappeared from her face. "Oh. Cash. That bastard!"

"Why do you call him that? What has he done?" I asked.

"Perhaps I shall tell you a secret first." She looked down at the table, picked up a knife, and began to fiddle with it. "As you know I worked for Bloomfield Weiss for two years before I moved to BLG," she began. "Well, after a year or so I built up a good group of clients. I was doing lots of business. I was happy, the clients were happy, Bloomfield Weiss was happy. Then Cash Callaghan arrived from New York. He had a big reputation and a big salary to live up to, and he didn't have any existing clients in Europe. So he stole them."

"How did he manage that?" I asked.

"Subtly at first. He would work out which of the big accounts salesmen did not have enough time to cover properly. He would 'help them out.' Eventually, the client would end up wanting to talk to Cash rather than his original salesman. I suppose in a way that was not too bad, the client got better coverage and the firm did more business. But then Cash began to use more drastic methods.

"In my case he had his eye on my two or three largest customers. If ever I was out of the office, he would call them. But they were loyal, they wanted to stay with me. So then he began a rumor about me and a client. I am afraid I cannot tell you his name."

"What was the rumor?"

"He said that I was sleeping with this client, and that the client was giving me all his business because of it," she said, her voice burning with anger. "It was ridiculous. Completely untrue. The reason my client did most of his business with me was that I gave him good ideas, and he made money out of them. I would never have an affair with a client. Never. It would be completely unprofessional."

She looked up at me, her eyes alight with fury. Then she laughed. "Oh, Paul, don't look so disappointed."

I could feel my face redden with embarrassment. Her declaration of professional conduct with clients had shattered some half-hope at the back of my mind. I had no idea that my disappointment had shown.

She went back to her story. "I didn't know anything about this. Nor did my client. But everyone else was talking about it, or so I am told. It became one of those stories that circles around and around, so that after a month or two you have heard it from several different sources and it has to be true. I am sure my boss must have heard about it, but probably only whispers. Of course I could not deny it. I didn't know there was anything to deny.

"One day Cash went to my boss. He said that my 'affair' was making Bloomfield Weiss the laughingstock of the City. He had some numbers, which he claimed came from a source inside my client's company, that showed that my client was doing ninety-five percent of his business through me. Cash must have fabricated those numbers. I know my client did a lot of business with other brokers.

"So I was called into my boss's office and told I could either resign, or my boss would have to suspend me pending the launch of a formal investigation. He said this would probably damage my client as much, or more than me. I was shocked. Then I am afraid I lost my temper. I shouted and screamed at him, called him every foul name I could think of, and told him what he could do with my job. BLG had being trying to hire me for months, so I started a new job with them within a week."

"But wouldn't it have been better to be a bit calmer? You could have cleared your name. Cash wouldn't have been able to prove anything."

"The damage was already done. I wasn't prepared to have my integrity questioned in public, and my personal life examined under a microscope, just for the privilege of continuing to work with scum like that."

"I see," I said, feeling anger rise myself. "You're right. What a bastard. This business is rotten. So many people running around making so much money. They think they are geniuses, but half the time they may just as well have stolen it. If they all just got on with doing their job in a straightforward, principled way, there would still be plenty for all of us." I could not keep the anger from my voice, and I could feel the words coming faster and louder.

Claire laughed. "Oh, Paul! You are so sweet. So concerned. So idealistic. But the world doesn't work the way you want it to. You have to be tough to do well. The biggest bastards earn the biggest bucks. I'm okay. I am doing the same job for better people at a higher salary." Her big, liquid eyes smiled at me beneath long lashes. "But you were going to tell me your secret."

I calmed myself down. "I'm afraid I can't tell you the exact details yet, partly because I don't know them myself. It is important, though, that nobody finds out what I have been asking about." I lowered my voice. "Last year De Jong bought a private placement from Bloomfield Weiss issued by Tremont Capital. It was Cash who sold it to us. Do you know anything about it?"

"Tremont. Tremont Capital," Claire murmured, her forehead knitted in concentration. "The name sounds familiar but I don't. . . . One moment! I know! Wasn't the deal guaranteed by the Industrial Bank of Japan?"

"Not quite, it was Honshu Bank. But you are close enough," I replied.

"Yes, I do remember it vaguely. It was only a small deal, wasn't it?"

"Forty million dollars." I nodded. "Did you sell any?"

"No. It was one of Cash's 'special deals.' I think he cooked it up himself. None of the rest of us got a look in at selling it. All the commission went to him."

Special deals. Special customers. Cash did a lot of special business. "Do you know anything at all about the company?"

"Tremont Capital? Nothing at all. I have never heard of it before or since."

"Would anyone else?"

"No. When Cash put together deals, he kept them to himself until they were finished and he could proclaim them from the mountaintops."

"He must have had some help from someone in the firm to do the documentation, or structure the deal," I asked. "Was there anyone in corporate finance he used to deal with?"

"Not in London, I don't think. But he did talk to someone in New York on some of his special deals. I met him once when he was over in London. A short fat guy. Waigel. Dick Waigel, I think his name was."

"Can you remember who bought the rest of the issue?"

"Yes, I think I can. I remember hearing Cash selling it to De Jong. It didn't take him very long. And then he just made one other call and sold the deal straight away. I remember thinking how amazing it was to be able to sell a whole deal in just two phone calls. I detest Cash. But I have to admit he is a good salesman."

"Who was the other buyer?"

"I knew you would ask me that," she said. "Let me think. . . . I know! It was Harzweiger Bank."

"Harzweiger Bank? That's a small Swiss bank, isn't it?"

"Not necessarily small. Certainly low profile. But they manage a great deal of money very confidentially. Cash deals with them a lot."

"Who did he talk to there?" I asked.

"A man named Hans Dietweiler. Not a very nice man. I spoke to him a couple of times."

I had found out all I was going to find out from Claire. At least about Tremont Capital.

"One more question," I asked.

"Yes?"

"Who is Gaston?"

"Gaston? I don't know any Gaston." Then she chuckled. "Oh, you mean Gaston my boyfriend in Paris? I am afraid that was just a story for Rob."

"That was cruel. He was very upset."

"He was very persistent. I had to put him out of his misery somehow. This seemed like the best way. And he is strange, that one."

"Strange?"

"Yes. There is something about him. He is so intense, he seems unstable. You don't know what he will do next."

"Oh, that's just Rob," I said. "He's harmless."

"I don't know about that," said Claire. "I am glad I got rid of him." She shuddered. "Besides, I told you. I never sleep with my clients."

As she said this she sipped her wine and looked over the rim of the glass at me. She seemed to smolder, her lips very red, her eyes very dark. My throat was dry.

"Never?" I said.

She held my eyes for several seconds, sending messages whose precise meaning I could not decode.

"Almost never," she said.

After that lunch it was difficult to focus on work. With an effort I managed to put to one side thoughts of what sex with Claire would be like, although they kept on trying to reemerge. I had to make a phone call to Herr Dietweiler.

I looked up Harzweiger Bank in the *Association of*

International Bond Dealers Handbook and found the number. It had a Zurich area code.

A woman answered.

"Can I speak to Herr Dietweiler?" I asked.

"I am sorry, he is not in now. Can I help you?" The reply was in excellent English.

"Yes, perhaps you can," I said. "My name is Paul Murray, and I work for De Jong and Company in London. We hold a private placement which I believe you also bought. Tremont Capital eights of two thousand and one. We would like to buy some more and wondered whether you were interested in selling."

"Oh, Tremont Capital! Finally we find someone who will trade in it. I don't know why we bought it. The Honshu Bank guarantee is very good, and the yield was nice, but nobody trades it. We are supposed to have a liquid portfolio here, not this garbage. What is your bid?"

This was tricky. The last thing I wanted to do was end up buying more of the bloody bond. This woman sounded as though she would sell it at any price!

"It's not for me, it's for one of our clients," I lied. "He was interested in buying our bonds, but they are not for sale. Before I can go to him to see whether he would buy them from you, I need to be sure that you are a seller."

"I see. Well, we had better wait for Herr Dietweiler. He bought the bonds originally. He should be back in an hour or so. Why don't you call back then?"

"That sounds like a good idea. Tell him to expect my call."

Good. It was Dietweiler I wanted to speak to.

Exactly an hour later I dialed the Zurich number again.

A gruff voice answered the phone, "Dietweiler."

"Good afternoon, Herr Dietweiler. It's Paul Murray from De Jong and Company here. I talked to your colleague earlier about a bid for the Tremont Capital eights of two thousand and one that you own. I wonder if you would be interested in selling?"

"I am afraid you are mistaken, Mr. Murray." The heavy Swiss accent sounded less than friendly. "I do not know where you obtained your information. We do not own that bond, nor have we ever done so."

"But I spoke to your colleague about that very bond," I said. "She said you had it in your portfolio."

"She must have been mistaken. She probably confused it with another Tremont Capital bond. In any event, we view the contents of our portfolio as highly confidential information that we never disclose. I have just reminded my colleague of that. Now good-bye, Mr. Murray."

As I put down the phone I felt sorry for the friendly Swiss girl. I was sure she had not enjoyed being reminded of her duties by Herr Dietweiler. A nasty piece of work. And not a good liar. There were no other Tremont Capital bonds. Harzweiger Bank owned the same bonds we did.

But why didn't they admit it?

This was serious. There was a good chance that De Jong had lost $20 million. Unless we found the money, it could cripple the firm. I supposed that we would not be legally bound to recompense our clients whose money we had lost, but I was sure they would not remain our clients for much longer. I had to tell Hamilton what I had discovered. He wasn't at his desk. Karen said he was out all afternoon and wouldn't be in until late the next morning.

He came into work at lunchtime the next day. I watched him go over to his desk, take off his jacket, and turn on his screens. He sat down in front of them and stared.

I strode over to his desk. "Excuse me, Hamilton," I said, "have you got a minute?"

"It's now one twenty-seven. The unemployment figures come out at one thirty. I have three minutes. Will that be enough?" he asked.

I hesitated. What I had to tell him was important. But

I didn't want to rush it. If Hamilton said he only had three minutes, he only had three minutes. "No, I'm afraid it will take a little longer," I said.

"In that case sit down, you might learn something."

Stifling my impatience, I did as he said.

"Now tell me what's been happening to the treasury market." Hamilton meant the market for U.S. government bonds, the biggest, most liquid bond market in the world, and the one that most investors use to express a view on long-term interest rates.

"It's been going down for the last month," I said. "People are looking for yields to go higher." As treasury prices fall, their yields go up, reflecting an expectation of higher interest rates in the future.

"Why has it been going down?"

"Everyone is frightened that the U.S. may have reached full employment. Last month's unemployment figures were five point two percent. Most economists think that it will be impossible for unemployment to get much below five percent and that once it gets down to that level, inflationary pressures will build up in the system. It will get more difficult for businesses to find workers, and so they will have to pay higher wages. Higher wages mean higher inflation, which means higher interest rates. So treasury prices go down."

"So what's going to happen after the figure?" Hamilton asked.

"Well, the market expects that the unemployment number will be down to five percent. If that happens, lower unemployment will mean higher inflation. The market will sell off yet again."

It always seemed to me ironic that what was good for jobs was bad for the bond market. I could remember the day I had been on the trading floor of one of the big brokers. On the announcement that a few thousand more people had lost their jobs than expected, a huge cheer had risen round the room, and the treasury market had roared ahead. Talk about an ivory tower!

"You are right that nearly everyone thinks that the number will be five percent and that the market should sell off. So what should I do about it?" Hamilton asked.

"Well if we had any treasuries left, we could sell them," I said. "But since we sold what we had a month ago, I suppose we can just sit and watch."

"Wrong," Hamilton said. "Or at least you can sit and watch."

The green television screen in front of us showed where the market was trading at that instant. A dense array of little green numbers winked as bonds were bought and sold, and prices changed. The key treasury bond we were looking at was the thirty-year bond, otherwise known as the "long bond." Its current price was 99.16 meaning 99 16/32, or 99 1/2.

With one minute to go until the release of the figure, the green numbers stopped winking. Nothing was trading. Everyone was waiting.

The minute seemed to last forever. All over the world, in London, New York, Frankfurt, Paris, Bahrain, even Tokyo, hundreds of men and women were sitting hunched in front of their screens, waiting. The bond futures pit on the floor of the Board of Trade Futures Exchange in Chicago would be silent, waiting.

A muffled beep came from our Reuters and Telerate screens. A second later a little green message flashed up, "U.S. July unemployment rate falls to 5.0 percent versus 5.2 percent in June."

Two seconds after that the number 99.16 by the long bond flashed to be replaced by 99.08 meaning 99 8/32, or 99 1/4. I was right. It was a bad number and the market was falling.

Two more seconds, and our phone board was dotted with flashing lights. The salesmen did not know what Hamilton was thinking but they knew he was thinking something.

Hamilton picked one up. I was listening on the other line. It was David Barratt.

"I just wanted to let you know our views on . . ." he began.

"Offer me twenty million long bonds," Hamilton cut in.

"But our economist thinks . . ."

"I'm glad you have an economist that thinks. Now get me that offer!"

David shut up, and went off the line. He was back five seconds later. "We would offer them at ninety-nine four. Watch out, Hamilton, this market is crashing off!"

"I'll buy twenty at ninety-nine and four thirty-seconds. Bye."

The green number by the long bond on our screen was flashing constantly. It now read 99.00. I didn't know what on earth Hamilton was doing but I knew he knew exactly what he was doing.

Hamilton picked up the next line. It was Cash. "Offer me thirty million long bonds."

Cash didn't argue. Someone wanted to buy thirty million bonds in a falling market, that was fine with him. "Our offer is ninety-nine the buck."

"Fine, I'll take them," Hamilton said. He put down the phone and stared at the winking screen intently. So did I.

The price kept flashing, but it was no longer plunging straight down. It was wobbling between 99.00 and 99.02. Hamilton and I sat motionless in front of the screen. Every time the number 99.00 flashed, I found myself holding my breath, expecting to see 98.30 follow it. We could lose a lot of money on a $50 million position. But the 99.00 level held. Suddenly it flashed up at 99.04, then 99.08. Within seconds the price had moved up to 99.20.

I exhaled. Hamilton had done it again. We had managed to buy fifty million long bonds at what appeared to be the lowest prices for months. And it looked like the market was going back up. I studied Hamilton closely. He was still staring at the screen. His expression was unchanged. He wasn't smiling, but

I thought I could detect a slight relaxation of his hunched shoulders.

The price flashed up to 100.00.

"Shouldn't we sell now?" I asked.

Hamilton slowly shook his head. "You don't know what is happening here, do you?" he said.

"No, I don't," I said. "Tell me."

He leaned back on his chair and turned to me. "You have to be one step ahead of what the market is thinking," he said. "Market prices move when people change their minds. The market will go down if people suddenly decide that they would rather not buy or hold bonds, they would rather sell them. This often happens when there is a new piece of information. That's why the market often moves when an economic figure is released. Are you with me?"

"Yes," I said.

"Now, over the last couple of months a lot of people have been changing their minds, deciding to sell. As each piece of bad news has come out, more and more people have sold, driving prices ever lower. The situation has got so bad that by this week everyone expected more bad news and a further fall in the market.

"When the bad news came out, it was just what people had expected. Sure the dealers moved their prices down, but all the sellers had sold long before. Like we did a month ago. There were no sellers left."

"Okay, that explains why the market didn't go down for more than a minute or so, but why is it going up?" I asked.

"Well, when a market is falling, natural buyers tend to delay their purchases until they think all the bad news is out of the way," Hamilton said. "And there are people like me who are tempted to buy bonds at low prices." Hamilton talked slowly and deliberately, and I hung on every word, trying to extract the maximum amount of knowledge I could from what he had to say.

"But what about the economic fundamentals? What

about the threat of inflation if the U.S. has full employment?" I asked.

"That fear has been in the market for at least a month. Prices have been discounting that for weeks."

I thought about what Hamilton had said. It did make some kind of sense. "So one of the reasons the market went up was because everyone was so pessimistic?"

"Precisely," Hamilton said.

"One last thing I don't understand," I said. "If all that was the case, why did the market wait until the release of the figure before moving up?"

"Before taking the decision to buy, investors wanted to wait until the last major uncertainty was out of the way. Once they saw that the unemployment figure, although bad, was no worse than expected, they had no reason to put off their decisions. They bought."

I had a lot to learn in this business, I thought. I knew you needed a cool, calculating mind to be a good trader. But Hamilton was more than just an expert at analyzing numbers or economics. He analyzed human nature, weighing up the exact balance between fear and greed among the thousands of individuals who collectively make up "the market." And he was very good at it.

"I think we can leave this market to its own devices now," Hamilton said. "You wanted to see me about something."

I told Hamilton everything that Debbie and I had found out about Tremont Capital. I told him it looked to me as though we would never see our $20 million again.

In all the time I had worked with Hamilton I had never seen him shaken. He was shocked now. He had lost control, a rare feeling for Hamilton.

"How could that happen? Didn't we check the documentation?"

I shook my head slowly.

"Why didn't I get Debbie to check the documentation?" he muttered, biting his bottom lip. "That bastard Callaghan! He must have known about it all the time!"

"I heard Cash sold you the bonds."

"He certainly did. At the time those bonds were yielding one and a half percent more than U.S. governments. Not bad for bonds with a triple A guarantee. They were the cheapest bonds around at the time."

"And you think he knew that the guarantee was worthless?"

"He must have done," said Hamilton bitterly. "If the library at Bloomfield Weiss knows nothing about the bonds, you can bet no one else there does. He must have set this thing up himself. I do my best never to rely on that man. I can't imagine how I let him get away with it."

"Couldn't Cash have been passing on the bond prospectus in good faith? Perhaps someone in his corporate finance department is behind this? Claire mentioned a chap named Dick Waigel."

"Maybe. But I don't think so. I think it's Callaghan."

I hesitated. I wasn't sure whether to mention what was in my mind. Quietly, I asked, "Do you think Cash had something to do with Debbie's death?"

Hamilton looked at me, puzzled. "That was an accident, wasn't it? Or suicide? Surely not murder?"

"I'm not sure what it was," I said. "Remember I told you that I saw a man just before Debbie's death?" Hamilton nodded. "Well, that man turned out to be Joe Finlay, Bloomfield Weiss's U.S. corporate trader. Now, I told the police this, but it appears that Joe had a couple of friends who said they shared a taxi with Joe immediately after they all left the boat."

"Joe Finlay?" said Hamilton. "I've met him. He's not a bad trader. But from what you said, the police have ruled him out?"

I sighed. "Yes, they are going to put Debbie's death down as an accident. But I just don't believe it."

Hamilton looked at me for a second. "I suspect the police know what they are doing. In any event, I doubt that Cash had anything to do with it." He lapsed into silence, an unusual fire in his cold blue eyes. Then, slowly, he began to relax. He rhythmically stroked his beard. He was back in control. Thinking. Calculating all the angles.

"What shall we do?" I asked. "Shall we confront Cash? Go to the president of Bloomfield Weiss? Go to the police?"

"We shall do nothing," Hamilton said. "At least not for a while. My guess is that Tremont Capital will continue to pay interest for several years so as not to arouse suspicion. It is the principal we will never see again. So we have time. It is our turn not to arouse suspicion. As soon as Cash finds out we are on to him, then the money will be gone and we will never see it again. So we act as though nothing is amiss."

"But we can't just do nothing!"

"We won't just do nothing. We will get our money back."

"But how?"

"I'll find a way."

And somehow, I thought he would.

I HAD QUITE A backlog of work to catch up on. Accounting discrepancies, monthly valuation commentaries, a pile of reading. I plowed through it all afternoon and the early part of the evening.

I left the office at half past seven and sauntered down Gracechurch Street toward the Monument underground station. I couldn't work out how we could try to get the Tremont money back. I had no idea how Hamilton would go about it, although he seemed confident he would think of something.

I was interrupted by a voice next to me and a hand slipping through my arm. "Paul, why so miserable?"

It was Claire. I caught the same subtle scent she had been wearing in Luc's the day before.

"I'm not thinking, I'm just preoccupied."

"With work. But work is over for the day! It's time to play."

I smiled weakly. I couldn't tear my mind away from the Tremont Capital disaster.

"Look, you've been worrying too much lately," Claire said. "You take it all too seriously. I am meeting some old friends of mine tonight. Do you want to come?"

I hesitated.

>>>

"Oh, come on!" she said. She raised her arm at a passing taxi that screeched to a halt. She bundled me in. I didn't resist. She was right. All that I had learned over the last few days was weighing heavily on me.

Claire directed the taxi to a small wine bar in Covent Garden. It was dark and wooden and crowded. Her friends were there already. Denis, Philippe, and Marie. They had all been to the university together at Avignon. Denis was working on a Ph.D. in Anglo-Saxon history at King's College, London. Philippe and Marie were both teachers in Orléans; they were in England on vacation— and only Denis spoke English.

My French is barely up to conversational standard, but I did my best. I was encouraged with enthusiasm by the others, who derived no end of amusement from my Yorkshire-French accent. I got by pretty well, although the conversation took some strange paths because my comments were dictated more by what words I knew rather than what it made sense to say. The wine flowed. The volume of the conversation rose, punctuated by bursts of hysterical laughter. No one mentioned bonds, markets, interest rates, Tremont, Joe, or Debbie.

As the night wore on I found it more difficult to focus on what was being said or where the conversation was going. I just sat back in my chair and watched.

In particular, I watched Claire. God, she was sexy! She was perched cross-legged on her chair, her tight black skirt riding up over her well-shaped thighs. Her white blouse was tucked firmly into her skirt, stretching over the curves of her breasts, as she leaned forward to make a point. Her lips were full and pouted frequently as she talked. The French language was made for lips like hers, I reflected.

Suddenly, at a signal that I had missed, everyone stood up. I looked at my watch. It was midnight. We left the wine bar and spent five minutes on the side-walk outside in a confusion of good-byes. Then Denis disappeared in one direction and Philippe and Marie in another, leaving Claire and me alone.

Claire put her arm through mine and we wandered down toward the Strand. We wended our way through groups of people shouting good-bye to each other, hailing cabs, and laughing excitedly. The night air was warm and relaxed.

"I forgot to ask you whether you could speak French," said Claire. "You were good."

"After all those years of learning it at school, some of it was bound to sink in, I suppose," I said.

"That was a nice evening, wasn't it? Don't you like Marie? And Denis is very funny, isn't he? Oh, we all had such fun together at Avignon."

"I enjoyed it very much. Thank you for bringing me along."

"Shall we share a cab?" asked Claire. "Where do you live?"

"Kensington, and you?"

"Oh, that's fine. I live just off Sloane Square."

We walked along the Strand, trying to get a cab. Eventually, we caught one coming over Waterloo Bridge from the south side of the river.

Neither of us said anything in the taxi, but I was acutely aware of Claire's presence beside me. She let her head rest gently on my shoulder.

We pulled up outside her flat. She clambered past me, opened the door, and dropped to the curb.

"Good-bye," I said, "I'm glad I bumped into you this evening."

The taxi had stopped under a streetlight, so I could see Claire's face clearly. Her eyes smoldered, dark and sensual, just as they had in the restaurant. She smiled. "Come on," she said.

I hesitated for a moment, then swallowed, climbed out of the taxi, paid the driver, and followed her into the building. Her flat was on the second floor. It was comfortable, stylishly furnished, with two large abstract paintings hanging on one wall.

That was all I had time to notice. As soon as we were inside, Claire turned and pulled my head down to hers. A long kiss, our bodies pressed against each other, both feeling the other's excitement. Eventually, Claire drew her lips away from mine, chuckled hoarsely, and whispered, "What do you want?"

I didn't get a chance to answer. She led me into the bedroom. She didn't turn on the light, but the curtains were open and the orange glow from the street lamps outside lit the room. She loosened my tie and undid the top buttons of my shirt. I took off my jacket and undressed. In a moment Claire was standing before me, naked. The headlights of a passing car illuminated her. Her body was round and firm, almost muscular. I only just had time to take my socks off before she pulled me down onto the bed.

Claire was a vigorous, energetic lover. The bedclothes were soon strewn all over the floor. After an exhausting hour of the most intense pleasure, I rolled over onto my back, short of breath, sweating, spent. Claire lay down beside me and we talked and laughed as she ran her fingers over my chest and stomach.

Within a few minutes, relaxed and contented, I rolled over and fell straight asleep.

I was awakened by Claire kissing me lightly on the nose. She was fully dressed in a blue suit.

"Some of us have to go to work," she said. "Make sure the door locks behind you." She was gone before I could reply.

I dragged myself out of bed, pulled on my clothes, took a taxi home, and had a bath. I was late into work that morning.

Hamilton had been thinking as promised. He beckoned me into the conference room.

"This isn't going to be easy," he said. "We need to find out more." He leaned forward over the sparkling white pad on the table in front of him. All energy and purpose. I listened, ready to follow instructions.

"We can attack this problem from two angles. I suggest I tackle one of them and you the other."

I nodded.

"Firstly, there is the Netherlands Antilles. I have been through the Tremont prospectus word for word. It calls for a number of conditions precedent before the money can be drawn down, including the signature of the Honshu Bank guarantee. Now that means that Van Kreef, Heerlen must have had sight of that document before the money was paid out. Either they saw a document that was a forgery, or they allowed the money to be released without seeing anything.

"There is also a requirement for accounts to be audited annually. The auditors are a local firm of accountants. There is nothing in the prospectus that gives us the right to look at the accounts, but they might be filed somewhere.

"Lastly, the money must have been invested or transferred somewhere from the Netherlands Antilles. Professional advisers will probably have been involved there."

"There may well have been lawyers and accountants involved in all these stages, but they will never tell you anything," I said. "The Netherlands Antilles has a reputation for absolute confidentiality to maintain. If they lose it, then half the money invested through the islands would leave tomorrow."

"That's true. It would be very difficult to find these things out by myself," said Hamilton. "But I spoke to Rudy Geer last night, one of the top lawyers in the islands. He is going to help me. As far as he is concerned, the last thing he wants the islands to be known for is as a good place to base a fraud. Apparently, Van Kreef, Heerlen sail a bit close to the wind. I hope I will be able to mobilize the local establishment to take our side. They would much prefer the money to be returned quietly without anyone knowing about it, than have an international scandal. I shall fly out there the day after tomorrow."

"Okay, so what do I do?" I said.

"Check out Cash," said Hamilton. "You are going to New York soon, aren't you?"

"Yes, in a couple of days," I said.

"Are you going to see Bloomfield Weiss?"

"I intend to."

"Good. See what you can find out about Cash and the Tremont deal. But be very discreet. It is essential that Cash isn't tipped off."

"Okay," I said. "What about this guy Dick Waigel?"

"I've come across him in the past," said Hamilton. "A nasty little man. I wouldn't be surprised if he was involved. He's too clever for his own good. See what you can find out about him, but be careful. If he is working with Cash on this, then he will be wary of people asking questions."

"What am I looking for?" I asked.

"It's difficult to say," said Hamilton. "Anything that ties Cash in to Tremont and in particular anything that suggests what Tremont will have done with our money. The prospectus just mentions investments in securities, without specifying what those might be." I had no clue how I would be able to find out what Hamilton was looking for. He saw the look of concern on my face. "Don't worry, even if you don't turn up anything I should be able to discover something in Curaçao."

I felt distinctly uncomfortable about all of this. "Shouldn't we tell someone?" I said. "The police perhaps, or at least Mr. De Jong?"

Hamilton sat down again. He opened his fingers in front of him and sighed. "I thought about that last night as well. I don't think we should."

"But this is a major fraud. Surely we have to report it?" I protested. All my instincts told me to go to the police and leave it with them.

Hamilton leaned forward in his chair. "Remember I told you I thought I had found a new investor in Japan? Fuji Life? Well, I am pretty sure that they intend to give us five hundred million dollars of their money to manage. All being well, we should get it next month. You know what the Japanese are like. If a group with the prestige of Fuji Life are prepared to give us that much money, others will follow." He was talking more quickly now. "This could be the breakthrough De Jong needs. It could make us one of the major fund managers in London." Hamilton looked me straight in the eye. I could feel the power of his conviction and his will. He wanted to be the most powerful fund manager in London; it was an ambition he was determined to achieve. And I would be cheering him on all the way.

He relaxed. "You know George. He would want to tell our investors immediately. We wouldn't be able to talk him out of it. And once he does that, the reputation of our firm will be significantly harmed. It may never recover. We would certainly never see the money from Fuji Life. And as for the police, that would be even worse."

Hamilton could see I wasn't quite convinced. "Look, you and I have a terrific opportunity to really make something of this firm. Can I rely on you to help? If we can get the money back in the next two or three months, then it will be a lot better for the firm and for George De Jong. If we have got nowhere by Christmas then we will tell him. You've done your duty by telling me about it. You're safe. This mess is my responsibility and I am going to clear it up."

I thought about it for a moment. $500 million from Fuji Life would bring who knows how much money with it from Japan. We would do some serious trading with funds like that behind us. We would move markets, people would have to sit up and take notice of us. And there was no doubt that I would be part of it all; Hamilton had referred to the two of us as a team. I liked that. We had everything to play for. I knew Hamilton was right about George De Jong; he would want to go straight to all our investors and spoil it all.

Well, Hamilton had asked for my help and he would get it. "Okay. You are right. Let's find that money."

I walked back to my desk excited and a little bewildered. It would be fun working with Hamilton to recover the money. But how on earth would we do it? I had no idea how I would get the information Hamilton had asked for. All I could do was try my best to see what I turned up. Whatever happened, I didn't want to let him down.

On my desk I found a note that Claire had called. I rang her.

"BLG."

"Hello. It's me, Paul."

"Ah, good morning. I am glad to see you made it into work. I have some prices for you." At the best of times Claire's voice sounded sensual. When I heard it that morning, it brought back the previous night's activities.

"I enjoyed last night," I said.

"So did I. It was fun."

"We must do it again sometime."

There was silence on the other end of the line.

"You know, Paul, I don't think we should." I had been half expecting this. "What I said about it being unprofessional for a salesperson to have a relationship with her clients is true. We had a great night. No harm was done. We had better leave it there."

I was disappointed. There is no pretending I was not disappointed. If she thought professionalism was so important, what had she been up to last night? But . . . she was right. No harm had been done. And for the first time in a long while I had a really good time. I should just chalk it up to experience.

"Now, about those prices . . ."

>>>

The Gloucester Arms was as crowded and smoky as usual. In one corner four or five New Zealanders were chatting up a similar number of giggling Italian students. A group of large men propped up the bar, their beer-developed stomachs peeking out underneath too-small T-shirts. A mildly eccentric old man muttered to himself as he puffed at his pipe and perused the *Daily Telegraph*. The seats on either side of him were empty, he looked just a little too crazy for comfort.

The Gloucester Arms was by no means the most attractive pub in London. But it was my local. I probably spent more time in there than I should, unwinding from the day's tensions, reliving good trades and forgetting bad ones. As I sat in the corner watching the laughing, gesturing crowd of people, and slowly sipping a pint of Yorkshire bitter, the cauldron of competing anxieties that had been bubbling in my head cooled down to a gentle simmer. Debbie, Joe, Piper, and Tremont were still all there in the background, but I could worry about them properly tomorrow.

I looked up and saw Rob's chubby face over the other side of the room. He caught my eye and pushed through the drinkers toward me. Every now and then we would have a beer in the Gloucester Arms. He lived quite close, so the pub was convenient for both of us.

"Hi. Can I get you another?" he asked. I nodded my assent, and he was soon back with two pints of Yorkshire.

He took a deep swallow of his, closed his eyes, and loosened his shoulders. "I needed that," he sighed.

"Bad day?"

"You could say that," Rob said. He shook his head. "It's my own fault. I bought a load of Bunds yesterday, because I thought today's money supply figures would be lower than expected."

"So what's the problem?" I asked. "You were right, weren't you?"

"Yeah. The market went up a point. But instead of taking my profit, I bought more."

"Why?"

"I don't know, it just felt right. Then that bastard Poehl says that the Bundesbank is still worried about inflation despite the good money supply figures, and the market came off a point and a half."

"Oh dear," I said, as neutrally as possible.

"That's right," said Rob. "Oh dear. I don't know why I didn't sell right after the figures came out."

Rob stared gloomily into his pint. I didn't know why he hadn't sold either. But then I didn't understand why he had put on the position in the first place. He had no carefully worked out reason for thinking the money supply figures would be low. It was just "gut feel." That was certainly not the way Hamilton would have played the situation, but then more traders were like Rob than like Hamilton.

Rob looked up from his beer. "That was quite some trade Hamilton did yesterday, wasn't it?" he said. "I couldn't work it out. Neither could Jeff. In fact I think it upsets him a bit." Rob reported to Jeff Richards.

"What does?" I asked.

"Hamilton calling the market right all the time."

"Well, Jeff does all right himself, doesn't he?" I said.

"Yes, he does on the whole," Rob said. "But he can spend days poring over economic research and statistics before deciding which way the market will go. He then has to wait weeks sometimes for the market to catch up with him. I think seeing Hamilton call the market just right, against all that fundamental analysis, irks him. How does he do it?"

"He thinks of everything," I said. "He leaves as little to chance as possible, and when the odds are heavily stacked in his favor, he makes his move. You can learn a lot from him."

"I can see that," said Rob. "Bit of a cold bastard, though, isn't he?"

"Yes, I suppose so," I said. "But he is fair. I like working for him. Seeing him in action, like he was yesterday, is quite incredible."

He was a great man to learn from, I thought. One day, if I watched and listened closely, I would be just as good as Hamilton. Secretly, I thought I could be better. That was my ambition. And I was determined enough to make sure I achieved it.

Rob nodded his head in agreement and sipped his pint. "Aren't you going on a boondoggle soon?" he asked.

"Boondoggle? I am about to embark on a grueling business trip, if that's what you mean." I smiled at him.

"To Arizona?"

"Yes, to Arizona. Although I am going to spend a few days in New York beforehand, to catch up with what is happening on Wall Street. And then of course I will have to spend a day in Las Vegas to check out the Tahiti."

"If that isn't a boondoggle, I don't know what is," said Rob. "Mind you, I have an exciting trip ahead of me myself."

"Oh yes? I didn't know Jeff approved of the expense."

"Well, he has made a special exception in this case. It's a two-day seminar on Central Bank approaches to controlling exchange rates. It's in Hounslow. Do you want to come? I hear Hounslow is very nice this time of year."

"Very kind of you, but no thanks," I said, smiling. Somehow, Hounslow didn't quite shape up to Phoenix. "Anyway, enough of work. How's your love life?"

Gloom instantly returned to Rob's face.

"Not so good?" I asked.

"Terrible," Rob answered.

"You are still chasing Cathy Lasenby, I take it."

Rob nodded miserably. "I had this great idea," he said. "Cathy has been avoiding me, there is no escaping that. But I wasn't going to let her go, just slip away. So I thought I ought to engineer something."

Rob took out a cigarette and lit it. I hardly ever saw him smoke; never at work and only occasionally outside, when he was worked up about something. "I sent her a fax," he went on. "I said I was impressed with her ideas on the treasury market, but that before doing business with her, I and my colleagues wanted to meet her properly. So I suggested dinner at Bibendum in Chelsea."

Rob saw my puzzled expression and laughed. "I signed it John Curtis of Albion Insurance."

"You did what?" I exclaimed.

"She had told me that Albion Insurance was her biggest prospective customer. She had to come. I gave her De Jong and Company's fax number to reply to, so that Curtis wouldn't find out what was going on. Sure enough she replied.

"Well, I booked two tables for eight, one in the name of Curtis for four, and one in my name for two. I arrived ten minutes early, and propped up the bar. I don't know whether you have ever been to Bibendum?"

I shook my head. "No, but I've heard of it."

"It's quite stylish. It's in the old Michelin Building, 1920s architecture, great service, delicious food. A good choice. Anyway, Cathy arrived ten minutes late. She looked stunning in a black dress that showed everything off. The waiter led her past me to her empty table, which was right by where I was standing. She made a half-hearted attempt to ignore me, but couldn't really get away with it; she was only ten feet away.

"She caught my eye and I walked over to her table. We both discovered we were waiting for someone—I told her I was waiting for my uncle. She agreed to have a drink with me at the bar. She was nervous, and looked like she needed one.

"I ordered a bottle of Taitinger, saying that my uncle always drank it, and would order one anyway. We had a glass and then another glass. Cathy took a while to relax. She told me she was very keen to make a good impression on Curtis. After a while she wound down. By nine o'clock neither my uncle nor Curtis had turned up. I suggested that if they didn't show up in the next ten minutes, we should have dinner together. She agreed. Not surprisingly, nobody showed. The dinner was marvelous. The champagne flowed. We had a great evening."

"So far, so good," I said.

Rob smiled to himself as he took a swig of his beer. "We had just finished a terrific summer pudding, and were sitting back replete, when Cathy said that she was glad that Curtis hadn't made it. We agreed it had been a wonderful evening. And then . . ."

"Don't tell me," I said, seeking refuge in my pint. But there was no escape.

"Then I told her that I had set the whole thing up. My uncle wasn't coming. Curtis and his colleagues weren't coming."

"And she didn't like that?"

"She didn't like that," Rob admitted. "She didn't like that one little bit."

"What did she do?"

"She went wild," Rob said. "She went bright red. She said she had never been made such a fool of. She said I was devious and totally untrustworthy." Rob paused, clearly uncomfortable at the memory of the scene. "I told her that I loved her, and I knew she loved me."

"What did she say?" I asked.

"She told me to go to hell," Rob answered miserably. "She said I was an idiot, and I should make sure I never bothered her again. Then she got up, and left."

"Bibendum, eh? That must have set you back a bit," I said.

"It did. It would have been worth it if she had stayed. I can't work out why she didn't. I mean we got on so well. I know we had a good time together, she would have to admit that."

I shrugged my shoulders. "Well, there is not much you can do now."

"I don't know," said Rob. "Maybe if I did something dramatic. You know, really romantic. Something that would make her realize how important she is to me. Women like that sort of thing, you know."

I raised my eyebrows, but didn't say anything. I dreaded to think what Rob would classify as "dramatic." I thought about trying to talk him out of it but decided it was a waste of time. When Rob's mind was made up, his mind was made up.

It was extraordinary the way he was able to switch his affections from one woman to another, and within a week or so form a passionate attachment to someone completely new. Almost the mirror opposite of myself, I thought. I remembered Debbie's encouragement to me to get involved with women again.

It was hard to think of Debbie and Rob together. Debbie's bubbly repartee and Rob's earnest declarations of devotion didn't seem to me to mix very well. Perhaps that is why the relationship had not lasted very long.

Almost without thinking I said, "I miss Debbie."

Rob looked at me. "Yes," he said, his voice firmly in neutral.

"You and she saw a lot of each other at one stage, didn't you?" I asked.

"Yes we did," Rob answered. He clenched his pint in front of him. His face reddened noticeably.

"It's funny, I never would have guessed," I said.

"We were very professional about it. We never let it interfere with work. Anyway, once it was over it was over."

That wasn't what Felicity had said. I remembered what she had told me about Rob pestering Debbie just before she died, to ask her to marry him. I needed to know what had happened.

"I saw Felicity the other day. You know, Debbie's flatmate."

Rob didn't say anything so I plowed on. "She said that you asked Debbie to marry you the week before she died."

Rob stiffened, and looked at me sharply. He was bright red now, the blood had spread out from his cheeks to his ears and his neck. He breathed deeply, his whole body racked with emotion. His chin shook, and his eyes blinked. For a long, painful moment he couldn't bring himself to say anything.

I had gone too far, and I regretted it, but there was nothing I could do to take my words back.

Finally it all came out in a torrent of words. "The stupid, stupid, stupid bitch. I loved her. She knew that. Why didn't she say yes? If she had only said yes, she . . ."

He broke off and stared at me through watery eyes. He bit his lip, slammed down his beer on the table with such force that I was surprised the glass did not shatter, turned away from me, and left the pub.

I sat there for several minutes, stunned by the heat of Rob's outburst. I had never seen anyone so emotional. It had seemed to me to be a mixture of anger, regret, with a vicious undercurrent of pure misery. I felt terrible that I had been responsible for setting him off. I had never taken Rob's passion for women seriously, I couldn't quite believe that it was for real. I now knew it was. I would treat it with much more respect in the future.

I drained my glass and left the pub. I was beginning to see what Claire had meant when she had said there was something strange about Rob. No normal person would behave like he did. His outburst had frightened me. I wondered what those phone calls with Debbie must have been like. No wonder she had been shaken by them.

And now, less than a month later, his attentions had turned to Cathy. Still, she looked like she could take care of herself. They probably deserved each other.

It was a nice warm evening, and the glow of the beer slowly restored my spirits. It had rained heavily earlier in the day, and the headlights of passing vehicles danced with the street lamps in the puddles, occasionally joined by the darting orange of the signal of a turning car. A group of youths were shouting incoherently outside a pub on the other side of the road. I turned to look at them as they began to make their unsteady way up the street. As I turned away from them, I caught something in the corner of my eye.

Joe.

He was there, sitting by the window of the pub, watching me.

Or was he?

I looked more closely, and saw a lean figure inside the pub stand up and move away from the window. It was his size, but I couldn't be sure it was him. I had only caught a glimpse of him. Perhaps I was imagining it. Or perhaps . . .

I hurried down the road and suddenly turned right into a mews. It was dark. Too dark. My feet splashed through the newly formed puddles lurking against the side of the road.

I stopped for a second. I thought I could hear a rustle behind me. I felt as much as heard footsteps, but I couldn't wait to check if anyone was there. There was an illuminated phone booth a hundred yards ahead, just outside a wine bar.

I strode rapidly toward the source of light, reflected off the pools of water in the road and the glistening leaves of the privet hedges that loomed up on either side of the street. The back of my neck tingled, I expected at any moment to feel an arm round my throat or an iron bar on the back of my head.

I jumped as a couple tumbled out of the wine bar right in front of me. I paused to let them pass, laughing and swaying, on their way back to Gloucester Road.

I made it to the phone booth. I pushed the door and squeezed myself inside. From what I could see, there was no one in the mews. The problem was that because the phone booth was lit from the inside, it was very difficult to see anything outside.

I lifted the receiver to my face, ready to dial 999 at any sign of trouble.

There was none.

This was ridiculous. After a couple of minutes I replaced the receiver and left the phone booth. I walked briskly down a narrow pathway, and then along a road next to a church. There was a path through the churchyard that formed a shortcut to my flat. I took it.

I had only walked a few yards when I thought I heard a soft thud behind me and to my left. Even though I was in the middle of a city, the churchyard was eerily quiet. The usual urban sounds were reduced to a muffled far-off rumble by the wall and the church. I waited, eyes and ears straining to pick out any sound or movement. Then I thought I saw a shadow flit behind a gravestone.

I ran.

I sprinted through the churchyard, flying past gravestones and moon shadows, concentrating on the churchyard gate. I reached it unscathed, and although it must have been almost five feet high, I hurdled it without slowing down. I ran on through another mews and on to the main road and didn't stop running until I reached my flat.

I let myself in, poured myself a large whiskey, and threw myself onto the sofa, still gasping for breath.

As my pulse and my breathing began to settle down, so did my brain. I was jumpy. Way too jumpy. I had never actually seen Joe clearly. I had thought I had seen and heard someone following me, but could I be sure? Was I going to spend every day from now on looking over my shoulder, running from shadows? I was a little drunk and more than a little scared.

I pulled myself together. Yes, I was up against some unpleasant people. They were unpredictable and probably dangerous. Joe, in particular, didn't seem to like me very much. But there was nothing I could do about that. I wasn't going to let him ruin my life. If I was careful and kept my wits about me, I would be all right. Or so I told myself as I took another gulp of whiskey.

CHAPTER
>>>> 11

IT WAS A RELIEF to get out of the country. I had spent two days looking over my shoulder everywhere I went. Not knowing whether my apprehension was justified hadn't helped at all. As soon as I got on the plane, I felt a huge weight lift from my shoulders. Somehow I doubted that Joe would track me down in New York.

I was glad that Cathy and Cash were not on the plane. They were following more or less the same itinerary I was. They were spending a couple of days at their head office in New York first, then moving on to Phoenix for the conference, and finally joining their clients for a visit to the Tahiti. Cash, especially, I was not looking forward to meeting. It was hard enough to think of him as responsible for the Tremont Capital fraud. What bothered me even more, was the question of whether he was involved in Debbie's death. I was still no nearer finding out who had killed her. I wasn't even sure why she had been killed.

It was going to be difficult to talk to Cash on this trip, but I was going to have to do it. I had lots of questions to ask him, and I would have to be subtle. I also needed to find out what I could about Dick Waigel, and look for some trace of Tremont Capital at Bloomfield Weiss's New York office. I was due to spend the whole of my first day there, and Cash had fixed up a lot of people for me to meet, so I was hopeful that I would find something out. I was still not exactly sure how.

Despite this, the task excited me. It was a challenge with a lot at stake; $20 million and De Jong & Co.'s reputation. Hamilton was going to meet me for dinner in New York on his way back from the Netherlands Antilles. I would make sure I had something to tell him.

My arrival in New York was just as intimidating as always. Although it was half past seven local time when I left the airport, it was after midnight according to my own biological clock. Not the right time to deal with the stress of New York's welcome.

As I emerged from the terminal, I beat off a chauffeur who offered to give me a lift in his boss's limousine for $100. I grabbed a yellow taxi. The driver, whose name, according to the license pinned to his dashboard, was Diran Gregorian, did not seem to speak English. He didn't even acknowledge the words *Westbury Hotel.* But he started his taxi and drove off toward the city at full speed.

Fortunately, his headlong flight was hindered by the Long Island traffic jams. We crossed the Triboro Bridge with New York's skyline welcoming us on the left. I tried to pick out as many of the buildings as I could. Most prominent was the Empire State Building, incomplete without the figure of King Kong clambering up it. In front was the smaller and more elegant Chrysler Building, whose peak rose like a minaret, calling the faithful money makers to their desks each morning. I picked out the Citicorp Building, the top right-hand corner of its roof cleanly sliced off, and in the distance the green rectangular slab of the United Nations Building jutting out into the East River. Other lesser structures clustered round these in the middle of Manhattan. Then, to the left stretched a plain of the low, brown tenements of Soho, the East Village, and the Bowery, until the huge twin peaks of the World Trade Center dwarfed the Wall Street office blocks surrounding them downtown. My pulse quickened despite my fatigue. Among all those buildings were lights, noise, traffic, and people. Millions of people working and playing. They beckoned even the tiredest traveler to join them.

We finally made it to the hotel. I threw down my bag without bothering to unpack it, and flopped into bed. I fell asleep immediately.

I wasn't due at Bloomfield Weiss until ten o'clock, so I could linger over the excellent Westbury breakfast. One of the great pleasures of being away from the office was the opportunity to have a long, leisurely breakfast, instead of cramming down a stale pastry at my desk at half past seven in the morning. The Westbury is Manhattan's "English" hotel. I had been booked in there because it was the hotel Hamilton usually stayed in when he was in New York. It had elegance without opulence. A tapestry in the foyer, Regency furniture and nineteenth-century landscapes could almost persuade you that you were in an English country hotel and not in an eight-story block of stone in the middle of Manhattan.

Finally sated, I caught a taxi, Haitian driver this time, and bucketed down to Wall Street, a local French-language radio station blaring in my ears.

I was a few minutes early, so I asked the taxi driver to drop me off at the top of Wall Street so I could walk the last few blocks to Bloomfield Weiss's offices. Walking down Wall Street was like descending into a canyon, with huge walls shooting up on both sides. Although it was a sunny day, the giant buildings threw the street into shadow, and at this time of morning it still felt cool. Halfway down the street I turned left and then right, down narrower streets, the buildings coming ever closer together, the shadows ever deeper. Finally I came to a fifty-story black tower, which looked more sinister than those surrounding it. The words *Bloomfield Weiss* were printed in small gold lettering above the entrance.

I had been told to go up to the forty-sixth floor and ask for Lloyd Harbin, the head of high-yield bond sales.

I waited in the reception area for a couple of minutes before he came round to get me. He was of average height but had a very compact frame. His shoulders were broad and his neck bulged with muscle. He strode across the room, hand outstretched and voice booming, "Hi Paul, how are you? Lloyd Harbin."

I was prepared for the iron handshake. I had learned at school that if you pushed your hand hard into the joint between thumb and forefinger of your adversary, it was impossible for him to grip your hand tightly. I had developed this technique so that it was not obvious, but was still very effective against the American marine types. It momentarily put Lloyd Harbin off his stride.

But Lloyd was not going to be disconcerted by a young wimp of a Brit and recovered himself in a moment. "Have you seen a Wall Street trading floor before?" he asked.

I shook my head.

"Well come and see ours, then."

I followed him through some gray double doors. Bloomfield Weiss's trading floor was not quite the largest on Wall Street and certainly not the most modern, but it was the most active. Stretching out on all sides were hundreds of dealing desks. Large electronic boards proclaimed the latest news, stock prices, and the time all round the world. Milling around the desks were an army of men in regulation Brooks Brothers white shirts, interspersed with a few women, mostly wearing tight dresses, lots of makeup and elaborate hairdos. Trading floors are still male dominated, the women were nearly all assistants and secretaries.

The floor was alive with the urgent buzz of voices, passing information, arguing, abusing, ordering. Standing on the edge of that room, I found myself in the throbbing heart of capitalist America, the place from where all the money was pumped around the system.

"Here, come over to my desk, and I will show you our operation," Lloyd said.

I followed him through the trading room, picking my way through the jumble of wayward chairs, papers, and wastepaper baskets. Lloyd's desk was in the middle of a close-knit group of men in white shirts. I felt conspicuous as the only man in the room wearing a jacket, and so took it off. I still felt conspicuous as the only man in the room with a striped shirt, but there was nothing I could do about that.

Lloyd pointed out the two groups of people involved in trading junk bonds, the salesmen and the traders. It was the salesmen's job to talk to clients and try to persuade them to buy or sell bonds. It was the traders' job to determine at what price these bonds would be bought or sold. The traders were responsible for managing the bond positions owned by the firm. Traders bought and sold either from clients or from other traders at other companies, collectively known as the Street. It was generally much more profitable to trade with clients, and it was only by talking to clients that the traders could get the information on what was going on in the market that was so important to running a profitable position. Thus the salesmen needed the traders and the traders needed the salesmen. However, this symbiotic relationship had its rough side.

An argument was right then in progress.

"Look Chris, you can bid higher than eighty-eight. My client has to sell. He's been told by his management to sell today. We put him into this bond, we've got to take him out." The speaker was a blond, youngish man, well groomed with a friendly face. His voice was reasonable but firm. A salesman.

He was talking to a short hyperactive man who was almost frothing at the mouth. "Hey, this is the asshole who took me short the Krogers last week, and then went around and lifted the rest of the Street," he shouted. "I still haven't been able to buy them back. Let him suffer. It's about time we made some money out of him for a change."

The salesman turned to Lloyd. "Do something with this jerk, will you," he said quietly.

Lloyd walked up to the trader, who was bristling for a fight. "Where did you make those bonds this morning?" he asked him.

"Ninety to ninety-two, but the market's down."

"Fine, we will bid the customer eighty-nine."

Howls of protest from the trader and a disappointed shake of the head from the salesman. Lloyd's voice rose in volume just a touch. "I said we will pay eighty-nine. Now get on with it."

They got on with it.

Lloyd came back to his desk. We talked for a few minutes as Lloyd explained how his group worked. He then introduced me to the traders. There were five of them, all on edge. Although they were all polite, they couldn't keep their attention on me for long. After thirty seconds of conversation, their eyes would wander back to their screens or their price sheets. There followed a few painful minutes of small talk at which all the traders said they loved to do business with clients, especially those based in London. Lloyd pulled me over to another desk.

"Why don't you spend a few moments with Tommy here. Tommy Masterson, this is Paul Murray from De Jong."

Tommy Masterson was the salesman I had seen arguing earlier. Despite that, he had a much more relaxed demeanor than those around him.

"Take a seat," he said. "So you are from London?"

I nodded.

"Not many people buy junk bonds over there, I bet."

"Not many," I agreed. "In fact we are just starting. Your traders seemed very anxious to help us get into the market."

Tommy laughed. "You bet they are. They can't wait. They will take advantage of you so bad, you'll forget how many fingers you were born with."

"How will they do that?" I asked.

"Oh, quoting low prices when you are a seller and high prices when you are a buyer. Trying to offload their worst bonds onto you with stories about how great they are. It's difficult for them to get away with that sort of thing with the large U.S. accounts. But a small foreigner? Lamb to the slaughter."

"Well, thank you for the warning." I had known I was going to have to be careful dealing in the junk market, but I didn't realize I had to be that careful.

"If you have a good salesman, you should be protected," said Tommy. "Who is your salesman?"

"Cash Callaghan," I said.

"Oh, dear. Now there is a slippery customer. But I'm sure I don't need to tell you that."

"I have seen him in action," I said. "But you tell me what he was like in New York. We hear he was the top salesman in the firm."

"He was. But that doesn't mean he was the straightest salesman. He was like a good card shark. He would let the punters have some successful trades, make a bit of money, get the hang of trusting him. Then he would persuade them to do very large trades, which generated Cash a fortune in sales commissions. The customers lost their shirts. He could fool even the smartest customers. Usually, they didn't even realize they were being taken and would come back for more."

I thought of Hamilton. Cash had even managed to hoodwink him.

"Was any of this illegal?" I asked.

"Not that I know of. Unethical? Yes. Illegal? No."

"Would you be surprised if Cash did something illegal?"

"Yes, I would. Cash is too smart for that." Tommy sat up in his chair and smiled. "Have you got anything specific in mind?"

"No," I said, although I could see Tommy was not convinced. I changed the subject. "Cash still does a lot of business with one American customer. It's an Arizona savings and loan."

"That would be Phoenix Prosperity," Tommy said. I was thankful for his frankness.

"Oh, would it? Does he con them too?"

"I don't know. I don't think so. They have always done a ton of business with him. In fact it's amazing how much business they do for such a small institution. They are pretty aggressive. They used to be covered by a fellow called Dick Waigel. He developed them into his biggest account, and then Cash took over when Dick moved to corporate finance."

"I've heard of this chap Dick Waigel," I said. "What's he like?"

"He's a real jerk," said Tommy emphatically. "He thinks he is the smartest thing on earth. To hear him talk, you would think he was personally responsible for half this firm's income. But he and Cash are good buddies. Go back a long way. Lloyd thought the sun shone out of his ass."

"Did he? I wouldn't have thought Lloyd suffered bullshit gladly," I said.

"He sure doesn't. He's not very smart though, so he doesn't always recognize it. But he's tough. He can be a real asshole. He is going places in this firm, and that's because anyone who stands in his way gets mowed down. It's not talent. Management by fear is his style. Every now and then he'll fire someone, just to encourage the others."

"But not you."

"No, not me," Tommy smiled. "He'd love to. He doesn't like my attitude. Too Californian. Not gung-ho enough. But he can't afford to fire me. For some strange reason, I'm the top salesman on the desk. And I don't even lie and cheat to achieve it."

I looked at Tommy and could believe him. I had no doubt that his friendly, frank manner encouraged people to deal with him. And, unlike Cash, I doubted whether he would betray their trust.

"We can't sit around here talking all day," said Tommy. "You've got lunch at one o'clock with Lloyd, haven't you?"

"Yes, I think so," I said.

"Okay, well it's twelve thirty now. Tell you what. It's the ten-year auction today. The U.S. Treasury is auctioning nine billion dollars of new ten-year government bonds at one o'clock. Do you want to see the Bloomfield Weiss machine in action?"

I certainly did. Bloomfield Weiss was renowned for its trading muscle in government bonds. He took me over to the other side of the room and introduced me to a grizzled gray-haired man in his fifties.

"Fred, have you got a minute?"

"For you Tommy, always." He grinned.

"I'd like you to meet Paul Murray, one of our clients from across the ocean. Paul, this is Fred Flecker. He is our head government bond salesmen covering New York accounts. He has been in the market forever. I bet the first long bond you sold matured long ago, right Fred?"

"Just about," replied Fred. He held out his hand and I shook it. "Have a seat," he said. I found a small stool, and squatted between him and the other men frantically working the phones around him. I felt a bit like just another wastepaper basket, there to get in the way. "Do you understand what's going on?"

"No," I said. "Tell me."

"Okay. At one o'clock our firm, together with all the other investment banks on Wall Street, will be bidding for a certain amount of ten-year treasuries at a certain yield. There are nine billion dollars' worth for sale. The bidder who bids the lowest yield will be sold bonds first, then the next lowest bidder, and so on.

"We will be bidding on our own and on our clients' behalf. Obviously, the more demand we see for the bonds, the more we will bid for on our own behalf. My job is to talk to the major New York clients and reflect their bids to our head government bond trader, John

Saunders. He is sitting over there." He pointed to a thin man frowning with concentration at a desk thirty feet away. People were constantly hurrying up to him, passing messages, and hurrying back.

Just then the squawk box on his desk crackled into life. "Fred, what are you hearing?"

"That's John," Fred said to me. And to the squawk box, "It looks good. We've received bids for six hundred million from New York alone. People seem to like the market."

"Yeah, I'm hearing that from Chicago and Boston," John's voice crackled.

"Are you going to take this one?" Fred asked.

"I'm sure thinking about it."

I watched and listened as Fred took calls from several more clients, most of whom placed orders for the auction. Given the sums at stake, I was amazed by the calmness of Fred's voice. Quiet and measured, it inspired confidence and trust.

At twelve fifty-five, only five minutes before the auction, John walked over and whispered something in Fred's ear. He smiled. He looked at me and said, "What you see now you keep to yourself, understand?"

I nodded. "What's going on?" I asked.

"We're going to make a shutout bid," he said. "We will bid for most of the auction at a yield so low that none of the other dealers will buy any bonds. Most of them have sold ten-year bonds short with the hope of buying them back during the auction. But they won't be able to, because we will own them all. As they scramble to cover their short position, and as other customers realize that their orders will not be filled, everyone will be trying to buy the bonds. The market will go up and Bloomfield Weiss will clean up. Now, I must make a couple of calls. We want to cut our friends in."

The first was to one of the largest corporations in America.

"Hello, Steve, it's Fred," he said. "You put in a hundred

million order for the ten-year auction. I think you should consider increasing that."

"Why?" asked the voice at the other end of the phone.

"You know I can't tell you that," Fred said.

There was silence. Then, "Okay, I'll play. Put me down for five hundred million."

"Thank you," Fred said and hung up. They had obviously done this many times before.

He made a similar call to another large institution who agreed to increase its order to $300 million.

I was intrigued to see Cash hovering over by John Saunders's desk. He must have heard something, because suddenly he rushed over to a nearby empty desk and made one phone call. I could guess who it was to.

At two minutes to the hour Fred got a call from a firm called Bunker Hill Mutual.

"Hi, Fred, how's it going?"

"I'm fine, Peter. But I don't think this auction will be. None of my customers are interested."

"What do you think Bloomfield Weiss will do?" the man called Peter asked.

"I don't know, of course, but I think we will bid to miss."

Peter grunted his thanks, and put the phone down.

"Why did you tell him that?" I asked.

Fred chuckled. "Oh, he always rings round all the investment banks just before an auction. He is as leaky as a sieve. If I told him what we are really up to, it would be all round the Street."

The whole trading room lapsed into silence as the clock moved to one o'clock. It could be up to ten minutes before the results of the auction would begin to be known.

The minutes ticked by.

Then the squawk box crackled into life. "Okay, it looks like Bloomfield Weiss owns all nine billion of this one. Get on the phones and tell your clients what is happening. Let's scare out those shorts."

I looked around me. Smiles everywhere as salespeople eagerly phoned their customers to tell them the result. Within seconds the green numbers on the screens on Fred's desk started winking as the market began to move up.

Bloomfield Weiss, and its most favored customers, made a lot of money that day.

I was a few minutes late for lunch, which was in one of Bloomfield Weiss's dining rooms. It was spectacular. Forty-seven floors up, the dining room was high enough to peek over the building between it and the harbor. I had never seen such a view of New York Harbor. The sun shone off the silvery-blue sea, ferries bustled back and forth between Staten Island and the terminal directly below. The Statue of Liberty thrust her torch defiantly up toward us, taking no notice of the two helicopters buzzing around her ears. In the distance the elegant curves of the Verrazano Bridge lay astride the horizon, a focal point for the dozen or so ships making their way out toward the ocean.

"Anywhere else, you'd have to pay a couple of hundred dollars for a meal with a view like this," said Lloyd, as he approached me.

Silly me, for a moment I hadn't appreciated the dollar value of the view.

Cash was behind Lloyd, and next to him, a short balding man of about thirty-five with thick glasses.

The sight of Cash made me feel sick. I was furious with myself for ever being deceived by all that good humor and amiability. But I would have to talk to him as usual, forget what he had done to De Jong, what he might have done to Debbie.

"Hi, Paul, how are you doing?" he boomed, holding out his hand.

I hesitated a second before shaking it. Then I pulled myself together and replied, "Oh, I am fine. Your colleagues here have been very kind in showing me round."

"Good, good," said Cash. "Now you met Lloyd this morning, but I don't think you have met my old friend Dick Waigel."

The short, balding man shook my hand vigorously, and gave me an unnatural smile reeking insincerity. "Pleased to meet you," he said. "Any client of Cash's is a friend of mine."

"Now, why don't we all sit down?" Lloyd said. "What would you like to drink, Paul, iced tea?"

I had forgotten that lunches in Wall Street investment banks were dry. I had found it difficult to get used to the American habit of drinking cold tea at lunch, but I supposed they found the English warm beer just as confusing. I thought I ought to enter into the spirit of the thing. "Iced tea would be very nice, thank you," I said.

For a while the conversation followed the usual tedious paths of these occasions; discussions were had on the weather in England, which was the best airline these days, how the market was quiet and how difficult it was to make money.

I looked around the restaurant at the other diners. They were at odds with the breathtaking view around them. Either big and beefy, or short and wiry, they ate their food rapidly, spearing errant pieces of steak with forks and shoving them into mouths lowered as close as possible to the table. They didn't look at all comfortable in the hushed surroundings. Conversation was not the relaxed murmur of a normal restaurant, but rather a series of staccato whispers. I could see a number of other clients among the Bloomfield Weiss executives; the difference in levels of aggression between them and their hosts was obvious from twenty feet.

As I scanned the room, my eye caught the profile of one of the men at a small table in the corner opposite us. He had his back to me, but was turning to talk to the man on his left. I knew that profile. Joe Finlay.

One of the people at his table must have seen me stare, because Joe turned round and stared straight back at me. He twitched the corners of his mouth up in that same quick false smile that he had used on me at the boat, and turned back to his food.

What the hell was Joe doing here? It was bad enough having Cash to deal with in New York, the last person I needed to see was Joe.

I leaned over to Cash. "Isn't that Joe Finlay over there?"

"Yeah, that's him," said Cash.

"What's he doing here?"

"Same as all of us. Spending a few days in New York and then going to the conference in Arizona."

"But you didn't tell me he was coming," I said.

Cash looked puzzled. Then he laughed. "Hey, Paul, I can't tell you the names of everyone going to this damn conference. You got me and Cathy looking after you. What else do you want?"

Cash was right, of course. But Joe's presence still unnerved me.

Waigel looked over toward Joe's table. "That guy sure is a good trader. Or at least he has a hell of a reputation. Speaking of which, how's your boss Hamilton McKenzie? I haven't seen him for years."

I tore my eyes away from Joe's taut frame and on to the pudgy, oily face of Dick Waigel. "Very well indeed. He is doing a great job at De Jong. Our clients like him. The money is pouring in from investors impressed by his performance."

"He always was a bright guy," said Waigel. "We were at Harvard Business School together. When he went off to join De Jong, I joined Bloomfield Weiss."

"And what did you do here?" I asked.

Waigel took a deep breath, clearly pleased with the opportunity to talk about his favorite subject, and began. "Well, I used to be a salesman covering accounts in the Southwest. I did well at it, but I didn't feel it was providing the right challenge for my talents. Selling is a rather narrow activity, you know." At this the two salesmen sitting at the table stiffened. But Waigel went on.

"So I took a job in corporate finance, responsible for private placements. We find that sometimes a particular investor will want a bond issue tailored specifically to his needs. So I find a company to issue such bonds and place them privately with him and perhaps one or two other investors. That's how I came to work with Cash here. Since he has such good relationships with his customers, we do a lot together, trying to structure transactions which fit their needs."

This was Waigel's connection with Cash on Tremont Capital, which had been a private placement.

"I am not too familiar with private placements," I said, "but isn't it true that they give investors less protection? Normal bond issues in the United States have to be scrutinized by the Securities and Exchange Commission. Who does the due diligence on private placements?"

"Oh, we do. And I would say the investor is better protected with a Bloomfield Weiss private placement. We have very high standards, Paul, the highest on Wall Street. I can assure you that nothing irregular has happened in any of our transactions." With this, Waigel looked me straight in the eye through his thick glasses, and gave me another one of his insincere smiles.

"I don't think we have ever bought a private placement from you since I have been at De Jong," I said. "Did we buy any before I arrived?"

Waigel opened his mouth, and closed it again. For a rare moment he seemed at a loss for words. Finally he said, "No, I don't believe you did."

Cash interrupted, "Come on, Dick. Don't you remember that Tremont Capital deal? The triple A bond with the huge yield. A sweet deal. I sold half of that to De Jong."

"Oh yes, I remember," said Waigel. "Yes, that was a good deal. Have you looked at it, Paul?"

"I have seen the bond in our portfolio," I said, "but I am not familiar with the details. Can you tell me more about it?"

Waigel looked uncomfortable, but Cash bailed him out. He enthusiastically told me all about the deal, and how the Honshu Bank guarantee made the transaction creditworthy. "One of the best deals I ever sold," Cash finished off.

"Very interesting," I said. I turned to Waigel. "How do you go about putting a deal like that together?"

Waigel looked even more uncomfortable. "One of the problems with corporate finance is that you owe a duty of confidence to everyone involved. We make it a rule never to discuss the details of a transaction, even after it is completed."

"Baloney, Dick," said Cash. "There is nothing you like to talk about more than one of your own deals."

Waigel didn't find this amusing. "Cash, you can be as indiscreet as you like, but to me it is unprofessional. My predecessor may have been unprofessional, but I am sure I am not going to follow him in that."

Lloyd interrupted, suddenly finding himself on a subject close to his heart. "Aw, Greg Shoffman wasn't unprofessional, he was just a wimp. He had no guts. We had some great junk-bond deals that he refused to do because he said they were unethical. Unethical! What did he think we were running, a charity?" Lloyd pulled himself up as he remembered my presence. "Now, Paul, don't get me wrong, all the deals Bloomfield Weiss do are above board. But in today's markets you have got to be a tough competitor to survive, and this fellow Shoffman just wasn't tough enough."

Shoffman! I had heard that name before. I rifled through my memory. That was it. The man from Honshu Bank had said a Mr. Shoffman had called him a few months before Debbie.

"This Mr. Shoffman was your predecessor?" I asked Waigel.

"Yes," he replied. "He was a nice enough guy. But as Lloyd says he didn't have what it takes. You need the killer instinct to get things done, especially against the competition out there. That's something I have and he hadn't."

Somehow, I could believe Waigel had the killer instinct. "So, what happened to him?" I asked.

"About two years ago he was transferred to our documentation department and Dick here took his place," said Lloyd.

"Is he still working for Bloomfield Weiss?" I asked.

There was a silence. The others looked to Lloyd to break it. Eventually, he obliged them. "No," said Lloyd. "One day several months ago, he didn't come in to work. He just disappeared. The police couldn't find any trace of him. He probably ended up in a back alley somewhere. You know what this city is like nowadays."

"Did they find out who did it?" I asked.

"They don't even know for sure he is dead. The police think it's most likely he was murdered in the streets for his wallet."

The police might think that. I thought it strange that both the people who had called Honshu Bank about the Tremont Capital guarantee were now dead. With a shock I remembered that there was now a third person who knew about it. Me.

"That's what you get for living in the city," said Waigel, waving a finger at me. "I used to live in the city until it got too dangerous. Now I live in the 'burbs. Montclair, New Jersey. Life is much safer now. Mind you, it takes a whole lot longer to get to work these days."

The conversation drifted on to commuting times and then back again to how talented Waigel was. When lunch had finally finished, I went back down with Lloyd to the trading floor. I strolled over to Tommy's desk.

"Have a nice lunch?" Tommy grinned.

I made a face.

"You could hardly pick a nicer bunch of guys," said Tommy. "Lloyd Harbin, Cash Callaghan, and the odious Dick Waigel."

"I must admit I found him very unpleasant," I said.

"One of Bloomfield Weiss's finest," said Tommy.

I smiled. I gestured to Tommy's phone. "Do you mind if I watch you at work?" I asked.

"Sure." He picked up the phone and motioned for me to take a second earpiece.

I heard him through a number of phone calls. He was good with his clients. He sounded friendly and helpful with all of them, but he changed his manner subtly with each one, hearty with one, nerdish with another. He gave his clients plenty of information quickly and efficiently, he seemed to know exactly what bonds they were holding at the moment even when some of them were doing their best not to tell him, and he made no attempt at all to sell the Macy's position that Bloomfield Weiss had picked up by mistake and were desperate to get rid of. A good salesman.

After an hour or so, we were interrupted by Lloyd, who tapped Tommy's shoulder. "Can I see you for a moment?" he asked.

"Sure," said Tommy and they disappeared round a corner. I stood around for a minute or two, and then sat in Tommy's chair to watch what was going on around me.

After a few minutes Lloyd returned. I made as if to get up, but Lloyd motioned for me to stay seated.

"Stay there, Paul," he said. "Use that desk for the rest of the afternoon as a base if you wish. The head of our research group will be up in a few minutes to take care of you."

I wanted to ask him where Tommy was, but something told me not to. The salesmen who were sitting round Tommy's desk glanced at me furtively. I had the impression they were not looking at me, but rather at the chair I was sitting on. Tommy's chair.

I felt as though I was desecrating a grave, sitting there. I leaped out of the chair. I felt a bit foolish, standing around, being ignored by everyone on all sides. I wanted to tell them it was not my fault that Tommy had gone.

I knew what they were thinking. Tommy was unlucky. It could easily have been one of them. Tommy had gone from successful salesman to failure in five minutes. They couldn't be seen to be associated with that failure. They wanted nothing to do with it, at least in public anyway.

A man in gray overalls with a large blue crate walked up to me. "Was this Mr. Masterson's desk?" he asked.

I nodded. He carefully placed everything that looked personal into the crate. As he walked off, dragging the crate behind him, I saw he had left Tommy's jacket on the back of the chair. "Hey!" I shouted, but he didn't hear. My English accent sounded out of place in that big American trading room, and several people turned to look, although not of course those sitting nearest me who remained steadfastly ignorant of my presence.

At last, I was saved by the head of research who came along to whisk me away. I spent the rest of the afternoon with a number of analysts talking about the pros and cons of various junk bonds. I found the subject interesting. Separating those companies that would succeed from those that would fail was a challenge that was as much an art as a science. I learned a lot from the Bloomfield Weiss analysts which I would be able to use later.

At about half past five I came to the end of my meetings. I went back into the trading room to say good-bye to Lloyd. He made no mention of Tommy, so I said, "If you see Tommy, wish him luck from me."

"Sure will," said Lloyd, "he's a great guy."

I walked with him to the elevators trying not to let my anger show. Bloomfield Weiss seemed to breed very unpleasant characters: Cash Callaghan, Dick Waigel, and Lloyd Harbin. I supposed that sometimes some people had to be sacked. But I doubted the genial and successful Tommy deserved to be one of those people. And he had not just been sacked. His memory and every trace of him had been expunged from Bloomfield Weiss before the afternoon was even over.

As I said good-bye to Lloyd, I again managed to disrupt his bone-crushing handshake, which gave me a small shred of pleasure.

The elevator was empty as I got in, and I heaved a huge sigh as the doors closed behind me. I had enough of ruthless bastards for one day.

The elevator fell one floor and stopped. The doors opened to let in the tall figure of Cathy. She looked quite upset. Her cheeks were flushed, and her lower lip was trembling.

"Bad day?" I said.

"Bloody awful day," she said.

"Nasty place, this."

"Horrible place."

"There are some real bastards working here."

"Real bastards," she said. She looked at me and gave me a small smile.

"Do you fancy a drink?" I asked on an impulse.

She hesitated. "Oh, why not? Do you know anywhere round here?"

We went to Fraunces Tavern, an old, redbrick building squatting among Broad Street's skyscrapers, with a warm, dark interior. We sat down and ordered two beers.

"What's up?" I asked.

Cathy winced. "Let's just say there was a clash of personalities."

"And you came off worse?"

Cathy sighed, and leaned back in her seat. "I just had a big fight with Cash," Cathy said. "For all his nice-guy image that man can be very difficult to work for."

"What did he do?"

"It was the usual thing. Cash was trying to stuff one of our clients. The trading desk in New York is long fifty million of a dodgy insurance company. There was some bad news about it in *The Wall Street Journal* this morning, so the prices are being marked down and our traders can't give away the bonds."

Her long slim fingers fiddled with the coaster in front of her. "Well, this is Cash's chance to look good with the bosses in New York. So he rings one of our clients in London with a cock and bull story about how the article is wrong and the insurance company is really doing much better than everybody thinks it is. They believe it, and are falling over themselves to buy the bonds. They'll find out their mistake soon enough, when they try to get a price for them."

She sighed. "It isn't even really his client. It's someone I have been trying to develop a relationship with for months. They were just beginning to trust me. After this, they won't want to talk to me again. Cash will look a hero, and I will lose a client." She looked up at me. "I shouldn't be telling you all this, should I? It's just sometimes I get so sick of the whole thing I could explode. And it's nice to talk to someone about it."

"Don't worry," I said. "I had worked out Cash wasn't a hundred percent trustworthy myself. Does this sort of thing happen a lot?"

"All the time," she said. "I hate lying. I'm not really much good at it. I'm sure the only way to develop relationships properly is by building up trust." She looked up from her beer. "We may have had our differences in the past, but I have always been honest with you, haven't I?" Her eyes looked for support and encouragement.

I thought about it. She was right. And she had been very straightforward with me in telling me about her run-in with Cash. I nodded. "I can't think of a time when you haven't been straight."

Cathy was pleased with my response. "It's frustrating. I do my best to tell the truth to my customers, and they don't deal with me. Cash lies through his teeth to them, and they do masses of business. It's like that with De Jong, isn't it?"

"I haven't really thought about it. I suppose it is," I admitted.

She looked glumly down at her coaster. "But I shouldn't go on about my troubles. What about you? You didn't look too happy yourself in the elevator. Have you had a bad day too?"

I told her about the disappearing salesman act I had witnessed and about my lunch with the obnoxious Waigel.

"Oh, him. He's known as 'the poisonous frog.'"

I laughed. That did seem an apt description.

"There are a lot of people like Dick Waigel and Lloyd Harbin at Bloomfield Weiss," she said. "In fact they are actively encouraged. It's the same with most of the Wall Street firms. Competitiveness and aggression are extolled as virtues. Only the toughest will survive. It makes me sick."

This seemed a bit rich. "You don't always give that impression."

She looked at me inquiringly. Then she sighed. "Yes, you are right, I know I can be aggressive. I think that's why they gave me a job. And I play up to it. They like it, even if my customers don't. The problem is, I hate it."

"Why do you do it then?"

"I want to succeed, I suppose. I want to make a lot of money at Bloomfield Weiss."

"Why?"

"Why? Isn't it obvious?"

"Not really."

"Mm. No, I suppose you are right. It isn't obvious." She paused to think. "Both my parents are university professors, and they have always had great ambitions for me. My brother is the youngest director of one of the merchant banks in London. He got a scholarship to Oxford, so I had to get a scholarship to Oxford. Now I have to do well in the City. Silly, really, isn't it?"

I nodded. It was silly. But I had to admit it was a motivation that applied to lots of people toiling in banks and brokerage firms. And the frankness of her reply impressed me.

"Do you enjoy it?" I asked, trying to make my voice more friendly.

"Yes, in many ways I do," she said. "I like the excitement of the markets. I like dealing with people. And I think I am genuinely quite good at it. What I don't like is the lying, the posturing, the politics, the need to show that you are tougher than the next man."

"Well, why don't you just give up the tough-guy image?" I asked.

"No," she said. "Bloomfield Weiss would eat me alive. You are just going to have to put up with it." She laughed, not looking at all like the all-conquering corporate woman.

In fact, shorn of her cool self-assurance, she seemed like a normal, intelligent woman, with lovely eyes and an attractive smile. A few moments of silence passed, both of us trying out each other's company.

"Tell me about Rob," I said.

She smiled. "You tell me about Rob," she said.

"No. I asked you first."

"Okay," she said. "He's a nice enough guy. Quite sweet really. We went out together a couple of times and had some fun. Then he suddenly got serious. Very serious. It was scary. He wanted to marry me and we hardly even knew each other. I felt bad, because I thought I must have led him on without realizing it, although thinking back, I can't see how I could have.

"So, I thought the best thing to do was to try to avoid him. I didn't want him to persist with the wrong idea. But then he lured me to a restaurant, pretending to be a client of mine. I felt such a fool. I was furious. I haven't heard from him since then, thank God." She paused. "Is he always like this?"

"Quite often, I'm afraid," I said. "In your case he seems to have got it pretty bad. I don't think you have heard the last of him."

"Oh dear," she said. "If there is anything you can say to him to put him off, please do. I have tried everything I can think of. He's a nice guy, but enough is enough."

I thought about what Felicity had told me about

Rob's phone calls to Debbie, about Claire feeling that there was something weird about him, and about what I had seen of him myself that night in the Gloucester Arms. "Be careful," I said.

Cathy raised her eyebrows at this, but I refused to explain further. We carried on talking for an hour or so, lingering over another beer. Cathy coaxed me to talk about my family, something I am usually reluctant to discuss with strangers. I told her about my father's death, about my mother's illness, and about how I had dashed my mother's hopes of me becoming a farmer. She was sympathetic. Much to my surprise, I didn't find her sympathy embarrassing, nor did it make me bitter as it sometimes did when given insincerely. It was comforting.

"Is Hamilton McKenzie the cold fish he seems?" she asked. "He must be difficult to work for."

"He isn't a very easy person to read," I admitted. "And he can be a bit of a taskmaster. He is very sparing with praise."

"But you like him?"

"I wouldn't say exactly that. But I do admire him. He is so good at what he does, one of the best in the market. He is an excellent teacher. And he has this way of making me work hard for him, of bringing the best out of me. To tell you the truth, I would do anything for him."

"It must be good to work for someone like that."

"Yes, it is."

"A bit like having a father?"

I squirmed in my chair. "I hadn't thought about it that way. But I suppose you are right."

Cathy reached across the table to touch my hand. "I'm sorry, I shouldn't have said that," she said.

"No, no, that's okay. It's a relief to be able to talk to someone like this. Someone who understands. One of the worst things about losing a parent is that it imposes a sort of loneliness upon you. It is one of the most important things in your life, but you can't share it with anyone."

Cathy smiled. We sat in silence for a few moments. Then she looked at her watch. "Is that the time? I must be off. Thanks for the drink. I feel much better now." She got up to leave.

I found myself reluctant to let her go. "So do I," I said. Much better.

We parted, each of us heading toward our separate subway stations.

FIRST THING THE next morning, I canceled my meetings for the day. Something had come up, I said. I wanted to spend my day in New York following up on what I had heard the day before.

Two questions intrigued me. First, what had happened to Shoffman, and second, could I find out anything more about how Waigel had put the Tremont Capital deal together?

I tried to deal with the first one first. I called information to find out the number of the nearest police station to Bloomfield Weiss. I suspected that would be where his disappearance would have been reported by the firm. I dialed the number from my hotel room.

I was transferred a couple of times until I ended up with a friendly woman who told me that the disappearance had been reported to that station, but that the enquiry had been taken up by another precinct on West 110th Street, which was near where Shoffman had lived. I thanked her, left my hotel room, and took a taxi up to the Upper West Side.

Fortunately, the police station was fairly quiet. Even more fortunately, the desk sergeant turned out to be one of that rare breed of ardent Anglophiles that are scattered throughout America.

"Hey, are you English?" he asked in response to my greeting.

"Yes, I am," I said.

"Welcome to New York. How do you like it here?"

"Oh, I think it's a fine city. I always enjoy coming here."

"So you're from England, huh? My mother was from England. A GI bride, she was. Where are you from in England?"

"London."

"Oh yeah? So was my mother. Maybe you know her family. Name of Robinson."

"I'm afraid there are quite a few Robinsons in London," I said.

"Yes, I'm sure there are. I went over there to visit them a couple of years ago. I had a great time. Anyway, how can I help you?"

The policeman standing next to him was big and beefy, and his name tag had *Murphy* written on it. His scowl deepened as he listened to this conversation.

"Yes, I am trying to find something out about an old university friend of mine, Greg Shoffman. He was reported missing at this station four months ago, and I would like to try to find out what happened to him."

"Sure. Wait a moment and I will see if I can find his file."

I waited for about five minutes, and then the policeman returned, a very thin file in his hands.

"We don't have much on him. He was reported missing on April twentieth. No trace of him found at all. No body, no empty wallet, no driver's license. His credit cards remained unused. The investigation is closed."

"But how can a man disappear without a trace?" I asked.

"This is New York. We have six murders a day here. Sure, we find the bodies of most of them. But not all of them."

"Where was he last seen?"

The policeman referred to his file. "The last reported sighting was when he left his office at seven o'clock on the nineteenth. Neither his doorman nor any of his neighbors reported seeing him arrive at his apartment. He lived alone. No wife, no girlfriend we know of."

"What was his address?"

The policeman glanced at me, his eyes narrowing a little. "I thought you said you were an old friend of his," he said.

"Yes, I'm sorry. I left his address in England. I have his work number, so when I came over here I called him at work to fix up dinner. Then they told me about his disappearance. It was a real shock. I would very much like to find out what really happened."

The policeman's face softened. He gave me an address just two blocks away from the police station. Then he said, "Look, mister. You are not going to find out anything however hard you look. I have seen dozens of cases like this in the past. Unless the victim's body or his possessions are found and reported to the police, you never get anywhere. It's true that if we had more man-power and less murders we could have spent more time on this case, but I doubt whether we would have got any further."

I thought about it. He was probably right. I sighed and thanked him for his trouble.

"Not at all. A pleasure to help. And have a pint of bitter for me when you get back."

I assured him I would and left, thinking how lucky I had been to come across such a helpful New York cop. His Irish colleague's scowl followed me all the way out of the police station.

I walked the two blocks to Shoffman's apartment building. It was in one of those frontier neighborhoods, where the more adventurous young urban professionals made forays into the run-down districts of Harlem. Neat brownstone buildings, built toward the end of the nineteenth century and renovated toward the end of the twentieth, rubbed shoulders with disused warehouses and builder's merchants. A Korean fruit and vegetable store stood on the street corner, spick and span, ready to sell its wares to returning office workers. At this time of the morning the streets were nearly empty. An old black man shuffled along the sidewalk, muttering to himself.

It is impossible for an Englishman to understand the real workings of a neighborhood such as this. Brought up on a diet of TV cop shows and lurid news stories, it is all too easy to see New York as a battleground between white professionals and a black underclass. Shoffman lived right in the middle of the battle lines. The reality of the situation is probably infinitely more complicated than this, but as an Englishman dressed in a suit walking those streets on the outskirts of the notorious Harlem, I found it easy to believe that Shoffman could have become a casualty of this war.

The lobby of his apartment building was well furnished and there was a doorman sitting behind a desk guarding the passage to the elevators. I asked him about Shoffman, giving him the old-friend-from-England routine.

Yes, he remembered Mr. Shoffman. Yes, he had been on duty on the evening of April nineteenth. No, he had not seen Mr. Shoffman come home, neither had the doorman who relieved him at midnight. Yes, he would have remembered, he had been looking out for him to give him a parcel. No, the parcel was nothing special, just some books from a book club. No, he could not show me the apartment, it had a new owner.

I left defeated, hailed a cab, and went back to the hotel.

Back in my room I flopped onto my bed, stared at the ceiling, and thought.

It looked as though I had drawn a blank on the answer to my first question. I only had a day left in New York. I was sure the policeman was right. My chances of finding out what really happened to Shoffman were very small. But I was still convinced that his disappearance so soon after his phone call to Honshu Bank was not a coincidence. Someone had found out that he had discovered Tremont Capital was a fraud and he was now dead.

That still left the second question. How had Waigel put together the Tremont Capital deal? Who had he been dealing with? Where had the money raised by the private placement been paid?

There must have been some paperwork associated with the transaction. Hamilton would soon be looking for traces of it in Curaçao. But there must also have been some at Bloomfield Weiss. The librarian in London had been adamant that none of it was in any central filing system. Of course, it might have all been thrown away. But on the other hand the shell company still existed, it was still paying interest. No, it was quite possible that Waigel might have some of the records concerning the deal in his own private files. How could I get to his filing system?

I called Lloyd Harbin.

"Hello. This is Paul Murray. I was just calling to thank you for showing me around yesterday." I tried to keep the insincerity out of my voice.

"Oh sure, think nothing of it," Lloyd said in a get-off-the-phone-quick-I've-got-something-better-to-do voice.

"I wonder if you could give me Tommy Masterson's home number?" I asked.

"I'm afraid Tommy has been terminated. He no longer works here."

"Nonetheless, I would be very grateful if you could help me. You see I loaned him my pen, and he didn't get a chance to return it. I have owned it for several years and it means a lot to me."

"I am sorry, Paul. I just can't give out information about former employees."

I should have known the sentimental approach wouldn't work with Lloyd Harbin. I would have to speak to him in his own language. "Lloyd, listen carefully. De Jong and Company is soon going to start a buying program of junk bonds. It will total two hundred million dollars. [A lie, but who cared?] Now we can either buy them from Bloomfield Weiss or we can buy them from Harrison Brothers. The choice is yours."

It worked. "Now, hold on, don't do anything rash. I'll just get it for you." He was back in less than half a minute. "Three four two, six six oh seven."

"Thank you. It will be a pleasure to do business with you," I lied, and hung up.

I caught Tommy at home and asked him if he would mind meeting me for lunch. We agreed on an Italian restaurant, Café Alfredo, near where he lived in Greenwich Village.

Tommy without a job seemed much the same as Tommy with a job. The same laid-back air, the same amiability.

"I was sorry to see you let go yesterday," I said, using the standard euphemism for "getting fired."

"Thank you," said Tommy. "It was a bit of a surprise."

"I was amazed at the way they did it. Is that how it normally works? You get hauled off to some office somewhere and don't even get a chance to go back to your desk."

"That's the way it works," said Tommy, "although usually you get a little more warning of what is going to happen."

"Why did he do it?" I asked.

"He doesn't like me," Tommy said. "My 'attitude did not fit in with the Bloomfield Weiss culture.' And, I was 'undermining his authority.' I don't think they like too much independent thought at Bloomfield Weiss. They don't like people who call a rip-off a rip-off instead of a 'unique investment opportunity.' Still, without me they will sell less bonds and make less money, so that is something to be grateful for."

"You must be angry," I said.

"Oh, I'll be all right. This has probably been a good thing. It will force me to go and find somewhere better to work, somewhere that employs human beings. I may even go back to California and let the Bad Apple rot."

For all the brave face he was putting on it, Tommy could not suppress the bitterness in his voice. Good, I thought.

"I wonder if I could ask you for some advice," I said.

"Sure."

"My firm is the proud owner of one of those 'unique investment opportunities' you were talking about. In fact it's so unique, I am pretty sure it's illegal. I can't do anything about it until I have some hard evidence."

"What was the transaction?" Tommy asked.

"It was a private placement done eighteen months ago called Tremont Capital. Dick Waigel structured the deal."

"Never heard of it. I'm afraid I can't give you any advice on that."

"I don't need any advice on the deal itself," I said. "But I do need advice on how to gain access to Waigel's files."

I looked at Tommy closely, hoping I had not gone too far.

He looked back. "I can't do that," he said. "What if they found out I helped you?"

"They can hardly fire you," I pointed out.

"True," Tommy smiled. "But if they did catch me, their lawyers would have me for breakfast."

"I'm sorry, Tommy," I said. "I had no right to ask you. Please just forget we ever had this conversation."

There was silence for a moment. Then Tommy relaxed again and smiled. "Hell, why not? I don't owe them anything and it sounds like they owe you a lot. I'll help."

"Great!"

"Waigel runs a department of five or six people. They all work in one room, but he has had his own office built. It takes up half the space, and has curtains for greater privacy."

Typical Waigel, I thought. His ego required as much space as all six people who worked for him.

"I know Waigel's secretary, Jean, quite well. She's a nice woman, but she can't stand his guts. She's on the point of quitting. I think she will probably help us, especially when she hears what has happened to me. She can let us know when he is out. We go up there, and she shows us into his office, as though we have an appointment with him. Simple."

"Good," I said. "But how do we get in the building? Haven't they taken your pass away?"

"Yes they have, but I am sure Jean can take care of that."

"There's no need for you to come," I said. "I can go by myself."

"Oh, yes there is. If Jean's going to let you into Waigel's office, I am going to have to be there too."

"Is there anything between you and this Jean?" I asked, smiling.

Tommy laughed, "Oh, no, nothing, I promise you."

We finished our lunch, I paid, and then we set off for Tommy's apartment so that he could call Jean. I needed to get into Waigel's office that afternoon.

Tommy's apartment was on the third floor of an old brownstone on Barrow Street. We walked up the stairs, and as Tommy fished for his keys, he hesitated. "Oh, I have a friend of mine staying with me. Gary. He works in the evenings, so he may well be in."

He opened the door, and I followed him through a small hallway into a tastefully decorated living room. There was an expensive oriental rug on the floor, and another on one wall. A number of attractive abstract paintings adorned the other walls. Gary was sitting in a comfortable leather armchair. He shouted a welcome as we came in.

Gary had a full moustache, a crew cut, and was wearing tight light blue jeans, the uniform of the gay New York male. So this was why Tommy had laughed when I had mentioned the possibility of a relationship between him and Waigel's secretary. I looked again at Tommy. There was no outward sign of his sexual orientation.

Tommy caught my look. "Okay, so I'm gay. Does it surprise you?" he said.

"I suppose it does a little," I said. "But I'll get over it." I couldn't suppress an involuntary chuckle.

"What are you laughing at?" asked Tommy, looking at me suspiciously.

"Oh, I was just thinking of Lloyd Harbin's face if he ever found out."

Tommy smiled. "Yes, I see what you mean. Mind you, I saw him in a bar on Christopher Street a few months ago with some very unsavory company. Do you want some coffee?"

Tommy made some coffee and then called Waigel's secretary. While he was on the phone I sipped my coffee and chatted to Gary.

After three or four minutes Tommy put down the phone. "Waigel's out now, and won't be back for an hour. If we are quick, we should be able to find what we want before he comes back. Just wait a moment while I get changed."

A minute later Tommy emerged from his bedroom in a suit. I put down my coffee, said good-bye to Gary, and followed Tommy out of the door. We quickly found a cab, and headed downtown to Wall Street.

We pulled up outside the great, black, looming building of Bloomfield Weiss. We took an elevator up to the reception area on the forty-seventh floor, which was where corporate finance was located.

Tommy walked up to the receptionist and said, "Tommy Masterson and James Smith to see Mr. Waigel."

The receptionist looked at Tommy and said, "Don't you work here, Mr. Masterson? I thought you were on the trading floor."

Tommy gave her a friendly smile. "I used to work here until very recently," he said.

The receptionist looked at her book. "Well, if you have an appointment, I guess it's okay." She tapped some buttons on her phone. "Jean? Mr. Waigel's guests are in reception." She put the phone down. "Please wait here, gentlemen."

Jean was out in a flash. She was a tall woman with round Lennon glasses and long brown hair plaited down her back. She had a baggy blouse and a long skirt. She looked as much like a hippie as one can look on Wall Street, which is not very much. She showed no hint of recognition of Tommy. She led us through some corridors and into an open plan office. There were six desks cramped into a small area. Five of them were occupied with people hard at work. One guarded a glass-encased office on one side of the room. There were curtains on the inside of this office, making it impossible to see in.

"I am afraid Mr. Waigel is not expected back for another half hour," Jean said. "I am terribly sorry for the mix-up on appointment times. I can't think how it could have happened. Would you like to wait or come back later?"

"We would like to wait if we may," Tommy said.

"Well, why don't you wait in Mr. Waigel's office until he returns?" said Jean.

As she showed us into the office, Tommy gave her a broad wink. She smiled back at him and closed the door on us.

The office was large, with a big desk, two armchairs, a sofa, and a coffee table. The room was littered with "tombstones," advertisements of previous deals encased in clear plastic blocks. Waigel had done a lot of deals, and he wanted everyone to know about them. There were two framed photographs on the wall, one of Waigel shaking hands with Lee Iacocca and another with Mayor Ed Koch. The Koch one would have done any New York Chinese restaurant proud.

Along one wall was a row of wooden file cabinets. Two full cabinets were marked "completed deals." I tried them. They were locked.

Tommy went outside, and under the pretext of asking for some coffee, came back with a key from Jean. He opened the cabinets.

Inside were rows of files in alphabetic order. I quickly flipped through until I came to T. No Tremont Capital. Damn. I began to look back through some of the other files. I noticed that many of them had titles that were obviously code words.

"What do we do now?" Tommy said.

"There's nothing for it but to go through each file individually," I said.

"But there are at least a hundred. It will take an hour! We only have twenty minutes."

"We've got no choice. I'll start at A and you start at Z and work back."

"Just a moment. Let me see if I recognize any of the code words," Tommy said.

I was rifling through my second file, which turned out to be about the takeover of a beauty products company code named Adonis when Tommy whispered, "Here, I've got it!" He held up a file labeled "Music Hall."

"How did you work that one out?" I asked.

"Tremont Capital reminded me of Tremont Avenue in the Bronx. There was a music hall there that used to be very popular."

"Well done!" I said, and grabbed the file. I hadn't connected the word *Tremont* with the Bronx. Interesting.

I laid out all the documents in the file on the desk and worked my way through them. There were drafts, and then the final version of the prospectus I had looked through back in London. There was correspondence with the lawyers Van Kreef, Heerlen discussing a number of detailed legal points. One letter dealt with how to ensure that the ownership of Tremont Capital was kept strictly anonymous. Needless to say the owners were not mentioned there.

Then I found a letter with the Harzweiger Bank

letterhead. It was from Hans Dietweiler. It confirmed account numbers for the payment of funds raised by Tremont Capital from its bond offering.

Damn. If the money De Jong had paid for the private placement had gone into Switzerland, it would be next to impossible to trace it.

I moved on. Then I found it. It was just a scrap of yellow legal pad paper. Scrawled on the top was the word *STRUCTURE*. Below were a series of boxes. It laid out the complete structure of the fraud.

I took a piece of paper from Waigel's desk and copied out the diagram. I was interrupted by a tap on the door. It was Jean. "You guys had better hurry up. Dick will be back any minute now."

I hurriedly finished the diagram, carefully reassembled the Music Hall file and placed it back in the file cabinet. Tommy and I checked the office to make sure everything was as we had found it. My eyes fell on Waigel's desk diary. I quickly checked the week Debbie had been killed. It was filled with appointments, all of which seemed to be in New York. There was no mention of canceled meetings or flights to London.

"Come on," said Tommy, and I followed him out of the door. Looking irritated, Tommy stopped at Jean's desk and said, "Tell Dick we waited for him. Mr. Smith has another appointment, and we are already late. Have him call me, please."

"I can't think what can have happened to him," said Jean. "I am very sorry you and Mr. Smith had to wait so long. I am sure he will be back in a minute."

"We can't afford to wait any longer. Good-bye." With that Tommy and I marched out of Waigel's department into the corridor. Our act had drawn one or two bored glances from the people working in the outer office. It was enough to be plausible, not enough to be memorable.

We waited for what seemed an age for an elevator to come. Finally one arrived. It was crowded with Japanese businessmen, clients of Bloomfield Weiss. They went through a complicated dance to decide which one of them should get out of the car first. Behind them all, ushering them out, was the short, bald figure of Dick Waigel. I saw him before he saw me.

"Quick, Tommy. Fire exit!" I said.

Without dithering, Tommy darted to the stairway. I couldn't follow him because I was caught up in the melee of Japanese. Waigel saw me.

"Paul, what brings you here?" he asked, his eyes suspicious.

"Oh, I was in the building and I thought I would drop by to follow up on one or two of the comments you made at lunch yesterday," I said. "I found them very interesting."

"Oh good," said Waigel, staring at me thoughtfully, trying to decide whether I was telling the truth.

The group of Japanese were looking at Waigel expectantly. I coughed nervously and said, "Well, this doesn't look like a good time for you. If you are going to be at the conference in Phoenix, perhaps we can chat then."

I knew I wasn't convincing. Waigel's stare hardened. I stared back. Something was wrong. He didn't know what, but it unsettled him. He hesitated for a moment, but his guests were waiting. "See you then," he muttered.

I got into the elevator and breathed out loudly as the doors closed in front of me. My heart was beating rapidly, and I could hear the blood rushing round my ears. I hoped Jean would be able to bluff her way round the awkward questions Waigel would be bound to ask her. But at least I had the diagram.

I met Tommy in the lobby. He was clearly enjoying his afternoon. "Wow, that was close!" he said, eyes shining. "I just caught the gleam of his bald head, so I beat it. Did you speak to him? Did he suspect anything?"

"I don't know," I said. I shuddered. "What a nasty little man!"

Tommy laughed. "One of Bloomfield Weiss's finest."

"I hope Jean is all right," I said.

"Don't worry. The worst Waigel can do is fire her, and she wants to quit anyway. So what did we find? Was the mission successful?"

"It was indeed," I said, patting my pocket. "I think this diagram will explain a lot."

"Well, let's get it out and look at it then."

"Look, I'm sorry. I don't think I can show it to you."

"Why the hell not?" Tommy was upset. "I just risked getting fired for the second time in one week. I have a right to know. Come on, let's get a cup of coffee and you can tell me all about it."

"I would, but . . ."

"Yes?"

"I know this may sound corny, but I don't want to put you in danger."

Tommy took me by the arm and looked me in the eye. "You're right, it does sound corny. Look, if you really are in danger, maybe I can help you out. It's no good. You've got me hooked on this thing. I can live with the risk. Let's get that cup of coffee."

"Okay, I give in."

We found a Greek coffee shop and ordered two cups, and I began.

"About a year ago, Bloomfield Weiss sold us twenty million dollars of a private placement for a company called Tremont Capital NV. Tremont was supposed to be guaranteed by Honshu Bank. It turns out that this guarantee never existed. Neither Honshu Bank nor Bloomfield Weiss have any record of it. The only security we have for our investment is an offshore shell company."

"That's bad," said Tommy.

"What's worse is that two of the three people who have discovered this are now dead."

"Wow," Tommy whistled. "Was one of them Greg Shoffman?"

"Yes," I replied. "The other was a woman called Debbie Chater who worked for us in London."

"Do you know who did it?" Tommy asked.

"No. Debbie fell into the river Thames. I think she was helped. By whom, I just don't know. But I'm going to find out."

"So who is behind Tremont Capital?" Tommy asked.

"I can guess," I said.

"Who sold the deal to you?" Tommy asked.

"Cash Callaghan."

"And Dick Waigel structured it?"

"Dead right," I said.

"Jeez-us," Tommy said as he leaned back in his chair. "Well, I am not surprised by that snake Waigel. But Cash? I can imagine Cash bending the rules, but I wouldn't have thought he would go that far. What scum!"

Tommy gulped his coffee, thinking it through. "So Shoffman and your Debbie Chater are dead? Who's the third person?" Tommy paused and whistled again. "That's you. Man, you had better watch yourself."

"I know," I said, "and you can see why I was reluctant to make you the fourth."

Tommy laughed, "Don't worry about that. They don't know I know. I'll be all right. So what happened to the money?" he asked.

"I don't know," I said. "That's why I wanted to take a look at Waigel's files. Let's have a look at that diagram."

I pulled it out of my pocket and spread it out on the table.

It consisted of a series of boxes, one underneath the other. Connecting them were arrows, all pointing downward. They showed the direction of the flow of funds in the transaction.

The first box was labeled "2 investors." That was presumably De Jong & Co. and Harzweiger Bank.

An arrow with $40 million written by it pointed down to the next box, labeled "SPV." That must stand for "special-purpose vehicle," which was Tremont Capital. This represented the $40 million raised by Tremont from the private placement.

The next box down was labeled "Swiss bank a/c." That would be the account referred to in Dietweiler's letter.

Next came a more puzzling box: "Uncle Sam's Money Machine." I had no idea what that could be. Below this were a series of boxes marked "high return investments." By the arrows were the numbers "$150 to $200 mm." I could see the power of Uncle Sam's Money Machine. A total of $40 million went into it, and $150 to $200 million came out of it. A money machine indeed.

Underneath the diagram were some notes explaining things a bit further: "Yrs 8–10 sell investments. Sell or break money machine. Take the profits out of SPV in dividends. Estimated dividends $50 million. Bond repaid if possible."

"What do you make of that?" Tommy asked.

I thought for a minute or so. "Well, I don't know what Uncle Sam's Money Machine is, but I think I understand most of the rest.

"The forty million raised by Tremont Capital from the private placement is deposited in a Swiss bank account. From there it is used to purchase, or perhaps build, the mysterious money machine. There the money is somehow turned into two hundred million. This money is put into high return investments. After eight years or so these are sold. The proceeds, which by that time are presumably quite large, flow back to Tremont Capital. The forty million is then repaid. Any profits from the investments over and above the interest costs on the private placement are paid out by Tremont Capital in dividends. Waigel estimates these to be fifty million. So, Waigel and his accomplices borrow forty million, use this money to generate a further fifty million in profits for themselves, and then give the original forty million back, with nobody any the wiser."

"Why do they do that?" asked Tommy. "Why don't they just keep the forty million."

"That's the clever bit. By giving the money back, no one will know that a crime was committed. They can carry on living normal lives and perhaps try the same trick again, fifty million dollars richer. If they were to get greedy and not repay the forty million they had borrowed, then an investigation would be started, and they would run the risk of getting caught."

"They raised twenty million from De Jong. Where did they get the other twenty from?" Tommy asked.

"From Harzweiger Bank in Zurich," I said. "I spoke to a Herr Dietweiler there who pretended they had never bought the deal. He must have got some kickback for getting involved. That must be why they use accounts at Harzweiger Bank where Herr Dietweiler can keep his eye on the funds."

"Okay. So how do they manage to make all this money out of borrowing forty million dollars? What is this Uncle Sam's Money Machine?"

I shook my head. "I don't know. It seems to be the key to the whole thing. I don't know what the hell it is."

"Perhaps it's a government agency?" suggested Tommy.

"Maybe," I said. "But I don't see how anyone ever got rich by giving money to a government agency."

"Uncle Sam could refer to the army," said Tommy. "Lots of people make money out of that. Defense contractors and such like."

"Could be," I said. We discussed the possibilities for several minutes without coming to a satisfactory conclusion.

"So, how can I help?" Tommy asked.

"Are you sure you want to?" I said. "You know what happened to Debbie Chater and Greg Shoffman."

"Hey, I don't have a job, and I need something to do. This beats selling bonds. And the more I stir up that sticks to Bloomfield Weiss, the better."

"Well, you could try to find out a bit more about Greg Shoffman," I said. I told him about my attempts to discover more about his disappearance. "I would like to know who killed him. Just as important, I would love to know what he found out before he died. He may have turned up some useful evidence against Cash and Waigel. I would do all this myself, but I won't be in New York for very long. If you come across anything, call me at the conference in Phoenix."

Tommy said he would do his best. We paid for the coffee and then left.

I liked Tommy. For a moment I was concerned that I had needlessly put him in danger by telling him what I knew. No, that was silly. I knew more than Tommy. And I wasn't in any visible danger.

I got back to my hotel room hot and sweaty. The red light on the phone was on. I left it there and jumped straight into the shower, letting the cool water lower my blood temperature. Feeling much better, I went to the phone and rang the message desk. Hamilton was coming into New York the next day. He wanted to meet me for lunch at a fashionable Italian restaurant on the Upper East Side. It would be good to see him. Everything was jumbled in my mind. Talking it through with him, I knew it would all fall into place.

The next day was my last in New York before flying to Phoenix. I was scheduled to see a couple of investment banks in the morning. At one of them a persistent little man called Kettering insisted on lecturing me on the opportunities in South American debt, even though I had no interest. He regaled me with a mixture of beration and abuse. He succeeded in making me feel stupid for not agreeing with him about the financial wonders of that continent and in irritating the hell out of me.

Tired and battered by the morning's hard sell, I decided to walk from the investment bank's offices up to the restaurant. I needed the air, even though it was only New York's hot atmosphere, which managed to be both dusty and clammy at the same time. I sauntered diagonally through side streets and up the main avenues, slowing myself down, just looking.

I walked along a deserted side street, high buildings on either side. Thin eerie music echoed off the walls of the canyon. A group of short square men wearing what looked like shawls and bowler hats clustered round some rugs, acoustic equipment, and a set of primitive drums. They had dark, wind-beaten skin and high, hardened cheekbones. There was just me and them alone on the street. I stopped to listen. The music had a magical quality to it, evoking sheer mountainsides, swooping birds of prey, the age-old loneliness of the Andean altiplano. I don't know how long I stood there, bewitched by the music. Eventually, they paused, and only then acknowledged my presence, smiling shyly. I bought one of the tapes they had laid out on the sidewalk. The cover was a picture of the group looking very serious, with the caption *Las Incas.* I walked on, the music still swirling and swooping inside my head. Within a minute I was back in the blaring bustle of Third Avenue.

The restaurant was light and airy. Skylight and metal tables suggested an informal garden trattoria in Italy. The other diners' sober suits or chic dresses confirmed what it really was: an expensive New York restaurant currently enjoying its brief turn as the place to be.

I saw Hamilton lost in a sheaf of papers. He looked quite out of place among the other tables of smart diners. As I drew up a chair, he glanced at his watch and frowned slightly. I looked at my own and saw it was 12:33 P.M. Three minutes late. Who but Hamilton would care?

Stuffing his papers into his briefcase, he asked, "How are you finding New York?"

"Oh, I like it," I said. "It's so"—I paused—"unexpected."

I told him about the Peruvian band I had encountered on my way.

Hamilton looked at me, slightly puzzled. "Yes, I see," he said. And then, with an edge to his voice, "You have seen some investment banks, haven't you?"

As usual with Hamilton, I felt slightly foolish. Of course, Hamilton was not interested in my thoughts of New York as a city, he wanted to know what was going on on Wall Street.

I told him the highlights of what I had heard. He questioned me closely about one or two conversations I had had that I thought were completely unimportant. He probed me with questions that I realized I should have asked and hadn't, digging to discover who was buying what. My self-confidence began to wane as I recognized that by Hamilton's standards I had done a superficial job of finding out what was really going on. The waiter had been hovering throughout this interrogation, nervous of interrupting Hamilton. Finally, he saw his chance and, after forcing a hurried glance at the menu, coaxed an order from each of us. Hamilton stuck with a Caesar salad, which seemed a bit Spartan to me, given the exotic attractions of the menu. Reluctantly, I forbore the appetizer, and after a swift glance, asked for a complicated looking meat dish. Hamilton ordered a large bottle of mineral water. I looked enviously at the next table where a couple were enjoying a long, relaxed meal and were already onto their second bottle of Montrachet. Why come to a restaurant like this and gallop through some lettuce and a glass or two of water? Oh, well.

"How have your other investigations gone?" Hamilton asked.

I told him everything I had found out: how Waigel had been evasive about his involvement in the original deal, about Shoffman and his disappearance, and about the diagram I had found in Waigel's office.

Hamilton listened carefully to every word. When I had finished I looked to him for a response. He was silent for what seemed an age, gently stroking his beard. Then he smiled. "Good work, Paul. Very interesting. Very interesting indeed."

After my poor showing earlier in the conversation, I was pleased. "So what do you think Uncle Sam's Money Machine might be?" I asked.

"What do you think?"

I had thought about this hard over the last twenty-four hours, but had not come up with anything. "A government defense agency? Some sort of computer? Some kind of government bond fraud?" I guessed wildly, looking to Hamilton for a reaction. He didn't seem too impressed with these ideas.

I shrugged. "I don't know. What do you think?"

Hamilton paused. "We have no way of knowing. We don't have enough to go on yet, but it's a start. Well done." He took a peck at his salad. "I think you are right, though, finding out what this thing is, is the key to getting our money back."

"How did you get on in the Netherlands Antilles?" I asked.

"It was a bit difficult, since I didn't want to tip off Van Kreef, Heerlen that we are suspicious. Rudy Geer was very helpful. My cover was that the recent tax reforms had caused us to look at the possibility of asking for a change in domicile for Tremont Capital. As part of the process, Geer had to check all the documentation."

"Did he find anything?"

"It's interesting. Van Kreef, Heerlen claim that they did see the Honshu Bank guarantee. When Geer asked them to produce it, they said they couldn't find it in their files. This is, of course, a terrible thing for any firm of lawyers to admit, so Geer suspects it must be true."

"What do you make of that?" I asked.

"I don't know. I suppose the most likely thing was that the guarantee was a fraud that was somehow removed from Van Kreef, Heerlen's files. Perhaps by one of their own lawyers who is on the take. It is going to be difficult to kick up too much of a fuss without causing our concerns to get back to whoever owns Tremont Capital."

"Very interesting," I said. "Anything else?"

"Well, it looks as though we will get a court order forcing Tremont Capital's auditors to show us a copy of their accounts. Hopefully, that will give us some clue where the money has gone. The court order won't be granted until early next week, and they will have a couple of weeks to comply. There's not much I can do until I hear back from Geer and actually get my hands on those accounts."

"So, what now?" I asked. "Do you think we have enough to go to the police?"

Hamilton leaned forward, his blue eyes boring straight into mine. "We have to get that money back," he said. His voice was calm, his tone level, but there was an edge of absolute determination to it. "You remember I told you about that lead I had in Tokyo? Well, I think we really might get it. And they are talking five hundred million dollars. That could transform De Jong." He sipped his mineral water, never taking his eyes from mine. "If they hear we have lost twenty million dollars in a fraud, our credibility will be blown, and no one will give us their money to manage. Even if it wasn't our fault."

It was our fault, I thought. Or at least Hamilton's. He had been sloppy in checking the documentation. A rare mistake on his part, but I was not about to try to get him to admit to it.

"But if we go to the authorities, won't they help us find the money?"

Hamilton shook his head. "The police's top priority is to catch the criminal, not find the loot. That's why most cases of fraud never get to the police or the public. If you can sort it out yourself, you have a much better chance of coming out whole." There was a slight smile on his lips, mocking my naïveté.

"All right," I said, not really feeling all right about it at all, "so what do we do next?"

"Well, you've done a good job so far. Keep plugging away, asking questions. There will be a lot of people from Bloomfield Weiss at the conference in Arizona. See what you can find out there. In particular, see if you can find out anything about this Money Machine. I'll do what I can in London, while I wait to hear from Curaçao."

Hamilton saw the concerned look on my face. "Don't worry, we'll find the money."

Hamilton brushed away the dessert trolley, dripping with temptation, and paid the bill. We went our different ways, with me taking a taxi downtown to Harrison Brothers.

The afternoon dragged. I was tired and edgy and found it difficult to concentrate. I was nervous about going along with Hamilton. I felt out of my depth, and although I would normally trust Hamilton to do anything, I had nagging doubts that he was out of his depth too.

Finally five o'clock came, and I could respectably leave. I was due to meet one of Harrison's government bond salesmen at eight o'clock for dinner. That was three hours away, so I decided to head back to the Westbury. I walked to the Fulton subway station and boarded the Lexington Line Express heading north. I changed at Grand Central to get the local.

It was rush hour and the train was crowded. New York in early September is still very hot and very humid. The train was one of the few on the subway system that had no air-conditioning. I felt the sweat run down my body, soaking my shirt and even my trousers. My tie looked as though it would curl up in the heat.

The train stopped for an age. Passengers were crammed together. Tempers were short. People were muttering under their breath, cursing the goddamn subway system. Even in these conditions, everyone was following the golden rule of the New York subway—never, ever catch another person's eye. He might be a coke head, a rapist, a serial murderer, a Jehovah's witness.

I stared at the advertisements. There was poor Walter Henson, an architect famous throughout New York City for his hemorrhoid complaint. There, too, were big, black, ugly cockroaches crawling into a Roach Motel with the caption *"Las cucarachas entran pero no pueden salir."*

The train lurched forward. My gaze wandered along the car. It stopped with a jolt.

There, at the end of the car, was Joe.

He was staring at me, expressionless. Although I was looking straight at him, he gave no sign of recognition. I tried to regain my composure, but I was sure he must have seen the alarm that I felt when I spotted him.

I tore my eyes away from him and looked the other way. Since catching sight of Joe in Bloomfield Weiss's dining room, we had avoided each other, much to my relief. But now he was right here, in the same subway car as me. It must be a coincidence, mustn't it? It had to be.

I tried to ease myself down to the other end of the car. I was flustered, and I stepped on the toe of a mild-looking man in a business suit reading *The Wall Street Journal.* I put all my weight on it.

"What the fuck are you doing, you dumb fucker!" he screamed at me. "Get the fuck off my fucking toe or I will smash your fucking face in!"

I glanced at the swearing man without really focusing on him. I pushed past him.

"Jerk," he muttered to me and to everyone standing round us.

I was glad of the attention. It would be impossible for Joe to do anything to me on a crowded subway train, and when we got to Sixty-eighth Street there ought to be plenty of people around.

I was right. A stream of office workers spilled out of the subway entrance on their way home. I latched onto a group of noisy young bankers who were heading in the same direction as my hotel. Looking over my shoulder, I could see Joe following a block behind.

I peeled off from the bankers on Park Avenue and walked the block to the Westbury as fast as I could. I paused by the awning in front of the hotel and could make out the figure of Joe standing on a street corner, still a block away.

I told the man at reception to make sure I was not disturbed by anyone. He looked at me a little strangely but promised me he would do as he was asked. I went up to my room, turned all the locks and bolts on my door, and flopped onto my bed.

If Joe was following me, it could only be because he wanted to get even with me. Perhaps the police had been round to his house again. Or perhaps, despite my caution, I had stirred something up with my questions about Greg Shoffman and Tremont Capital. But why should that bother him? Maybe he was just brooding over the fact that my little finger was still intact.

I paced up and down the small bedroom worrying about Joe. After ten minutes or so, I became less agitated. It must have been a coincidence that Joe had got on the same subway train as me. He had probably followed me just because he was curious; perhaps he thought it would be fun to scare me. Well, he had succeeded.

I debated whether to call off my dinner. I decided I should be safe if I took a taxi to and from the restaurant. There was nothing Joe could do in broad daylight right outside the hotel. So at half past seven, having showered and put on a new shirt, I made my way down to the lobby.

There was a group of people clustered round the entrance, waiting for taxis. The doorman was in the middle of the street blowing his whistle full blast. But there were no empty taxis to be seen. It was still light, although the sun was glowing red, low over Central Park. I looked up and down the street. No sign of Joe. He definitely wasn't in the lobby either.

After ten minutes, the doorman had only nabbed one taxi and there were still two people in front of me. Joe wasn't anywhere to be seen. I decided to walk over to Fifth Avenue and try my luck for a taxi there.

I had almost reached the avenue when I heard soft footsteps right behind me. I felt a sharp prick through the fabric of my suit. I shot up straight, arching my back, and turned my head slowly.

It was Joe, dressed like a jogger in a dark tracksuit. And he was fondling his favorite instrument. A knife.

CHAPTER
>>>> 13

"WE'RE GOING FOR a walk in the park," Joe said.

I looked up and down Fifth Avenue. A few people sauntered along the street, enjoying the evening, but none of them seemed obvious sources of help. New Yorkers knew the rule. If you see someone in trouble, ignore it, you might get hurt. Besides, it would take Joe less than a second to plunge his knife between my ribs. He knew how to use it.

So I did as he said. We crossed Fifth Avenue and walked down a bank of summer-burned grass toward the small boating lake. A boy of about ten was guiding his radio-controlled yacht across the water. His mother urged him to hurry up, concerned at the gathering gloom. There were still some people around, but they were all heading in the opposite direction to us, out of the park.

Joe's knife was hidden, but I knew it was there, only inches from my back.

"I told you to call the police off," he hissed. I could feel his breath on the back of my neck.

"There was nothing I could do," I replied, somehow keeping my voice calm.

"Oh yeah? Why did you give them all that crap about me and Sally in the first place?" he said, prodding my back with the point of his knife. "They've taken Sally away from me. And Jerry. It's not good for a man to be away from his wife and child. How do you feel about being responsible for that?"

I didn't say anything. I was glad that Sally had escaped Joe's beatings, and I was glad I was responsible for it. But it didn't seem a good idea to tell Joe that. Joe's voice was flat and toneless, but I imagined that this was the sort of thing that could get him pretty upset.

We were much deeper in the park now, and there were very few people around. We walked down toward a statue of an old Polish king charging toward a baseball cage. A broad field opened up to the north of it, with the tall buildings of Central Park West beyond.

I knew what Joe was planning to do. He was going to take me to the quietest, most inaccessible part of the park. Then he was going to kill me.

I had to get away.

Joe's grip on my arm wasn't very tight. But his other hand, holding the knife, was only inches from my ribs. I had to take the risk.

I snatched my arm away, sprung clear, and sprinted toward the field. I felt a rush of exhilaration as I realized there was no knife stuck in my back. But Joe was quick to follow me. I looked over my shoulder; he was only three yards behind. And he was closing. I pumped my legs harder. If I could only keep clear of him for the first hundred yards or so, I was sure I would outdistance him. I was still fast. But Joe was very fast. I glanced behind me, and saw him a yard closer. Not for the first time in my life, I cursed my lack of sprinting ability. I tried to force my legs to move harder, faster. No response. A couple of seconds later, I felt Joe's hands on my shoulders as he dived to pull me to the ground. I wriggled and twisted, but he soon had me pinned.

Two lovers fifty yards across the field stared at us as we struggled. Joe saw them too. Witnesses.

"Get up!" hissed Joe. He dragged me to my feet and propelled me into the woods to the south of the field. His grip on me was much tighter. I could feel the knife again.

We walked deeper into the trees. It was getting quite dark. Central Park is New York's playground. By day it is populated by joggers, cyclists, softball players, sunbathers, roller skaters, old ladies, children, and a host of other New Yorkers furiously pursuing their chosen passion. At dusk they all go home. At night the park is a playground for different types of people.

Shadows flitted silently between the trees. We passed groups of youths talking loudly, or sitting on benches, silently smoking. Men shuffled past, rolling their eyes and muttering to themselves. They were either crazy or drugged or both.

We walked deeper into the wooded section of the park. We followed narrow footpaths winding round large black rocks looming twenty feet above us in the twilight. The wind gently moved the trees and bushes, the undergrowth growing deeper and more tangled as the light failed. I completely lost my sense of direction. It was impossible to believe we were right in the middle of the city.

I began to think about dying. I thought about my mother. I thought it would be the last straw for her. Faced with the death of her son as well as her husband, she would withdraw from reality altogether.

I thought about Cathy. Would she care about my death? To my surprise, I desperately wanted to believe that she would. And I thought about Debbie.

"Did you kill Debbie?" I asked.

"No," said Joe. "But that doesn't mean I won't kill you. Killing people used to be my job. I am good at it."

I believed him. "Then who did kill her?"

"You never give up, do you?"

We walked on. We stumbled down a winding path between two large overhanging boulders, surrounded by thick trees on all sides.

"Stop here," he said.

I could just make out the empty lake through the trees in the evening gloom. Apart from the occasional rustle of the wind creeping through the branches overhead, all was silent. A quiet, lonely place to die.

"Move back," said Joe.

I was facing him with the boulders behind me. I did as he said, my ankles brushing against some brambles, until I felt the rocks, warmed by the day's heat, against my back.

Joe moved closer, his dead eyes locked on mine. The whites shone with a yellow gleam in the twilight. A thin smile played over his face. He was perfectly balanced, the knife held lightly in front of him. This time I was not going to get away.

Suddenly, I heard soft footsteps on the pathway behind Joe. He grabbed my arm and placed his knife firmly against my back. A group of five or six black kids emerged from the gloom. They were tall and athletic, making little sound as they rolled along in their expensive air-cushioned basketball shoes.

They walked up to us. One of them laughed. "Yo, tooti-frooti! Having fun, guys?"

A tall kid with strange patterns carefully carved into his close-cropped hair came up to me very close. "Hey man, do you get high?"

He was menacing, but less menacing than Joe behind me. I saw my chance. "Yes, sure," I said. "What have you got?"

I turned to look at Joe. He was still holding my arm, but his knife was hidden. I guessed he would rather not stab me there and then. The kids looked dangerous, and there was no knowing what weapons teenagers in Manhattan might carry in Central Park at night.

I walked into the middle of the group, trying to put a yard between me and Joe.

"I got some ice here, just a dime," said the tall kid. He had a lopsided grin on his face. He didn't really believe that we had come all this way into the park just to buy crack from him, but he was willing to play along.

"A dime?"

"Yeah, ten bucks, man, just ten bucks." He held out a small packet. I reached into my pocket as if to dig out some money. Joe looked on, not sure what to do.

Suddenly, I shouted, "Run!" and snatched the packet from the kid's hands. I pushed my way through the group, brushing one of them off, but two of the others grabbed me.

I heard a shout, "Hey, that mother's got a knife!" There was a sharp cry from one of the kids holding me, and his grip loosened.

I saw flashes of steel, as two more leaped on Joe, knives in hand. There was another scream, which was cut short.

One of the kids still had a grip on me. I swung round, fist clenched, and landed a perfect punch into his solar plexus. He went down on his knees, gasping. Then I felt a blow on the side of my head, I couldn't see where it came from. It was hard; it left my ears singing and my eyes unable to focus. It was followed by a boot in the ribs that knocked the breath out of me and threw me off balance.

I rolled over and saw Joe surrounded by three kids, all with knives. Two others were on the ground, one completely still, and the other holding his leg and groaning.

The kids tried to lunge at Joe, but Joe was very quick, turning from one to the other. One of them didn't pull his arm back fast enough, and let out a howl of pain as Joe's knife slashed his forearm.

Joe backed toward me as the other two came at him warily, feinting on one side and then the other. I saw my chance. I stretched out my leg, and kicked at Joe's ankle. He lost his balance. He didn't fall, but he gave one of the kids an opening. Half a second was all it took for a knife to be plunged into Joe's side. As he doubled up, the other kid stuck him deep in the back.

Joe spun round and fell to the ground. He looked at me, his face screwed up in pain, but his eyes as cold as ever. Then he coughed, some blood trickled out of the corner of his mouth and that expressionless stare was locked forever.

I scrambled to my feet and took off. One of the kids tried to follow me, but I was too fast, spurred on by large doses of adrenaline.

I ran all the way back to the Westbury. I dashed straight up to my room, into the bathroom and threw up. I rang the restaurant where I was supposed to meet the man from Harrison Brothers, and told him I would not be coming. I ordered a bottle of whiskey from room service, and when the room became fuzzy round the edges, I went to bed, to a night of fitful sleep.

I AWOKE WITH a headache and a strong desire to leave New York. In those indistinct seconds between sleep and wakefulness, I once again saw Joe's eyes fixed in their final stare as he lay beneath the boulder in the park. Fortunately, I was booked on an early flight, so I lost no time in getting showered and dressed, and heading for the airport. It was only when I felt the aircraft leave the runway at La Guardia, and saw Manhattan Island receding into the distance beneath and behind me, that I finally began to relax.

Even at nine o'clock in the morning Phoenix was hot. It was a physical shock to walk out of the cool, dark terminal into the bright reflection of the sunlight. Locals ambled past in short-sleeved shirts, sunglasses, and deep tans. In less than a minute I was sweating in my suit as I carried my bags over to the large sign that read, "Bloomfield Weiss High-Yield Bond Conference."

They had laid on white stretch limousines to take the conference participants to the hotel. Within seconds, I was back in air-conditioned quiet again. I passed on the Scotch in the minibar and sat back to watch the wood and concrete structures of Phoenix glide by. I supposed that it was perfectly possible to spend all of your life in Phoenix at 65 degrees Fahrenheit, with only brief bursts of extra heat as you transferred from air-conditioned house to air-conditioned car to air-conditioned office.

After half an hour's drive, we reached the hotel. I dumped my things in my room, and went for a stroll. The rooms were grouped in small whitewashed buildings with red tiled roofs surrounding little courtyards. Bougainvillea was everywhere, adding splashes of purple and green to the white and blue of buildings and swimming pools. There seemed to be pools everywhere. Most of the little courtyards had one, and there was a large central pool just by the main building. Sprinklers strained to ensure that the immaculate patches of green approached the perfection of AstroTurf.

I walked into the main building. Immediately, the dazzling colors outside gave way to dark muted creams and browns. The air-conditioning roared in the background. Although attempts were made to perpetuate the Mexican atmosphere, there was no disguising the impression of a financial center in temporary accommodation. Signs abounded, telling me to do a hundred things at once. They were dominated by a large banner proclaiming, "Welcome to the fourth Bloomfield Weiss High-Yield Bond Conference." Everywhere tables were piled with conference documentation and registration forms. I had a peek into one of the conference halls, a dark cavern bristling with electronic gadgetry.

A number of people were wandering around aimlessly. Clean-cut, with carefully ironed slacks and short-sleeved shirts, you could tell they had been plucked only a day ago from the investment offices of New York, Boston, Minneapolis, or Hartford. They all had badges giving name, rank, and organization. I felt naked without one, and set off in search of the right registration desk to pick mine up. Properly labeled, I went back to my room to pull on some running shorts and get some exercise.

It was mid-morning, and the temperature was rising steadily. I stretched, and then set out at a gentle jog toward a long low hill with two humps, which I later learned was called, appropriately, Camelback.

I soon found myself climbing up a rocky desert slope. The only vegetation was thorny bushes and cacti. Lizards and insects scurried from sunshine to shade. I ran slowly and methodically. It was still very hot and the temperature combined with the incline took it out of me. One of the digital thermometers that adorn buildings all over the United States claimed that it was ninety-one degrees. But it was also very dry, and in a way more pleasant than the lower temperatures but higher humidity of New York in summer.

Halfway up the hill, I paused for breath. It would be foolish to push myself too hard in this heat. I turned to look at the city sprawling below me. European cities evolve over the centuries out of their natural setting, nestling in a valley or at the confluence of two rivers. Phoenix looked as though a giant hand had drawn a square grid over the desert and dropped neat blocks of buildings onto it, one by one. Which wasn't too far from what had actually happened. It was a tribute to the inventiveness and prosperity of Americans that such a city could exist in such an inhospitable climate. Of course with air-conditioning, a vast water distribution network, and swimming pools, this unfriendly environment could be transformed into the ideal setting for the modern American dream. That was why Phoenix was one of the fastest-growing cities in the country.

I decided running in this temperature was a bad idea and spent a pleasant hour or so lying on a rock alone on the hillside, letting the sun beat down on my face and remove some of the tension of the last few days.

Every investment bank with any pretensions to deal in the junk-bond market hosts a high-yield conference. They are schizophrenic occasions. The organizers, following the lead given by Drexel Burnham Lambert's notorious "Predators' Ball," feel the need to create an extravaganza in exotic locations, where powerful controllers of billions of dollars can do deals and have fun. There is a bit of the showman in every high-yield salesman, and this appeals to his ideal of what the whole thing should be about.

Unfortunately for the organizers, most of their customers are earnest young men and women whose overriding concerns are such questions as "Will Safeway's new inventory-control systems really increase margins by half a percent?" These people demand a grueling schedule of presentations that start at eight o'clock in the morning and often don't finish until seven at night. This was the first such conference I had been to, and while I was looking forward to seeing some of the presentations by companies issuing high-yield bonds, I also wanted to meet some other investors and perhaps catch an hour or two by the pool. It might help me unwind.

I showered and just made it to lunch. I munched my way through an exotic Mexican salad, half-listening to a Bloomfield Weiss economist drone on about the importance of recent nonfarm payroll figures in the deliberations of the Federal Open Market Committee.

The first presentation after lunch was by Hank Duralek of Beart, Duralek & Reynolds, the kings of leveraged buyouts. Their firm had just bought the biggest cookie manufacturer in the world, for a breathtaking $27 billion, easily the largest deal in history. Duralek was convincing, arguing that it would be easy to make enough cost savings to finance the mountain of debt that the company had taken on. I was intrigued, but I thought I would wait to see what happened to the company over the next year. It was just a little too risky for De Jong's first investment in junk bonds.

Then came an extraordinary presentation from the notorious Marshall Mills. As he himself said, his greatest achievement was to marry an actress a third of his age. He was a short, stocky man in his sixties, who breathed heavily as he talked. A handkerchief was never far from his balding brow. But his eyes were tough and beady, full of energy as they darted about his audience. As he began to speak, the atmosphere in the room became electric. The earnest young men polished their glasses, stuck out their jaws, and glowered. Mills's audience didn't like him. But he didn't care.

He told us the story of his success. Thirty years ago he had inherited his father's small oil company based in Tulsa, Oklahoma. Over the next couple of decades he had grown the company from a little cluster of nodding donkeys to one of the largest private oil and gas concerns in the state. He had used innovative financing techniques to achieve this growth. *Innovative financing techniques* was a phrase that reappeared regularly in Mills's talk. I soon realized it meant finding a sucker and borrowing as much as you could from him in the hope that whatever you had bought with the money he had given you went up in price. If it did, you made millions; if it didn't, then the sucker lost. It was a strategy followed successfully by a number of America's great entrepreneurs.

In 1982, after the second oil price hike, Mills had made his boldest move. He had borrowed several hundred million dollars to finance the development of oil finds in Utah and Colorado. Mills portrayed the episode as a dramatic success. My recollection of events was that the drilling had been left unfinished as oil prices dove below $15, instead of rising above $50, as had been predicted. Somehow Mills's original businesses had ended up with all the cash, while the non-recourse subsidiaries held all the debt and a few half-drilled holes in the Rocky Mountains.

He had pulled the same stunt five years later in an attempt to use innovative financing techniques to build a network of gas fields across the U.S. Southwest. Once again, it had all ended in tears for Mills's hapless bond holders. The way Mills told it, though, they had been honored witnesses to one of America's great entrepreneurial successes.

The audience was restless during this self-eulogizing.

When his speech was over and he asked for questions, a dozen people leaped to their feet. It was clear that a number of them had participated in some of these innovative financings. After the fifth hostile question, Mills's patience wore thin. He interrupted an inquiry about why his refining company had failed to make an interest payment when it had $50 million of cash on its balance sheet by saying, "Look, you guys are lucky. You buy my bonds, and you have Marshall Mills working his guts out for you night and day. There are many people who would give their right arms to have Marshall Mills working for them. Now I have something to tell you, which really will give you something to worry about." Suddenly there was silence in the hall. It gets worse? "You may not have Marshall Mills working for you much longer." The wheezing became more pronounced. "My doctors have diagnosed a heart condition. I could live ten more months or ten more years. But I think it will be prudent for me to retire soon and spend more time with my darling wife."

The audience cheered up at this. No doubt many of them hoped that the actress would be more comfortable with the notion of repaying debt than Mills was. Two or three people quietly sneaked out of the conference hall. Later, on the way to dinner, I was not in the least surprised to hear that most of the bond issues of Mills's companies were up five points.

I joined the two hundred other participants in a huge ballroom dotted with tables laid for dinner. I walked over to my table. Cash was there with Cathy and Waigel from Bloomfield Weiss. Apart from myself, there were two other clients there.

"Hey, Paul, how're you doing?" Cash yelled across the table. "Glad you could make it all this way. Let me introduce you. This is Madeleine Jansen from Amalgamated Veterans Life, and this is Jack Salmon from Phoenix Prosperity Savings and Loan. Madeleine, Jack, this is Paul Murray, my best client in London."

We exchanged smiles and nods. Madeleine Jansen was a small quiet-looking woman. However, as she smiled and said hello her eyes displayed a striking intelligence. Jack Salmon was a tall, thin man a few years older than me. He had slightly buck teeth and fidgeted nervously with his left hand as he shook mine with his right. I found I was seated next to him, with Cathy on my other side.

"I have heard a lot about your institution," I said to Jack.

"Oh, yeah?" he said, clearly pleased. "I didn't know anyone had heard about us outside Arizona, let alone in London."

"Ah, but you make quite an impression on the eurobond markets, don't you," I said, consciously trying to flatter him.

"As a matter of fact we do a lot more in those markets than you would think for an institution our size," said Jack.

"Such as in a recent much-maligned deal for a country not a million miles north of Denmark?" I said, putting on a sly smile.

Jack returned it. "Now you come to mention it, yes. How do you know about that?"

"I make it my business to know," I said. "Actually we took a lot of that deal ourselves. I think we and you were about the only investors to buy the deal when it originally came out. It's not often that one gets a chance to clean up like that."

Jack laughed, "As Cash would say, 'That was a sweet deal!' I sure enjoyed that one." He took a large gulp of wine.

Stroking this man's ego was not going to be difficult. "It's strange for someone based so far away to be so successful in the London markets. How do you do it?" I continued.

"Well, we like to think we are quite cosmopolitan at Phoenix Prosperity. More so than your average investor in the States. I like to keep up with European news and events. I spent three months there when I was at school. And we know Cash Callaghan from way back."

Ah, the real reason, I thought.

"Do you do much of your business with Cash?" I asked.

"A fair amount," said Jack. "He has a very good handle on the markets and comes up with some good analysis. He seems to be able to relate to my ideas."

I bet he does, I thought. Phoenix Prosperity was an ideal account for Cash. I could imagine him inciting Jack Salmon to buy and sell all manner of bonds all day, while he steadily notched up sales commissions. "Yes, we find him good too," I said.

"Have you been involved in the junk market for long?" Jack asked.

"No, we are just starting. And you?"

"Oh, we've been doing it for a year or so."

"How have you found it?"

"It's a blast. But you have got to have balls. If you find a good deal, and it gives you a sixteen percent return, and you are comfortable with the credit, then you have got to buy a lot of it, know what I mean?" Jack gave me a knowing smile.

I nodded. This guy is dangerous, I thought.

"But they won't let me do it," Jack went on. "If I buy more than one or two million they panic. I tell you, it makes it hard to make any decent money."

So there was someone sensible, somewhere, controlling Jack.

"Are there any companies I should look out for tomorrow?"

"Yes, there is one I like. Fairway. I think they have a good story."

"Fairway?" I said. "What do they do?"

"They make golf carts. You know, the little buggies you drive around golf courses."

"I know. Thanks, I'll make sure I see them speak," I

said. We ate on in silence for a minute or two. "Are your offices near here?" I asked.

"Pretty close. They are about ten miles away, downtown. But I'm staying at the hotel for the conference. It's a good opportunity to meet some of the other people involved in the business."

"Do you have a big operation?" I asked.

"No, only two or three of us on the investment side. I make most of the trading decisions. But you don't really need a lot of people to throw around a lot of money."

"We are a small operation too," I said. Then I started angling, "It would certainly be interesting to compare what you do to what we do. Although we live on different continents, I get the impression we have a similar outlook."

Jack took the bait. "Hey, when the conference is over, why don't I show you round. Could you spare a couple of hours?"

I smiled, "Thank you. That will be very interesting. I look forward to it."

Cash had been chatting away to the woman from Amalgamated Veterans Life. At first she had been very aloof, but she was slowly beginning to warm to Cash's charm. After half an hour or so, her laughter was ringing out to match Cash's.

I murmured to Cathy, "Cash seems to be hitting it off with that woman. Why does she get the star treatment?"

"Amalgamated Veterans is one of the largest investors in the U.S.," Cathy said. "Madeleine Jansen is the senior portfolio manager there. She decides what strategy to follow. When she changes her mind about a market, that market moves. She's supposed to be very good."

"I see," I said. "But Amalgamated Veterans isn't one of Cash's clients, is it?"

"Precisely," said Cathy. "But, you never know, one day it might be. Cash likes to make sure he knows as many of the major investors as possible. When he moves back to the States, he will probably call her up to see how she is doing."

"And what will the salesman from Bloomfield Weiss who covers her think of that?"

"That's Lloyd Harbin. He isn't here this evening. A perfect opportunity for Cash."

I didn't say anything. I supposed stealing a client off one of your colleagues was nothing compared with stealing $20 million from one of your clients. I thought of Debbie Chater. But I couldn't tell Cathy my suspicions. I shook my head. "Cash seems like a nasty piece of work to me."

"I can see how you might think that," said Cathy diplomatically. "It's true some people don't like him, but he's not always that bad really.

"Okay, I admit he can be untrustworthy, he does take advantage of his customers now and then, and he is a notorious thief of other people's clients. But I wouldn't say he is the devil personified."

I shrugged.

"Oh, no. He wouldn't hurt a fly. He's quite a softie. Wants everybody to love him. Even me. Although I grumble about him, he does stand up for me. A couple of months ago, they told me I wasn't getting a pay raise this year. I had worked hard, and I deserved one. Cash threatened to resign unless they gave it to me. So they did. There aren't many bosses at Bloomfield Weiss who would do that for their staff."

I was impressed by Cathy's loyalty, but I wasn't convinced. I let it drop.

Cash broke off his conversation and called over to us. "Hey, Paul, I'm getting a complex here! First of all you conspire with Jack. That makes me nervous. Two of my clients plotting against me. There are some awkward stories you two could share about me. And if that isn't enough you start turning my very own partner against me."

"Yeah, you had better look out, Cash, Paul here has told me all your secrets," Jack said.

This last comment made me distinctly uncomfortable.

I knew Jack was joking, but did Cash? I looked carefully at Cash, but he just laughed. I could see no indication that he was concerned.

Waigel butted in. "There are quite a few secrets about Cash I could tell you. Remember Sheryl Rosen?"

"Hey, Dick, be fair," laughed Cash. "That was a long time ago."

"You two have known each other for a while?" I asked.

"Oh, yes," said Cash. "We go back a long ways. We both grew up in the same neighborhood. Dick was the smart one. Always top of the class. Columbia University, then Harvard Business School. I was just good at drinking beer and getting to know girls like Sheryl Rosen."

"You should have seen his bar," said Waigel. "Full every night. Lots of kids having a great time. It's a shame you had to shut that down."

"Was that near Tremont Avenue?" I asked as innocently as I could manage.

"Right around the corner," said Cash. Waigel looked at me narrowly. I held his gaze for a second or two, doing my best to look innocent. I wasn't sure I succeeded. Waigel thought I was up to something; I would just have to make sure that I didn't give him any evidence to back up his suspicions.

Cash went back to his task of charming the woman from Amalgamated Veterans. Waigel turned to Cathy.

"Tell me, how do you like the conference?" he said.

"Oh, it's fascinating," she said. "It's amazing how well a lot of these companies are run. Having piles of debt to service really seems to focus the mind."

"Yes, there were some great companies talking today. Did you see Chem Castings? That was a deal I structured myself. Great management. That's a company that is really going places."

I had seen Chem Castings' presentation. The management did seem to be competent, and the underlying business was a good one. But, thanks to the advice of its investment bankers Bloomfield Weiss, the company had taken on too much debt and would struggle to meet even its next interest payment.

"Yes, I saw that one," said Cathy.

"It's a shame we can't sell deals like that into Europe," said Waigel. "Why is that, I wonder?"

Cathy stiffened. She didn't say anything for a second or two. I could feel the tension rising beside me, and I focused on my plate, pretending to ignore it. "I don't know," she said, carefully. "Our clients just don't seem to have any interest."

"Of course, it's very difficult to know whether it's the clients that lack interest or the salesmen," said Waigel. He was chewing his steak noisily as he said this, staring defiantly at Cathy. The sweat shone under his thinly plastered hair. "Selling that Chem Castings deal was very important to the firm. We were left with a block of bonds that lost us a bunch of money. If we had proper international distribution, we just wouldn't have had that problem."

Cathy kept her cool. "The problem is that most of our clients just don't like the risk of junk bonds. You can't force them to change their views."

"You can't force them, but with a body like yours, you could sure as hell persuade them." Waigel laughed as he said this, took a gulp of wine, and winked at me. I glowered back.

Cathy looked confused, unsure whether to take this as a joke or the insult it clearly was. In the end she smiled thinly.

"Aw, come on, what are you upset about?" said Waigel with a leer. "A good-looking girl like you could sell anybody anything. I bet you have built great relationships with your clients. After an evening out with you, I'm sure I could be persuaded to take whatever you were selling." He turned to me, with another wink. "Am I right, or what?"

"Dick," muttered Cathy through clenched teeth, "remember there are clients here."

Waigel had drunk a lot of wine. "Paul here is a man of the world. He knows how things work. Now, listen, Cathy, I'm an important man in Bloomfield Weiss, and I am going to become more important. You should get to know me. I can be a great help in your career. How about just you and me having a quiet glass of champagne after dinner?"

Waigel was sitting opposite Cathy. Cathy had very long legs. She slid down in her chair slightly. A moment later Waigel let out a cry of pain, and seemed to clutch his napkin in his lap. Cathy stood up, excused herself, smiled curtly to everyone at the table, and walked off, her sharp high heels clacking on the wooden floor.

I got up and followed her to the bar. Her eyes were smarting, and she had to bite her bottom lip to stop it trembling.

"Not very subtle, is he?" I said.

"Bastard!" she muttered.

"Still, I thought you dealt with him quite well."

"Yes, I enjoyed that," she smiled. "But he's right, you know. I'm not going to get very far in my career by kicking Bloomfield Weiss's rising stars in the balls."

"Sod him. Sod Bloomfield Weiss. Have a drink," I said.

I got Cathy a glass of wine and myself a Scotch. Cathy sipped her drink. "Did you hear about Joe Finlay, one of our eurobond traders?" she said.

My pulse quickened. "No?"

"It's terrible. He was murdered yesterday in Central Park."

"Really? How awful." I tried to give my voice just the right amount of concern. Enough to acknowledge the awfulness of murder, not enough to suggest anything more than a brief acquaintance with Joe. "What happened?"

"Apparently he had been out jogging. It was dark and he was jumped. He got one of his attackers. Killed him. He used to be in the SAS, so they say." Cathy shuddered.

I was glad Joe was dead, and I didn't feel the slightest guilt in my part in it. There was no doubt at all in my mind that he had been just about to kill me. And now I wouldn't have to look over my shoulder everywhere I went. Life could become normal again. I thought of Joe's wife, Sally. And Jerry. No doubt being brought up without a father would be bad, but it must be infinitely better than being brought up with Joe.

"Have the police caught anyone?" I asked.

"Not yet, but it's early days," she said. She took a nervous sip of her drink. "I know this sounds terrible, but I didn't like him very much. He seemed weird. Dangerous."

"I don't think that sounds terrible at all," I said a little too positively.

Cathy noticed my tone, and eyed me inquisitively. Then something caught her eye behind me. "Look at that!" she said.

I turned to see the bulky frame of Marshall Mills weaving his way through the crowd toward the bar. On his arm was a tall, curvaceous woman with fluffy red hair, big green eyes, and full bright red lips that never quite closed. She swung her whole body as she walked, her hips bumping gently into Mills's side with each step.

Just before the couple could make it to the bar they were stopped right next to us by Cash.

"Marshall!" Cash shouted.

"Who the hell are you?" spat an angry Mills.

"My name is Cash Callaghan. I'm a salesman at Bloomfield Weiss. And I would just like to say what an interesting and thought-provoking presentation you gave this morning."

"I hate salesmen. Go away!" growled Mills.

Cathy giggled. "Cash has finally met his match here," she whispered.

But Cash wasn't going to give in that easily. He thought for a moment, trying to figure out Mills's weak point. Finally he said, "Mrs. Mills, I loved your latest film. What was it . . . *Twilight in Tangiers*? I always knew from your photographs in the press that you were beautiful, but I had no idea you were such a great actress."

Mrs. Mills was as taken aback by this as Cathy and I were. But she recovered enough to dip her eyelashes and reply in a languorous Texan drawl, "Why thank you, sir."

"Not at all, not at all. I trust there will be a sequel soon?"

Marshall interrupted, his voice full of pride, "We are planning *Moonlight in Marrakech*. We should start shooting in a couple of months. I'm glad you liked *Twilight.* I think most of the critics missed the film apart from some illiterate bozos who wouldn't recognize Meryl Streep if she appeared in a school play." Mills was breathing heavily, sweat pouring from his brow.

"Now now Pooky, watch your blood pressure," Mrs. Mills drawled.

"Sorry, Poppet," replied Mills.

"Let me introduce you to two of your most loyal bond holders from England, Cathy Lasenby and Paul Murray."

My mouth gaped open for a moment, but Cash winked at both of us, and I found myself playing along. We both made polite noises. Mills was clearly surprised that he had any loyal bond holders left, even as far away as London.

"I hear you are looking for some finance for your latest development," said Cash.

"Yes, it's a great property off the coast of Ecuador, but I'm told that none of these dumb idiots here want to give me any money. I could teach them a thing or two about investing. What these idiots don't realize . . ."

"Pooky," admonished Mrs. Mills.

"I'm sorry, dear."

"Well, I think I know someone who may be able to help," said Cash. I was shaking my head furiously, determined that I would not let Cash railroad De Jong into this one. The revenues from the oil field might look good, but only a fool would trust Marshall Mills. Fortunately, Cash pulled Mills and his wife off toward where Madeleine Jansen was standing.

"He must be crazy if he thinks he can get her to even talk to Mills, let alone give him any money," said Cathy. "Amalgamated Veterans lost a packet on one of his companies a year ago."

We watched them talk for several minutes. After about a quarter of an hour, the group broke up and Cash walked back up to us. He had a huge grin on his face and was literally rubbing his hands with glee.

"Bartender, a bottle of Dom Pérignon please," he called. "And three glasses."

As he poured the champagne, Cathy said, "Surely you don't expect us to believe that Madeleine Jansen agreed to give him any money."

"Fifty million," Cash said.

"How on earth did you manage that?" she asked.

"Partly price. He's going to have to pay two percent more than the average yield for a new junk issue. But the key is the security. If Mills defaults, or tries any funny stuff, Amalgamated Veterans will have the right to take possession of the copyright of both *Twilight in Tangiers* and *Moonlight in Marrakech* and prevent any further distribution of the films. That ought to keep him straight."

"Oh, I see. And if his heart gives out, it should keep his widow in line as well," I said.

Cash laughed. "Having seen Lola Mills in *Twilight in Tangiers*, I am surprised his heart didn't give out long ago. That woman sure is some gymnast."

I couldn't stop myself from laughing with Cash. I had to marvel at his amazing ability to get two such totally different people to do business together.

I DUTIFULLY ATTENDED breakfast and the morning's presentations. I made sure I was at the Fairway talk. Jack Salmon was there as promised. I sat next to him.

Of all the enthusiastic managements I saw at the conference, Fairway's was the most enthusiastic. There was nothing they didn't know about golf or golf carts. Demand for golf was growing in the United States. More people wanting to play could be accommodated in two ways, both of them good for Fairway. One was to build more golf courses, which would need new fleets of golf carts; the other was to make the use of golf carts compulsory on existing courses, to get more people round a course in a single day.

Gerry King, Fairway's chief executive officer, knew everyone in the industry. He was unscrupulous in the way he used his contacts. He used top players to sponsor his carts and to suggest minor alterations to make better vehicles. He knew the top course designers in the country, who could recommend Fairway machines on new courses. And he went to great lengths to explain his close ties with distributors.

The company was winning market share from its competitors, and its cash flow had grown 25 percent for each of the last two years. It had borrowed heavily to finance its growth, and I realized I would have to do some careful analysis when I got back to London to make sure it could support this debt. Provided the results of that were positive it looked to me as though Fairway would make a good investment.

After the presentation, Jack said, "Wow! How do you like that company? I can't wait to get my hands on some of those bonds. What do you think, Paul?"

"Hmm, it does seem rather good," I said.

Jack laughed. "Rather good," he said, mimicking an English accent, "it's goddamn dynamite!"

"I'll see you at your office tomorrow," I said, and left him.

Outside the room there was a woman taking names for the trip to Las Vegas the next afternoon. There were to be visits to three casinos. The high point was to be the newly opened Tahiti. I went up to her table and added my name to the list. I still wasn't sure why Debbie had been killed. It could have something to do with Tremont Capital. Or it might have something to do with Piper. I was looking forward to seeing him. There was a lot more I wanted to find out about Irwin Piper.

The lunchtime speaker was a famous American talk-show host whom I had never heard of. I decided to skip lunch and find a nice spot by a pool to have a nap.

In addition to the main swimming pool, there were a number of small pools dotted round the hotel grounds. There was one I had noticed earlier that was out of the way on the edge of the hotel premises. It was in the middle of a Spanish-style courtyard, and looked like an excellent place to while away an hour or two.

There was no one by the pool, and I found a spot in the sun, lay down, and closed my eyes.

I must have drifted off, because I was awakened by the gentle splash of someone diving into the pool. I opened my eyes and saw the long, lithe form of Cathy gracefully stroking through the water. She was an excellent swimmer, scarcely causing a ripple as she glided up and down the pool.

After a few minutes she hauled herself out of the pool

and dried herself on the other side of the courtyard from
me. I wasn't sure whether she had recognized me or not,
because I was lying face down on a lounge chair. Out of
one eye half-closed in the sunlight, I watched her as she
slowly rubbed her towel over first one long, slim golden
brown leg, and then the other. As she stood up to dry
her shoulders, I admired the gentle curve of her back,
teasingly revealed by her bathing suit.

She lay down and closed her eyes. After five minutes
or so, someone else entered the little courtyard. I recognized the balding head of Dick Waigel. A spare tire of
fat rolled over the elastic of his Bermuda shorts. I don't
think he even noticed me as his attention was immediately caught by the prone Cathy. He waddled over to
her, squatted down beside her, and began to talk. I
couldn't hear what was said, but I could see Cathy sit up
and talk politely back.

Then I saw Waigel let his hand drop almost casually
onto Cathy's thigh. She brushed it off immediately, but
he replaced it more firmly, and began to move his other
arm over her shoulders.

Without waiting to see Cathy's reaction, I leaped to
my feet and ran round to the other side of the pool. I
grabbed hold of one of Waigel's arms, and pulled him to
his feet. Waigel was small, surprised, and caught off balance. I made the most of my advantage by landing one
clean blow straight on his chin. He went flying backward
into the swimming pool.

He was momentarily unconscious, but as his head
submerged under the water he spluttered and came to.
He gasped for breath and waded through the water to
the opposite side of the pool from where I was standing.
He hauled himself out, water and fat slopping onto the
paving stones. "What the fuck did you do that for?" he
screamed at me, his wet face red with anger. "I was just
talking to the bitch. You can't hit me like that and get
away with it. You had better watch your ass! I'll trample
all over you, Murray!"

He picked up his towel and stalked out of the courtyard, still muttering insults and threats. I just watched him go.

Cathy was sitting hunched up on the lounge chair, her chin resting on her knees.

"Do you think Waigel is finally going to get the message that every time he makes a pass at you he is going to get hurt?" I said.

"I hope so," she said, staring at a point on the ground just in front of her feet.

I sat next to her on the lounge chair. Neither of us said anything. I could feel the anger seething within her slowly subside.

"I hate this company, and I hate the people who work for it," Cathy muttered.

I didn't reply. I felt sorry for her, having to work for scum like Waigel, to do his beck and call, to put up with his lechery. No wonder she hated it. I didn't know why she took it. She seemed a strong person, why didn't she just tell them to shove it and walk out? She just didn't like to give up, I supposed.

We sat together for several minutes, both wrapped in our own thoughts. Finally, Cathy uncurled herself and stood up. She gave me a quick, nervous smile. "Thank you," she said in a small voice. Biting her lip, she grabbed her clothes and ran out of the courtyard.

Presentations began again at two o'clock. I watched the chief executive of a cable TV company explain his plan to operate the biggest and best network in the country, but none of it sank in. Nor did the presentations of the two companies that succeeded him. My mind was preoccupied with Cathy. In those few minutes by the pool, I had felt so close to her. Her vulnerability still tugged at me. The aggressive corporate woman whom I had first seen in De Jong's offices in London had become a brave but persecuted girl who needed a protector.

The program for that evening was drinks and a barbecue by the main swimming pool. A breeze blew down
from Camelback, cooling the air and ruffling the surface
of the pool. The reflections of the glowing charcoal, the
white tablecloths, and the milling crowd of blazers and
summer dresses, danced across the water as I
approached. The sound of relaxed laughter carried
across the pool toward me, mingling with the chuckling
of the crickets. All this was under a starlit sky that
looked like the backdrop to a Hollywood musical.

It was a lovely evening, and I drifted among the
earnest young men and women who were winding down
after a hard couple of days. I chatted lightly and pleasantly to a number of people always keeping one eye open
for Cathy.

Looking over the crowd, I caught Waigel's eye. This
man is not going to forgive and forget, I thought.

"Paul?" I heard a woman's voice call my name from
behind me. I turned round. It was Madeleine Jansen.

"Oh, hello."

"How are you finding the conference?"

"Oh, um, very interesting," I said, looking over her
shoulder.

Madeleine said something else, and looked at me
expectantly.

None of it sank in. "Sorry, I'm afraid I didn't catch
that. It's been a busy day," I said.

"Did you see any companies you liked?"

"Yes, there was one. Fairway. I thought they were
good." Where was she? She had to be around somewhere.

"Oh, yes?"

Finally I saw her. "Excuse me," I said to Madeleine
and pushed my way through the crowd toward her.

She was talking to Cash amid a small group of people.
I stood for a moment just looking at her, admiring her.
The glow from the barbecue danced across her face,
lighting up her smile. The shadows made her dark eyes

even larger than usual. I fought my way over to her. "Cathy," I said.

She turned and looked at me. For a moment, her smile changed from polite to radiant. She reddened a little and said, "Hello."

"Hello."

A pause. Not awkward or difficult, just a pause.

"Are you feeling better?" I asked.

"Oh, you mean after this afternoon?" she said. "Yes, I'm fine. Thank you for what you did." Her voice told me she meant it, she wasn't just being polite. She smiled.

I looked around at the crowd of people under the canopy of the desert night. "Have you ever been to anything like this before?" I asked.

"No, but I've been to Phoenix once," she said, "on a Greyhound bus. It was several years ago. I was a student then, so we didn't stay anywhere like this. We slummed it all over America."

"Did you go alone?"

"No. With a boyfriend."

I pictured Cathy as a student traveling through the Arizona heat. Jeans, a T-shirt, long hair tied back, carefree. "Lucky chap," I thought, and then reddened myself as I realized I had spoken it out loud.

Cathy laughed. "I haven't seen him in years."

"Is there anyone you do see? Now, I mean?" I blurted it out. Only once I said it did I realize how important the question was to me, and how desperately I hoped for the right answer.

She gave it. "No," she said. "No one." She paused, and looked up at me. "And you?"

I immediately thought of Debbie. Her round face, her smiling eyes and the conversation we had the night before she died. That conversation had unlocked something. A realization that life was there to be enjoyed, and to be shared with other people. One of those other people could have been Debbie. But although she was gone her vitality lived on; I could almost hear her urging me on with Cathy, teasing me for being shy. But I couldn't explain all this.

"No, nobody," I said. It seemed to me that Cathy seemed to relax at this. I was encouraged. "So, where else did you go on your bus?" I asked.

She told me all about her trip around America and about many other things besides. Friends, family, university, books, men. And I talked too, long into the night. We sat on a grassy bank overlooking the pool, watching the other conference attendees slowly drift off to bed. Finally, at two thirty, long after everyone else had gone, we got up to leave. Afraid of risking anything that might ruin the evening, I said good night, kissed her cheek, and made my way back to my own room, singing softly to myself.

I took a taxi downtown to keep my appointment with Jack Salmon. I looked out of the window at the forest of billboards and sun-baked wooden stores that lined the road into Phoenix, and thought of Cathy, her dark eyes and intelligent face glowing softly in the starlight, and of the vulnerability I had felt in her as we had sat together by the pool the day before.

But she was not the only one who was vulnerable. My own feelings were exposed, laid bare to the open air, for Cathy to do with them what she wished. Since my father's death I had been careful to protect my emotions, to shield them away from outside events, such as my mother's mental illness. I had channeled my emotional energy first into running, and now into trading. Willpower, determination, and self-discipline. That is what had got me an Olympic medal. That is what would make me a great trader.

And now I found myself wanting to loosen this iron grip that I had developed over the years. I was a bit scared, but also exhilarated. Why not? The risk was worth it. I was curious to see what would happen.

But would she have me? Rejection would be hard to take. Very hard.

Phoenix Prosperity's offices literally shone in the sunlight as the taxi approached them. They looked to be built of the same type of glass as those sunglasses in which you can see your reflection. The giant gleaming cube rose above the debris of concrete, tarmac, wood, and dust that was the undergrowth of a modern American city.

The taxi pulled into the parking lot, which was three-quarters empty. I got out and walked toward the building. Despite the traffic speeding along the road nearby, the building had a quiet menace about it. No one walked in or out. It reminded me of one of those secret evil installations that crop up toward the end of James Bond movies. I expected to be greeted by impassive automatons in exotic uniforms. In fact an overweight security guard glanced up from his paper, and waved me toward the elevators.

The investment department was on the third floor. I was met by a secretary who asked me to sit down in one of a cluster of four leather armchairs set in the middle of a vast empty reception space.

I sat and waited. Phoenix Prosperity's annual report rested on the low table in front of me. Under the caption "Bringing you Prosperity from the Ashes" was a picture of Phoenix's office building set against an unnaturally azure sky. I leafed through the document. There was lots of worthy coverage of work Phoenix Prosperity had done in helping to build the community. The savings and loan had twenty branches throughout the Phoenix region.

The chief executive, one Howard Farber, had written a statement. In it he referred to the financial difficulties that had been faced by the institution two years ago, but then mentioned a substantial capital injection which had strengthened the balance sheet. No mention of where this capital injection had come from.

I took a look at the balance sheet. Capital had grown

from $10 million two years ago to about $50 million. This must reflect the new funds. Assets too had grown sharply, from $100 million two years ago to $500 million now. The report was studiously vague about what all these assets were. Perhaps Jack would be able to enlighten me.

He came into the waiting area just then. "Hi, Paul, good to see you," he said, holding out his hand.

I shook it. "Nice to see you too," I said.

"Come on through." He took me down a narrow passageway and into a spacious office with four fully equipped dealing desks in the center of it. "This is it," he said. "Take a seat."

"So, tell me what you do all day," I said.

"Do you know how a savings and loan operates?" asked Jack.

"Isn't it a bit like one of our building societies?" I said.

"Well, that's how many of them started out," he said. "Small community savings banks, raising money locally to lend for local mortgages. Everything very conservative, everything very boring."

"You don't look like the kind of chap who writes mortgages all day," I said.

Jack grinned. "I'm not. Several years ago, savings and loans were deregulated. Now they can invest in all kinds of things: speculative real estate, eurobonds, even junk bonds. We can make all kinds of interesting investments."

"But why would depositors place their money with you if all you are going to do is gamble with it? What if your investments went wrong? Local people would lose everything."

"That's the beauty of the whole thing," Jack said, smiling. "All deposits are guaranteed by the U.S. government through the Federal Savings and Loans Insurance Corporation. We can borrow as much money as we want to play with however we want. The depositor doesn't care because he can rely on Uncle Sam to bail him out. It's easy."

"But what happens to the shareholders? They may lose everything, surely?"

"Yes, that's true. But the potential returns are huge. For every ten million dollars they invest, they can borrow another ninety million, government guaranteed. That means if they invest well they can earn several times their original investment. As long as they can afford to lose the original stake if they are unlucky, then it's great odds for a bet."

So, that was it! Uncle Sam's Money Machine was a savings and loan! The $40 million investment on Waigel's diagram referred to Tremont Capital buying a savings and loan. Using a government guarantee to borrow money it could turn the initial $40 million into several hundred million dollars. And if the savings and loan got it wrong, well then Tremont Capital would just have to default on its bonds. It was just the kind of innovative financing technique that Marshall Mills himself would be proud of. I had a pretty good guess which Money Machine Tremont Capital had bought. I hoped Jack would confirm my suspicions.

"I was reading your annual report outside," I said. "It mentioned a sizable capital injection a year or so ago. Where did that come from?"

"I'm sorry, I'm afraid I can't tell you that," said Jack.

Oh well, I thought. I could probably check it up later.

"What are the more interesting things you invest in?" I asked.

"Oh, real estate, junk bonds, a theme park, even a casino."

"A casino. That sounds fun. Is it one I might have heard of?"

"Well it's this really neat place in Las Vegas," Jack began. Then he cut himself off. "I'm sorry, I think some people would be quite upset if they knew I talked about it. Let me just tell you it's big. Real big."

I was sure Jack was sorry too. He was dying to brag about his investment.

"Sounds interesting. I'm sure you can tell me something about it. No need to tell me the name," because I can guess it already, I added silently.

"It's a great deal," he said. "We teamed up with a top-class operator to build one of the best, if not the best casino in the country. The project is almost completed. All we need to do is wait for the junk-bond financing to be closed and we will get paid out."

"What sort of return will you make?" I asked.

"Oh, double our money," Jack said, smiling.

"Whew! Not bad, not bad at all," I said. So Uncle Sam's Money machine was taking government-guaranteed money from local depositors and using it to buy a piece of Irwin Piper's Tahiti. The question was, who was behind Phoenix Prosperity's investments? It was obvious Jack Salmon wasn't the brains behind the operation. "Are you given guidelines on what you can invest in, or can you do what you like?"

"It varies," said Jack. "Sometimes they tell me what to buy. Sometimes they just accept my suggestions. I think they value my judgment. Hey, tell you what. I've been thinking about that Fairway deal. Do you want to help me buy some bonds? I fancy picking up five million."

"I'd love to," I said. "But I think I should just watch. You go ahead."

"Okay. Just a minute while I call the boss."

Jack dialed a number and drew away from me so that I couldn't hear. Up until then he had been all braggadocio, but now he took on a sort of submissive posture, rather like a naughty puppy expecting a beating from his master. After a few minutes of solemn conversation where Jack did most of the listening, he put down the phone, his eyes shining.

"Wow, he really liked that one," he said. "He doesn't want me to buy five million, he wants me to buy twenty million. At last these guys are beginning to appreciate my ideas. Let's get to it." The puppy was wagging his tail. His master had given him an unexpected bone.

I watched as Jack set to work to purchase his twenty million dollars of Fairway bonds. For all his claims of extensive experience, he did a lousy job of it. Buying twenty million dollars of bonds in the junk-bond market requires extreme delicacy. I knew how Hamilton would do it. He would subtly nose around the market, trying to find dealers who owned the particular issue he was looking for. He would disguise his inquiries by throwing in several red herrings, so none of them could be sure what he was about. Then, when he had found the dealer who seemed to be able to provide him with the most bonds at the cheapest price, he would open up to him, telling him exactly what he wanted to do. The dealer could then work hard to try to buy the bonds from his customers quietly without disturbing the market.

Jack started off by asking ten brokers for prices in the issue. He bought two million each from the three that had the lowest prices. So far so good. The problem was that when Jack tried to buy the rest, lo and behold, the price had gone up three or four points. All the dealers had worked out what he was trying to do, and what was worse, they knew that every other dealer knew. Jack spent most of the rest of the morning shouting at dealers for putting up their prices against him. When I left him, he still had eight million left to buy and was in a thoroughly bad mood.

I took a taxi back to the hotel. Before checking out I made a quick phone call to Tommy in New York.

"Good to hear from you," came Tommy's voice, relaxed as ever. "I trust you are sporting a nice tan after your vacation in the sun."

"If I hear one more smug chief executive talking about operating synergies and enhancing shareholder value, I think I will explode," I said. "How are you getting on?"

"Nothing, yet. The police aren't very cooperative. Also, it's difficult to get hold of Shoffman's files. But don't worry, I haven't given up. Have you found anything?"

"Yes, I have done rather well." I told him about my chat with Jack Salmon and my discovery of what Uncle Sam's Money Machine was. "I wonder if you would do me one more favor," I said.

"Sure," said Tommy.

"See if you can find out who it was who took over Phoenix Prosperity sometime in the last two years. They paid forty million dollars. Some of the press-cutting databases may have something, although I suspect that the deal was kept private. I bet Bloomfield Weiss had something to do with it. They could have been advisers either to Phoenix Prosperity or to the purchaser. See if you can find anything about it there."

"It's tricky stuff snooping through corporate finance files like that. You can go to jail for that sort of thing."

"I know. I can have a good guess who the purchaser was, but I need evidence. Sorry, Tommy. If you don't want to do it, I will understand."

"Oh no. You can't get rid of me that easy. This is fun. I'll have the information for you. Where can I get hold of you?"

"I'll be at the Tahiti for a couple of days," I said, "you can get in touch with me there. Good luck."

I was glad Tommy thought the whole thing was a lark. I felt bad about asking him to do something that carried so much risk, but he seemed genuinely eager and willing. It gave him a chance to get his own back on Bloomfield Weiss. He had been fired, what else did he have to lose?

I was not quite so happy about the whole thing. Whoever was behind it all was dangerous. Debbie and Greg Shoffman had both died on the trail of Tremont Capital. I didn't feel at all safe following in their footsteps. But I was getting somewhere, especially with the discovery of what Uncle Sam's Money Machine was. If Tommy could get answers to my questions, I would be a long way toward figuring it all out. I was doing well; it would be impossible for Hamilton not to concede as much. I would show him he had been right to place his trust in me.

C H A P T E R

> > > > **16**

WE TRAVELED TO Las Vegas in style. Irwin Piper had laid on his own private jet for certain valued investors. To my surprise, I was one of them. Jack Salmon and Madeleine Jansen were there. There were also three or four other investors from some of the biggest money managers. Cash and Waigel were also present. So was Cathy.

Cash was having a whale of a time. The plane was fitted out to cater for the high rollers that Piper wanted to transport to his casino. There was a bar, including several bottles of chilled champagne. Cash lost no time in breaking into these, forcing everyone to take a glass. Within a few minutes the plane was buzzing with chatter and laughter; Cash had started his party.

Much to his delight, Waigel found himself a TV with a selection of pornographic videos, which he hastened to try out on the machine. Cathy, whom he had jammed himself next to, stared out of the window in disgust.

I was sitting next to Madeleine Jansen. The champagne made its way up the plane to us. Madeleine lifted her glass. "Cheers."

"Cheers."

We both sipped from our glasses. The bubbles danced around my mouth and tickled my nose. Champagne always seems more active at altitude.

I looked out of the window down to the dry Arizona

desert below. We were passing over a range of low mountains. Here the desert buckled up into folds of browns, yellows, oranges, and blacks. Rock, sand, and shadow from the strong sunlight. There was not a patch of green in sight. Just one dead straight, man-made track bisected the landscape as far as I could see. Looking down from an air-conditioned airplane thirty thousand feet up, the landscape appeared cold and empty. The intense heat of the desert floor was difficult to imagine.

Madeleine glanced over her shoulder toward where Cathy was sitting. "You seemed a little preoccupied in Phoenix," she said.

My cheeks burned. "Yes, I'm very sorry. I was a little rude, wasn't I? I hope you will forgive me?"

"Yes, of course." She laughed. I was embarrassed that my absorption with Cathy had been so obvious. But Madeleine seemed to be no more than pleasantly amused.

"Have you been to Las Vegas before?" she asked.

"No, this will be my first time. I'm quite curious to see what it's like. And you?"

"Once or twice."

"On vacation or as an investor?"

"No, I haven't been there on vacation," she said, "but I have been to look at a couple of investments in the city."

"Are these junk-bond investments?" I asked.

· "Mostly," she said, "although we do have a couple of equity investments in casinos."

"Really?" I said.

"Yes. In fact we own a piece of the Tahiti."

At last! Someone who was prepared to be straight about what they owned.

"That's interesting. What do you think of the deal?" I asked.

Madeleine looked at me, amused. "What do you think of it?" she said.

I shuffled uncomfortably in my seat. This woman

obviously knew what she was talking about and I didn't want to make a fool of myself. On the other hand I had never liked the deal, even before I had discovered Piper's murky past. "I don't know much about casinos, so I may be wrong, but I am afraid I don't like it at all."

"And why is that?" Madeleine said, a slight smile on her lips.

"I'm not convinced that casinos are immune from a recession, especially those that cater for the family holiday. In a recession fewer people go on vacations, it's as simple as that. And there isn't much leeway in the financial projections for rooms and tables to be left empty."

She looked at me, interested. "Go on," she said.

"Well the other thing is Irwin Piper. Sure he's a savvy investor. But I get the feeling this is an ego trip for him. He wants to build the most spectacular hotel in the world, and will bend the finances to make it work." I sighed. "The real thing is I just don't trust him."

She looked at me long and hard. "I think you are right," she said.

"But, if you agree with me, why did you invest?" I asked.

"Amalgamated Veterans invested, not me," she said. "One of the people who work for me put the idea forward and fought for it very strongly. It has a lot going for it. It will be one of the most celebrated casinos in the world, and Art Buxxy has a good reputation for getting the customers in the door. But I didn't really like the smell of it. There was nothing I could put my finger on. In the end, my colleague insisted, and we went ahead. It was, after all, only thirty-five million dollars."

"What do you mean, only thirty-five million dollars?" I said. "That's an awful lot to lose."

Madeleine smiled. "I am in control of over fifty billion dollars. It's very difficult to find enough opportunities to invest that much. We make a host of investments of fifty million or less in projects like the Tahiti."

Although I was used to juggling with millions of dollars,

I still found it difficult to comprehend the sheer size of the American insurance industry. Companies like Amalgamated Veterans Life, Prudential, and Aetna played with amounts that were bigger than most countries' gross national product.

"Anyway, it looks like we will be all right. We provided bridge financing for the construction of the hotel. As long as the junk-bond issue gets placed, we will get our money back, and make a nice profit on top."

"How much of a profit?" I asked.

"Oh, we should make eighty percent or so," Madeleine said. "Not bad for a one and a half year investment."

That 80 percent matched Jack Salmon's claims that Phoenix Prosperity would be doubling its investment, allowing for some exaggeration on Jack's part.

"So why are you going to see the Tahiti if you are going to get your money back soon?" I asked.

Madeleine paused. "I don't want to put you off, but since you seem put off already, it doesn't matter. I am not sure that the new junk-bond issue will get done. I think people have some serious questions about Piper. We shall see."

If investors knew what I knew about Piper, I thought, then they certainly would have some serious questions. And the shareholders in the Tahiti, like Amalgamated Veterans, wouldn't double their money, they would probably lose most of it.

"Who else has invested in it?"

"There is one other institution apart from Irwin Piper himself," she said. "I'm afraid I can't tell you who it is."

"It's not a crazy savings and loan from Arizona, by any chance?"

"I'm afraid I can't say. Let's just say that the other institution doesn't give me any comfort that this is a good investment."

Just then, from the back of the plane Jack Salmon let out a whoop of laughter at something Cash had said, and Madeleine and I exchanged amused glances.

The Tahiti was located on Las Vegas's Strip, the area three miles from downtown that contained the glitziest casinos. There was no mistaking it as we approached. A tall, white octagonal tower housed the bulk of the hotel rooms. The entrance was up a short palm tree–lined drive. Big banners hung over the door announcing the grand opening.

The first steps into the Tahiti were breathtaking. The foyer was a huge atrium reaching a hundred feet into the sky. The floor was broken up into islands connected by walkways. Salty water lapped up against the island shores, in small waves. On the islands were a variety of seating areas, bars, fast-food counters, and the inevitable slots. As I walked through the archipelago, I was struck by the atmosphere, a mixture of warm flowers and slight salty tang, which really did conjure up images of the South Seas. Brightly colored fish and turtles swam between the islands, and coral reefs smoldered below the surface. On one side of the atrium, the water was fenced off. There, the thrusting triangles of sharks' dorsal fins plowed through the pool. Beautiful women in grass skirts and garlands glided among the trees with drinks and change for the slot machines.

I went up to my room to have a shower and change. It was one of the high-roller suites, although probably not the best. But the opulence made my stomach turn. Purple velvet and gold everywhere. Ankle-deep carpets. A huge heart-shaped bath. A bed itself the size of a small room. Above the bed was a complicated control panel. I pressed a couple of buttons gingerly. The bed started to undulate in a very disturbing fashion. I pressed the buttons again and it stood still. I decided to leave these alone and hoped to God that it wasn't set on a timer.

I stepped out on to the small balcony outside the window. Directly beneath me was a sprawling swimming pool of deep blue water. It, too, was dotted with islands, and swimmers were sitting in the water drinking and playing the slot machines.

The sight of women in bathing suits brought Cathy to mind. I smiled to myself, and went back into my room to give her a call. There was no reply from her room, and so I left a message for her to call me when she returned.

I set out to explore the casino. For all Irwin Piper's talk about high rollers, most of the floor space was devoted to parting the ordinary man in the street from his hundred dollars a night. There were a number of large rooms, decorated in various South Sea themes, with acres of roulette, blackjack, and craps tables. With the exception of some of the craps players who seemed to like shouting a lot, most of the proceedings were conducted in a deathly hush. Gamblers solemnly gave their money to the croupiers, who quickly and professionally gave some of it back.

And then there were the slots. Row upon row of machines, each one in control of its own human being, which fed the machine in a dazed, mechanical rhythm. There were no windows. It could have been day or night, the machines didn't care, and the humans did what they were told.

After walking round the Tahiti for a couple of hours, my mind became a blur of flashing dollar signs, lights, and faces, all devoted to the pursuit of money. It made me uneasy. As I had said to Piper half-jokingly, gambling was my job. Somehow the rush of adrenaline came more naturally when facing the winking green numbers on the screens at my desk than the relentless passing back and forth of money in Las Vegas. But perhaps I was just as trapped as the sad-looking individuals feeding the slots.

In a despondent mood, I had a sandwich and went to bed.

It was a great double act. Piper looking relaxed but dependable in a conservative lightweight suit. Art Buxxy, the showman, doing what he did well. It was a big moment for both of them. They had to secure $200 million from their audience.

Piper warmed up the crowd. In a reasonable, persuasive voice he talked in abstract terms about the remarkable financial opportunity that the Tahiti presented. There was talk of numbers, strategy, competitive analysis. Enough to make us think that the Tahiti was in safe hands, not enough to bore us. Despite the outward reserve, as he warmed up to his presentation, Piper did let some of the excitement he felt for the project show through. Standing there, tall, tanned, elegantly but conservatively dressed, speaking in a manner that was more suited to the Harvard Club than a casino, he gave his audience reassurance. Despite appearances, the Tahiti must be a respectable, conservative investment, or why would someone like Irwin Piper be involved with it?

Then it was Art Buxxy's turn. Buxxy was a small man with a nut-brown face, longish blow-dried gray hair, and bundles of enthusiasm. He was hardly ever still, and when he was, it was for a melodramatic pause, to let the full consequence of what he had just said sink in. His abrasive, rough-edged manner jolted his audience after the smooth Piper, but within a minute his energetic charm had already bewitched us all. Selling was his calling, and the Tahiti was the love of his life. He used all his skills. He told us about his childhood as a cardshark son of cardshark parents. His poor-gambler-made-good story neatly combined several elements of the American dream. He then launched into the details of how to run a casino. How to prevent croupiers from stealing money, how to spot card counters, how to use databases to analyze high rollers' personality profiles, and which promotional campaign worked best. We were captivated. And I think most of us were sold.

They took us on a tour of the complex. Seen through Buxxy's eyes, the tackiness, and the loneliness of a big casino disappeared. We saw the glamor, the glitter, the amazing technological effects. He took us to see the private rooms where the high rollers played, wallowing in sophistication, power, and money. By the time we had returned to the conference room where he had started his pitch, I could feel that the majority of the audience would write out a check there and then.

"Any questions?"

Silence. No difficult questions about Piper's background. No tedious questions about percentage drop of slots against tables, high-roller comps, or blue-collar busing costs. Even the most cynical investor was under the spell of the greatest casino on earth. At least temporarily.

I had thought through this moment carefully.

I stood up.

Piper's eyebrows pulled together slightly, in the barest trace of a frown. "Yes?"

"I have two questions for Mr. Piper." The audience was looking at me with mild interest. My English accent jarred in the glitzy Las Vegas surroundings. Piper was staring at me hard. "First, has the Nevada Gaming Commission scrutinized your previous investments?" The audience stirred a little, but not much. Piper stiffened. "Second, can you comment on an investment you made in a clinic for executive stress in Britain?"

I sat down. The audience reaction was mixed. Some faces bore disapproval; I was a spoilsport to try to take cheap shots at these great guys and their great casino. A few, including Madeleine Jansen, sat up and took notice.

Piper rose to his feet. He was as unruffled and urbane as ever. "I would be happy to answer those questions. First, the commission checks out all applicants for gaming licenses very thoroughly. Second, I have a large portfolio of investments. I believe a few years ago these included some properties in England, but I don't have the details of them at my fingertips. Any other questions?" He looked around the audience quickly.

This was a dangerous moment for Piper. Until now, he had his listeners eating out of his hand. But he hadn't answered my questions properly. If anyone pursued him on this, then doubts might creep in. But I wasn't going to push it any further. I had achieved my objective. He knew I knew, and he knew I would tell. I looked over at Madeleine. She opened her mouth as if to ask a question, but she was too slow. Piper was already wrapping up the meeting. She gathered her papers together thoughtfully and looked over toward me, trying to catch my eye. I avoided her glance.

Half an hour later, I was having a cup of coffee in the atrium, when a bellboy came over to me. "Excuse me, sir, Mr. Piper would like you to join him in his suite." That didn't take him long, I thought as I put down my cup and followed the bellboy to the elevators.

Piper's suite was on the top floor of the hotel. It was completely out of character with the rest of the Tahiti. There were no lurid scarlet furnishings, no mirrors or gilded fittings. There were a number of pieces of English antique furniture: a delicate sofa, six straight-backed chairs with embroidered covers, a small writing desk, and two or three deeply polished small tables. These rested on a large predominantly light blue silk carpet criss-crossed with intricate ancient Persian or Indian motifs. All this looked out of place against the large floor-to-ceiling window that overlooked the tall white structure of the casino next door and, beyond that, the dusty grays and browns interspersed with neon of the city of Las Vegas. The desert could be seen stretching away in the distance.

Piper was alone in the room. He beckoned me to a seat. I perched on the flimsy looking Georgian sofa, while he sat in one of the high-backed mahogany armchairs. Gone was all the civilized politeness. Piper was angry.

"What the hell do you think you were doing out there?" he said. "I am not some two-bit bond salesman you can play games with. I am a powerful man in this town. I've got money, and I've got lawyers. And if you mention Bladenham Hall one more time, or even allude to it, I will sue. I will sue you for so much that your great-grandchildren will still be paying off your debts a hundred years from now."

Piper, angry, was impressive. For a moment he had me on the defensive. If I had upset such a powerful man, I had surely made a mistake. The moment passed.

"I thought you would be interested in this," I said, untucking the newspaper I had been carrying under my arm. It was a copy of the Sun of several years ago. On page two, just opposite "Bubbly Belinda Baring All," was the headline "City Slickers' Saucy Retreat." Under this was a photograph of Bladenham Hall and an article about how a Mr. Irwin Piper was helping police with their inquiries. Lurid insinuations of businessmen indulging in sex orgies followed.

Piper went purple. "If you dare show that to anyone, I'll have my lawyers right on to you immediately. That is if I don't tear you apart myself."

Paradoxically, Piper losing control helped me stay calm. He didn't seem quite so powerful. "By 'your lawyers,' you presumably include Debbie Chater?"

"Hah! She's the one who told you, is she? I'll sue that toad Denny as well."

"She no longer works for Denny Clark," I said.

"I don't care where she works. If she breaches attorney-client confidences, she is in deep trouble."

"She's dead," I said. "Murdered."

This did cause Piper to pause for a moment. "She probably deserved it," he said. "I'm not surprised someone wanted to kill her."

"Was it you?" I asked.

"Don't be ridiculous. And don't repeat that allegation either."

"Do you know who killed her?"

"Of course not. I can scarcely remember the woman. I haven't seen her for years."

I believed him. He was scared about what I might say

about Bladenham Hall, but he didn't care what I said about Debbie, despite his bluster.

"You know the Phoenix Prosperity Savings and Loan?" I asked.

"I've heard of it," said Piper, thrown off balance again.

"Is it true that institution has an investment in the Tahiti?"

"That information is not available to the public."

"Did you know that Phoenix Prosperity obtained the money it has invested in the Tahiti by fraud?"

Piper clearly did not know this. He frowned, not sure what to say next. With an effort he collected himself. In a much calmer voice he said, "I don't respond to blackmail or lies, Mr. Murray. Kindly leave, and if I hear any of this repeated, you know what I will do."

I didn't leave. I stood up from the delicate sofa, and walked over toward the giant window. We were a long way up. The darkened windows took away the noise, the glare, and the heat of Las Vegas. The city floated away harmlessly below.

I turned to Piper. "I don't intend to blackmail you. I am just concerned. Concerned that a colleague of mine was killed a couple of months ago. Concerned that my firm has been defrauded of millions of dollars, which are now invested in your casino. This, I am sure, will concern an honest businessman such as yourself as well. After all, these things can be dangerous for one's reputation. It may be that I will need your help in the future to find who is behind this. I am sure you will be delighted to give it. In the meantime, I will certainly not mention Bladenham Hall to anyone." I smiled and made for the door. Just before I left, I turned and offered Piper my hand. He didn't take it. I shrugged and walked out of the room.

Piper had his own express elevator that took me to the ground floor. I felt elated after my encounter with him. I had got him just where I wanted him. I crossed over into another elevator and went up to my room to think.

After ten minutes or so, the phone rang. It was Tommy.

"I have found out some things that might interest you," he began. I wrenched my mind back to the Tremont Capital problem.

"Shoot."

"Well, first of all you asked me to find out about the acquisition of Phoenix Prosperity. I guessed that Waigel must have had something to do with it, so I got Jean to raid his files. Do you want the details?"

"Yes, please."

"It starts off with some correspondence from Howard Farber, the owner and chief executive officer of Phoenix Prosperity. It says that he is facing a bad year ahead and that he probably has only two choices, either file for bankruptcy or sell the business. That's dated about two years ago.

"Three months later Waigel wrote back to tell Farber that he had found a buyer. Lo and behold, that turns out to be our old friend Tremont Capital. There is a whole sheaf of correspondence documenting the deal. Tremont put in forty million dollars of capital in return for ninety percent of the company. Howard Farber remained CEO but someone called Jack Salmon was appointed liaison officer. His job was to liaise with the majority shareholder, Tremont Capital."

"Very interesting."

"Yes. And you know what else is interesting?"

"Tell me."

"Bloomfield Weiss only charged a twenty-five-thousand-dollar advisory fee. I can't imagine Bloomfield Weiss doing anything like this for less than one percent, which in this case would be four hundred thousand."

"I suppose Waigel didn't want to charge himself too much," I said. "Talk about conflict of interest. That's great! Well done. Did you discover anything else?"

"I didn't. But the police did. They finally found Shoffman's body in a wood in Montclair, New Jersey."

"Do they know how he was killed, or who did it?" I asked.

"No. It was hard enough to identify him after all this time. They are still working on it, but they are not very optimistic."

"Damn. I was hoping there would be something to tie his death in with all of this."

"There is."

"What?"

"Dick Waigel lives in Montclair."

"Really?" I said. I wasn't exactly surprised. "Okay, Tommy. Thanks very much for all you have done. Can you send copies of those documents to my office in London?"

"Sure," said Tommy. "It will be a pleasure. Let me know what you come up with."

"I will. Thanks again," I said and hung up.

Everything was falling into place. I had almost all the information I needed to piece together what was going on. I pulled out some sheets of paper, and spent the next two hours drawing as complete a picture as I could of Tremont Capital, the financing of the Tahiti, and the various people involved. After I had finished, there was still one key question left unresolved. Why had Debbie died?

That she had been murdered, I was sure. It seemed to me highly likely that the reason was something to do with Tremont Capital. Waigel seemed the most likely candidate: The discovery of Shoffman's body near Waigel's house in Montclair suggested he was certainly capable of it.

But Waigel's diary showed he was in New York the night Debbie was killed. And it was Joe, not Waigel, that I had seen just before she was killed. So what was Joe's connection with Waigel? There was none that I knew of, but perhaps Cash had put Joe up to it. I had no doubts about Cash's involvement in the whole thing. After all, it was he who had sold the Tremont Capital bonds to Hamilton in the first place.

As for motive, it looked to me as though Cash had somehow found out that Debbie had discovered the Tremont Capital fraud, and was going to see Mr. De Jong about it. She had to be silenced.

And yet . . . I wasn't convinced. Joe had been adamant that he had not killed Debbie, and I believed him. It didn't quite make sense yet.

Still, I had got a long way. I called Hamilton. His voice traveled crisply down the phone lines. "What have you got for me, laddie?"

"I think I have worked it all out, or almost all of it," I said, trying not to sound too proud of myself.

"Tell me," said Hamilton, unable to keep the eagerness out of his voice.

"Well, I am pretty sure that Waigel and Cash are behind the whole thing. Waigel created the Tremont Capital structure and Cash sold it to you."

"Sounds plausible," said Hamilton. "We know that Tremont Capital raised the money under a false guarantee, but have you found out where the money went?"

"I think so."

"Well, don't play games, tell me."

"Uncle Sam's Money Machine was a savings and loan. Phoenix Prosperity Savings and Loan, to be precise. Tremont Capital bought ninety percent of the company with the money raised from the private placement. They are using Phoenix Prosperity to make a series of high-risk investments funded with government-guaranteed deposits. One of them is Irwin Piper's Tahiti Hotel."

"Is he involved in Tremont?"

"I don't know," I said. "I am not sure who owns Tremont Capital itself. I expect Cash and Waigel are shareholders, perhaps Piper is too."

There was silence on the end of the phone. I could

almost hear Hamilton thinking it all through. "Well, it all adds up," he said. "You've done an excellent job! Excellent. Now all we have to do is figure out a way to get our money back."

"Don't we go to the police now?" I asked.

"Not when we are so close to locating the money. As soon as we have got it all back, then you can go to the police and tell them everything, but not until then, do you hear?"

I heard. And in truth I was enjoying this. I was a lot more confident that Hamilton and I would work out a way to get our twenty million back.

"I'll call Rudy Geer. I want to see how he is getting on in Curaçao. With this information, we might be able to crack Tremont Capital in the Netherlands Antilles. I had better get out there again soon."

"There is one thing I don't understand."

"What's that?"

I told Hamilton about the questions I still had about Debbie's death.

"Yes, I see what you mean," said Hamilton, his voice thoughtful. "There is still a lot we need to find out. But maybe if we find the money, it will lead us to Debbie's killer."

"Okay," I said, "What's next?"

Hamilton's response was clear. "I get hold of Rudy Geer. I go to Curaçao again. And I do some thinking."

"What about me?" I said.

"Don't worry, laddie, you've done enough. Put down the main points of what you have just told me on a fax, and send it over. Then just enjoy yourself, and I'll see you in the office on Monday."

As I put the phone down, I reflected that Hamilton must be pleased with me if he told me to enjoy myself. And frankly, I was pretty pleased with myself. There was no doubt that I had impressed him.

I scribbled my findings on a couple of sheets of paper, and went down to the hotel business center to send the fax. Not surprisingly, the Tahiti was fitted out with all sorts of sophisticated computers, photocopiers, and fax machines as well as two secretaries who were available to type copy for the hotel's customers any time of day or night. I declined their services, and insisted on sending the fax through to Hamilton myself.

It only took a couple of minutes. I strolled back to the bank of elevators, wending my way through the grass-skirted beauties who worked for the hotel and the over-weight punters who were its customers. Cathy was waiting in one of the elevators.

"Hello," I said, as I jumped in just before the doors closed. "Did you get my message last night? Do you fancy exploring the town later on?"

She bit her lip and looked down at the floor of the elevator. "No, I think I should like an early night."

"Oh, okay. Do you want to meet up for supper?"

"No, I'd better not. I promised I would eat with Cash and Dick. This is my floor." With barely a glance at me, she stepped out of the elevator.

I frowned. What was all that about? And since when was Cathy so eager to have dinner with the poisonous frog? Odd. I walked down the landing to my room feeling distinctly uncomfortable.

The more I thought about it, the surer I was that her aloofness was deliberate. She had decided to avoid me, to put me off. There was no other explanation, I couldn't hide from that conclusion.

But why?

I lay on my back on the bed, staring at the ceiling. I had no idea why. I couldn't think of anything I had said that might have put her off me. I lay there puzzled and afraid. It would hurt if I lost Cathy. It would hurt a lot.

I was damned if I was just going to let her drift away with a series of banal excuses about how she was too busy to see me. If she wanted to avoid me, I had a right to know why.

I dialed her room number. The phone rang five times.

No reply. Even though it was obvious she was not there, I let it ring and ring, just in case.

Eventually, I hung up. I leaped off the bed and paced around the room. I had to find out what was wrong. I had to.

I decided to wander round the hotel. There was a chance I might bump into her, and even if I didn't at least I wouldn't be moping in my room anymore.

She wasn't in the lobby. I looked in all the bars and coffeeshops, wound my way through the palm trees, the islands, and the machines. I walked slowly, to increase the chances of finding her.

This was ridiculous. I had no idea where she was. She had probably gone downtown or to one of the other casinos on the Strip. I gave up my loitering inside the building, and strolled round the gardens outside. Turf, shrubs, and palm trees had been transplanted onto what two months before had been a building site, and sprinklers were on constantly. The foliage was a deep green, interspersed with flashes of purple. It all seemed unnatural in the desert climate.

I trudged around the gardens for half an hour, and then made my way back inside. As I walked through the lobby I looked left and right on the off chance that I might see her. And I did. She was crossing the vast atrium, heading out of the hotel. I hurried after her. I caught her up on one of the bridges between islands.

"Hello," I said.

"Hello," she said, and quickened her pace.

"I want to talk to you."

"I'm afraid I don't have time right now. I'm in a hurry. Perhaps later."

I lengthened my stride and placed myself in front of her. "Look," I said, "I have to talk to you. And I'm going to talk to you some time. So you may as well get it over with now. Otherwise you won't get rid of me. Okay?"

Cathy looked at me, frowning. She nodded. "Okay."

We were standing on a small islet with some chairs and a table. We sat down.

"All I need is to understand," I said. "I felt I was getting to know you over the last few days. Getting to know you well. And the more I got to know you, the more I liked what I saw. You and I fit. I know that, and I think you know that. So I need to understand."

Cathy was staring straight ahead. "Understand what?"

"Understand what's wrong. Understand why you wanted to avoid me this morning. Why you don't want to talk to me now."

Cathy reddened slightly. "I'm not trying to avoid you. I had just agreed to do something else, that's all." She saw the look on my face. I waited. Finally she sighed. "You're right. You do deserve an explanation."

She still wasn't looking at me, but rather staring at a transplanted palm tree ahead of her. "I have grown to like your company. It's fun to be with you. When you are not around, I find myself looking forward to the next time I might bump into you."

I smiled at her. She still didn't meet my eyes. "I feel the same way," I said. "So what's the problem?"

"On the aeroplane coming here I sat next to Waigel. We had a chat. About you." She clasped and unclasped her hands, and resolutely looked away from me. "He said he thought that there was something going on between you and me. He said he didn't like it. He said it was unprofessional, bad for my career."

My anger was rising. "Waigel hates me, you know that. What does it matter what he thinks?"

Cathy went on in a low voice. "He said if it carried on I would be fired."

I exploded. "That's crazy. He can't fire you."

"Oh, yes he can. He and Cash are old friends, remember? He said he would check with Cash to make sure I wasn't seeing you. He said that there was some doubt about my future at the firm, and some prompting from him and Cash would be all it would take to get them to sack me."

"He's bluffing."

Cathy turned toward me, anger in her eyes. "No, he's not. You are quite right, he doesn't like you at all. In fact he hates you. And he will go to great lengths to get his way."

"But with what he's said and done to you, you could get him fired."

Cathy gave a shallow laugh. "You would have to be crazy to bring a sexual harassment suit against Bloomfield Weiss. Even if I won it, I would be finished."

"Well, then screw Bloomfield Weiss. After all you hate the firm. You said it yourself. So screw them."

From Cathy's reaction, I realized immediately I shouldn't have said this. "That's easy for you to say," she said. "It's my career we are talking about. You know how difficult it is being a woman in this business. People don't treat you seriously. Men like Waigel assume you are a bimbo whose job it is to seduce clients for the firm. Well, I refuse to prove Waigel right. I have put a lot into this job. I have fought hard to achieve what I have achieved, and I'm just not going to let all that go to waste."

"Okay, okay, I'm sorry," I said. "But you've got to mold your job to your life, not your life to your job."

"Oh, yes, I see. So the moment I see a man and fall in love with him, I should resign and do a crash course in cooking and household management." Cathy's voice was heavy with sarcasm.

"That's not what I mean," I protested.

"Oh, yes, well what do you mean?"

The argument had got out of hand. Waigel was blackmailing Cathy to stay away from me, and somehow we were arguing over a woman's right to a career. I searched for the words to answer her, but was too slow.

"Look, I thought I liked you, but I don't really know you at all," Cathy continued. "I am not about to jeopardize years of work for you. And that is that." With that she stood up, turned away, and walked quickly back to the elevators.

I sat on the chair overcome with anger. All the muscles in my body were clenched tight. My fists were white and shaking. That bastard Waigel! My contempt for him had grown as I had discovered more of his role in the Tremont Capital fraud. He had probably murdered Shoffman. He may have had something to do with Debbie's death. He had pestered Cathy in the most unspeakable way. And now he had chased her away from me. That turned contempt into hatred. I would get him. I would nail him properly.

I was also angry with Cathy. The girl whom I had grown increasingly fond of had reverted to the arrogant Bloomfield Weiss executive woman I had first met. But perhaps I was being unfair. Perhaps it really was unreasonable to expect Cathy to risk her job for me. The trouble was, I didn't really feel like being broad-minded about this. I had lowered my emotional defenses for perhaps the first time in my life, and Cathy and Waigel between them had trampled all over the exposed nerves.

I stalked over to one of the bars and ordered myself a beer. We were all supposed to be visiting a couple of other casinos that issued junk bonds that afternoon. I decided to skip them.

I finished my beer in a couple of minutes and ordered another. Slowly, my fury began to subside. I looked around the large atrium at the assorted people milling about, some in a desperate hurry, most just hanging around. I recognized one of them. I choked on my beer as I saw a figure approaching me from the reception desk. It was Rob! What on earth was he doing here? He should have been at the office, or possibly at his own conference in Hounslow.

Then I focused on the large yellow bouquet he held in one arm. Oh no! I knew why he was here. He was making the dramatic gesture he had promised me that evening in the Gloucester Arms.

He walked with a determined stride. As he came up to me he didn't stop but just grinned. "Close your mouth, Paul, you never know what kind of insects they might have in a place like this," he said as he strode past me on his way to the elevators.

I realized my mouth had indeed been gaping open. I shut it and watched him disappear into an elevator.

I propped up the bar, waiting for Rob to return. What would she say to him? After our conversation, she couldn't possibly accept his advances, could she? Or could she? The thought filled me with horror. I had to admit it was quite a dramatic gesture. But Cathy was sensible. She wouldn't fall for that, would she?

An agonizing ten minutes passed as I stared at the bank of elevators. At last I saw Rob emerge from one. He saw me at the bar and wended his way through the island walkways to where I was sitting. His face was totally impassive. I couldn't tell whether he was elated or dejected. He was apparently deliberately suppressing his emotions. Why?

He walked up and stood right in front of me, silently. Say something! I wanted to scream at him. I needed to know what she said.

Instead, I just said, "Hello, Rob."

"You shit," he said. He said it slowly and deliberately, looking me right in the eye.

"Why?" I said. "What have I done?" I could hear my voice emerging weak and hoarse.

"You utter shit," he said again. "I meet the girl who I want to spend the rest of my life with. I fly six thousand miles out here to tell her so. And what do I find? My friend has got there before me.

"She told me all about you," he continued bitterly. "And the worst thing is you knew how I felt. You pretended you didn't like her, trying to put me off her, when all the time you had your own designs on her." I saw tears begin to well up in Rob's eyes.

"Rob, it's not like that . . ." I started.

"Go fuck yourself," Rob spat. "I won't forget this. You won't get away with it. Neither of you. I'll kill her. And I will kill you too." He stormed off, kicking a pile of coconuts out of his way and sending a latex humming-bird spinning across the floor.

I gulped the rest of my beer and ordered another. What right had Rob to get so angry with me? He was crazy if he thought Cathy would have anything to do with him. She had told him what she thought of him before. And besides I hadn't done anything wrong. I hadn't intentionally chased after her. I had been com-pletely honest when I had told Rob I didn't like her. Whatever had happened had just happened, that was all. There wasn't much I could do about it.

I had never seen Rob angry before, and he had looked very angry then. When he had threatened to kill Cathy and me, it looked like he really meant it. I shuddered. With Rob, anger wasn't something that would be gone as soon as it had come, I thought. He had been deeply hurt, and he would not forget. I felt bad. I should have restrained myself. I should have realized Rob would not appreciate any relationship between Cathy and myself.

Slowly, I began to feel sorry for him. Poor guy! The ticket to Las Vegas must have cost him a fortune. It was bad enough to be turned down after flying all that way. But Rob had been turned down before, he was used to it. It must have made it so much worse to find a friend there between him and his goal.

I thought about trying to find him to apologize. No, that wouldn't work, at least not for a while. He wouldn't believe my protestations. In fact, they would probably make his hatred of me deeper. It was probably best to avoid him and hope that time would heal the rift between us.

But at least Cathy hadn't said yes to Rob. In fact he had said that she had told him all about me. What had she told him? She must have admitted that there was some sort of relationship between us, some sort of bond.

Otherwise Rob would not have been so upset. Maybe she had decided to give up her fears of "unprofessionalism." Perhaps she had felt guilty about giving in to Waigel. I wanted to find out.

I went back up to my room and rang her number. She answered the phone. "Hello?"

"It's me," I said. "I wondered if you had thought more about our conversation. The invitation for dinner tonight is still open."

"What is it about all you men at De Jong?" she answered angrily. "You are all so persistent. No, I do not want to go out with you this evening. I just want to be left alone to get along with my life and my job. Okay?"

"Okay, okay," I said. I hung up.

I had a miserable evening. Worries about Cathy gnawed away at the edges of my mind, and forced themselves further toward the fore. I could feel everything getting out of proportion; I had lost the ability to think clearly.

I ordered a steak and a bottle of zinfandel from room service, ate the meat, drank the wine, and went to bed. I lay awake for what may have been many hours or perhaps was just one. Finally, deadened by the alcohol and battered by confused thoughts and fears, my brain stopped churning, and I drifted to sleep.

THE SUN SHONE down on the gray concrete and glass buildings of Gracechurch Street as I joined the familiar throng of office workers on the way to their desks. The street was packed indeed, because it was five to nine, much later than normal for me. I had allowed myself to sleep in to get over the jet lag and the fatigue of the long journey.

I had flown to Los Angeles from Las Vegas, and from there direct to London. Twelve hours in airplanes and four more at Los Angeles International Airport had been a strain. And not just physically. Cash, Cathy, and Rob had all been on the same plane, although because Rob was paying for his own ticket, he was flying in the back. The whole thing was very uncomfortable. There had been an intensely unpleasant two-minute period when we were lining up to board the plane. Rob and I were just ten feet away from each other. He just stared at me, mouth clenched, eyes lit with anger. I turned away from him, but I could still feel his stare piercing my back. It hurt.

Once on the plane, Cathy was polite but cool toward me. I accepted this and was polite but cool back. Rob avoided both of us and kept himself to himself. The most distressed by all this was Cash. He tried to lavish his bon-homie on all three of us, but no one responded. Eventually Cash gave up, mumbling something to himself about "tight-assed Brits." He finally cheered up when he discovered he was seated next to an old rival from Harrison Brothers. My sleep on the plane was interrupted by ever more far-fetched tales of past trades, as each good-humoredly tried to outdo the other.

But, as I made my way up Bishopsgate toward De Jong & Co., I couldn't help smiling. I was pretty pleased with the way I had got to the bottom of the Tremont Capital scam. Now it was just up to Hamilton to get the money back.

The smile was still there as I entered the trading room and nodded a welcome to everybody. The markets were busy; everyone was working the phones. I got to my desk and scowled at the pile of research waiting for me. I checked the screens and the position sheets, to see how my old positions had fared and what new ones had been put on in my absence. With Hamilton, me, and Rob out, not much had changed, although Gordon and Jeff had been quite busy.

I had only been at my desk for a couple of minutes when Hamilton came over.

"Hi, Hamilton," I said. "How did you get on? We have a lot to talk about."

I was taken aback by the grave expression on Hamilton's face. "We certainly do," he said. "Let's go into the conference room." Uneasily, I followed him into the small room just off the trading floor.

"What's up?" I asked.

Hamilton didn't reply. "Tell me about your trip first," he said.

I ran through what I had discovered. Hamilton listened intently and took notes. When I had finished, he leaned back in his chair. "Well done, Paul, that's excellent. It corroborates a lot of what I have discovered."

There was silence. Hamilton frowned deeply. I wanted to ask him what he had discovered, but I couldn't. There was something else hovering in the air. Something momentous. Something bad.

"Paul," Hamilton began, "tell me about Gypsum."

I didn't understand this. I thought we had discussed the position I had taken and why I had taken it. Besides, it looked as if the bond price had gone up even further since I had been away.

"The bonds looked good value," I started, but Hamilton held up his hand.

"Not the bonds, the shares," he said. "You bought the shares of Gypsum Company of America days before it was taken over."

Alarm bells started ringing. Why would he ask me about that? He's talking about insider trading, I thought. But I hadn't done anything wrong. I was sure I hadn't. Well, pretty sure.

"Yes, that's correct. But I didn't have any information that the company was going to be taken over. I was just lucky, that's all. And so was Debbie," I said before I could stop myself. Exactly how lucky had she been?

"Well, there are some people who think you did have inside information."

"That's absolutely not the case," I said.

Hamilton looked at me for a few seconds. I held the gaze of his piercing blue eyes. I was telling the truth and I wanted him to know it. Finally, he nodded. "Well, I'm sure you are right. But it's not me you have to convince. There are two men here from the TSA who would like to ask you a few questions. Would you like me to be present?"

This was extraordinary! Ridiculous. Crazy. I didn't yet feel scared. Shocked, yes. And bewildered. But I was glad the men were here to interview me. With luck, I would be able to sort it out there and then.

"Yes, please," I said quietly.

Hamilton left the room to collect the two men from reception. I looked around the conference room. It was a lonely room. All internal walls, no windows. Expensive-looking, but characterless reproduction furniture. Idiotic clippers sailing nowhere across the walls. White crisp notepads and sharp yellow pencils on the table. Yes, it would serve as an interrogation room.

Hamilton returned, followed by the two officials. I supposed they must have been waiting there when I came in, but I hadn't noticed them. Although it was early September and it hadn't rained for days, they both carried fawn raincoats over their arms. They unburdened themselves of these and their briefcases, took out their own pads of paper, and sat down opposite me. Hamilton sat at the head of the table between us. I wished he had positioned himself right next to me. The three feet between us seemed a long way.

One of the men began to talk. He was mostly bald, the dark hair that remained was cropped close to his skull. He had a prominent nose and chin, but there was very little distance between the two features, giving his face an unpleasant squashed look. He wore black-rimmed glasses with very thick frames. He must be almost blind, I thought. The corners of his thin mouth turned up as he introduced himself. "Good morning Mr. Murray. My name is David Berryman, I work for The Securities Association. This is my colleague Rodney Short." The other man, thin and timorous, nodded. That was the closest I would get to communicating with him. He was there to keep quiet and write everything down.

I knew all about The Securities Association, commonly known as the TSA; I had recently sat an examination to become a member. It was one of a number of self-regulatory organizations that had been set up following Big Bang to police the City. It promulgated dozens of rules and had its own staff to ensure that they were complied with. It had the power to fine or expel members. In cases in which criminal charges could be brought then the TSA would hand over its investigation to the Fraud Squad or the Serious Fraud Office.

"Do you mind if I ask you a few questions?" Berryman began.

"No," I said, my voice suddenly hoarse. Berryman

strained to hear. Pull yourself together, I said to myself. I mustn't look nervous, after all I had done nothing wrong. "No," I repeated loudly, too loudly to be natural.

There was a pause as Berryman looked at me through those big lenses. I smiled a helpful, friendly smile. "I will tell you anything you like." My smile was not returned as Berryman fumbled through his notes. His sidekick, Short, was already writing furiously, what I had no idea.

The questions began. "Your name?"

"Paul Murray."

"Are you employed by De Jong and Company?"

"Yes."

"For how long have you been in their employ?"

"Eight months."

"In what capacity?"

"Portfolio manager."

These questions came quickly, and I answered them quickly and clearly.

"Did you on the sixteenth of July last purchase Gypsum of America bonds to the value of two million dollars on behalf of De Jong and Company?"

"Yes, I did."

"And did you on the same date buy a thousand shares of Gypsum of America common stock for your own account?"

"Yes."

"You will be aware that later that day the share price of Gypsum of America rose from seven dollars to eleven and a quarter dollars. Within a few days an offer to acquire Gypsum of America was announced. Did you have any knowledge that this offer was pending?"

"No, I didn't."

"Then why did you buy the bonds and the shares?"

I knew my answer to this question was important. I leaned across the desk and tried to look Berryman in the eye. It was difficult with those bloody lenses.

"Bloomfield Weiss had offered to buy a small position of Gypsums that De Jong had held for a while. I did some research on the company, and it seemed to me that a takeover was a distinct possibility. The company had been badly run, and the previous chief executive had died recently. He had always blocked a takeover in the past."

"I see." Berryman tapped his chin with a pen and thought for a moment. "There was nothing else that made you suspect a takeover was imminent. What you have told me seems precious little on which to risk De Jong's capital, let alone your own."

"Well . . ." I started, and then cut myself off.

"Yes?" Berryman raised his eyebrows so they were just showing above his spectacles.

I had to finish. "I was suspicious that Bloomfield Weiss knew something. It seemed odd to me that they were willing to pay such a high price for the bonds, all of a sudden."

"Who was it at Bloomfield Weiss who expressed interest in the bonds?"

"Cash Callaghan, one of their salesmen."

"I see. And Mr. Callaghan gave no indication that the company was about to be taken over."

"No, he didn't. But then he wouldn't, would he? Not if he wanted to buy the bonds from me cheaply?"

"Are you suggesting that Mr. Callaghan knew about the proposed takeover?"

I hesitated here. For a moment I thought this could be the chance I had been looking for to nail Cash. But only for a moment. I was on dangerous ground; I had better play it straight. But Berryman had noticed my hesitation, no doubt he was putting his own interpretation on it.

"No, I'm not. I have no idea what Cash knew or didn't know. I am merely saying, that at the time I suspected that he might."

Berryman didn't believe me. I could tell he didn't. In a way I wished he would come right out and say it, give me a chance to convince him of my innocence. I thought of launching into an impassioned plea to be believed, but I held back. It would probably just make things worse.

"This is an important question, Mr. Murray." Berryman leaned forward. "Did you discuss with Mr. Callaghan the possibility of buying shares in Gypsum of America for your own account?"

"No, I did not," I said firmly.

"Are you quite sure?"

"Absolutely sure." I wondered where Berryman had got this idea from. Perhaps Cash had been trading on inside information himself. Perhaps he had claimed that he had tipped me off. I didn't know.

The corners of Berryman's mouth twitched upward again. He seemed very satisfied with my response. I felt as though I had fallen into a trap, but I couldn't for the life of me work out what the trap was.

Berryman continued. "Did you call the compliance officer at Bloomfield Weiss shortly after the takeover was announced?"

My heart sank. Berryman saw this. "Yes," I said.

"Why did you do that?"

"Our compliance officer here was a woman named Debbie Chater. She died recently. When I was clearing up her desk, I found a note to her from Bloomfield Weiss about an investigation into the Gypsum of America share price movements. It asked for her to give them a call. I called the man at Bloomfield Weiss, a Mr. Bowen I think it was, to see if I could help."

"I see." Berryman rummaged through his notes. "You told Mr. Bowen that Miss Chater had informed you about the Gypsum investigation."

"No. Not at all. Well, I mean . . ." Christ, what had I said? "I think I said that we had been working on Gypsum together, which we had, in a manner of speaking."

"Hmm. Mr. Bowen is of the opinion that you had discovered that Miss Chater had tipped him off about her suspicions about the movements in the Gypsum share price, and you called him to try to find out how the investigation into yourself, Callaghan, and others was going."

"That's just not true."

"It's convenient that Miss Chater died just then, isn't it?" Berryman went on, his tone wheedling.

I exploded. For the last ten minutes I had become confused and afraid, not sure exactly what they thought I had done or even really sure whether what I had actually done was right or wrong. I had been on the defensive, reeling from one veiled accusation to another. But this last insinuation went one step too far. I wasn't exactly sure who had killed Debbie, but I knew for sure it wasn't me.

"I don't have to take all this crap. Just because you don't have a clue what happened you can't throw allegations around at random hoping one will stick. Debbie was a good friend of mine. I didn't kill her, and you have no grounds for thinking I did. If you think I did, let's go to the police and discuss it. If you don't, then shut up."

Berryman was taken aback by my outburst. He opened his mouth to say something, and then thought better of it. He turned to Hamilton, who had been watching all this impassively.

"Do you mind if I ask you a question or two?"

"I will answer questions of fact, not unsubstantiated allegations." Hamilton's voice was reasonable but firm. Berryman shrank.

"Was Murray authorized to purchase the Gypsum bonds?"

"Of course he was," Hamilton replied. "He is authorized to trade for the firm."

"Did he receive specific authorization to buy the bonds?"

"No. I was in Japan at the time. But he didn't need authorization from me."

"When you returned, did you approve of the purchase?"

Hamilton paused. Berryman waited. Eventually Hamilton said, "No, I didn't."

"Why not?"

"Paul had a hunch that Gypsum of America would be taken over. In my view, he didn't have enough information to back that hunch."

"But if Murray had known for certain that Gypsum was going to be taken over, then the trade would have seemed a good one?"

"Yes, of course. A sure way to make money."

"In retrospect, doesn't it seem likely that Murray did in fact know for certain that Gypsum was going to be taken over and that is why he purchased the bonds?"

Hamilton stood up. "Now, Mr. Berryman, I told you that I would not respond to unsubstantiated allegations. I think you had better leave."

Berryman tidied up all his papers and put them in his briefcase. The other man, Short, scribbled on for a few seconds and did the same.

"Thank you for your cooperation," Berryman said. "I should be grateful if you could send me copies of your own internal records of the bond and share purchases made by Mr. Murray and the tape of all Mr. Murray's telephone conversations on the sixteenth of July." All phone calls in trading rooms are taped, either to settle disputes on who said what or, very occasionally, to assist the authorities in their enquiries.

Hamilton showed the two men to the elevator. I sank back in my chair, shocked and confused. Berryman clearly thought he was on to something. What false trail he could have picked up, I didn't know. Whatever it was, it didn't look good for me.

Hamilton came back into the room. "Well?" he said.

I sighed. "I bought the bonds and the shares because I guessed Gypsum was going to be taken over. I had no inside knowledge that it would be."

Hamilton smiled. "Okay, laddie, I believe you."

I felt a surge of relief rush over me. It was good to know someone believed me. "It didn't sound too good, did it?" I said. I wasn't at all sure how I had done, and I needed to know what Hamilton thought.

He stroked his beard. "They can't prove anything yet, but they seem quite sure they have something on you. Look, why don't you just tidy up your desk for the next few minutes and then go home. You are in no fit state to trade."

I nodded thankfully, and did as Hamilton suggested. As soon as I got home, I put on my running clothes and set off pounding round the park. I did two circuits, eight miles, pushing myself all the way. The pain in my legs and lungs tugged my mind away from the morning's interview, and the steady emission of adrenaline into the bloodstream soothed my nerves.

As I lay soaking in a hot bath afterward, the problem fell into perspective. I had done nothing wrong. I had no inside information. A successful prosecution was highly unlikely; the record of any of the financial regulators on that score was appalling. As long as De Jong continued to support me I would be all right, and Hamilton seemed firm on that score.

I had been in the bath for twenty minutes when the phone rang. It was difficult to summon up the energy to answer it, but eventually I did. It was Hamilton.

"How are you, Paul?"

"Oh, I've just been for a run and I feel much better."

"Good, good. I've just spoken to Berryman. I told him that it was important to De Jong and to you, that they should sort this problem out soon. Either you did something wrong and they can prove it, or you didn't and they can stop pestering us. They said they should be in a position to let us know by the end of the week. So, why don't you take the rest of the week off? You'll be no good at a trading desk anyway with this hanging over you."

"Okay," I said. "I'm glad they think they can clear it up so soon. I'll see you next Monday."

But as I hung up the phone, I felt uneasy. If they were confident of resolving the case by Friday, it seemed more likely that it was because they felt they were close to proving my guilt, than because they were close to giving up.

I was pulling on my clothes, my spirits sinking again, when the phone rang once more.

It was my sister, Linda. "Now then, Paul, how's life been keeping you?" she said.

"Fine, fine, and you?" I replied, wondering what on earth she could be calling about. We scarcely ever spoke to each other, and when we did it was only because we were both with my mother at the same time. This was something Linda tried to avoid. I suppose we didn't like each other. It wasn't an active dislike. Like everything else it had its roots in my father's death. Linda had felt it was my role to be the man of the house and had disapproved deeply when I had gone to Cambridge and then London. She herself lived only ten miles away, in the neighboring dale. She had married a farmer, a big brute of a man whom I disliked intensely. She worshiped him, and compared me unfavorably to him at every opportunity. As I said, we didn't talk much.

"What's up," I said, wanting to get to the point. "Is it something to do with Mum?"

"Yes," Linda said. "Don't worry, she's not ill or anything. It's her house. You know Lord Mablethorpe died a couple of months ago?"

"Yes, Mum told me."

"Well, his son has told her she has got to get out."

"What? He can't do that. Lord Mablethorpe promised her that house until she dies. His son knows that."

"There's nothing on paper about that," Linda continued. "He says he can do what he likes. He says he has received a very attractive offer for it from a television producer who wants to use it as a weekend cottage."

"What a bastard."

"Just what I said. I told our Jim to go round and give him what for, but he said that was your job."

Typical of our Jim, I thought, but he had a point. "Okay, I'll see what I can do."

I thought of getting in touch with the new Lord Mablethorpe in London, but decided it would probably be best to see him in his ancestral home. Maybe then he would think about his ancestral responsibilities.

I rang Helmby Hall. Fortunately, Lord Mablethorpe was there all week shooting grouse. I made an appointment to see him the next day and called my mother to tell her I would be staying the night. She sounded distressed, but was relieved I would be coming.

I set out on the long drive early. I successfully put the Gypsum investigation out of my mind. There was, after all, nothing I could do about it. Similarly, my desire to unravel the mystery surrounding Debbie's death and the Tremont Capital fraud had faded a little, or at any rate become less immediate. I was in a sort of limbo, and in a way I was grateful to this latest family problem for providing me with a distraction.

I arrived at my mother's in time for a late lunch. Over the shepherd's pie, she chattered on about her house and garden, about how it was so central in the village. She obviously was going to be very upset if she had to leave. I hoped I would be able to find her something else in Barthwaite. Without the considerate neighbors who knew and liked her, eccentricities and all, she would find life much more difficult.

It took just ten minutes to drive to Helmby Hall. An assortment of Range Rovers, Jaguars, and Mercedes were drawn up outside, no doubt Lord Mablethorpe's shooting guests. I parked my little Peugeot beside them, walked up to the huge front door, and rang the bell. A butler showed me into a study where I waited.

The study was a comfortable place, full of the day-to-day bits of paper and books that the old Lord Mablethorpe had needed. I remembered the several occasions when I had been in this room as a boy, watching my father and Lord Mablethorpe laughing by the fire. Lord Mablethorpe had a huge laugh. His red face would split into a big grin and his massive shoulders would heave up and down. His hands were as large and well worn as my father's as they cradled the whiskey that he always broke out for these occasions. I checked the bookshelf behind me. Sure enough, a quarter-full decanter was propping up some old editions of *Whitaker's Almanac*.

Finally, Charles Mablethorpe arrived. He looked very different from his father. Thin and anemic, I was surprised he could survive a whole day striding across the moors in search of grouse, let alone a whole week. He was about my own age, and an assistant director in the Corporate Finance department of an old, but now very minor, merchant bank.

"Hello, Charles. Thank you for taking the time to see me," I said, proffering my hand.

He shook it limply. "Not at all, Murray, have a seat."

He gestured to a small chair by the side of his desk. He sat in a large chair behind it.

I bridled at being treated as a loyal retainer by this prat, but sat down.

"I've come to talk to you about my mother's house," I began.

"I know," Mablethorpe interrupted.

"You know that when my father was killed, your father promised my mother that she could live there until she died."

"Actually, I don't. In fact, I can't even find a tenancy agreement for the cottage. It would appear that your mother is living there illegally."

"That's ridiculous," I said. "She isn't paying rent because she is living there rent free. There isn't a tenancy agreement because there was no need for one. Your father was very happy to let her live there."

"That may well have been the case; my father was a very generous and charitable man. But we only have your mother's word that he promised her the cottage for life, and she isn't exactly reliable now, is she?" Mablethorpe drew a packet of cigarettes from his pocket and lit one. He didn't offer one to me. "The problem is I have fearsome inheritance taxes to pay. I have got to sell off part of the estate, and fifty thousand pounds would come in very handy, thank you."

"You can't throw her out," I said. "It's illegal. She's a sitting tenant. And don't think you can intimidate her to leave."

"I'm terribly sorry, Murray, but I am afraid I can. You see, she has never paid any rent, and so she is not a tenant. She's really just a sort of squatter, you know. Don't worry, I have checked everything with my solicitors in Richmond. Technically, it may be difficult to evict her if she barricades herself in, but we will get her out eventually."

"Your father would be furious if he knew you were doing this," I said.

Mablethorpe pulled deeply on his cigarette before replying. "You have no idea what my father would have thought. My father had many qualities but financial acumen wasn't one of them. There is a lot of capital tied up in this estate, and it has to be made to provide a decent return. In the modern world, you can't just leave assets lying around generating no income. You work in finance, I am sure you can see that."

"I know that you can't run an estate like you would the balance sheet of a bank," I said, but I could see that there wasn't much I could do to change Mablethorpe's mind. Pleading with him wouldn't work, and I had nothing to threaten him with. There was no point in hanging around. I got up to leave. "Dad always said your father thought you were a fool, and now I know why," I said as I turned on my heel and walked out of the room. A cheap shot, but it made me feel better.

CHAPTER
>>>> **18**

THE COLD DAWN AIR bit into my lungs with every breath. The muscles in my calves twisted and jarred on the stony path. I had forgotten how hard running up steep hills was on them. I was following the route I had run almost every day as a kid. Four miles up the steepest slopes in the area. The top of the hill was only two hundred yards away, but my progress was interminably slow. It felt bad enough now—I wondered at how I managed it as a twelve-year-old.

I recognized each odd-shaped stone, each sudden twist in the path. Recognition brought the pain of those runs flooding back. I had sought it out, looking forward to the daily struggle against the steep paths and the cold wind. It wasn't just a means of driving out that other pain of the loss of my father, although that was how it had started. I had developed a dependence on it, a need to focus my mind and my whole body on overcoming the pain and discomfort. It was a kind of self-indulgence, an opportunity to wrap myself up for an hour or two every day in my own world, which had my body and its aching muscles at its center and the sometimes glorious, sometimes terrible hillside scenery as its backdrop. Every day a hard-fought battle, every day a well-deserved victory.

Eventually, I broke the brow of the hill and began the half-mile canter along the ridge between Barthwaite and Helmby. I loped along, dodging the sharper stones and the thicker clumps of heather that lurked along the old sheep track, waiting to jar a foot or ankle. A brace of grouse darted out of the heather and flew fast and low along the line of the hill, before swooping out of my sight. The mist was just lifting from the valley floor around Barthwaite, and I could see the silver ribbon of the river sparkle in the morning sunshine, before turning sharp left behind the shoulder of a purple hill. I looked behind me at the broad desolate brown and purple expanse of the fell at the head of the dale. But I was running away from that, down toward the neatly parceled green fields of the valley floor and the gray stone village, where the first signs of morning activity could be heard; a tractor spluttering to life, dogs barking for their breakfast. I arrived back at my mother's house sore but refreshed, and with a decision made.

I couldn't hope to change Mablethorpe's mind. Even if I found a way to fight him legally, he would get my mother out in the end. The effect of that on her delicately balanced psychology was incalculable. But perhaps I could buy the cottage. That would provide both me and my mother with the comfort of knowing she had a secure home for the rest of her life.

The trouble was, I couldn't afford fifty thousand pounds. But, with my ten thousand pounds of savings mostly made up of my Gypsum investment, I could just afford to borrow another twenty, after taking into account the existing mortgage on my flat. How to get the cottage for only thirty thousand pounds?

Swallow my pride and ask him, I supposed. I rang the Hall and made another appointment for later that day. We met in the same study as the day before. I told Mablethorpe my proposition, the cottage for thirty thousand pounds. I regretted my parting comment of the day before, but Mablethorpe was a little more conciliatory; maybe some of my remarks had got through after all.

"Thirty-five thousand," he said. "No less."

"Okay, thirty-five thousand," I said and held out my

hand. I hoped I would get the finance from somewhere. He shook it limply. I think we were both aware of the strong friendship that had existed between our fathers and felt ashamed at letting them down. We parted on cool but not cold terms.

My mother was very pleased when I told her. She insisted I stay another couple of days, which I did. After the strain of the last few weeks the enforced idleness and change of scenery did me good. I tried, and broadly succeeded, in banishing concerns about my future at De Jong & Co. Time enough to worry about that. I was less able to free my mind of Cathy. I wondered whether she would like Barthwaite. Idiotic thought! There was no reason on earth why she would ever have cause to consider the question. I kicked myself more than once for somehow screwing up what seemed to have been the start of a very promising relationship.

And then I had to borrow twenty-five thousand pounds from somewhere. It ought to be possible, just. After a year or two in the bond-trading world, my salary should rise quite rapidly, and it should quickly become more affordable. That was as long as nothing came of the TSA's investigation.

We were sitting in the De Jong conference room, the same one in which I had been grilled by Mr. Berryman from the TSA. On the polished mahogany table was a tape recorder. On the other side of the table was Hamilton.

When he had called asking to see me at eleven o'clock on Monday morning, my fears had been awakened. If I had been cleared by the investigation, then surely I would have been asked to report to work at seven thirty as normal.

Hamilton's demeanor was grave. Taciturn at the best of times, the most he could manage in terms of small talk now was a curt, "Good week off?"

Without taking any notice of my mumbled answer, he said, "Listen to these tapes."

I was completely still. I attempted to sift through all the conversations of the last two months, trying to think of one which could incriminate me. It was difficult to think what could be on the tape, since I hadn't done anything wrong.

Hamilton flicked the switch.

The volume was on high. Cash's voice boomed, "Change your mind about the Gypsums?"

"No, I haven't," I said. It is always strange listening to your own voice on tape. It didn't sound like me, it was slightly higher pitched, and the accent stronger than I knew it to be. The tape went on. "I wonder if you could do me a favor?" Me again.

"Sure." That was Cash.

"How can I buy some stock on the New York Stock Exchange?"

"Oh that's easy. I can get an account opened for you here. All you have to do is call Miriam Wall in our private client department. Just give me five minutes and I'll warn her you are coming through."

Hamilton switched off the tape recorder. Neither of us said anything for a moment.

Eventually, I broke the silence. "That doesn't prove anything," I said, and then regretted it. It sounded just like the sort of thing a guilty man might say.

Hamilton's slight frown suggested the same thought had occurred to him. "It doesn't prove anything conclusively, no," he said. "But it doesn't look good when put alongside the other evidence the TSA is pulling together against Cash. It sounds to them as though Cash is telling you how to buy stock for your own account in a company about which he has inside information. A classic way of bribing your clients to do business with you. That's how it sounds."

"Well it wasn't like that," I protested.

"The shares you were talking about were Gypsum of America, were they not?"

"Yes."

"And Cash did go out of his way to help set up an account for you?"

"Well yes. But he was trying to help me out as a client." I paused trying to collect my thoughts. I felt cornered, and I couldn't think of a clever way of dodging out. In the end I just repeated the truth. "Debbie and I decided to buy shares based on the analysis of the company I did myself, which suggested it was likely to be taken over. Neither of us had bought shares in American companies before, and Cash seemed the natural person to ask how to do it. It's as simple as that."

Hamilton looked at me for a long time. There is no better judge of character than Hamilton, I thought. He will know I am telling the truth.

But he didn't quite. "It does seem odd to me that you would do something like this," he began. "But the TSA are quite convinced that you and others traded on inside information. You are right that they don't have conclusive proof. Prosecutions for this kind of thing are expensive and frequently don't succeed. However, they do always ruin the lives of those involved, whether guilty or innocent."

He paused, and looked down at the table in front of him. "I also have the interests of the firm to think of. It would be easy for the TSA to publicize this, and even fine us. I need hardly tell you what effect that would have on the institutions who give us money to manage. As you know, we are in the middle of discussions with some potential Japanese clients that could have great significance for this firm. I will not allow those discussions to be jeopardized."

He looked up at me again. "So I have done a deal. In the circumstances, quite a good deal for all involved. I will accept your resignation today. You will serve a two-month notice period, which should be enough time for you to find suitable employment elsewhere. During that period, you may come into work if you wish, but under no circumstances will you trade on behalf of the firm. No one outside this room will be made aware of the reason for your resignation.

"I'm sorry," he said, "but this is best for all of us, especially you."

There it was. A fait accompli. A nice little deal done so that De Jong could carry on as though nothing had happened. And there was nothing at all I could do about it. That was hard to accept.

"What if I don't resign?" I said.

"Don't even ask," said Hamilton.

For a moment I felt like making a stand, refusing to go along with him, demanding a full investigation. But there was no point. I would be crucified. At least this way I could get another job.

I said nothing and just stared at the conference table. I could feel the color rising to my cheeks. I felt several emotions all at once. There was anger, there was shame, and underlying both of these was a strong pull of despair. I opened my mouth to say something, but couldn't. I breathed deeply. Control yourself. You can sort it all out later. Don't say anything, don't blow your top. Just keep your composure and get out.

"Okay," I said hoarsely. I stood up, turned away from Hamilton and left the conference room. There were one or two things I would need from my desk. Phone numbers, that sort of thing. I entered the trading room. All activity stopped. I could feel everyone's eyes on me. I plowed through the atmosphere thick with discomfort. I didn't look at anyone. I just focused on my desk, my face set tight. My cheeks were still hot. No one said anything as I walked over to my desk, picked up my phone numbers and a couple of other things, put them in my briefcase, and walked out. God knows what they thought. I didn't want to worry about that now.

I grabbed a taxi on the street outside the building. The journey home went quickly by. By the time I reached my flat I had at least separated most of the emotions that boiled inside me. I placed them all in their own compartments; divided, I would conquer them.

Anger first. Anger at the injustice of being found guilty without having the chance to defend myself. My guilt had been accepted because it was easiest for everyone. Anger at the way Hamilton had let them do it. Surely, he could have done something to protect me? Hamilton of all people should have been able to come up with a way out of this mess. He had put the firm before me. I thought I meant more to him than that. But, as I thought about it, I supposed Hamilton had in his usual fashion weighed the pros and cons of fighting it out to the bitter end and had alighted on this as the better alternative. And it was pointless just screaming "It's not fair."

Then there was sorrow. I was beginning to fit into De Jong. I was learning how to trade and enjoying it. And for all that Hamilton had let me down, I had learned a lot from him. There was a lot more to learn; it was difficult to see how anyone else could be such a good teacher. But at least my time at De Jong had convinced me that I wanted to trade and shown me I had the potential. I would just have to start again with someone else.

What if I couldn't get another job? A rush of panic flew to my head at this thought. What if I would never trade again? I didn't think I could face that possibility. And I needed to get a well-paid job too if I was going to raise the money to buy my mother's cottage. It would be impossible to raise twenty-five thousand pounds without a job. God knows what she would do if Lord Mablethorpe threw her out. I could already see the look of contempt on Linda's face when she found out I had failed to prevent it.

But the panic soon subsided. People lost their jobs all the time. If they were any good, they soon got new ones.

I am a stubborn individual. I was buggered if I was going to be put off trading by what was no more than a piece of awful luck. You make your own luck. Sure, sometimes it runs against you, but if you keep plugging away, eventually events will run your way. The key was not to give up; every time something went wrong, just try harder.

So, I pulled out a pad of paper and sketched out a plan of campaign for how I would get another job. Within half an hour I had outlined a series of steps that I was fairly confident would get me something. To work.

I called two recruitment consultants I knew, and arranged appointments. I spent a couple of hours perfecting my CV. So far so good. The headhunters were pleased to have a new client, and I thought my CV didn't look at all bad.

The problems started the next morning. I had decided that a good place to begin would be the salesmen I spoke to every day. They would probably know who was hiring, and they should have a reasonable idea of my abilities. After careful consideration, I called David Barratt first. He had been around a long time and knew a lot of people. He should have some ideas.

So I dialed Harrison Brothers. It wasn't David who answered the phone but one of his colleagues. He said David was busy but would get back. I left my number and waited. Two hours later and still no phone call. I tried again.

This time David picked up the phone.

"Hello, David, it's Paul," I began.

There was a short pause before David responded. "Oh, hello, Paul. Where are you ringing from?"

"From home. You've heard then?"

"Yes I have." A pause. "Have you found anything yet?"

"Well, not yet. In fact I am just starting. That's why I am calling. Do you happen to know if there is anything interesting around at the moment?"

"Not much, I am afraid. The job market is quite quiet now," David said. "Look, I have got to go. A customer on the other line."

"Before you go . . ." I said quickly.

"Yes?"

"I wonder if you could spend half an hour to chat about what I might do. You know the market much better than I do. . . . "

"I'm afraid I'm quite busy at the moment."

"Whenever you like," I said, hearing the desperation creep into my voice. "Breakfast, after work, I can come round to your place."

"Paul, I don't think I can help you." The voice coming over the phone lines was polite but firm. Quite firm.

"Okay," I said dully, "I'll let you go," and hung up.

I couldn't make sense of it. David was always helpful. For him to refuse to come to my assistance now was significant. I thought for a moment I had totally misjudged him. Perhaps he was a completely different person with clients than with ex-clients. But that didn't really seem to be like David.

With some trepidation I called another salesman. Same result. Polite unhelpfulness. The third was even worse. I overheard the salesman say, "Tell him I'm not here. And if he calls again tell him I am off the desk."

I sat staring at my phone. This did not look good. Who else could I call? Cash was out of the question. With a pang I thought of Cathy. But I couldn't bear to receive the same brush-off from her as I had from the others.

Claire! She would give me some time, surely.

I called her. As soon as she heard my voice, she broke into a whisper. "Paul. Is it true what they are saying?"

"I don't know. What are they saying?"

"That you were caught insider trading?"

At last! Someone who was direct enough to say what they were thinking.

"No, it is not true. Or at least, I wasn't actually insider trading. But it is true the TSA thinks I was. That is why I resigned."

"Resigned? Everyone is saying you got the sack!"

"Forced to resign, then." I almost left it at that. A further denial seemed wasted breath. It seemed as though everyone accepted my guilt. In the end I quietly said, "I didn't do anything wrong."

"I know," said Claire.

A small burst of relief and gratitude came over me. "You know? How can you know?"

Claire laughed. "You, you are the last person in the world to get involved in insider trading. You are the straightest person I know. Much too serious. Much too boring."

"I don't deny it," I said, my spirits lifting slightly.

Claire's tone slipped to a conspiratorial whisper. "Tell me what happened."

I told her all about my purchase of Gypsum shares and why I had done it. When I came to Cash's involvement, she interrupted me. "That worm! I should have known he would have something to do with this. My God! It is incredible he is allowed to keep trading."

She had a point there. It had sounded as though Cash were under some sort of investigation. Perhaps his days at Bloomfield Weiss were numbered too. That was some consolation. However, I thought that if anyone could wriggle out of trouble somehow, it would be Cash.

I told her about the reaction of David Barratt and the others to my requests for help. "Hmm, I am not surprised," she replied. "Everyone is talking about it. You have achieved notoriety. Even people who don't know you are chattering. I can assure you there is no chance of anyone giving you a job in a hurry."

I reeled under the blow. That was blunt even for her, and she realized it. "Oh, I'm sorry Paul, I didn't mean that," she said quickly. "They will forget in a month or two. You will find something." I didn't say anything. "Paul? Paul?"

I mumbled good-bye and put the phone down.

There it was. Staring me in the face. I was not going to get another job in the bond market. Not now. Probably not ever. Simple. Finite.

It was a truth that I had known since the evasive phone call with David Barratt, but one that I had forced to the back of my mind. I had believed that willpower alone would get me another job. But willpower could not make people forget that I was that most notorious of financial criminals, an insider trader.

It struck me as ironic that such a simple misdemeanor as the one I was supposed to have committed should be treated with such contempt by people who routinely lied and cheated against their customers, their employers, even their friends. But insider trading was different. It was contagious. The great plague of it which had ended up claiming the mastermind of the junk-bond market, Michael Milken, had crept through Wall Street, slowly passing from investment banker to investment banker until almost every house in New York was diseased in some way. The remedy was easy. At the first outbreak, any diseased member should be isolated and cut off. That was what had happened to me.

The consequences were difficult to take. To trade was quite simply all I wanted to do. To trade well was my ambition. Until a week ago it was something that looked clearly within my grasp, given a couple of years of effort. No chance now.

I suppose some people drift through life happily enough without any goal. Not me. When I focus on an objective, I strive for it with all my heart. Subsume my life to it. Sure, when I finally accepted I was not going to be the fastest eight-hundred-meters runner in the world it had been hard, but I couldn't deny to myself that I had achieved a lot to get close. To be denied even a clear shot at trading was more than I could take.

The next two weeks were the worst of my adult life. I still sent off letters and even went to a couple of interviews, but my heart wasn't in it. I knew it was a lost cause.

Depression quickly set in. A deep black depression that I had never experienced before. I was dispirited down to the bottom of my soul. It became difficult to do anything. After a day or so, I gave up running, always telling myself that one more day's rest wouldn't hurt. I tried to read novels, but couldn't concentrate. I spent a long time in bed, just staring. I went for long aimless walks round London. But the din of traffic, the exhaust fumes, and the heat left me tired and jaded. The collapse of will, for one who has drawn sustenance from it for so long, is debilitating indeed.

I was also lonely. It never usually bothered me to be by myself, but now I craved someone to talk to. Someone who could help put everything into perspective. But who was there? I could hardly talk to anyone from work. I did not have the courage to admit what had happened to me to the odd scattering of friends and acquaintances I had picked up over the years. I should have done, but I didn't. And the last person on whom I could lay the burden of my troubles was my mother. I was well aware that I would soon have to instruct solicitors about buying her cottage. How would I get finance for it? Indeed, with trading now closed to me, it would be impossible for me to get a job that paid enough.

I ignored that problem, or tried to. But the longer I left it, the more it gnawed away at me. I was responsible for leaving my mother without a home; I was too feeble to do anything about it.

In my moments of loneliness, thoughts of Cathy frequently emerged. When I wished to myself that there was someone I could talk to, that someone always became her. I thought of the easy understanding we had developed in America, her sympathy and interest in my life. I needed someone to be interested in it now.

And then her rejection came back to taunt me. Her accusations that I was ruining her career, my crass pleas to her to come out to dinner with me. She would no doubt have heard about what I had done—correction, was supposed to have done. She would be thanking God that she avoided getting involved with me and kicking herself for even considering it. A relationship with an insider trader would be no help at all for her progress up the greasy pole.

IT WAS THURSDAY AFTERNOON. I was watching track-and-field from Oslo on television. It was profoundly depressing, but somehow I couldn't bring myself to turn the set off. As I saw the eight hundred meters being won by a Spaniard whom I had beaten on several occasions, I asked myself yet again why I had given up. I had been so good! Why the hell had I bothered with trading? And it was too late to go back to running now. I would never be able to recapture my old form. It was all gone. There was nothing left for me to do but sit here and regret it.

I gazed round my small flat. My bronze Olympic medal mocked me from the mantel. God, the place was a mess! It was so small, it didn't take much to make it untidy. There was a big pile of dirty laundry in the corner behind the door. I really ought to take it to the launderette, I thought. No, it could wait another day. I hadn't quite run out of clean clothes.

The phone rang. It was probably one of the recruitment agencies. I had recently told them to give up searching for trading jobs and asked them to look for a vacancy for a credit analyst instead. They had muttered about how difficult the job market was these days. I had evidently worked my way swiftly down on their list of likely placements from near the top to near the bottom. I let the phone ring ten times before pulling myself out of my chair to go and get it.

"Hello?"

"Hello, is that Paul?" Cathy's voice came clearly down the line.

My heart started beating fast. A brief surge of elation was quickly tugged down by my surly mood. I had played over that rejection a hundred times in my mind in the past two weeks; I didn't have the strength for another one.

"Paul, is that you?"

I cleared my throat. "Yes. Yes, it is. How are you, Cathy?" I could hear my own voice cold and formal. I didn't mean it to come out like that, but it did all the same.

"I'm very sorry to hear what happened. It must have been awful for you."

"Yes, it was a bit."

"There were all sorts of silly rumors flying around about why you left."

What was she trying to do? Gloat over the gory details? Pick up some good gossip? I wasn't going to help her. "Yes, I'm sure there were."

"Look, I was thinking," she began nervously, "it's a long time since we saw each other, and it might be nice to catch up." Catch up on what, I thought cynically. "I wondered if you were doing anything on Sunday afternoon?"

My pulse quickened again. "No, no I'm not."

"Well, I wondered if you would like to come for a walk in the country somewhere. I know a lovely place in the Chilterns, it's only an hour away. That is if you'd like to." Cathy's voice trailed off at the end. She must have plucked up some courage to call me, and I was not being exactly helpful.

"Yes, I'd like that very much," I said, trying to put some enthusiasm into my voice and, to my surprise, succeeding.

"Good. Why don't you pick me up from my place at two?" She gave me an address in Hampstead.

It would be an exaggeration to say that my depression

rolled away, but the sun was definitely shining through the clouds. I managed a passable interview with a Japanese bank the next day, and spent much of Saturday methodically going through the Financial Times, looking for help wanted ads and getting up to date on the current financial news. I was going to have to get some sort of job soon, I reasoned, and so I may as well get as good a one as I could. That was a great step forward from the beginning of the week.

"Tell me what happened, Paul."

I had known she would ask this. We were walking down the side of a grassy hill toward a small stream. A group of black-and-white Friesian cows stared at us from the other side of the field, debating whether they had the energy to amble over to get a closer look. In the end they decided it was too far, and bent down for more grass. It had rained the day before, so the air was fresh. In the sunshine it felt more like spring than September.

It was a question I had wanted to avoid. I knew I was innocent; the rest of the world held me guilty. There was nothing I could do to change their minds, so why deny it? There seemed to be more dignity in keeping silent than in professing innocence to all and sundry. And Cathy was the last person in the world to whom I wanted to appear a whining complainer.

I had been apprehensive on the way to Cathy's Hampstead flat. I had run through all the points of potential conflict in my mind. Our argument about her career, Cash, my failure to get another job, and this. I was prepared for a difficult afternoon picking through the minefield.

But it hadn't been like that at all. Cathy had been obviously pleased to see me. We had chatted comfortably on the way up to the Chilterns. We had parked near an old Saxon church, and Cathy had led the way. We had strolled through a medley of typical English settings, a village, an old beech wood, a farmyard, and then this small green valley leading down to a stream.

So when she asked, I told her. She listened carefully, accepting everything, so I told her more. Not just about how I had got into the mess, but also about how I had felt over the last couple of weeks. It was easy. The words tumbled out to be met with sympathy and concern. As I talked I relaxed. I realized I was no longer striding through the countryside with Cathy struggling to keep up with me; we were now slowly meandering our way along the side of the stream. My words also put the last two weeks into perspective. I saw my indulgent self-pity for what it was.

Eventually, the torrent abated. "I'm sorry for talking so much," I said. "You are very patient."

"No, that's okay," she said. "It sounds as if you have had a horrible time." She climbed down the bank to the stream. "Why don't we stop here a bit? We must have walked four miles. I could do with a paddle."

She took off her shoes, rolled up her jeans, and stepped into the fast-running stream. She let out a yell as the cold water rushed around her ankles. I lay down on the bank and let the sun beat down on my face. Through half-closed eyes I watched her pick her way around the wet stones. She was wearing a white shirt and a pair of old jeans. Her hair blew into her tanned face as she jumped from stone to stone. She had a carefree, tousled scruffiness I had not seen before. And I liked it. I liked it very much. I smiled and closed my eyes.

I was pleasantly dozing on the cool grass of the bank, when I felt a gentle tickle under my nose. I sneezed, spluttered, and opened my eyes. Cathy was lying next to me poking a long blade of grass under my nose. I made a half-hearted attempt to grab it but she pulled it away, giggling. Her face was only six inches away from mine. Her big brown eyes were shining as she looked down at me. The smile drifted from her lips. I reached up and pulled her down to me. We kissed tentatively at first, and then fell into a deep embrace. Cathy pulled back, giggled slightly, pushed the hair away from her face, and kissed me again, hungrily this time. Just then I heard a shout not fifty yards away, "Benson, come here! Come here, you bloody dog!"

We broke apart, laughing. Cathy got to her feet. "Come on, we've still got three miles to go before we get back to the car."

"Okay." I sighed and stood up.

We made our way farther down the stream in silence. As we turned up the other side of the valley Cathy said, "It was sad about Debbie."

Another difficult subject, but once again I found myself able to talk about it. "Yes, it was."

"I didn't know her that well," Cathy went on. "Did you?" She looked at me inquiringly.

I understood her question and smiled. "No, not in that way. But we got on very well. I liked her."

We walked on a few yards farther.

"What happened to her?" Cathy asked.

"What do you mean?"

"Well, they said she committed suicide, but that can't be right. And an accident seems unlikely."

"Hmm," I said.

"You know what happened, don't you?" Cathy said.

I nodded.

"Will you tell me?"

I took a deep breath. Suddenly I wanted to tell her everything. Wanted to tell her very badly.

"Okay." We were walking up a steep bit now, and I waited until we had reached the brow of the hill before stopping. I looked down on the small stream gurgling through the little valley. A quiet, innocent corner of England.

"She was murdered."

"I guessed as much," said Cathy quietly. "Do you know who did it?"

"No. At first I thought that it was Joe Finlay, but he denied it. And I believe him."

"Oh. Well, do you know why she was murdered?"

"I think so." I told her all about how I had discovered that the Honshu Bank guarantee for Tremont Capital did not exist; about how I suspected Debbie had discovered this before me. I told her about my investigations in New York, about my encounter with Joe in Central Park, about Phoenix Prosperity Savings and Loan, and about its investment in the Tahiti.

Cathy listened, eyes wide, taking it all in. "How do all these companies link together?"

"Tremont Capital issued forty million dollars of bonds with a fake guarantee from the Honshu Bank. Cash then sold twenty million to De Jong; because of the fake guarantee, Hamilton didn't get the documentation checked. He then sold the other twenty to Harzweiger Bank in Switzerland. Herr Dietweiler was no doubt bribed in some way to buy it on their behalf. It looks as though Cash was pretty heavily involved. He and Waigel go back a long way.

"The forty million raised by the private placement was used to buy the majority of the savings and loan, Phoenix Prosperity, or 'Uncle Sam's Money Machine.' With the extra capital, Phoenix Prosperity was able to borrow large amounts of money with a government guarantee. It, in turn, intended to invest this money in a number of high-risk, high-return ventures. One of the first of these was a twenty percent stake in Irwin Piper's Tahiti Hotel.

"So far so good. Then things started to go wrong. First, Greg Shoffman became suspicious. He called the Honshu Bank and discovered that the guarantee was bogus. I don't know what else he may have discovered or how they knew he was on to them. But he was murdered, probably by Waigel, and his body was dumped near Waigel's house. Then Debbie Chater became suspicious. And she was murdered."

"So who do you think is behind all this?" Cathy asked.

"I don't know. Whoever are the shareholders of

Tremont Capital. I am sure Waigel must be one of them. And . . ."

"And what?"

"Well, I wouldn't be at all surprised if Cash was in on it too."

"And anybody else?"

"Maybe. I just don't know."

"And who killed Debbie?"

"That is a difficult question. We know it wasn't Waigel, because his diary shows he was in New York at the time of Debbie's death. As I said, Joe denied it completely, and I am inclined to believe him. It could have been Cash, or it could have been someone else entirely."

"Like Irwin Piper?"

"No, I don't think it was him. I confronted him in Las Vegas, and he seemed genuinely surprised that Debbie had been murdered."

"So who was it?"

I turned to look at Cathy. "It must be Cash. He must have known what he was selling to Hamilton. He's also the one with the relationship with Phoenix Prosperity Savings and Loan. And he and Waigel are old friends."

She frowned. There was silence as we both mulled over everything I had said. We trudged on. "I know this may sound odd to you," Cathy said "but I don't think Cash would be a part of something like this. He's sleazy, and he looks after number one. But he does have his own set of moral principles that he wouldn't breach."

"What do you mean?" I said. "He is one of the slimiest people I have ever met!"

"He may be most of the time," Cathy said. "But I have worked closely with him for a year now, and I don't think he is all bad. I just don't think he would have anything to do with anyone being killed."

"What about that bloody Gypsum of America business. That was hardly straight, was it?"

"Oh, didn't I tell you? The investigation cleared Cash of all involvement. It was Joe who was trading on inside information. The Gypsum bonds were on his book, and he bought a bucketload of shares through some nominees."

"Really? That does surprise me. I was sure Cash had known something about the takeover." I digested this new piece of information, and tried to put it together with what else I knew. I still couldn't quite believe in Cash as the bond salesman with principles.

"Apparently they are still investigating who else was involved," Cathy said.

"Meaning me?"

"I haven't heard. I suppose so," said Cathy. "We did have a policeman come round on Friday night asking questions about you."

"A policeman? Not the TSA? Are you sure?" I thought the deal that Hamilton had come to was that the TSA would not pursue their investigation against me as long as De Jong agreed to fire me.

"Yes, I'm sure. His name was Powell. Inspector Powell. He asked a lot of questions about you and Debbie."

Now that did seem strange. I had thought Inspector Powell had closed his investigation into Debbie's death. Why was he asking questions about me? Odd.

We walked on. The village where I had parked my car was just in sight now, watched over by the squat church a hundred yards or so away from the rest of the village, on a slight mound. The site of a pre-Christian place of worship, I thought vaguely.

"So what are you going to do about it?" Cathy asked.

"About what?"

"About Debbie's death. About Tremont Capital. About Phoenix Prosperity."

"Nothing."

"Nothing?"

"Why should I? There is not a lot of point, is there?" I said sullenly.

"Bullshit," she said. I looked at her. "Bullshit," she said again.

"What do you mean?"

"It's about time you pulled yourself together, Paul. Okay, you've had a tough break. But someone, or some people, have stolen forty million dollars and killed two people in the process. If you do nothing they will get away with it. You can't just let that happen, can you?"

She was angry. Her eyes were burning and her cheeks had reddened. But I got the feeling she was angry with me rather than against me. I shrugged my shoulders. "You are absolutely right."

She smiled and took my arm. "Good. I'll help you. What shall we do first?"

"Well, I suppose I should talk to Hamilton, but I don't see how I can do that with this Gypsum business hanging over me."

"I see what you mean," said Cathy. Then a thought struck her. "If Cash has been cleared, shouldn't you be? I mean, if he didn't have inside information, how could he have passed it to you?"

I looked at her. She was absolutely right. Hope began to flow through my veins.

"Let me talk to Cash about what happened to you. I am sure he will be able to help."

"I don't think that's a good idea," I said.

"Look, I am quite certain he had nothing to do with killing anyone, let alone Debbie Chater. Let me talk to him."

"Okay," I said. "But don't mention the Tremont business."

"I won't."

The village was much closer now. I spied a pub. "Enough of all this. I'm thirsty. Let's have a drink."

We sat outside the sixteenth-century inn and dawdled over a couple of drinks as the sun set over the wooded hills. It was a magical evening, and neither of us wanted to end it. So, because the pub had a dining room, we stayed for a supper of home-made steak-and-kidney pie.

"Have you seen anything of Rob since we got back from America?" I asked.

"Yes, I have," said Cathy unenthusiastically.

"What's the matter? Has he been bothering you?"

"Yes, I'd say he has," Cathy said, looking down at her plate.

I waited for her to say more. She didn't. I was interested. More than that, I was worried. I could not easily forget the venom of Rob's words in Las Vegas. "What has he done?"

"Well, I have bumped into him once or twice at various functions. And recently, he has taken to hanging around Bloomfield Weiss's building and following me on my way home. He always comes up to talk to me, and he is always rude."

"What does he say?"

"Oh, he says I am shallow and fickle. He says I betrayed him. He calls me a tease. And he says some pretty unpleasant things about you."

I sighed. "I'm not altogether surprised."

"He told me that you had something going together with Debbie." Cathy looked up at me, her eyes questioning.

"Well, that's wrong. I told you that. We just worked together and became good friends."

"Rob said he saw both of you having a romantic dinner on a boat, just before she died." Cathy saw the shocked look on my face. She smiled. "Don't worry, I believe you. Anyway, it's none of my business who your girlfriends are."

I waved my hand. "It's not that. I was just thinking how Rob could have seen us on the boat. We left him in the office that night. He must have followed us."

"Why would he do that?"

"I'm afraid you are not the first woman Rob has behaved like this with. He once went out with Debbie. She got rid of him, but Debbie's flatmate said Rob had been bothering her recently. He had asked her to marry him and been turned down."

"Wait a second! If Rob saw you together just before Debbie died, then he might have seen who did it," Cathy said. Then she saw my face. "You don't think it was him, surely?"

I sighed. "It could be, I'm afraid. You've seen what he is like when he is angry. And he doesn't give up. I must admit, when he said he was going to kill both of us, I almost took him seriously."

Cathy shuddered. She looked scared. We ate on in silence. Finally, I broke it. "Well, there is nothing we can do about it now. Let me get another bottle of wine, and let's change the subject."

So we did. We talked on through the evening, our conversation gliding happily from subject to subject. We listened and laughed at each other's inconsequential stories. Eventually, the publican hovered over us, and looking around, we saw that the pub had emptied. Reluctantly, we got up from the table to leave. My eyes caught a sign. "It says they do bed and breakfast here." Cathy looked at me and grinned. "Does it?"

They had a vacant room with a warped ceiling, cracked oak beams, and a small crooked window out of which we could see the silhouette of church and mound against the full moon. We didn't turn on the light, but undressed in the moonlight slowly and carefully. Naked, Cathy stepped over to me and nestled her head in my chest. I gently pulled her close to me. Where our bodies met, the first touch of skin against skin sent a shiver through both of us. We savored the intimacy of that embrace, gradually getting accustomed to each other's body. My fingers drifted slowly down her spine and round the smooth firm curve of her buttocks.

She looked up at me, her dark eyes bigger than ever in the moonlight. "Come to bed," she whispered.

I looked out of my window sipping a well-earned cup of tea as the early-evening sun glinted on the rush-hour traffic creeping along the road beneath my flat. I had had a good day.

It had been a busy day, a day when my life had begun to slip back into some sort of order. Cathy and I got up at five thirty so that I could drive her back to London in time for her to get changed and get to work. I went for my first run in two weeks, just a gentle jog to get the circulation going. I rang headhunters and pestered them. I applied to a few of the firms that I had seen advertising over the previous week, and for the first time I called a few old contacts in banking who I thought might be able to help. If only I could clear my name with the TSA, there was a future for me.

My thoughts were interrupted by the buzzer of the intercom. I looked down and saw a police car parked right outside my building.

I pressed the intercom button. "Yes?"

"Police. Can we come up?" What did they want? I remembered what Cathy had said about Powell asking questions about me.

"Certainly." I pressed the button to let them in downstairs, and opened my own door. Two uniformed policemen clumped up the stairs, and asked me to accompany them to the station.

I thought for a moment, and didn't see the harm in it. Besides, I was curious to find out what Powell had discovered.

I joined them in their car, and we drove off to a police station somewhere near Covent Garden. I tried to make small talk, but without much effect. They all but ignored me. This did not look good.

They led me into the police station, and into an interrogation room furnished only with a table, four chairs, and a file cabinet. I sat on one of the chairs, declined a cup of tea, and spent half an hour reading and rereading the brightly colored posters that urged all the villains who sat where I was sitting to lock their cars and look after their handbags.

I felt guilty sitting there. I didn't know what of yet, but I definitely felt guilty.

Finally, the door opened and Powell came in, followed by Jones. Powell was on his home territory and clearly felt much more comfortable now than he had when I had met him in De Jong's polished conference room. He sat down on a chair opposite me. Jones pulled out one of the other chairs, placed it by a wall, and sat on it, notebook in hand.

Powell leaned forward, and stared at me hard for what seemed like a full minute. I already felt uncomfortable. This didn't make it any easier. But I managed to sit motionless, legs crossed, hands resting on my lap.

"Have you got anything to tell me, Murray?" he asked, his voice quick and powerful.

"About what," attempting to make it sound casual. But it was ridiculous to pretend that it was usual for me to be hauled into a police station on a Monday night. I was nervous, and Powell knew it.

"About the murder of Debbie Chater."

"Murder? I thought you said it was an accident or a suicide."

Powell didn't like to be reminded of his earlier views. "We know now it was murder."

"That's just what I told you all along," I said.

Powell leaned even closer to me. "Don't get clever with me, sonny. I know it's murder and you know it's murder. And we both know who did it, don't we?"

Oh, my God, I thought, he thinks it's me. I just looked at him blankly.

"Now take me through that evening again," said Powell.

I went through it in as much detail as I could, but Powell wanted more. I became uncomfortable when he asked me about my trip back on the tube from Temple station. All I could remember were my thoughts about Debbie; I remembered those vividly. But I couldn't remember what time I had got on the tube, or when I had got off at Gloucester Road, or indeed very much else about the later part of the evening.

Powell sensed my discomfort. When I had finished he said one word: "Bollocks."

I looked at him blankly.

He stood up, and began pacing round the small room. "Let me tell you what I know. The victim and you left the boat together. Some drunks bumped into you. You both set off toward the Embankment station. It was dark, raining hard, and visibility was poor. When you thought no one was watching, you picked up the victim and threw her into the river."

I swallowed. Why the hell did I feel so guilty? This was ridiculous. I should be outraged. But all I could manage was a simple no.

Powell moved up to me in two swift paces. He didn't touch me but put his face three inches away from mine. I could smell onions on his breath, see his shiny acne-marked skin. "I know that's what happened, Murray, because I have a witness who saw it all."

A witness? That was crap. Suddenly, I pulled myself together. My brain cleared.

"Who was the witness?"

"I can't say."

"Why not?"

"Look, Murray, it doesn't matter who it is, I have a sworn statement."

"From someone who knows me?"

"I said I wouldn't tell you."

Rob! It had to be. Cathy had mentioned that he had seen me and Debbie go to the boat together that evening. What the hell had he told the police?

"So, do we get a statement? We know you did it." Powell was pacing again. "It would be better for all of us if you told the truth, now. There is no point in pretending that what happened didn't. As I said, we have a witness. We have proof."

I was damned if I was going to let Powell intimidate me any more. I nodded to Jones, who had been taking notes furiously. "Get him to type up what I have said already and I will sign it. Until then I will not say any more without a solicitor present."

I remained silent for the next five minutes as Powell tried various approaches to goad me into saying something. Finally he gave up. "You're a stubborn bastard, Murray. But don't worry. I'll be seeing you again shortly."

Powell and Jones left me alone in the interview room while I waited for my statement to be typed. I checked it carefully, signed it, and left the police station. My knees felt weak as I spilled out into the street. I was in a very dangerous position. I knew Powell had been trying to scare me into saying something I shouldn't. I assumed he must not have gathered enough evidence yet to arrest me, but there was no doubt I was in trouble. Powell wouldn't have gone to the effort of resurrecting the case if he hadn't been convinced that he had good cause.

Powell himself worried me. I had seen that he was a man who made judgments quickly. He was tough and impatient, and I had no comfort that he would be scrupulous in the way he gathered evidence. He knew I was guilty and he was going to nail me one way or another.

And I was sure Powell usually got his way.

Murder! Insider dealing had seemed a bad enough crime to be accused of, but it was nothing compared with murder. And of Debbie as well, of all the injustices.

As soon as I got home, I called Denny. Luckily, he was working late. His advice was clear. Treat Powell's suspicions seriously. However, it was unlikely that Powell had enough evidence to charge me yet. If Powell wanted to talk to me again, I should refuse unless Denny was present. Until then all I could do was wait and see what happened.

THE BAR WAS COOL, dark, and almost empty. It was still quite early. I nursed my pint of Davy's Old Wallop, while I waited for Cash and Cathy to arrive.

I heard Cash before I saw him. His voice echoed round the empty cellar as he came down the stairs from the street above. "Jesus, Cathy, it's like a morgue down here."

I had selected somewhere quiet to meet. Perhaps that was a mistake. Cash's voice would carry much farther in an empty bar than a full one. I looked round. Three sets of canoodling couples who were also looking for quiet and darkness, and a group of men in their early twenties, swiftly getting drunk. It should be safe.

I was apprehensive about meeting Cash; he did not seem at all apprehensive about meeting me. He bustled into the bar and headed straight for me, hand outstretched, and a big smile on his face. "Paul! Good to see you. How have you been?" He pulled up a chair. Cathy followed him a couple of steps behind. She gave me a discreet but very sweet smile as she joined us at the table. "Boy, that was really rough what happened to you. Cathy told me all about it. I can't believe they did that to you."

I found myself warming to him. His concern did seem genuine and it was nice to hear somebody believe me. Watch out, I warned myself, trusting Cash is a dangerous business.

"Hello, Cash," I said coldly, briefly shaking his hand. He looked hurt at my coolness. I relented. "Can I get you a drink?" I said, trying to be polite, if not exactly friendly.

"Sure, I'll have whatever it is you've got there," he said, pointing to my tankard of Davy's. It took me only a minute to get it, together with a Perrier for Cathy.

There was a distinctly awkward atmosphere at the table as I returned. I didn't say anything as I set the drinks down.

Cash took a sip, grimaced, and said, "Interesting." He was uncomfortable with the silence, as was Cathy. I found I didn't really want to talk to Cash and regretted agreeing to the meeting. "You haven't missed that much these last two weeks," Cash said to break the silence. He chattered on for five minutes about the market, with me giving him minimal help.

As this one-way conversation petered to a halt, Cathy interrupted. "I got you two together, because I think you have a lot to say to each other. So why don't you start, Paul," she said firmly. "Tell Cash about the TSA's investigation."

I hesitated a moment, and then I told him. Cash listened closely all the way through. At the end he said, "It sure seems flimsy to me. It doesn't look like they have any direct proof."

"What happened when you were interviewed by the TSA?" I asked.

"That whole thing scared the life out of me," he said. "First you tell me that Bowen's on to you. Then I get grilled by Berryman. And then you get the sack for insider trading."

Cash took a gulp of his beer. "That really worried me. I mean, I knew I hadn't done anything wrong, but firms like Bloomfield Weiss are happy to look for fall guys if there is any dirt flying around.

"Then suddenly last week, I got called into a meeting with the head of the London office. He told me that evidence had been found that Joe Finlay had been buying large amounts of Gypsum of America stock for his personal account based on inside information. He had also built up a sizable position in the bonds for Bloomfield Weiss, but the authorities were now convinced that no one else in the firm was involved. I can't tell you how relieved I was."

Cathy listened with interest to this, her brows knitted in concentration. "What I can't understand," she said, "is why Paul isn't in the clear. If the TSA thinks Cash had nothing to do with it, then unless it thinks that Joe and Paul were in regular contact it should prove that there was no channel for Paul to get the information."

"You're right," I said.

Cash nodded. "She is right. You should see someone about it. Either De Jong or the TSA. I'll back you up."

I smiled. "Thanks, Cash." And I was thankful. Having escaped unharmed, there was probably nothing Cash would rather do less than reopen the whole question. It was good of him to offer to do so. "I'll phone the TSA in the morning."

I sipped my beer. "I wonder if Joe knew Debbie was on to him?"

"What do you mean?" said Cash.

"Well, Debbie tipped Bowen at Bloomfield Weiss off that something funny was going on. If Joe found out about it he would have been quite upset."

"You mean he might have killed her?"

I raised my eyebrows. "Maybe."

"Jesus, maybe he did," Cash said. "But I am not so sure that Joe was acting completely alone in all of this."

"Why is that?" I asked.

"Well, he had to get the information from somewhere. I mean, a German company taking over an American target. How would a bond trader in London hear about that?"

"Careless talk?"

"Maybe. Maybe not."

I thought for a second. "What about Irwin Piper? He specializes in just that sort of thing, doesn't he? Did Joe know him?"

"I was just thinking along those lines," said Cash. "Yes, he did. I'm not sure how they met, but somehow or other they had gotten to know each other pretty well."

I rubbed my chin and thought about it some more. "It is possible. But how can we find out?"

"We might be able to work out something from his trading tickets!" said Cathy. "They should still be around somewhere. I'll have a look tomorrow."

"It's worth a try," I said.

"Well, I am glad we are getting somewhere," said Cathy. "Now there is something else we wanted to talk to you about, Cash."

I looked sharply at Cathy. I was prepared to believe Cash had nothing to do with the Gypsum insider trading, but that did not mean I trusted him on everything else.

"Paul, I think we should tell him," she said. "Trust me."

I hesitated. I was tempted to accept Cathy's plea to trust her. I found it difficult myself to believe that Cash was the brains behind the Tremont operation. What the hell, I thought. Why not confront him with it? I had been dodging around for weeks trying to get answers from people without alerting them. I was getting impatient. I wanted to know. Now.

"Okay," I nodded my head. "Let me get you another drink, Cash, you'll need it with what I am about to tell you."

So I bought Cash another drink, and told him more or less everything that happened from Debbie's death on. It was the first time I had ever seen Cash at a loss for words. His jaw literally dropped as I went through my story. When I finished it, I looked him straight in the eye. "Well?" I said.

It took a while for Cash to collect his thoughts. "Christ!" he said. Then "Jesus!"

"Do you mind if I ask you a couple of questions?" I asked.

"No, sure, go ahead," said Cash absently, his mind still going over the implications of what I had just told him.

"Did you know that the Honshu Bank guarantee on the Tremont Capital bonds never existed?"

"No, I didn't," he said. Then his eyes flared up with anger. "You think I'm involved with this, don't you?"

Cash's response seemed genuine enough, but his ability to bend the truth was legendary. I didn't know whether he was lying now or not. "The thought had crossed my mind," I said.

In a moment the anger was gone. "Yeah, I suppose it would," he said. He paused. "Look, you've had a rough time, and I like you." He saw my eyebrows move up at this but held up his hand, "No, honestly I do. Some of my customers are jerks and some of them are smart, and I rate you as one of the smartest. I'm not schmoozing you; after all, you are hardly my top client right now, are you?" I had to agree with that last statement.

"Anyway, I'd like to help you in any way I can. I wasn't involved in any of this. I know you don't believe me, but that doesn't matter for now. Between the two of us we ought to be able to figure out who is really behind all this. Until we do that, you can keep me on your list of prime suspects if you like."

I could feel myself wanting to believe Cash. It was difficult not to. His offer certainly seemed worth a try at least.

"Okay," I said. "Let's start with the launch of the Tremont Capital bond."

Cash smiled. "Good. Let me think. It was Waigel's deal through and through. He had the relationship with the issuer, and he was the only one working on it in New York. He gave me a call one day, described the deal, and asked me whether I could place it. I remember he said it had to be done quickly."

"How did you decide who to approach?"

"Come to think of it, Waigel suggested I should try the Harzweiger Bank. De Jong seemed a natural as well. This sort of thing is right up Hamilton's alley. A little complicated, a little obscure, a nice yield if you are smart enough to get it." I nodded, it was the kind of bond Hamilton would like to buy. "In fact, the week before, Hamilton had asked me to look about for high-yielding triple A deals for him. In the end, the deal was easy. All placed in a morning. No need for anyone else on the sales desk to get involved. Sweet deal."

"And very convenient for Waigel. The fewer clients and salesmen involved, the less chance of discovery."

Cash sighed. "I guess you are right."

"Now, what about Phoenix Prosperity? Did you know that it was owned by Tremont Capital?"

"No. I had no idea who owned it. But something very strange was going on there. Come to think of it, it all started quite soon after we placed Tremont Capital."

Cash took a sip of his beer. "I had been doing great business with Jack Salmon. He would buy and sell bonds all day, taking a profit whenever he made an eighth of a point and sitting on big losses whenever he got it wrong. A salesman's dream. Big-buck commissions.

"Then, suddenly, things changed. He was still active so I was happy, but he started to make money. He would put on these large, very risky trades. You know, junk bonds, derivatives, CMO strips, reverse floaters, all kinds of complicated stuff. Some went badly wrong, but he was certainly making more than he was losing."

"It seems a bit odd that Jack Salmon made money out of those things," I said.

"It certainly does," said Cash. "But it wasn't him. He never made any major decisions himself. Of course, he pretended it was him deciding what to do, and I went along with it, but I always made sure he had time to put the phone down and consult with whomever he needed to before coming back to buy my bonds."

"That makes sense," I said. I told Cash about how I had seen Jack consult someone before buying the Fairways.

We were silent for a bit.

"I knew Dick was a bastard, but I didn't know he was that much of a bastard," Cash said, mostly to himself.

"You knew him when you were a kid?"

Cash sighed. "Yeah, I did. We weren't real close. I guess I was a bit more popular than Ricky. He didn't call himself Dick until much later. He looked like a nerd, and acted a bit like one. He used to get a hard time from the other kids until . . ." Cash tailed off.

"Until?" I said.

"Until he started selling drugs. He teamed up with two big mean apes and supplied all the drugs to the kids in our neighborhood. Oh, Ricky never sold the stuff personally. He was too smart for that. But he was behind it all.

"I remember there was another kid who tried to muscle in to Ricky's territory. He ended up with a knife in his kidneys. Everyone knew it was one of Ricky's guys. I guess Ricky must have been behind it."

"But you are still a friend of his."

"Oh, yes. I mean, Ricky was smart. He realized there wasn't a great future in peddling drugs in the Bronx. So he got himself into Columbia and then Harvard Business School and then a top job in investment banking. It doesn't take just brains to do that. It takes a lot of dedication.

"I told you how I was proud of putting guys onto Wall Street. Well, Ricky was one of the most successful of us, and I guess I kind of admired him. Sure, I knew he sailed close to the wind, but you have to get things done somehow. And we did some sweet deals together, so I could overlook the odd misdemeanor. But killing Debbie Chater, and Greg Shoffman?" Cash shook his head.

"We don't know who killed Debbie," I pointed out. "It looks like it wasn't you, and Waigel was in America. But the police think they know."

Cathy and Cash looked at me inquiringly.

"Inspector Powell is convinced that I killed her," I continued. "He says he has a witness."

Cathy looked horrified. "That's ridiculous. He's not serious, is he?"

"He's very serious."

"But he hasn't got proof."

"I don't think he has got all the evidence he needs yet. But I am afraid he might find it," I said.

"But how could he?" Cathy asked.

"Someone could feed him some more. And I wouldn't put it past Powell to make it up for himself."

"So who's his witness?" asked Cash.

"I suspect it's probably Rob," I said. "Cathy mentioned he saw me with Debbie that evening. But why he would lie to the police is beyond me."

"Perhaps he killed her," said Cash.

"Perhaps he did." It could have been him. Or it could have been Joe, or Waigel, or even Piper. But Rob was in love with Debbie. Joe had denied that he had killed her. Waigel was in New York at the time. And Piper had seemed genuinely unaware of Debbie's death. We just didn't know. It could even be someone totally different, a professional hit man hired by Waigel, who, once he had dealt with Debbie, had disappeared into the dark and rain.

We discussed all this for an hour without getting anywhere. Finally, we gave up. We drank up and headed upstairs into the dusk of the September evening. Cash bade Cathy and me good night as he got into a cab. His almost lascivious grin suggested that the latest development in our relationship had not escaped him. Cathy and I walked the mile or so to a romantic little Italian restaurant near Covent Garden and had a very pleasant meal washed down with a bottle of Chianti. Afterward, we tossed a coin, I lost, and joined Cathy in a taxi headed for Hampstead.

I got back to my flat at eight the next morning. As soon as I walked in the doorway, I sensed something was wrong.

I shut the door carefully behind me, and stepped into the sitting room. Everything was untouched, just as I had left it the day before. A draft of air blew in from the direction of my open bedroom door. Cautiously, I looked in.

Bloody hell! Another break-in. I had been broken into only three months before. I didn't know why they bothered. There wasn't anything much to steal.

With a rush of panic, I looked back in the sitting room. My medal was still there. So too were the replacement TV and cheap stereo that I had bought after the last time. I opened my small liquor cabinet. Nothing seemed to have been touched there either.

I went back into my bedroom, and took another look at the window. Someone had forced the latch and crawled in. I cursed myself for leaving it unlocked, but I usually slept with it open during the summer, and it was too much of a bore to get out the key and lock it every morning.

I spent ten more minutes checking the flat again, but as far as I could make out, I hadn't lost anything. I sat down and thought about it for a moment. I couldn't for the life of me think why anyone would want to break in and not take anything.

Odd.

For a moment, but only for a moment, I considered reporting it to the police. After my recent experiences that did not seem an appealing prospect. Besides, there was nothing really to investigate.

So, I got down to work.

The TSA was a disappointment. After following through Cathy's logic, I was convinced that they would see that if Cash was cleared of insider trading, then I had to be as well. But Berryman was having none of that. He admitted that there was no conclusive proof implicating me but said I was still under investigation. I asked him about the deal he had made with Hamilton by which the TSA had promised to call off the investigation if I was fired. He refused to comment on this, simply saying that arrangements between De Jong and me were none of the TSA's business. He then referred darkly to "parallel investigations." That must be bloody Powell.

I was angry when I put the phone down. I had counted on total exoneration there and then. More fool me. I was also annoyed, but not entirely surprised, about Berryman not recognizing his deal with Hamilton.

Still, it wasn't all bad. Berryman didn't have anything concrete against me, and in time I would be cleared. If Powell didn't get me first.

My brooding was disturbed by the phone. It was Cathy. She had been back through the trading tickets that Joe had written relating to his Gypsum of America position. It had taken her a couple of hours, but by working through them chronologically, she was able to piece together how Joe had built up his position and what he had done with it. Half of it had been sold to the nominee account of a small Liechtenstein bank. Cathy had never heard of it, but Cash had. It was the bank Piper used occasionally for very sensitive trades. It was not traceable to him; only Cash, Joe, and perhaps two or three other trusted market operators knew about it. It would be difficult to prove absolutely that Piper had bought the Gypsum bonds, but it was clear enough to us that he and Joe had been working together.

I got out a pad of paper, and began scribbling short notes, and crossing them out. I felt I was so close to unraveling the tangle. Tremont, the Tahiti, Gypsum of America, Piper, Joe, Waigel, and Cash all seemed to be connected. Yet the more I thought about them the more jumbled the connections became. And then there was

Rob. Rob who had threatened Debbie, had threatened me, and who had threatened Cathy. Passionate, unpredictable. But not a killer, surely?

My thoughts were interrupted by the buzzer of my intercom. I looked out of the window. It was the police again.

I let them in downstairs, and stood at the door of my flat. There were four of them, Powell, Jones, and the two uniformed men.

"Can we come in?" asked Powell.

"No. Not without a warrant," I said.

Powell smiled, and handed me some papers. "Which I happen to have just here," he said. He barged past me into the flat. "Come on, lads."

The flat looked even smaller with four large policemen and me in it. There was nothing I could do. "What are you looking for?" I asked.

"Let's start with the records of all your share dealings, shall we?"

Reluctantly, I showed him where my share contract notes, all four of them, were kept. I was not one of the stock market's most active traders. Powell pounced on them, and quickly pulled out the Gypsum of America contract.

"We'll keep this, thank you," he said.

The other three policemen were standing at his shoulder, waiting for instructions.

He turned to them. "Okay boys, take it apart."

They systematically did as they were told. They searched without much enthusiasm, very aware of Powell watching them. I tried to keep my eyes on everything they touched, especially Powell. I might have been paranoid, but I didn't want Powell "finding" something that I had never seen before. But I couldn't watch all four at once.

There was a cry from my bedroom. "Sir! Look at this!"

Powell and I rushed through. One of the policemen

was holding an earring. It was cheap, but bright, a long red droplet hanging down from a gold coupling.

"Well done, lad," said Powell, grabbing the earring from the young policeman. He held it in front of me. "Do you recognize this?"

I did recognize it. I felt cold. I nodded. "It's Debbie's," I said, my voice hoarse.

"It certainly is," said Powell triumphantly. "She was wearing one just like it when we found her body. And only one."

His eyes never left my face, watching for every reaction.

"Where did you find it?" I asked.

The policeman pointed to a half-drawer in the chest by my bed. "Right in the back of there." The drawer was pulled fully out, my socks strewn all over the rug by my bed.

"You know exactly where it was," said Powell, grinning.

I felt a rush of anger. I had been right to be suspicious of Powell. "You planted that," I muttered.

Powell just laughed. "They all say that. Every time. You could have thought of something more original, a bright boy like you. Come on, lads."

With that he left the flat, clasping the earring and my share contract notes, the three policemen trooping after him.

As he passed me by the door, he leered. "Just you wait, boy," he said. "We're nearly there. A couple more days and we will be having some very long talks. See you soon."

I tidied up the mess, and went for a run. I pushed myself harder today, driven on by my anger. As I sped round the park, my determination grew. Cathy was dead right. I had wallowed for far too long. I was in a mess, but I would fight my way out of it. I wasn't quite sure how but I was determined to find a way.

Powell was really beginning to worry me. I had no

idea how the earring had got into my flat. He must have planted it.

I pounded on.

Of course! The break-in last night. Someone must have planted the earring then. That was why nothing was stolen. Somehow whoever it was had known that Powell was planning to search my flat today. Unless, of course, that person had tipped Powell off himself.

Powell had said he would see me soon, and I had no doubt he would. A murder charge was serious. In theory, I should be happy to put my faith in the British justice system to clear an innocent man. But Powell obviously thought he had a good case against me. And he did have the air of a policeman who always got his man.

Innocent men go to jail all the time.

I was moving very fast now, but I was scarcely aware of any pain in my legs or lungs. I followed my usual route automatically, dodging round the walkers in the park without slowing.

And it was all because of Rob! He must have told the police he had seen me push Debbie. Perhaps he had even planted the earring. Why? I resolved to find out.

Rob lived in a basement flat just off the Earl's Court Road. It was only a fifteen-minute walk, but I decided to wait until half past seven to be sure that he was in. I opened an iron gate and walked down some steps into a small patio. Some sad little shrubs grew in pots with weeds in them. I rang the bell.

Rob answered the door. He was barefoot, and wearing a T-shirt and an old pair of jeans. He held a can of Stella in his left hand. He wasn't pleased to see me. "What do you want?"

"Can I come in?"

"No."

I pushed my leg into the doorway. Rob shrugged and

turned toward his living room. "Okay, come in then," he said.

He flopped into a big gray armchair that was pointed at the television. The room was neat, simply furnished, unostentatious. There were already three or four empty beer cans on the floor by his chair.

I followed him in and, unasked, sat on the sofa.

Rob took a swig of beer from the can. He didn't offer me any. "So what do you want?"

"I'll be quick," I said. "I know you were following Debbie the night she died."

Rob looked at me steadily, his face registering neither surprise nor denial.

"And why would I do that?"

"Because you were jealous of me and Debbie."

"That's ridiculous."

"You had an affair with her a couple of years ago."

"As you say, that was a couple of years ago."

He annoyed me, slouching arrogantly in that big chair. My voice rose. "Look, Debbie's flatmate, Felicity, told me you had been bothering her just before she died. And Cathy said you told her you followed Debbie the night she was pushed into the river. So, you see I know. And I think it's sick creeping around after women like that."

My last comment hit home. Rob suddenly came to life. Anger sparked in his eyes. His cheeks flushed. He waved his can at me, spilling some of the golden frothy liquid onto the carpet.

"You're a bastard," he spat. "You're a fucking bastard. First you take Debbie from me, and now Cathy. Well let me tell you, you can't just steal my women like that and get away with it. You can't!" He shouted the last words.

"I didn't mean to take Cathy away from you," I said. "You just lost her all by yourself."

Rob didn't like that. He pulled himself out of his chair, and screamed, "Don't talk shit. You knew what you were doing. You have made my life hell. Complete hell. So don't just sit there and say you didn't mean to, you smug bastard."

He swayed, and collapsed back into his chair. "I loved Debbie. How I loved her! It was hard when we split up." His voice fell almost to a whisper. "In a way, all those other women I chased after were just a means of taking my mind off her. I did a good job of it. I buried my feelings deep."

He took another gulp of beer. "Then you came along. I could see that Debbie liked you. The way she used to flirt with you, and go off to lunch or a drink with you. I knew what was happening; I could see it right in front of my eyes, and I had to do something about it.

"So, I asked Debbie to marry me. She said no, but I didn't give up. In the end she told me to get lost. I was shattered. Then a week later, she was killed."

He swallowed. He pulled back his head, and rubbed his eyes. They were glistening.

"I was devastated. And then along came Cathy. The one woman who I had ever met who was as nice as Debbie. And so attractive. I felt confused, but she made everything much clearer. I feel right with her. Really right. And then I discover that all the while you were plotting to get your way with her as well."

Rob stared at me, his eyes full of hate. He wasn't going to forgive me, I thought. I had become the focal point for all the dissatisfaction he felt with himself and his relationships with women.

But I wanted answers. "So, did you see who killed Debbie?" I asked.

Rob relaxed. He took a swig of beer from his can, and smiled. "Maybe."

"Did you kill her?"

"Of course not," still smiling.

I struggled to control my own anger. "You told the police that you saw me push Debbie in the river, didn't you?"

Rob just smiled. I wanted to hit him.

"Because if you did tell them you saw me, both you and I know it was a lie. And there can be serious penalties for perjury."

Rob seemed unconcerned. "The police interviewed me, naturally. Whatever I told them will probably come out in court eventually. And I can assure you that I will stick to whatever I have told them, which is, of course, the truth."

"What about the earring?"

"What earring?"

"Debbie's earring. The one she was wearing the night she died. The one you planted in my flat."

Rob looked genuinely puzzled. "I don't know what you are talking about. But I should remind you that trying to intimidate witnesses is also a serious business. I will call Inspector Powell as soon as you have gone, and let him know of your visit."

I could see I was not going to get anywhere, except possibly into more trouble than I was already in. Rob had lied to the police, but would stick with his lie. It would be his word against mine. I didn't stand a chance.

I got up and left.

A quarter of an hour later, I was home. I was tired, confused, and angry. Rob hated me, Rob had lied to the police, and I would soon find myself charged with murder.

And there was nothing I could do about it.

Thoughts of Rob, Debbie, Waigel, and Joe spun around in my head. My brain was so tired, it was on the point of giving out. Exhausted, I flopped into bed.

DESPITE MY FATIGUE, I slept fitfully. When the black outside my window turned to gray, I crawled out of bed, pulled on my running things, and set off round the park. I did two circuits. On little sleep it was hard work, but it did calm me down. I got home, had a bath, some toast and some coffee, and felt a bit better. I called Cathy at Bloomfield Weiss. She had just arrived at work. I asked her and Cash to come round as soon as they could. I said it was urgent.

They arrived about ten. I told them about Powell's search of my flat, and about my visit to Rob's. I also ran through all I had been thinking the previous day.

I summed up. "So, we don't know who killed Debbie. We can be sure that Waigel was involved, but he wasn't in the country when she was killed. I suspect Rob might have something to do with it, and I also think that the Tremont Capital fraud is important. But for the life of me I can't put it all together. In the meantime, I am in serious trouble. All I need is for Powell to come up with one more piece of evidence, which it seems plenty of people would be happy to manufacture, and I will be arrested. Unless I can work out who killed Debbie, I will be facing a murder charge. Have either of you got any ideas, because I sure as hell haven't?"

Cash exhaled. "Jeez. This is all a bit complex for me. I don't know."

Cathy didn't say anything. She was thinking. I kept quiet, hopeful she would come up with something.

Finally she said, "Okay, try this. What do we know about Debbie's murderer?"

"Well, he must have been in London when Debbie was killed," I said.

"Right. And he may well have been the man pulling the strings at Phoenix Prosperity."

I nodded. "That's true. Jack Salmon was certainly talking to somebody. And that somebody knows the markets." I thought some more. That somebody had approved Jack Salmon's proposal to buy Fairway bonds.

I had told Hamilton I thought Fairway was a good investment.

My thoughts were interrupted by Cathy. "Waigel was lucky that no one checked out the Tremont Capital guarantee. He was running a risk there."

"It was a private placement," I said. "The documents didn't have to be filed anywhere, and there was a restricted list of customers."

"Very restricted," said Cathy. "Two, in fact. De Jong, and Harzweiger Bank."

"You said Waigel suggested Harzweiger, and you came up with De Jong yourself?" I asked Cash.

"That's right," he said. "After Hamilton had indicated his interest in high-yielding triple As."

"Well, we can be pretty sure that Dietweiler was working with Waigel; he probably stuffed the Tremont bonds in client accounts hoping no one would notice," I said.

"Which leaves De Jong," said Cathy.

"Mm. It is very odd Hamilton didn't check the guarantee, or at least get Debbie to check it," I said. "A rare mistake."

The inevitable conclusion was there, staring us all in the face.

Hamilton.

It couldn't be true. Hamilton might have sacked me,

but he was still important to me. I admired the man; he was the one person who was straightforward in this whole filthy mess. It just didn't make sense. I wasn't prepared to believe it.

But, as soon as I accepted Hamilton as a possibility, things began to slip into place. In partnership with his old business-school buddy Waigel, Hamilton had set the whole scheme up. He had bought the Tremont Capital private placement from Cash knowing exactly what it was. He was responsible for Tremont's investment in Phoenix Prosperity and for directing Jack Salmon's trading while he was there.

But worst of all, he had killed Debbie.

He had seen the appointment with Mr. De Jong in Debbie's diary. He had seen the marked-up Tremont prospectus on her desk. He knew she was going to talk to De Jong about the fake guarantee and he had to stop her.

So he killed her.

I felt numb. In shock. My body was physically unable to accept that conclusion.

"Paul? What's wrong?" Cathy reached over to touch my hand.

Stammering, I told them what I was thinking, the words coming out with difficulty.

They both just looked at me, too stunned to say anything.

I pulled my hand away from Cathy, and walked over to the window of my little living room. I looked over the street, bathed in morning sunlight.

The more I thought about it, the angrier I became. I felt foolish and betrayed. I wanted revenge, for myself, and for Debbie.

"I don't believe it," said Cash. "Hamilton is as prim and proper as they come. He isn't my idea of a master criminal. He's too . . ." Cash searched for the word and then found it: "boring."

"Oh, I do," said Cathy. "I never liked him. He's not a human being, he's a machine. But I wonder why he did it?"

I had an answer. I knew how Hamilton's mind worked. "Hamilton thinks life is all about playing the markets and winning. He is obsessed by making money. It's not the money itself he likes, it's the act of making it. And he is a risk taker. I think he got bored with straight-forward trading, he wanted something a bit more exciting. This was the perfect crime. He would steal tens of millions without ever being discovered. I bet he got a great kick out of it," I muttered bitterly.

"Why steal it, when the suckers give it away every day of the week?" Cash said, chuckling.

It was true, as long as there was one born every minute, Cash would never be short of money.

"So what about you?" Cathy asked. "How come he let you nose around for so long?"

"I suppose he didn't have much choice," I said. "Once I was suspicious, he knew I would ask questions. He was probably better off knowing what I was doing and directing me, rather than letting me go off on my own. He did persuade me not to tell anyone what I found out under the pretext of avoiding alerting the fraudsters before we had got the money back. I must admit I thought he would figure everything out. I suppose all that business about lawyers in the Netherlands Antilles was made up. Perhaps he didn't even go there."

"But why didn't he kill you like he killed Debbie?"

I paused. "I don't know why he didn't kill me. I suppose two dead employees in one month may have looked a little careless." Perhaps he was too fond of me, I thought to myself. The pride of being Hamilton's star protégé was difficult to shake. I felt a fresh wave of disgust for him wash over me. To think I ever admired a man like that!

He had tried to stop me, though, and nearly succeeded. Suddenly the Gypsum investigation slotted into place. "Berryman was right, Hamilton never did a deal with the TSA," I said.

Cathy looked at me, puzzled.

"He used the investigation into my Gypsum share dealing as an excuse to fire me. Once I had resigned, it was easy for Hamilton to spread a rumor around that I had been caught insider trading, which made me unemployable in the bond markets. Then, just to make sure, he got Rob to set me up as a murder suspect and broke into my flat to plant one of Debbie's earrings that had fallen off when he pushed her into the river."

"But why did Rob help him?"

I had no answer to that one. Perhaps he just didn't like me.

"So what do we do now?" asked Cash.

"Go to the police?" said Cathy.

I shook my head. "We can't. We don't have any proof. As soon as Hamilton realizes the police are investigating him, De Jong will never see its money again. And remember, I am still the man Powell wants behind bars. He won't be thrown off the track that easily."

Cathy nodded, worried. "You are still on the hook for that. Powell won't be impressed when you try to tell him that your old boss who fired you is really Debbie's murderer."

"Besides," I said, "I want to nail the bastard myself."

"So, what do we do?"

"We get De Jong's money back."

The other two looked at me blankly.

"We get De Jong's money back," I repeated. "And in the process we expose Hamilton's involvement in the whole affair. Powell will have to listen then."

"Well that's all fine and dandy," said Cash. "But how in hell's name are we going to do that?"

"I may have an idea. Let me think for a moment."

They were quiet as I stared out of the window.

There was a way, I was sure.

I outlined the germ of an idea. We discussed it and refined it over the next couple of hours, until we had quite a workable plan.

>>>

I joined Cash and Cathy in their taxi back to Bloomfield Weiss. I waited in the reception area for an hour or so. Eventually Cathy came back with an armful of prospectuses, annual reports, and computer printouts. I took them from her and headed back to my flat.

To work. I had information on five American companies that were currently in deep trouble. I laid the collection of 10Ks, 10Qs, price histories going back two years, and reports from Standard & Poor's, Moody's, Value Line, and various brokers in five neat piles. I began to work through them. I needed to pick one company that looked just right. I had to look at each one from three different angles: what I personally thought of the company's real prospects, what Hamilton would think, and what the market would think. I had to get the combination of these perceptions exactly right.

I broke off at three. I needed to make some phone calls. The first was to De Jong & Co. Karen answered the phone.

"Hi, Karen. It's Paul. How are you?" I said.

Karen sounded pleased to hear my voice. "I'm fine, how are you?"

"Is Hamilton there?"

Karen's voice became much more serious. "I'll just have a look."

I waited a few seconds, and then Hamilton's voice came down the other end of the wire, "McKenzie."

I was not prepared for the response hearing Hamilton's voice would arouse in me. It was a physical revulsion; the blood rang in my ears, and the hairs on my skin suddenly became very sensitive, so that I could feel my shirt rubbing against them. A feeling of sickness welled up somewhere near my diaphragm. Rationally, I knew Hamilton had betrayed me. I was not aware until then how deeply I felt it emotionally.

"Hello, Hamilton, it's Paul."

"Ah, Paul, how are you?"

"Fine, I suppose. I wanted to ask you something."

I could almost feel Hamilton stiffen on the other end of the phone line. "What's that?"

"I wonder if I could come in to the office to work out the rest of my notice period? I haven't had much luck getting another job in the bond market, so I am applying for a number of banking jobs. I would very much like to brush up on my credit skills. Besides, I am getting bored sitting around at home."

There was a second's pause while Hamilton thought this through. "That will be fine. You will be very welcome. I am afraid I can't let you trade, of course, but we would be happy to have you. As a matter of fact, there are one or two analyses that need doing."

"Good," I said. "I'll see you tomorrow morning."

So far so good. Next was Claire. As I expected, that was no problem; she was positively eager to help. Denny was more difficult. I knew I was asking a lot from him. He would have to do a fair amount of legal work for which he might not get paid if our plan failed. I didn't think that what we were intending to do was actually illegal, but it was certainly close. We talked for half an hour before Denny eventually said he would help, to my intense relief.

Now, the call I had been positively relishing. I dialed a Las Vegas number.

"Irwin Piper's office," said a secretarial voice, exuding cultivation, politeness, and authority. I asked for Mr. Piper. "I am afraid Mr. Piper is not here right now. Can I take a message?"

I had expected it would be difficult to get through to him. I had thought through my message beforehand. "Certainly. Can you tell him Paul Murray called. Can you tell him that unless he calls me back in the next two hours, I will call the Nevada Gaming Commission to discuss Mr. Piper's trading in Gypsum of America bonds through his Liechtenstein bank?"

It wasn't subtle, but it worked. Piper was on the phone within ten minutes. I didn't repeat my threat; I had made it once and that would be enough. I asked Piper politely for his help. I told him why it would be in his interests to give it, that helping me would solve his problem as well as mine. I explained what I wanted him to do.

I was surprised by his reaction. He was enthusiastic. "Sure, why not?" he said. "I went to a lot of effort to make sure the Tahiti is as clean as a whistle, and this Tremont Capital business nearly screwed all that up. It sounds fun. I was planning to come to England soon anyway. And it would be nice to get you off my back." I assured him I would forget all I had ever learned about him. We discussed dates and details for a few minutes and then hung up.

I dialed Cash. "How did you get on?" he asked.

"Everyone agreed to help. Piper even seemed to relish the idea," I said. "I think I have found the company we are looking for." I told him the name. "Can you check out how it is trading? Who owns bonds, whether there are any sellers likely to emerge in the next few days, that sort of thing."

"Okay. Talk to you later."

It was good to be in a suit again. As I walked into the Colonial Bank building and took the elevator up to the twenty-first floor, I felt tense but ready.

The small trading room froze as I walked in. Jeff, Rob, Gordon, and Karen all stared at me for a second or two, before putting their heads down to paper and telephone. Hamilton took no notice of my entrance. There was a young man with glasses sitting at Debbie's desk. Her replacement. I was glad that Hamilton had not yet found a replacement for me.

I strode into the room. "Morning, everyone," I said loudly. There were a few murmured responses. "Hello,

Karen. Miss me?" I shouted across to her. Karen at least smiled. It was something.

I walked over and introduced myself to the young man at Debbie's desk. He said his name was Stewart. "My name's Paul, I work here," I said. I saw Jeff stiffen out of the corner of my eye. Stewart was thrown into complete confusion, and blurted out something incoherent. He clearly knew who I was. He was torn between natural politeness and not wishing to be seen consorting with a criminal.

Hamilton finished his call, and came over. He was friendly enough, at least by his standards. "Morning, Paul. Nice to have you back. You can sit at your old desk." The word old jarred. "A couple of ground rules. I would rather you didn't have any contact with the market at all while you are in our offices, so don't answer the phone and don't make any calls to any salesmen."

"You don't mind if I use the phone to call head-hunters, do you?" I asked.

"No, that's fine." He dropped some papers on my desk. "I have got a couple of U.S. regional banks I would like you to take a look at. They have just been down-graded to triple B, and their bonds are yielding almost twelve percent. If they are safe, I would like to buy some."

Typical of Hamilton, I thought. He would make the maximum use of me that he could while I was there. But I was glad to have some real work to do. I would be more inconspicuous with my head buried in an annual report than hanging around trying to make work for myself.

No one talked to me all morning. I only caught the odd sideways glance. I couldn't really blame them, no one likes a crook. It was sad. They probably felt let down by me. Well, all that will soon be over, I thought. I tried to catch Rob's eye, but he was having none of it. He made sure that he was always deeply involved in phone conversations, eyes fixed on the screens in front of him.

The morning wore on. I looked at the clock on the trading room wall. Ten fifty-nine. At eleven o'clock precisely, I heard Rob call, "Hamilton! Claire on two."

I watched Hamilton as he spoke to Claire. I knew what she was saying, but it was impossible to see Hamilton's reaction. They talked for five minutes. After they had finished, Hamilton leaned back and stroked his beard. A good sign. He was nibbling at the bait. He sat like that for two or three minutes before suddenly getting to his feet and walking toward me. I quickly stared down at the balance sheet in front of me.

"Paul, I wonder if you would have a look at something for me?"

"Certainly. What is it?"

"It's a company called Mix N Match. Have you heard of it?"

I pursed my lips in concentration. "Yes, I think so. It's a retailer based in Florida. It has been having a tough time recently, I think."

"That's right," said Hamilton. "Do you know anything else about it?"

"No, I'm afraid not," I lied.

"Well, I got a call from Claire about it just now. The bonds are trading at twenty cents on the dollar apparently. Everyone expects the company to file for bankruptcy. Claire says there is a rumor it is about to be taken over by the Japanese."

I raised my eyebrows. Hamilton caught my expression. "Yes, I know," he said, "it's only a rumor. And Claire knows very little about junk bonds. But if she is right we make eighty cents, if she is wrong the most we can lose is twenty. I think it's worth a look. Claire should be faxing some stuff through soon. See what you make of it." He walked back to his desk and then hesitated. "But make sure you don't talk to anyone outside the firm on this."

"Right," I said, and set to work. I collected all the data we had on Mix N Match from our own files. I didn't have long to wait for Claire's fax. Then I set to work, surrounding myself with papers and tapping financial information into my computer.

I had selected Mix N Match as the best of the five companies I had looked at the previous day. It didn't look a bad investment at twenty cents; even in bankruptcy, bond holders should be able to get fifty cents on the dollar at least. With a takeover play to aim for as well, it made a hell of a good trade. Irresistible, I hoped.

For the next four hours I put together an elaborate analysis of the company in bankruptcy. I carefully valued all the assets, and put the results on a nice spreadsheet, which I printed off and showed to Hamilton. He had been hovering over my shoulder for much of the time and had read a lot of the material himself. He looked at the spreadsheet and stroked his beard, thinking.

I left him to it and made a quick phone call. Cathy answered. "He's ready. Get Cash on the phone to him now," I whispered and hung up.

Within thirty seconds, the light flashed on the phone board. Karen picked it up. "Hamilton! Cash on line one!" she called.

Hamilton was lost in thought. "Tell him I will get back to him," he said. Damn! I hadn't considered that Hamilton would play hard to get.

Karen got rid of Cash and called across, "Get back to him when you have a moment. It's about 'Mixer Mash' or something."

Hamilton stiffened slightly. I knew he wouldn't call Cash back straight away, that would appear too eager. He waited five minutes before picking up the phone. He and Cash spoke for half an hour. When he had finished he called over to me.

"Well, you picked a good day to come back. I'm glad you are here, you can make yourself useful. Mix N Match may be more interesting than we thought."

"Oh, yes?" I said. I didn't have to fake excitement.

"That was Cash. Funnily enough, he wanted to talk about Mix N Match. Apparently the Tokyo Stock Exchange is full of the rumor that the company is about to be taken over by a major Japanese retailer."

I interrupted. "You can't trust Cash on something like that, can you?"

"That's right, you can't. But it's nice that Claire's rumor is corroborated. The really interesting thing is that Cash is coordinating a consortium of investors to buy up the outstanding debt of Mix N Match."

"What's the point of that?" I asked.

"The idea is to form a special purpose vehicle that owns most of the debt of Mix N Match, and then force the Japanese to pay out par on the bonds when the company is taken over."

"I see. So who are the other investors?"

"Just one so far. But he is big. Irwin Piper."

"But he's a crook!" I said. "You don't want to have anything to do with him, surely."

"He might not be whiter than white, but he is smart," Hamilton said. "He is putting in twenty million dollars. Cash wants twenty million from us, and he thinks he has another investor in the States he can get another twenty from."

"So let me get this straight," I said. "De Jong invests twenty million in a special purpose vehicle, along with forty million from Piper and this other investor. The SPV uses the sixty million dollars to buy bonds on the open market. Mix N Match gets taken over by the Japanese, who find themselves facing a powerful owner of a majority of the outstanding bonds. We can negotiate a big payout under the covenants of the bond indenture."

"Exactly," said Hamilton. "And if the takeover doesn't happen, and the company goes into bankruptcy, then according to your analysis, we should still make a profit."

"Okay, so what next?"

"Apparently Piper has already got the documentation drawn up. He is using Denny Clark as his solicitors. He is arriving in the country tomorrow morning. We can meet him at Denny Clark's offices. You can come if you want." Rob was hovering, straining to hear as much of the conversation as he could. "Can I join you?" he asked Hamilton. "I would like to find out more about the junk-bond market, and you will probably need some help once Paul has finally gone." Rob said all this without once looking at me.

Hamilton raised his eyebrows, thought for a second, and then nodded.

I went back to my desk. Karen said there was a John Smith from the agency on hold for me. It turned out to be Cash.

"Couldn't you think of a better name than that?" I said.

"Hey, someone's got to be called John Smith," said Cash. "Did he swallow it?"

"Hook, line, and sinker," I said. "Let's just hope Piper manages to do as good a job as you."

"Don't worry. That guy is a real pro when it comes to conning people. How do you think he made all that money in the first place?"

"You have a point there," I admitted.

"I gotta go," said Cash. "I've got a deal to sell to a certain Arizona savings and loan."

HAMILTON, ROB, AND I walked into Denny's office. Four people sat around one end of the long conference table—Denny, Irwin Piper, Cash, and Felicity. The portrait of the ancestral Denny stared down at us, reminding us that we were in the offices of a very respectable law firm and we had better behave accordingly. Denny did the introductions, mentioning that Felicity had been responsible for drafting the documents. She looked tired, which wasn't really surprising. She had an awful lot to do in not very much time.

There were really only two people in the meeting, Hamilton and Piper. Piper began. "Cash has told me a lot about your operation, Mr. McKenzie. I must say it sounds very successful. I am familiar with a number of similar outfits in the U.S., and they all do very well."

Hamilton ignored the flattery completely. He came straight to the point. "Tell me about Mix N Match," he said.

Piper leaned back in his chair, and made an arch with his fingers, shooting starched white cuffs and monogrammed gold cuff links out from under his jacket sleeves. "I have been investing in companies one way and another for twenty years now, and I am pretty good at it. Once every decade comes an opportunity that's too good to miss, an opportunity to risk a substantial sum in the near certainty of making a killing. Everyone comes across such opportunities, but most people don't recognize them for what they are. They make a quick buck and nothing more. Now, Mix N Match is one of those rare opportunities. Limited downside, plenty of upside. This company will be taken over by the Japanese"— Piper paused to emphasize his conviction—"and when it is I am going to make a lot of money."

Hamilton gazed at him, expressionless.

"Do you want to join me?" said Piper.

Hamilton kept quiet, waiting for Piper to say more. But Piper was not going to say any more and refused to be pressured into it. The silence must have lasted a minute, with none of the rest of us daring to break it.

Finally, Hamilton asked another question. "You don't have much experience of retailing as far as I'm aware, Mr. Piper," he began.

"Just call me Irwin," interrupted Piper.

"Very well, Irwin," said Hamilton reluctantly. "As I was saying, you don't have much experience of this sector. How did you come across this opportunity?"

I shifted uneasily in my chair. We were on to dangerous ground here. This was one question we had not rehearsed.

Piper stood up and walked over to the window to look out at the quiet street below. He's playing for time, I thought.

He turned round. "My wife's family used to live in Japan, and she still has some Japanese friends. One of them is married to a senior executive in a Japanese retailing firm. She was over in America, and dropped in on us at the Tahiti. She was on her way to Florida to meet her husband, who was there on business. I checked out her husband's company. They had announced they were determined to make an acquisition in America this year. Mix N Match is the obvious target. I spoke to Cash, who got me some research on the company, and here we are." Piper held out his arms and smiled. "Of course, I would rather you did not repeat any of that outside this room."

Silence again as Hamilton weighed up Piper's answer. I found Hamilton's silence rude and intimidating, but Piper's urbanity seemed intact.

"So why should we work together?" Hamilton asked at last. "Why shouldn't I just trot off and buy the bonds myself?"

"I would be disappointed if you did that," said Piper, "especially since the idea came indirectly from me via Cash." Piper managed to imply with those words that what Hamilton had suggested was the lowest of the low ethically. He stood by the window, tall, sleek, and in control, looking down on the still seated Hamilton. I admired his ability to take the moral high ground in such murky circumstances. "But there is a more pragmatic reason for joining forces. If we act with one voice, we will be much more effective in negotiating with the acquirer of Mix N Match once it has been taken over. We will do that much better if we all own the bonds at the same price. And, if we all rush out and buy every bond we can in competition with each other, then the price will shoot up and none of us will end up with anything. Much better to do it slowly and carefully, pooling all our interests through one vehicle."

"I suppose I can see that," said Hamilton.

"Well, are you with us?" Piper said. "If we are going to move, we had better move quickly."

"I will need to think about it," said Hamilton.

Cash cleared his throat. "Hey, I understand you got to think about this one. But if you do decide to go ahead, as Irwin says, we got to move quickly. The rumors are already around the street. I know some big holders of Mix N Match bonds who are keen to sell, but we will have to go to them in the next couple of days. That means we will have to be ready to set up the SPV at short notice. Why don't you go through the documentation now? Know what I'm saying?" Cash nodded toward the pile in front of Felicity. You had to admire Cash's salesmanship, I thought, a great close.

But Hamilton wriggled. "I understand what you are saying, Cash. I agree we should check the documentation now. But don't take that as a sign of any commitment on my part."

Piper moved to the table. "That's fine, I understand perfectly well. I hope you will excuse me, Mr. Denny is aware of my views on the legal agreements. It's been a pleasure to meet you, Hamilton, and I hope we can do business together."

Power and charm oozed from Piper as he held out his hand to Hamilton. For once, Hamilton had been made to seem surly and pedantic, and he clearly didn't like it. He stood up, shook Piper's hand quickly, and turned back to the table and the pile of documents. "Let's have a look through these, then."

Cash made his excuses as well, taking Cathy with him, and Rob was not far behind. That left Denny, Felicity, Hamilton, and me to discuss the documentation. Felicity had not had time to draw up a thorough agreement. She hadn't done a bad job, but there were a number of holes. We had agreed beforehand that if and when Hamilton picked anything up, Denny would bow to any points he had. We could not afford to spend hours negotiating legal issues that were going to prove irrelevant anyway. Hamilton did put forward several objections, but after brief protestations, Denny gave in to them all. After two hours we had a document everyone was agreed upon. It was ready for Hamilton to sign, once he decided to join the consortium.

In the taxi back to the office Hamilton sat in silence. He stared out of the window at the flashes of red, black, and gray as buses, taxis, and suits milled back and forth. After five minutes he muttered something which I didn't quite catch.

"Sorry?" I said.

"I don't like it," said Hamilton.

I pondered his statement for a moment. "What don't you like about it?"

"It's too easy. It doesn't smell right. And Piper was lying about how he heard about the deal. I don't know what his game is, but he is up to something."

I didn't like the sound of this. Piper had seemed perfectly convincing to me, but he hadn't fooled Hamilton. I didn't want to seem too eager to persuade Hamilton to do the deal, but on the other hand, I desperately wanted him to commit. "What can he do?" I asked. "The documentation is watertight." Indeed it was. There was virtually nothing that Piper or anyone else could do with the SPV without asking De Jong & Co. first. De Jong had a right to veto the transfer of any assets in or out.

"I don't know," said Hamilton. "I can't work out his angle." He stroked his beard. "There's not much downside from a credit point of view, is there?" he asked, looking straight at me.

"No," I said, holding his stare. "Of course, you can never be sure what is hiding in any company, but it looks to me that with the debt trading at twenty cents on the dollar, bankruptcy would be a good thing; the debt should trade up anyway."

Hamilton looked at me and smiled, with what seemed to me to be genuine affection. "I'm glad you are working with me on this. It's nice to work with someone I can trust." The surprise must have registered on my face at such an unprecedented show of friendliness, as Hamilton, embarrassed, turned to look out of the window again. "I'm sorry you can't work with me any more."

Just for a moment I felt a surge of pride at this display. But only for a moment. I gently smiled to myself at the irony. Hamilton may think me the only person he could trust; I would soon show him how wrong he was.

We got back to the office and each went to our own desks. I called Cash. "Didn't Piper do a great job?" he said.

"Well, that's what I thought, but Hamilton is suspicious."

"Is he going to do it?"

"Not in his current frame of mind," I said.

"What's wrong?"

"It all went fine to start with," I said. "He couldn't resist the temptation to make a smart buck. But he doesn't trust Piper, and he doesn't trust you. He's sure you are up to something, but he doesn't know what. And I don't think he is about to risk real money to find out."

"Damn," said Cash. "Look, I'm sure I can talk him into it."

"It won't work. I'm afraid Hamilton is suspicious of you at the best of times. You will just confirm his worst fears about the deal."

"Well, what if Piper has another chat to him. Or perhaps you could talk him into it."

"He won't listen to Piper. And it would look odd if I came out in favor of the deal. Hamilton would think I had gone crazy."

We were both silent, thinking.

"How did it go with Phoenix Prosperity?" I asked.

"Jack Salmon loved the idea," said Cash. "But he has to think about it. That means check with Hamilton."

"And we all know what he will say in his current frame of mind. Call me if you have any ideas," I said, and hung up.

I was annoyed. We were so close to carrying out our plan, but it looked like it wouldn't work because of Hamilton's last-minute suspicions.

I was sitting there, racking my brains, when the phone flashed.

"I've got an idea." it was Cathy.

My pulse quickened. "Tell me."

"Hamilton might not believe Cash, or Piper or maybe even you, but he would believe me."

"You mean if you told him to invest in the deal?" I said doubtfully.

"No, if I told him not to invest in it." She told me her idea. It sounded a good one.

Cathy called at precisely half past three. I had made sure that I was talking to Hamilton at exactly that time, in the hope that he would let me listen in. Sure enough, once it became clear what Cathy wanted to talk about, Hamilton gestured to me to pick up.

I heard Cathy's clear voice speaking hesitantly. "Cash was very keen that I check to see whether you have made up your mind about joining the consortium." She managed to inject a hint of reluctance into her tone, as though she didn't really want to know the answer.

"I think it's unlikely," said Hamilton.

"Um, okay," said Cathy. "I'll tell Cash. He will be very disappointed."

"You do that."

Hamilton was just about to put the phone down when Cathy blurted, "Can I just ask you one question?" She sounded nervous.

"Yes?"

"Why aren't you going ahead with it?"

Hamilton paused. He seemed to decide there was nothing to be lost by telling the truth, and said, "It smells funny. I don't know why, but there is something else going on here that Piper didn't admit to."

"Oh, I'm very glad you said that," Cathy gushed, relief in her voice. "You are quite right, it doesn't seem at all straight. They are all absolutely certain that this takeover is going to happen. I don't know where they got the information from, but I am worried it is not legal. I would much rather have nothing to do with the whole thing. I don't know what to do. Should I report this to someone?" Hamilton didn't reply. Cathy went on. "Cash would kill me if he heard I had done that. And what if there is nothing wrong with the deal after all?"

Hamilton had tensed ever so slightly. He was listening carefully to everything Cathy said. "No, I wouldn't report it if I were you. As long as you don't know where they got the information from, you can't be implicated."

"Are you sure?"

"Quite sure."

"Okay, then." Cathy sounded doubtful.

"What will Cash do if I don't invest?"

"Well, there is another investor in the States who is thinking about it, but if he doesn't take it then we have got Michael Hall at Wessex Trust lined up to take the whole forty million."

Hamilton's eyes narrowed. Michael Hall was renowned in the City as smart money. He was often profiled in magazines and lauded for his ability to buy and sell at the right time. Hamilton refused to give interviews and claimed to scoff at Hall as a publicity seeker, but the reality was he envied him his reputation. If Mix N Match was indeed a golden opportunity, Hamilton would be incensed if Hall took it and he didn't.

"There is a small point I don't quite understand," he said. "Why should Piper want to get me of all people in on this?"

"Oh, he didn't," said Cathy. "Cash insisted on this. In fact I think he is behind this whole thing. He sees this as a way of getting his key clients to make a lot of money. I think he is worried that since Paul left in such difficult circumstances, he might lose your account. He's desperate to get you in."

"I see."

"So shall I tell Cash you are not interested?"

"Yes," said Hamilton and hung up.

Damn, I thought. Cathy had done an excellent job, but it looked like Hamilton still wasn't biting.

Rob strolled over. "Are we going to do this Mix N Match then?"

Hamilton leaned back in his chair stroking his beard. "That girl talks too much," he said.

"I think she is scared," I said. "It's a good thing we have let it go."

"I don't think we will let it go," Hamilton said. "I believe her. I think Cash does know something, and showing a sure thing to his favorite customers is just the sort of thing he would do. And I am damned if I am going to let that prima donna Hall get his hands on this one."

"So we do it?" Rob asked.

"We do it."

"Great!" said Rob.

Hamilton called Cash. When he answered, Hamilton said, "Cathy isn't on the line, is she?"

"No," said Cash.

"Well, I think you should watch out for her. I just spoke to her, and I think she is a little ah"— Hamilton searched for the word—"concerned about this deal. Just for my own conscience, there is nothing illegal about this transaction or the manner in which you got the information relating to it, is there?"

"Hey, Hamilton, you know I'm straight," protested Cash. "This deal is one hundred percent kosher, you have my word."

Hamilton didn't believe him, of course, but he wanted to cover himself in case anything went wrong.

"Good. Well, I'm in for twenty million. Send the documents round here by courier for me to sign. And don't let Cathy find out I have committed. Get her off the deal somehow." He hung up, turned to me, and smiled. "This is going to work," he said. "I know this is going to work."

I went back to my desk, and called Cathy. "Well done! You were brilliant!" I said.

"You think he's definitely going for it?" she said.

"Definitely."

"I am going to New York for four days tomorrow," she said. "I'm following up on some of the clients Cash and I saw when we were over there last month. Let me know what happens. Cash should be able to tell you where I am."

"Don't worry, I will," I said. Something made me uneasy. "Cathy?"

"Yes?"

"Be careful of Waigel."

"Why?"

"Just be careful. He's dangerous. I would hate you to get hurt."

"Don't worry. I won't go anywhere near him. Besides, there is no reason he should be worried about me."

"Okay, I suppose you are right." I wasn't convinced.

The documents were signed that afternoon, and Hamilton authorized $20 million to be paid into the account of the new SPV. Phoenix Prosperity also signed up that afternoon and transferred $20 million into the same account. Cash said that Jack Salmon had been raring to go and had been furious that his boss had not given him the go-ahead straight away. Piper signed the subscription agreement, but delayed transferring his $20 million subscription into the SPV's account.

So within twenty-four hours, the SPV was in existence and it had $40 million of funds at its disposal.

I found it very difficult to concentrate, or even pretend to be concentrating, on my work over the next couple of days. Hamilton was cool as ever, of course, just checking once to make sure that the prices of Mix N Match bonds hadn't fallen.

Once Denny, as trustee for the SPV, confirmed that the funds were in place, I acted. I didn't have much time. I had to wait until the brief quarter of an hour when Hamilton was away from his desk buying a sandwich. Most of the others were at lunch as well, although Stewart, Debbie's replacement, was at his desk, leafing through a bond market rag. He would probably hear what I was going to do. That was just tough.

First, I called Denny. Over the recorded phone, I sold to the SPV the $20 million Tremont Capital position held by De Jong at par. Then I sold De Jong's $20 million stake in the SPV back to it at par. It only took a minute. Stewart cast a quick glance at me while I was talking on the phone, and then went back to his magazine. He hadn't been able to hear what I was doing.

I then pulled out two sets of trading tickets and wrote in the details of the trades I had just completed. When the tickets were processed, they would ensure that the Tremont Capital bonds would be transferred from Chase, where they were held in custody for De Jong, to the SPV's custodian, Barclays. Similarly, the share certificates for the SPV that De Jong had just received from Denny Clark would be sent back round there by messenger. More important, De Jong's bank would be instructed to expect payment of $40 million from the SPV.

I looked at the clock. A quarter past one. Just time for a sandwich.

As I stood in the line in the small sandwich shop I ran through everything in my head one more time.The net result of all this juggling was that De Jong had received back the $20 million it had paid for the bogus Tremont Capital bonds. The SPV now consisted of $20 million of assets in the form of Tremont Capital bonds, funded by $20 million of share capital all held by Phoenix Prosperity. Because Tremont Capital's only asset was its investment in Phoenix Prosperity, or Uncle Sam's Money Machine, Phoenix Prosperity had just bought its own shares. When you unraveled all this, what had happened was that the $20 million that De Jong & Co. had unwittingly invested in Phoenix Prosperity via Tremont Capital had been repaid. All very neat.

Hamilton, Rob, and I were due to go round to Denny's office that afternoon, right after lunch. Denny had promised to have a reception committee for Hamilton. I was looking forward to that meeting.

I was pleased with myself. I had taken Hamilton on at his own game, and beaten him. I couldn't bring Debbie back to life, but at least her murderer would now face justice. De Jong would get their money back, and I should avoid a murder charge. All in all, a satisfactory outcome.

I walked back to my desk clutching a ham and cheese roll in a paper bag in one hand, and balancing a black coffee in a polystyrene cup in the other. The coffee from the shop was much better than the stuff that dripped out of the machine in the corridor. Stewart had popped out for a bite himself. The only two people in the room were Hamilton, who was buried in something, and Rob, munching a sandwich over a copy of the FT spread out on his desk.

I sat down and reached for the trading tickets.

They weren't there.

I scrabbled through the papers on my desk. I flipped through the pile of prospectuses. Had I taken them through to administration? No. Had I stuffed them in my briefcase? I was pretty sure I hadn't but I checked anyway. No. Had I hidden them? No.

I could remember what I had done with them. I had left them face up in the middle of my desk. And they weren't there.

My heart began to beat faster. I took a deep breath and turned round.

Hamilton was standing behind me holding the tickets out in front of him. He was reading them.

"What's this, Paul?" he said in a neutral voice.

I stood up and leaned against my desk, facing him. I tried to make my reply casual. "These trades get back the Tremont Capital money for De Jong," I said.

"Very clever," he said. He looked up and stared at me. His cold blue eyes looked right into me, piercing straight through my feeble attempt at nonchalance, uncovering the innermost workings of my brain.

He knew I knew.

"You set up Tremont Capital," I said. My voice sounded quiet and small, as though it belonged to someone else. "You killed Debbie."

Hamilton just stared.

The anger erupted inside me. How could anyone do that to her? How could Hamilton do all this to me? The man who had guided me into my chosen profession, who had patiently taught me everything I knew about trading, who had encouraged me to excel, was nothing but a thief and a murderer. Despite, or perhaps because of, his coolness, Hamilton had been more than a boss to me; he had been a mentor, a role model, a father. And all this time he was manipulating me, until finally I had become too dangerous and he had abandoned me.

"Why did you do it?" I said between clenched teeth. I was so angry it was a struggle to get the words out. "Why did you have to do something so bloody stupid? Why did you ruin everything we have got here? And why did you kill Debbie?" My voice cracked as I said these last words.

"Calm down, laddie," said Hamilton. "You're too emotional."

I lost it. "What do you mean calm down?" I shouted. "Don't you understand what you have done? This is all a fucking game to you, isn't it? We are all just pieces in some never ending puzzle for you to fiddle about with. But we are people, and you can't just get rid of us when we get in the way."

I paused for breath. "I respected you. God, how I respected you. I can't believe how fucking stupid I was. I don't know why you didn't just kill me."

Hamilton's stare didn't waver. "You're right," he said. "I should have killed you. That was an error. I was too soft. It was unfortunate Debbie had to die, but it was the only solution."

I had an urge to hit Hamilton as hard as I could, but I resisted it. I looked over to where Rob was sitting, bolt upright in his chair, watching us.

"I suppose he's in on it too?" I said with contempt. Hamilton must have told him to tell the police that I had killed Debbie.

"Oh, Rob's just a little scared insider trader," said Hamilton. "He made his five hundred pounds on Gypsum shares, and now he's afraid he is going to lose his job, just like you. So I asked him to tell the police a little story. Mind you, he seemed quite happy to do it. I don't think he likes you very much."

Rob reddened and shifted in his chair.

"And I suppose you planted Debbie's earring in my flat?"

Hamilton just shrugged.

I calmed down. "Well, anyway. It's all over now."

A thin smile played across his lips. "No, it isn't."

He sounded confident. "What do you mean?" I said.

"You are going to tear up those tickets."

No way was I going to do that. "Why?" I said.

Hamilton smiled again, and picked up the phone on the desk behind him. He dialed fourteen digits. America.

"Dick? It's Hamilton." A pause for a response from Waigel. "Listen, Dick, we may have some trouble here. I can't explain it all right now. But if I don't call back in five minutes, get hold of your friend and put our plan involving Cathy into action. Then get out of your office and disappear. Got that?"

Another pause as Waigel replied quickly. Hamilton looked up at the clock on the wall. "Okay, it's one thirty-three here now. If I am not back to you by one thirty-eight, do it."

He put the phone down. He turned to me. "I have been concerned about Cathy ever since she told me she was thinking about telling her bosses about Cash and Piper. So, just as a precaution, I have had Waigel organize someone to keep tabs on her so that if we need to dispose of her in a hurry, we can."

I suddenly felt cold. Cathy! She would be somewhere in New York right now, but she wouldn't be alone.

Someone was following her, watching her, waiting for the signal from Waigel to kill her. I couldn't allow that to happen, not after Debbie.

But was Hamilton bluffing? I didn't put it past him in a tight spot to come up with something like that. And if he was bluffing, I knew he would be convincing.

Hamilton followed my train of thought. "I'm telling the truth, you know," he said. "Anyway, you can't take the risk, can you? I may be lying, but you wouldn't risk Cathy's life on that outside chance."

He was right. We had been in enough situations where we had assessed risk together. It would be foolish to call his bluff, and he knew I wouldn't do it.

Hamilton's stare never left my face, reading everything he saw. He smiled. "So, you're fond of her, are you? She's more to you than just another saleswoman?" He chuckled to himself. "Well, well. You'll definitely have to tear up those tickets now, won't you?"

I was furious. He was right, I didn't have a choice. But I hated it. I hated to be outwitted by him when I was so close to nailing him. There he was in front of me, smiling slightly, calculating all the angles and getting it just right. As usual.

I looked at the clock. One thirty-five. Three minutes before he had to called Waigel.

Hamilton said, "Now, after you have torn up those tickets, write some replacements purchasing Phoenix Prosperity's stake in the SPV for twenty million dollars, for same-day settlement. I want you to tell administration to process the trade immediately, and call you back when the funds transfer is confirmed. I'll watch."

I thought Hamilton's last instruction through. It would allow him to make sure Phoenix Prosperity didn't lose their twenty million dollars after all.

Hamilton continued. "I will call Dick Waigel every five minutes. If you try any funny stuff, or if he doesn't hear from me, Cathy is dead."

I sighed. There was nothing to do but what Hamilton

wanted. I sat down at my desk and pulled out some blank tickets. Just then the line flashed. Hamilton held out his hand to stop me, but he was too late. "Yes?" I said.

"Paul, it's Robert Denny."

"Oh, hello," I said.

"I know you can't talk now," he said, "but everything's ready for you to come round with Hamilton and Rob. The police are here, waiting."

"Not Powell?" I said.

"Inspector Powell is here, but I've got his boss as well, Chief Inspector Deane. There are also two men from the Serious Fraud Office. And the FBI are standing by to snatch Waigel in New York."

Hamilton couldn't hear what Denny was saying, but he was watching me closely. I looked up at the clock. One thirty-seven. Hamilton's eyes followed mine. "One minute to go," he said.

"Are they right outside his office?" I asked Denny.

"Hold on," he said. I heard muffled voices on the other end of the line. They took forever. I watched the second hand race round the face of the clock, heading fast for the number twelve. I knew our clocks were accurate to the second. I hoped Waigel's would be equally precise. "Yes, they are right there."

"I won't call Dick Waigel back unless you hang up now," said Hamilton. I glanced at him. He meant it.

My mind raced. This was the best chance I would get to stop Hamilton. If I let it slip, there could never be any guarantee that Cathy would be safe. And I couldn't let him just walk away.

I took a decision.

"Listen closely," I said to Denny, speaking rapidly. "Tell the FBI to snatch Waigel right now. And send some police round here. Do it quick. We only have seconds. I'll explain in a minute."

"Right," said Denny, and hung up.

My heart was thumping at the risk I had taken. I put

the phone down and stood up straight looking directly at Hamilton. His eyes were wide open with surprise. He hadn't expected this. "I wasn't bluffing," he said. "Cathy is dead."

He bent down slowly, picked up his briefcase, and backed toward the door, his eyes never leaving my face.

I caught the movement of something rushing toward the desk beside Hamilton. Rob vaulted over it, sending a computer crashing to the ground, and hurled himself onto him.

They both hit the ground hard. Rob let out a cry and grabbed his shoulder. As Hamilton pulled himself to his feet, I leaped on top of him. He struggled, but Rob joined me, and in a few moments we had him pinned to the floor, Rob on his legs, and me on his shoulders.

"Tie his hands," shouted Rob.

I looked for something to bind him, and grabbed at the electric cord sticking out of the computer, which lay cracked on the floor. I yanked it out and tried to wrap it round Hamilton's hands.

It was difficult. Even with two of us, Hamilton was wriggling and thrashing, and we couldn't keep his wrists in one place long enough to tie them.

"Keep still!" I shouted.

Hamilton took no notice, and somehow managed to kick Rob hard in the ribs.

I took the cord and wrapped it round his neck, pulling his head back.

"Keep still, I said!"

He bucked and nearly threw me off his shoulders. I pulled back on the cord hard. Anger rushed through me. Here was the bastard who had betrayed me, deceived me, who had cheated, lied, and killed. He would have murdered Cathy as well if he had had the chance. In fact, he might already have succeeded.

I gritted my teeth and pulled harder. The blood rushed in my ears. The body underneath me stopped moving. I half heard Rob shouting my name.

Then I felt strong hands grab the cord and pull it away from me. Other hands picked me up off Hamilton. I looked down at him. His head flopped to the ground, and he took huge wheezing gulps of air. Spittle dripped down from his open mouth. His face was bright red.

I slumped back into a chair, the anger draining out of me. A small voice of common sense told me I was glad I hadn't killed him. A policeman was kneeling over him, and another had his arms firmly on my shoulders. Two more were watching, one talking urgently into his radio. My mind cleared. Cathy! I leaped to my desk and called Denny. He put me on a speakerphone with Chief Inspector Deane.

In a few seconds I told them what had happened. Deane had some questions.

I didn't answer them. I needed to know about Cathy. "Did the FBI get Waigel?" I said. "And had he made the phone call to the hit man? Can you find out right now?"

"All right," he said. He left me on the speakerphone. I could hear muffled radio conversation, but I couldn't make out the words. Two of the policemen handcuffed Hamilton and bundled him out of the trading room, still wheezing. I was glad he was out of my sight.

A very long minute later, Deane's voice came back on the phone. "They've got Waigel," he said.

"Had he made a phone call?" I said, my hopes raised.

"He was just putting the phone down when they entered his office." Deane's voice was grim. "He won't say who he was calling, but from the way he is acting, the FBI men there think it must be the hit man."

Oh, God. I had blown it. Oh, Cathy, Cathy, Cathy!

"Mr. Murray?" It was Deane's voice, insistent. "We need to know where she is."

"Right. I'll find out."

I hit the plunger button and called Cash.

"Y'ello."

"Cash. It's all going wrong. Waigel has put a hit man on to Cathy. Do you know where she is?"

"What's up? I thought you were going over to Denny's this afternoon. What happened?"

"Look, I have no time to talk. Just tell me where Cathy is, will you?"

"Okay, okay. I've got her itinerary here. Let me see." Come on. I willed him to hurry up. "Here it is. She has a meeting at nine o'clock at Arab American Investment. That's at five twenty Madison Avenue. She's staying at the Intercon. Knowing her, she's probably walking there right now."

"Thanks. Talk to you later."

I hung up and got back to Deane. I told him what Cash had told me. "Right," he said. "It's ten to two our time, that's ten to nine in New York. She should be almost there. I'll get the FBI on to it."

I put down the phone. I sat hunched at my desk staring at the screens. I didn't take in any of the green figures and letters in front of my eyes. I was looking at a New York street, searching for Cathy.

The clock ticked loudly. The police radios behind me crackled. I was in my usual position, sitting at my desk, waiting for the phone to ring. But this time it wasn't paper money at stake. It was Cathy's life.

How could I have been so stupid? Why had I taken the risk? This wasn't some damn trade. Stupid! Stupid! Stupid!

The phone flashed. I picked it up. Down a fuzzy line, I heard the sound of traffic.

"Paul! It's Cathy." I could hardly hear her voice, it was an urgent whisper. But she was alive! So far.

"Yes?"

"I'm scared. There's a man following me, I'm sure of it. He's followed me all the way up from the hotel."

"What's he doing now?"

"He's leaning against the wall of a church, reading his paper, acting as if he hasn't seen me."

"Is it crowded?"

"Yes. I'm right off Fifth Avenue. There are people everywhere."

"Good. Now where are you exactly?"

"I'm in a phone booth on Fifty-third Street, just by the entrance to the subway station."

"Hold on." I turned and gave this information to the policeman behind me, who relayed it into his radio.

"Now, Cathy, just stay where you are. The police will be with you in a few minutes. Stay on the phone."

"Who is he? What's he doing?" asked Cathy, sounding really scared.

"Waigel put him on to you. But don't worry, there's nothing he can do in a crowded street." I tried to make myself sound as confident as possible, and I hoped I was right, but I really didn't know.

We stayed on the phone, too tense to talk, waiting. The bustle of Fifty-third Street crackled down the phone lines: the noise of traffic, snatches of conversation from passers-by.

I watched the second hand crawl round the clock above me. Where were the police? Images of a gridlocked midtown Manhattan flashed before me. It could take ten minutes to go three blocks in the rush hour.

I started. Where was Cathy? I couldn't hear her. "Cathy?"

"Yes, Paul, I'm here."

Relief.

"Has the man moved?"

"No, he's still over by the church."

"Good. Tell me if he does move, won't you?"

"All right." A pause. "Paul, I'm scared." Cathy's voice sounded very small, very far away.

"Don't worry, it won't be long now."

Then I heard them. The wail of sirens, getting louder.

"Oh my God!" she said. "He's crossing the road. He's coming right to me."

"Drop the phone and run!" I shouted. "Run!"

I heard the clatter of the phone banging against the booth. Then a crack and the sound of splintering plastic.

Half a second's silence.

Then screams. Women shrieking, men yelling, the sirens getting louder. A shout, "She's been hit!" Another, "She's bleeding!" The sirens getting very loud. Large police voices ordering people to move back, make way.

"Cathy!" I shouted. "Cathy!"

Then her voice. Cathy's sweet voice. Strained, sobbing, but still her voice. "Paul?"

"Are you okay?"

"Yes. A woman's been hit, but I'm okay. I'm okay."

I WATCHED THE SCREEN in front of me with satisfaction. There had been a brisk rally in the treasury market during the morning, it was now a point and a half up on the day. Hamilton, as usual, had positioned the portfolio perfectly. We were going to make some money. I had heard rumors of a big new issue for the World Bank due out in the afternoon, and I wanted to make sure I got a piece of it. With the positive sentiment in the eurobond market, it would fly.

I looked up at the clock. Twenty past twelve already! It seemed only an hour or so since seven thirty when I had arrived back at my desk for my first full day's trading since I had been sacked. It had felt good. Jeff was nominally in charge in Hamilton's absence, but he had made it clear that he would allow me quite a lot of latitude. I was confident I wouldn't misplace his trust.

I was due to meet Denny, Cash, and Cathy at Bill Bentley's at twelve thirty. Denny had offered to buy us all lunch. I grabbed my jacket and headed for the elevators. As I got out of the car on the first floor, I saw Rob waiting for someone. I ignored him and walked across the foyer to the revolving entrance doors.

"Paul!" I stopped. He was calling me. "Got a minute?" He nodded to some chairs in a quiet corner of the entrance hall. I hesitated and then went over to join him.

We didn't sit down, we just stood by the chairs. Rob shuffled awkwardly from foot to foot. I wasn't going to make it any easier for him. Finally, he screwed up his eyes and his courage and said, "I'm really sorry I lied to the police about you."

I didn't say anything. I would find it impossible to forgive Rob. As far as I was concerned our friendship was over.

"I've been through a bad patch these last few months," Rob went on. "A very bad patch. I've done a lot of things I wish I hadn't. I just wanted you to know I am truly sorry for what happened."

"Okay," I said, neutrally. I knew Rob was in trouble. The TSA was investigating his purchase of Gypsum shares, and the police were not at all happy about the way he had given them misleading evidence. However, Rob had promised to testify against Hamilton and had been instrumental in his arrest, which would help. Whatever happened, he would probably lose his job at De Jong. I was glad about that. In my eyes Rob was weak rather than evil, but I certainly didn't want to see him every day. "How's Cathy?" asked Rob.

"Fine. She's fine."

"Good. She's a wonderful girl. Don't lose her."

It must have been difficult for Rob to forgive me for Cathy. I was surprised.

"I've got to go," I said and headed for the exit. As I walked out through the revolving doors, a very tall, blond-haired woman of about twenty walked in. She was wearing a skimpy T-shirt, no bra, and very short denim shorts, which showed off miles of golden brown leg. Heads turned all around, including mine. I paused just outside the building to watch as she bounced over to where Rob was sitting. His face lit up with that expression I knew of old, as he stood up and gave her a kiss.

How the hell did he do it? What did they see in him? I shook my head in wonder and turned down the street to the restaurant.

I walked down the steps into Bill Bentley's at half past twelve exactly. The bar was already crowded. Denny had booked a table downstairs.

Denny, Cash, and Cathy were already there. Cash and Denny shook my hand warmly. I kissed Cathy. It was great to see her alive and smiling.

"I'm glad to see you," I said.

"Me too."

"When did you get in?"

"This morning. The New York police lost the man who shot at me, so they told me it would be best to cut my trip short and come right home. But they don't think there is a longer-term threat. With Waigel and Hamilton locked up, it's very unlikely he would go after me."

"God, I was worried when I heard those screams down the phone," I said.

"You were worried! I was scared out of my wits. Fortunately, the woman who was hit is going to be fine, so I'm told."

Cash poured me a glass from the open bottle of champagne nestling in a bucket beside the table. "Here's to all of us!" he said, taking a large gulp. "And here's to Hamilton's vacation. I trust it's a long one."

We drank the champagne. I felt good. I had my job back. I would now be able to afford to buy my mother's cottage after all. And I was able to trade. But, most important of all, I had Cathy. I caught her eyes smiling at me over her glass.

I turned to Denny. "Thank you very much for all you have done," I said.

Denny held up his hand. "Not at all. It was a genuine pleasure to help you. Debbie was a good lawyer, and I'm glad I had the opportunity to help catch the man who killed her."

We ordered lunch, and Cash asked for another bottle of champagne.

"Have you heard anything from Jack Salmon?" I asked Cash.

"I spoke to him yesterday," said Cash. He paused while the waiter placed a bowl of soup in front of him. He slurped at it greedily. "He is in total panic. He says the investigators are in already. Of course, he told me he didn't know anything about it, but I doubt he will last past the end of next week."

"Another client bites the dust," I said.

"Yes, too bad," said Cash. "Phoenix Prosperity will just become another bankrupt savings and loan owned by the U.S. government. Still, they will have lots of bonds to sell." Cash paused for a moment as he considered the possibilities.

Just then the waiter came over to our table. "A phone call for Mr. Murray."

Cash's eyes watched me closely as I took the call by the bar. It was Jeff. "Paul, I'm glad I caught you. There is a new jumbo deal for the World Bank just coming out now. It looks very cheap. Harrison Brothers are the lead. Can you get back here right now?"

"I'll be right over," I said, and put the phone down.

I went back to the table and made my excuses.

Cash's eyes narrowed suspiciously. "What was that?" he asked.

"Oh, I've just got to go and buy a few bonds." I winked at Cathy, who grinned broadly back. I darted out of the restaurant with Cash scrambling to catch up to me.

"Hey, wait up," he shouted after me. "What's the deal? Who's the lead? I'm sure Bloomfield Weiss will have a good angle on this one. Don't do anything until I get back to my desk."

I ignored him and rushed back to the office, my mind already calculating how many World Bank bonds I would buy.